She first came to appre...

when as a child she charged her classmates a packet
sherbet dips to write their essays for them. Adopted at a
young age and always a daydreamer, she felt isolated
growing up in a small mining village and it was her writing
which kept her company. Jacqui has always written for
pleasure whether it be screenplays or stand-up, she is the
author of seven bestselling novels as well as the author of
two political thrillers written under a male pseudonym.
She is a keen equestrian and the owner of two horses and
spends most days riding.

Also by Jacqui Rose

Fatal

Jacqui Rose

avon.

Published by AVON
A division of HarperCollins*Publishers* Ltd
1 London Bridge Street
London SE1 9GF

www.harpercollins.co.uk

A Paperback Original 2019
3

A catalogue copy of this book is available
from the British Library.

ISBN: 978-0-00-828731-3

This novel is entirely a work of fiction. The names, characters
and incidents portrayed in it are the work of the author's imagination.
Any resemblance to actual persons, living or dead, events or
localities is entirely coincidental.

Typeset in Minion by Palimpsest Book Production Limited,
Falkirk, Stirlingshire
Printed and bound in the UK by
CPI Group (UK) Ltd, Croydon, CR0 4YY

MIX
Paper from
responsible sources
FSC
www.fsc.org
FSC® C007454

This book is produced from independently certified FSC™ paper
to ensure responsible forest management.

For more information visit: www.harpercollins.co.uk/green

To everyone who has experienced loss

Lex Talionis

– The law of retaliation

You must show no pity. Your rule should be life for life, eye for eye, tooth for tooth, hand for hand, foot for foot.

Deuteronomy 19:21

PROLOGUE

Alcuni anni fa . . .

Some years ago . . .

Standing by the grave in the pouring rain, Alfie Jennings felt the cold droplets running down his neck and inside his coat collar. He turned slowly to his friend Abel Gray, who until recently had been an unshakable force, a powerhouse amongst men. Wealthy and driven, a man at the top of his game. Selling and supplying weapons, Abel had been ruthless when it mattered, when he had to be, but at heart he was loyal and generous. But as Alfie looked at his face, drawn and haunted, he could see Abel now was nothing but a broken man.

'Are you going to be all right, Abel? Cos I can stay if you like.'

'I'll be fine, Alfie, I'd rather be left on my own anyway, but I appreciate you coming.' Abel paused as he reached out to touch the headstone gently. His voice hoarse, he added, 'We both do.'

Alfie shrugged uncomfortably. He was the only one who *had* come; over the last few months, Abel through his trauma and sorrow had pushed everyone away who cared, but Alfie was determined Abel wouldn't do that to him, no matter what he said, no matter what he did.

The two of them went back a long way, first business associates before becoming firm friends, so there'd been no question of him not making the trip to Abel's isolated thirty-acre country home. The estate, which sat on top of a hill, was tucked away in the New Forest of southern Hampshire, and Abel had insisted the burial take place within the grounds. But it still cut Alfie up to see him like this. The once physically imposing presence, the once sharp mind, all felt like they were crumbling, fading away in front of his very eyes. Sighing, he gave his friend a sad smile.

'I'll get off then, but Abel, if you need me, you know where I am mate. It don't matter what time of night or day it is, just call . . . And I'm sorry, truly I am. She was really special.'

As Alfie Jennings walked out of sight, Abel dropped to his knees, tears and rain mixing in the wet earth as he began to scrape away at the soil of the freshly filled grave. 'No, no, no, no, no, baby, no, it's all right, I'm here, I'm here . . . I'm coming, Natalia. I'm here.'

And as the rain poured down and Abel frantically dug, his fingers beginning to bleed, he remembered *that* night as if it were only yesterday.

'I'll ask you again, what did you do with my money?'

Panicked and desperate, Abel shook his head, his vision blurred as he stared through the stream of blood that ran from his head. 'I told you, I don't have it, I've no idea where it is.'

Nico Russo pulled out a blue handkerchief from his pocket and dabbed away the beads of sweat that sat on his olive skin like dewdrops. His eyes as dark as ravens, he gazed impassively at Abel, bloodied and tied to the chair. He spoke again, his voice unnervingly calm, heavy with a North Jersey–Italian twang. 'You need to speak up, I can't hear you, but it sounded like you were saying you don't have my money.'

2

With blood bubbling from the side of his mouth and the gash so deep on his forehead the bone of his skull was exposed underneath the flapping skin, Abel spluttered his words through lips that had been carved wide open, fear wrapping round him like a tight restraint. 'I don't! I don't have it, Nico! I never did!'

'Is that right?'

Abel nodded, flinching at the pain shooting through his body. He looked at Nico, pleading with him, desperate to persuade him somehow that he was telling the truth. 'Please, I swear. I can't tell you something I don't know.'

Nico Russo, a second-generation Italian-American who was built as powerfully as a herculean god, shrugged, his mop of unruly curly black hair pushed back far enough for Abel to see the deep lines of a frown appear. 'If that's the way you want it, so be it.'

'It's the truth, Nico!'

As he walked closer to Abel, Nico's words were rolled in sadness. 'You've been like family to me, and that's why this hurts me so much.'

'Nico, please, I'm telling—'

Nico's fist swung hard, striking and perforating Abel's eardrum. He breathed heavily and raised his hand to point at Abel. 'Never interrupt me, you know better than to show a lack of respect like that. Non mancarmi mai di rispetto. Never disrespect me. You understand? Never ever. Mai e poi mai.'

Agony shot through Abel as he felt the warm fluids drain out of his ear and down the side of his face. Barely capable of moving his head from the pain, Abel muttered his reply in Nico's mother tongue.

'Sì. Sì.'

'Good. However, that still leaves us with the problem of where my money is. So, you give me no choice . . . Salvatore! Salvatore!'

The wooden door to the cabin opened a few moments later. Salvatore Russo's features were more delicate than his elder brother's, but there was no mistaking the prominent sharp nose that determined the Russo family bloodline.

'Sì, Nico?'

Nico smiled, something he rarely did and rarely cared to do. 'You can bring it in now. Let's have some fun.'

With hatred and fear burning in him, Abel watched as Salvatore, always eager to please his older brother, nodded. 'Okay. No problem, Nico.'

As Salvatore stepped outside again, Nico turned back to Abel. 'You've no one to blame but yourself. It pains me, but I won't let anybody, not even you, who I loved like my own brother, steal from me.'

'I told you—' Abel's words were cut short as a woman was dragged inside by her hair and flung to the ground, knocking over one of the wooden chairs in the sparse, dimly lit cabin. She scrabbled to the back of the room and pushed herself up against the wall.

Nico turned to her and opened his arms in a welcoming gesture. 'Natalia, it's good to see you, though these are difficult times we all find ourselves in, but I hope we can come to some sort of an arrangement soon. How is your mother, by the way? I hope she got the flowers I sent her last week.'

Terror rushed through Abel. 'Let her go! Let her go! I told you, I don't know where your fucking money is! Jesus Christ, Nico, you sick bastard!'

Nico, bending down to Natalia – whose face, along with her clothes, was covered in blood – stroked her hair, whispering softly. 'Natalia, you know what needs to happen now, don't you, but all this could've been avoided if he'd only told me what I want to know.'

'Please, please, Nico, let me go!'

Nico pressed his fingers against her lips. 'Natalia, it's no good begging me. It's out of my hands now. It's him. Your fiancé you need to beg. Why don't you ask him to tell me where he's put it, Natalia? Then all this can just go away.'

Trembling, Natalia stared at Abel, her eyes filled with fear. 'Just tell him. Tell him what he wants, Abel. Tell him where the money is.'

Nico gestured, chuckling. 'You heard the lady, tell me.'

Tears rolled down Abel's face as he stared at Natalia, love and anguish ripping through his body. 'I don't have it! I never did! I swear, Natalia! Nico, please don't do this! Do what you want with me but leave her . . . Please God, just leave her.'

Nico stared with leisurely contempt. 'Cosa farai per amore. In Italian that means, what will you do for love? It seems, Natalia, even for love your boyfriend won't give me back my money. Va bene. All right . . . Salvatore, care to join me?'

Nico Russo nodded to his brother as he began to undo his trousers as he stood above Natalia. 'Watch and remember that this was your choice, Abel. All you had to do was tell me the truth. The blame lies with you, and only you.'

'Don't you touch her, you hear me? Don't you fucking touch her!' Abel struggled against his restraints, each movement sending shooting pains rippling through his body as Natalia, crying and shaking, begged him over and over.

'Please, Abel, please! Just tell him where the money is! Tell him! Abel, help me! Help me, Abel!'

'I swear I don't know, Natalia. Jesus Christ!'

As Nico continued to stand above Natalia smiling, Abel, helpless, stopped struggling, his heart breaking as he realised what was about to happen.

Smirking, Nico spoke in a lulling tone. 'Now, I want you to be nice, Natalia, you hear me? And Abel, you need to watch this. Don't close your eyes, because each time you do, I'll make sure it'll get a lot worse for her. Capito? Understand? I want you to always remember this.'

Natalia whimpered in terror, then, and without warning, Nico slammed her against the wooden wall. 'I said, be nice, and then I want you to be nice to my brother Salvatore. Such a pretty little thing, Natalia. You deserve so much better, but in the meantime . . . Baciami, Natalia. Baciami.'

5

Natalia stared, frozen.

'I said, kiss me, Natalia!'

Nico's fingers caressed her neck as he leant into her chest, kissing it gently.

'No, Nico! No! Please, don't! Please . . . Just tell him! Abel! Abel! Please, just tell him!'

Swallowing his bile, Abel's voice broke under the weight of his torture. He sobbed as he spoke, crying out. 'I swear, Natalia, I don't know . . . I just don't know.'

Then, knowing he had no choice but to watch the nightmare unfolding in front of him, Abel whispered, shaking, though his words were drowned out by Natalia's screams. 'You shall pay for this, Nico. One day I shall have my revenge. Avrò la mia vendetta.'

Suddenly, Abel's hand hit something hard, breaking his thoughts, taking him away from the memory that crushed his every breath. With the rain beating down, he brushed off the last bits of soft earth and threw the mud-covered white lilies to one side to reveal the lid of the casket.

'I'm here, Natalia, I'm here. I won't leave you in the dark, I promise . . . I promise.'

And as Abel wept, inconsolable with grief and guilt and love, he gripped the gold handle of the cherry wood casket and began to pull.

Part One

THREE MONTHS AGO

1

Cabhan Morton, a man with trouble on his mind, stepped out from the private luxury wooden lodge into the chill of the summer evening. Shivering in his white linen shirt, he watched the shimmering waters of Grand Lake, nestled at the bottom of the Rocky Mountain National Park, Colorado.

He let out a long sigh, feeling and pushing down his anxiety as he walked across the deserted glazed timber boardwalk against the backdrop of the snow-tipped mountains. The town of Grand Lake – a tiny community of about five hundred people – was the perfect place, away from prying eyes and ears, for the annual meet-up of the Russo brothers and the extended family. And foolishly, stupidly, through his own doing, he found himself at the heart of them.

If only he'd listened to the warnings; although if he were honest, he'd known the risks of getting involved with the Russos, but at the time he hadn't cared, hadn't wanted to listen to anyone. He'd just wanted to escape England then, and all the pain that came with it, but now, now was a different matter.

With his heart rushing in his chest, he glanced back at the lodge, checking no one was coming as he pulled out his phone and dialled a familiar number. He listened as Franny Doyle's voicemail clicked in straightaway. He needed to speak to her urgently, before it was too late.

'Franny, it's me. I'll try to call you back later, but it's not looking good at the moment. Seems like Salvatore's going to make it difficult for me to leave. I'm not sure what I'm going to do . . . Look, I'll speak to you soon.'

Scrolling down his contacts, Cabhan hesitated. He stared at Alfie's number, chewing nervously on his lip. Alfie had been the loudest objector when he'd come to work with the Russos, to the point he'd told him that if Cabhan did join them, Alfie would cut him out of his life, and that's exactly what had happened. But now he was desperate, so what choice did he have?

Resolute, Cabhan pressed dial, psyching himself up, but this time the phone rang twice before he heard Alfie Jennings chirpily inviting him to leave a message.

Frustrated, he cut off the call as a loud burst of laughter made him spin around. From the shadows, he watched Bobby and Salvatore Russo walking down the stairs of the luxury hideout, deep in conversation.

He'd been here too long. *Far* too long. And he wanted out, the quicker the better.

There were several reasons why he wanted to go back home, maybe not to Ireland, but at least to England. The main one was to take his beautiful daughter, Alice Rose – the daughter he didn't know he had until four years ago – away from this life. Because apart from Franny, whom he loved like his own, and Franny's father, Patrick, Alice, with her gentleness and innocence, was simply the best thing that had ever happened to him. She was by far the best part of him, and he was determined to take her back home to family. To Franny. Even to Alfie. To everything that had once made him feel safe.

Though, trying to get the Russo brothers to let him go was another thing entirely. He knew it'd be at a price, the problem was he wasn't sure what that price would be, and he didn't trust them, not one bit. So much so that, much to Alice's tears and protests, last year he'd moved her from the school she loved to a small, secluded convent in rural Iowa, in secret. Although at the time it'd felt like an extreme measure, somehow the Russos not knowing where Alice was made him feel better, allowing him to sleep at night.

Salvatore's loud, coarse New Jersey drawl cut through the air.

'Hey, Cabhan, hey, Cabhan, what the hell are you doing out here? We've got our guests to think about.'

'Just making a call.'

Shrugging, Salvatore looked to his brother Bobby as he continued to speak to Cabhan.

'You can't make the call inside? I thought we were all friends here? Family. What's so goddamn secret you need to hide out here?'

The cold stare Salvatore turned on him made Cabhan feel uneasy. Since he'd told the brothers he'd wanted to leave, suspicion and paranoia had set in, especially with Salvatore, who ran the main branch of the family business along the East Coast.

Cabhan's soft Irish lilt coated his words as he tried to sound calm.

'No, not at all, I didn't want to be rude. I thought I'd just check in with Franny and Alfie, see how they are. It's been a while since I've spoken to them. The time difference doesn't help. Apologies if I was out of line.'

Salvatore, his steroid-pumped muscular frame blocking out the light from the lodge doorway, continued to stare. 'Give me your phone.'

'What?'

'I said, give it me.'

Hesitantly, Cabhan – his face strained, his black velvet skin paling slightly – walked across to Salvatore and placed the phone in his outstretched hand.

He spoke evenly. 'Like I say, Sal, I was just calling home. See for yourself.'

11

Salvatore, holding eye contact before breaking it to scroll through Cabhan's call log, pressed last number redial. Staying silent, he put the phone to his ear, listening as the voicemail clicked in.

'This is Alfie, I can't answer right . . .'

Salvatore's laugh startled an old man standing by the door. Loud and menacing. He grabbed hold of Cabhan's shoulders, shaking him hard, pressing his flushed face into Cabhan's. His breath sweet and sickly, stinking of cigars. 'See what you've done to me, Cabhan, you've made me a bag of nerves. All this talk of you wanting to leave makes me edgy. Can't understand what the problem is. Why the big change? Maybe I should start looking over my shoulder.'

Cabhan, feeling the hard bone of Salvatore's forehead pushing on the bridge of his nose, knew better than to try to pull away. He also knew better than to show any weakness – showing any sign of fear to the Russos was just an invitation for them to go in with full force. The other thing he knew was that somehow he had to play this perfectly.

Nervously but hoping, *praying* that it didn't show, Cabhan kept his voice as light as possible. 'It's not personal, Salvatore. You know that. I just miss home. No big deal.'

Salvatore stepped back, looking up into the night sky. 'Not personal?'

'That's right, Sal. I appreciate everything you've done for me. Giving me a job and welcoming me as part of the family, but that's the point, I miss *my* family. Franny. Alfie. Like I say, it's not personal.'

Salvatore nodded, closing his eyes before whipping out a pistol from his pocket, smashing it and pressing it hard into Cabhan's face. 'And neither is this.'

Cabhan's hands shot up in the air as he stumbled back, fear gripping him. 'Sal, please.'

'Get on your knees . . . I said, get on your fucking knees, unless you want me to put a hole in you now.'

12

'Sal, please, Jesus Christ, you and me, we go back a long way. *Ti rispetto, ti voglio bene, Salvatore, tu e la tua famiglia.*'

Another burst of laughter came from Salvatore. 'You say you respect me? You love me and my family?'

Working hard to push down his panic, Cabhan nodded. 'I do.'

Salvatore flicked off the safety catch of the gun. 'Yet you want to leave and go back home. To me that doesn't sound like a man who loves and has loyalty to his friends. And a man who doesn't have loyalty is a dangerous enemy.'

Bobby Russo, his temper as violent and volatile as his brother's, had the ability to recognise discretion was sometimes needed. He spoke up as he watched more and more of their guests, curious about the commotion, come outside.

'Sal, why don't we sort this out tomorrow? We're celebrating. We've all had a good year. We've got the rest of the family to think of. They don't need this. Put the gun away. Cabhan was only calling Franny and Alfie. That's all. *Nessun danno fatto.* No harm done . . . Good? *Bene?*' Bobby kissed his brother on both cheeks. '*Bene?*'

Salvatore stared at Bobby, slowly nodding, his face showing a thousand thoughts. He answered slowly. '*Sì. Bene.*'

A grin spread across Bobby's pockmarked face, the handsome Russo genes not having passed down to him. 'That's right, Sal. All good. No harm! *Nessun problema.* No problem!' Bobby broke his hold, grinning at the guests. 'Nothing to see here, ladies and gentlemen! Please, continue to enjoy, we've talked business too long. Now we celebrate.'

Helping Cabhan to his feet, Salvatore slapped him hard on the back then pulled out a gold cigarette case from his pocket. He snapped it open, revealing several grams of finely cut cocaine along with an engraved toot. 'Have a line with me, Cabhan.'

'No, I'm fine.'

The ice ran back into Salvatore's words. 'I said, have one.'

Cabhan, realising he had no other choice, took the toot,

13

bending over the cigarette case as Salvatore watched him snort a line.

'Again . . . Have another.'

Cabhan hesitated slightly, but it was enough for Salvatore to step forward, his face pulled into a frown. 'Problem?'

'No, of course not, I—'

'Cabhan!' Alexandra Russo, Salvatore's spoilt sixteen-year-old niece, shouted loudly, breaking up Cabhan and Salvatore's conversation as she swayed her curvaceous body down the stairs.

'Cabhan, I want a lift home, now! I'm tired!'

Salvatore raised his eyebrows, chuckling nastily as he headed back towards the other guests with Bobby.

'You better do as she says, Cabhan. Hell hath no fury like a woman scorned and that includes not giving her a lift home . . . We'll talk tomorrow.'

Staring angrily at Cabhan, Alexandra drawled in the same New Jersey twang as her uncles.

'In fact, give me the fucking keys, Cabhan. I'll drive, and you can keep me company.'

Looking back at Alexandra, Cabhan hid his disdain whilst attempting to sound courteous.

'Ally, I'm happy to take you home, you know I am, but it's probably best if I drive.'

Ally licked her lips seductively before her face screwed up in annoyance. She poked Cabhan hard in his chest. 'Don't ever try to fucking tell me what's best, *especially* in public, or I might have to go and get my uncle Sal to teach you about respect. *Capito?*'

Evenly, Cabhan answered, remembering the last occasion Salvatore, on Alexandra's orders, had paid him a visit to remind him of the Russos' definition of respect. That particular visit had landed him two weeks in the Lower Manhattan hospital. 'Oh, I understand, Ally. You've made your point very clear . . . as you always do.'

14

A large smile spread across Ally's face. 'Then what are we waiting for, let's go.'

As Salvatore Russo watched them drive away, he smiled to himself, because although he'd been outvoted by the rest of the Russo family on permanently disposing of Cabhan, he was sure once he'd spoken to Nico that might change. After all, Cabhan had been privy to the family business and there was no guarantee he wouldn't start shooting his mouth off once he'd left. And the one certainty about dead men was that they couldn't talk.

2

Ally Russo gripped the wheel of her bright red McLaren GT – a sweet sixteen gift from her beloved uncle Sal. The wheels of the performance car gripped and burnt up the road as she took the corners of Highway 34 – Trail Ridge Road – at speed, winding up the Rockies as heavy mist began to obscure the surroundings, making it impossible to see the vast expanse of craggy mountains and aspen forests.

'Ally, for God's sake slow the hell down!'

Enjoying hearing the panic in Cabhan's voice, Ally shouted back, laughing as she did so, her Jersey twang emphasising the mockery in her voice. 'Are you scared, Cab? You a mama's boy who can't handle the speed? Why don't you try and grow a pair already?'

Cabhan, keeping his eyes on what was left of the road as the visibility worsened, shook his head, the high-purity cocaine he'd snorted earlier making him edgier than normal. 'No, I just value my life, and yours, come to think of it.'

Accelerating as she took the hairpin corner of Fairview Curve, Ally glanced across at Cabhan arrogantly as the deep roar of the supreme engine purred effortlessly into a higher gear. The force thrust the powerful car forward, causing Ally to lose grip on the steering wheel.

'Ally!' Cabhan yelled as he leant over, grabbing hold of the cream leather wheel, helping to regain control of the McLaren as it snaked dangerously into the sea of mist.

A slight look of fear passed over Ally's face before she took hold of the wheel again with a laugh. Relief mixed with adrenalin pumped out of her as she exhaled. 'That was a close one. What do they say, driving a fast car is better than sex . . .' She paused before glancing across again at Cabhan, purring, 'But I guess that all depends on who you're having sex with. You never did accept that blow job I offered you. What do you say, Cab? How about tonight . . .?'

Not interested in girls the same age as his daughter, especially a spoilt brat like Ally Russo, Cabhan's tone was hostile. 'Just pull the fuck over, you'll get us killed.'

Ignoring Cabhan, Ally continued to drive as the weather conditions worsened, the switchbacks on the road getting tighter with the five-hundred-foot drop, without guard rails, inches away from the screeching car's tyres. Below the road the mountain verge dropped away quickly into nothing but air.

'I said, pull over!'

'Fine, spoil my fun!'

Reluctantly, Ally slowed down, when suddenly a massive impact from behind shunted the car forward, causing the McLaren to swerve, running it up onto the stony edge of the road, smashing the car's axle along the rock-scattered terrain.

Panicking as the rear wheels began to lock, Ally screamed whilst Cabhan quickly glanced in the passenger mirror, but in the thick of the mist he couldn't see anything.

'Ally, you—' He suddenly stopped, feeling the first prickle of panic as blinding giant beams of light cut through the fog and a gigantic juggernaut appeared behind them.

Another huge bang propelled the car closer to the edge. Still screaming, Ally began to cry hysterically. 'Why aren't they stopping, Cabhan?'

Panic swirling through him, Cabhan spoke urgently. 'They can't see us and won't be able to feel the impact of the car in that massive truck. Ally, quick, you've got to blast the horn . . . Blast it!'

But as Ally sounded the horn, the juggernaut caught the back end of the car again, this time ploughing it forward, skidding the McLaren out of control. Ally fought frantically to keep hold of the steering wheel, which violently whirled through her hands as she choked on her tears.

As the McLaren bumped through the rocky terrain at the edge of the mountain, the low front spoiler ripped off as the car began to slide.

'Ally!' Cabhan screamed as his neck snapped forward, the front wheels hitting the edge of the precipice at well over a hundred miles an hour. The car hung suspended in the air for a moment before it crashed back down, smashing against the side of the mountain with bone-shattering force.

Further and further down the side of the mountain face the car fell, rolling and twisting, tumbling and flipping, bouncing and turning with Cabhan and Ally's screams echoing through the darkness until finally they came to a sudden stop. The impact sounding like roaring thunder.

The inside of the car seemed to be dripping with blood. Cabhan found himself jammed up against the door. Attempting to pull himself out of the wrecked vehicle, he crawled forward, and an excruciating pain exploded within him. He cried out as a torn piece of metal was embedded deeper in his calf, tearing open his flesh.

Knowing he had to try to get help, Cabhan, with sweat and blood covering his face, used all his strength, yelling out at the pain but refusing to let it stop him as he scrambled out of the car.

Panting with exhaustion, he looked around. They were under the mist now, allowing him to see clearly. The car had landed on a wide rocky shelf, three hundred feet down from the road they'd been driving along, with the drop below them another two hundred.

Stumbling round the car with his leg oozing, Cabhan bent down to where Ally lay, her face almost obscured by cuts and blood. He whispered her name. 'Ally, Ally, wake up! Come on, honey, wake up. It's okay, I'll get help. I'll get you out of there.'

Noticing part of the car's seat was pressing down on her chest, Cabhan took hold of Ally's shoulders, attempting to pull her into a better position, when suddenly her head, severed by the crash, rolled towards him. He recoiled, retching and scrabbling backwards towards the edge of the sheer drop. 'Oh shit, oh God. Please, no! Ally! Oh Christ!'

His hand shook as he quickly dragged his mobile out of his pocket and tried to focus on the numbers. He dialled 911, holding his side to halt the flow of blood, but he abruptly cut off the call before it connected. His gaze rested on the boot of the McLaren, which had torn open. Within the panels of the car, Cabhan could see several large packages of cocaine. His gaze crossed along the ground to more packages that had been scattered around. Urgently, he began to press another number. Salvatore. But another glance at Ally stopped him. There was no way he could speak to Salvatore now.

Cold, his body beginning to go into shock, Cabhan shook as he scrolled through his phone, then holding his bloodied hand against his ear he waited for his call to be answered.

'Franny! Franny! It's me. I need your help! I'm in trouble!'

3

'Cabhan, hey! How are you doing?'

'Franny, Franny, you've got to listen to me!'

Smiling, Franny twirled round as she tried to get a better signal in the heat of the Spanish sun. 'Cab, I can't hear what you're saying. Hold on a minute, let me go somewhere else.'

Eager to speak to Cabhan, Franny Doyle walked away from the busy market street in central Marbella looking for a quiet spot to take the call. It'd been a couple of weeks since they'd spoken – which was unusual for them – so she certainly didn't want to have to ask him to call back later. 'One minute.'

'Franny, just stop, Franny!'

Oblivious, Franny continued to walk around the corner to a quiet spot, which was drenched in the morning sun, her chestnut hair blowing in the warm sea breeze. 'That's better. I can hear you—'

Cabhan cut into Franny's words. 'There's been an accident.'

Panic rushed over Franny, but she quickly pulled herself together. 'What? Are you all right? What happened?'

'I'm okay, well, kind of, but . . . but Ally's not.'

'What do you mean?'

There was a pause before Cabhan said, 'She's dead, Fran.'

'Oh my God! How? Where are you?'

'Franny, my battery's going flat but I'm in a mess.'

Sitting down on a bench along the promenade with the sun beginning to get hotter, Franny was filled with worry, something she always fought so hard not to show or even to feel.

'Cab, what's going on?'

'Ally was driving and we came off the road. The car's totally trashed and, well, I managed to get out . . .'

Not understanding the timeline of events, Franny shook her head. 'Why didn't you call me before? When did this happen? Did they check you over in the hospital?'

'No, Fran, just listen to me, for God's sake. It's only just happened.'

Stunned, Franny asked, 'Are the emergency services there?'

'No.'

'But you've called them, right?'

'No.'

Puzzled and hating to feel out of control, Franny raised her voice. 'Then you've got to! Cab, what are you doing? How do you know Ally's dead? She might still have a pulse. Jesus Christ!'

On the other end of the line, Cabhan held his emotions together. He spoke matter-of-factly. 'No, Franny, she's dead all right.'

'I don't get it. Why aren't you calling anyone? What are you playing at?'

'If you'd *fucking* listen, maybe you'd understand.'

Franny, upset for Cabhan, knowing that he'd never normally speak to her like that, said, 'I'm sorry, Cab, go ahead.'

'No, *I'm* sorry, Fran, I just don't know what to do. The car's panels have come off and inside them there must be at least ten . . . twenty kilos of cocaine. I've also taken a few lines of coke myself and if they decide to do a blood test, well . . .' He trailed off before adding, 'So you see, I can't call the police.'

Closing her eyes for a moment as she took in the enormity

of the situation, Franny breathed deeply, calming herself, knowing that Cabhan needed her to be strong. She could hear her father's voice in her head, telling her that it wasn't emotions that won a war, it was action. It wasn't weakness, it was strength. It was having a heart of stone, no matter what. It was never allowing yourself to feel anything at all.

And with her father's teaching in mind, Franny pushed down any sort of dread and began to take control.

'First, Ally was driving, not you, they're not going to do any checks, so the only thing we've got to deal with are the drugs. But that's okay too. All you've got to do is hide them somewhere, then once you have, call 911. Get help. It's an accident, Cab, the police won't start searching the area, will they? It'll be all right. I promise.'

Franny could hear the panic in Cabhan as he answered. 'Fran, you don't understand, there *is* nowhere to hide them. We landed on a ledge when we came off Trail Ridge Road.'

Knowing the road well and how precarious it was, Franny's stomach went into knots, but again she rose above it. After all, she was a Doyle and, as her father, Patrick, always drummed into her, it wouldn't help anybody to break down and cry. 'You're lucky to be alive, Cab.'

'Fran, look, my battery's beeping, I'm going to cut out any minute.'

'Then you've got to listen to me, you've just got to get rid of the coke. You hear me? Break open the bags and throw it away.'

'I can't, Fran, it's probably worth about three million dollars with a street value of more. Salvatore's not going to accept that I just threw away his coke, especially after he finds out his niece is dead.'

'What else can you do, Cab?'

'Fran, they'll kill me. You know what the brothers are like. They'll chop me up in pieces and feed me to their dogs if I can't replace their coke. I just haven't got that kind of money.'

22

'I have.'

'What?'

Chewing on her bottom lip, Franny repeated what she'd just said. 'I have. I can get you two million pounds.'

'I . . . I . . . don't know what to say.'

'You don't have to say anything. Just promise me when you put the phone down you'll get rid of the coke and then call 911.'

'Fran, I can't take your—'

'I said, promise me!'

With overwhelming relief, Cabhan whispered, 'I promise.'

'Good. Because I'm not going to lose you, Cab. I love you. Throughout my life you've always been there for me, and now it's my turn to be there for you. And when *I* put this phone down, you're going to get help and I'm going to get on the earliest plane and come out there. Book yourself into a hotel room, lie low for now and call no one.'

'But what about Salvatore? I'll have to tell him about Ally.'

'No, leave that to the police. What you've got to do is once you're off that mountain, get hidden and stay hidden. We'll face Salvatore together . . . I'll see you soon.'

As the line went dead, Franny closed her eyes, taking another deep breath. There wasn't *anything* she wouldn't do for Cabhan. She'd known him all her life and regarded him as her second father, even if that 'anything' was taking the two million pounds Alfie and Vaughn had entrusted to her. The money that was meant to start their new business in England. The money they were waiting on and the money she was supposed to smuggle out of the country the day after tomorrow. Two million pounds. Alfie and Vaughn's two million pounds. The men's entire fortune.

At Malaga Airport waiting for her flight to Gatwick, which would then take her on to Denver, Colorado, Franny Doyle pulled out her phone and began to text.

Please don't be angry, Alfie, but something's come up. It's probably better if u don't know what. But trust me when I say I wish it could be different. I won't b coming to England. One day you'll understand why I've done this. If it's any consolation, I do love u. F.

Hearing her flight call, Franny turned off her phone. She wouldn't allow herself to have any regrets. This was something she just had to do and, if Alfie loved her the way he said he did, well, then he'd just have to understand. Two million pounds' worth of understanding.

4

Alice Rose skipped through the freshly cut meadow counting the white fence posts as she twirled around the trees, moving rhythmically in the warm Iowa breeze. This was her *very* favourite time of year, when all around her was an explosion of colours and scents.

The problem was, though, the happiness she felt often distracted her from giving a prayer of thanks for everything she had, and she knew that was wrong. *Sinful*. Her mother had warned her and her friend, Isaiah Thomas, on a daily basis what would happen if they forgot to say their prayers. She would be damned to eternal hell, cursed into everlasting fire prepared for the Devil and his angels, and *that* was something she *certainly* didn't want to happen.

Shivering at the thought, Alice decided she needed to try harder to remind herself that none of it would be possible without the good Lord's grace, especially a day like today. Only this morning her father had called to say that Franny was coming to visit them and, even though she missed Isaiah, she couldn't help but feel excited that Franny was making the trip.

The love she felt for Franny was the same love she'd felt towards her own mother; she was good and kind and compassionate.

God-fearing values, as her mother would say. Then, delighted just at the idea of Franny's trip to see her, a surge of pure joy ran through Alice. She jumped in the air, spinning around, feeling like the warm winds were sending her soaring towards the sun.

'Alice! Alice! Is that any way to behave? I don't think the Lord would approve of such behaviour, do you?'

Alice's long corkscrew curls tumbled over her beautiful brown face, chaotically dotted with freckles. She grinned at Sister Margaret, a nun whom most of the other girls found to be stern and unyielding, as she made them recite and write verses from the Bible each day, sit in silent reflection of their sins for hours on end – everything Alice's mother had done, and so Sister Margaret made her feel safe, reminding her of the world she'd grown up in.

Still skipping and spinning, coming across as much younger than her sixteen years, Alice laughed warmly, her words holding the purest sincerity. 'Sister Margaret, I think the Lord would be delighted that I'm celebrating what he made. After all, weren't you the one who taught us that *this is the day that the Lord hath made, and therefore we should rejoice and be glad in it*?' She paused, tilting her head thoughtfully before adding, 'Psalms 118, verse 24.'

'Alice Rose, I hope you're not being insolent?'

Panting and with her cheeks glowing, Alice walked across to the nun. She smiled, looking slightly puzzled, her tone a blanket of kindness. 'No, of course not, Sister Margaret! I was only saying that today like all days is a blessing . . .' Alice stopped, furrowing her eyebrows before adding, 'Am I wrong?'

Sighing, Sister Margaret, slightly ashamed of her grouchiness in the face of such godliness, smiled back, taking Alice's hands in hers.

Even though Alice was sixteen, she worried about the child; she wasn't cut out for the world they lived in. She'd been sheltered, brought up in a loving but strict religious community, and as

26

much as Sister Margaret wished it wasn't the case, Alice's background was a huge obstacle, coming with far too many challenges for a teenager required to live in modern society.

'No, I'm the one who's wrong, doubting your integrity, I should know better. And it's true, today *is* a blessing, like children are a blessing; a gift from God, and you, Alice Rose, are certainly that.'

Alice grinned, blushing at the nun's compliment. 'Thank you, Sister Margaret . . . anyway, I'd better get on.'

Skipping off, Alice wrinkled her nose, wincing as she heard the nun ask, 'Alice, what have you got in your hands?'

Swivelling around and dropping the mobile phone in the long grass, Alice decided that seeing as she had a good reason for not being *entirely* honest, the Lord would forgive her, and therefore she didn't have to feel guilty about what she was about to say. 'Nothing.'

Sister Margaret's tone was severe. 'Alice, you do know what the Bible says about lying and liars, don't you?'

'I do, Sister Margaret . . . *A false witness will not go unpunished, and he who breathes out lies will perish.* Proverbs 19, verse 9.'

'It also says *their throats are like open graves, with their tongues they deceive and the venom of poisonous vipers is under their tongue.*'

Paling, Alice stared at the nun as she whispered, 'Romans 3, verse 13.'

'Exactly. So I'll ask you again, what have you got in your hands?'

Swallowing hard and resolving that maybe it *wasn't* such a good idea not to be completely truthful, Alice brought her hands from behind her back, shaking at the thought of the snakes.

'There's nothing in my hand.'

Sister Margaret held Alice's gaze. 'Tonight in chapel, you'd do well to say an extra Hail Mary.' And with that the nun walked away.

Feeling deflated, Alice watched Sister Margaret disappear before daring to pick up the phone. She hadn't wanted to lie and she hadn't even seen it as a lie . . . well, not really, not like a real one anyway.

Normally, she didn't mind that they were only allowed their phones for a short time in the evening when supervised by the Sisters, but what she had to do, she didn't want anyone else to know about; she wanted it to be a surprise. So when she'd taken her father's call in Sister Margaret's office this morning, she'd also taken the opportunity to grab her phone out of the box they were kept in and slip it into her pocket.

Trying to push the feeling of guilt aside, Alice walked towards the far meadow where Mac, the convent's old dapple grey pony, was grazing.

Tearing a large handful of grass, she walked towards him, talking warmly. 'Here, boy, here you go . . . Come on, Mac, look what I've got for you.'

Lifting his head for a moment then turning away uninterested – quite satisfied with the grass already in his paddock – Mac sauntered off, leaving Alice to sit down by the large basswood tree.

She sighed deeply, worried about her father. He'd sounded strange – *stressed* – when they'd spoken this morning, and although she'd asked him if everything was all right and he'd told her he was fine, she knew something was wrong. Very wrong.

Perhaps he was working too hard, maybe business was bad . . . Not that she knew *exactly* what it was he did. Something to do with selling insurance was all he'd said when she'd asked. But it was obvious he was not feeling his best, which was even more of a reason for her doing what she was about to.

She wanted to do something special for him, something nice for his birthday next week. After all, he deserved it. He was always thinking about her or about Franny, making sure that everyone else was all right, and often neglected himself. So, this year she decided that she was going to make a fuss of him, and hopefully that might cheer him up.

Pulling out a piece of paper from her pocket, Alice began to dial a number. It rang twice before being answered.

'Hello?'

'Hello.'

'Who is this?'

'My name's Alice Rose. You don't know me, but I'm the daughter of Cabhan Morton.'

5

The splattering of blood covered the shower walls as Nico Russo stamped his boot into Don Lombardi's face. Don was a small-time crook who'd spent most of his life in and out of penitentiaries, but it was obvious to Nico that the one lesson prison life *hadn't* taught him was the most basic lesson of all: *never* steal from your own. So now he had to remind Don of *exactly* what happened to anyone who skipped that class.

'Hey, Don, had enough yet? What was that?'

Nico jumped in the air, bringing his foot down from a height. The weight and severity was so great that Don's mouth immediately flooded with blood while his front teeth were pounded out of his gums. Nico stamped his boot further towards the back of Don's mouth, pushing the rest of his teeth out of the way.

Avoiding the jets of water from the large communal shower-heads, Nico crouched down, panting from the exertion, inches away from hair-coiled soapsuds that mixed with Don's body fluids on the cracked tile floor.

Nico's tone was calm, reassuring. 'Don, *mio amico*, my friend, I want to give you the chance to tell your side of the story. I want to know if it's true what they said you did.'

There was silence save the running water and the gurgling

noises from Don Lombardi struggling to gasp for air. Nico pulled a face. 'I'll ask you again. Is it true that you stole the phone? Tell me.'

Sighing, Nico forced one hand in Don's mouth, yanking it open before putting his fingers between Don's bleeding gums to keep it open.

Bringing his eyes up to his men, Nico nodded. 'Give me them.'

Then without a word, a tall dark-haired man who stood impassively by the shower entrance handed Nico a pair of scissors from out of his trouser pocket.

Turning his attention back to Don, Nico said, 'You see this, Don? This is what happens to people who disrespect my friends by stealing from them. Respect to me is more important than family. *Rispetto*. Respect. The one thing I ask of all who know me, because without it, we are all just animals . . . And as you have nothing to say to me, you won't have any need of this.'

Don Lombardi shook his head with terror as Nico yanked at his tongue, digging the sharp scissors through the flesh as he began to extract it.

'Nico! Nico, do you have to do this in here?'

As Don choked and convulsed on the floor in an agony beyond pain, Nico threw the severed tongue to one side before looking up at the prison warden. Officer Johnstone was just one of several on his payroll. In fact, most of the correction officers in the facility, whether voluntarily or by various levels of coercion, were on his payroll in some way or another. It made for an easier life, making the hellhole he was in slightly less of a hellhole.

Armed and dressed in a dark green uniform, Officer Johnstone glanced down at Don Lombardi, his manner casual, almost weary. 'Get this cleared up. You hear me, Russo? And for Christ's sake, make sure someone takes him to medical.'

Standing up, Nico brushed down his clothes, running his hands under the icy showers to wash away the blood. He turned to smile at his men, though his tone was ominous and taunting, something Johnstone didn't fail to miss. 'You heard him. Clear this mess up. *Capito*? Understand? We'd hate to upset the officer, wouldn't we?'

'Good, make sure you do by the time I get back.'

Watching Officer Johnstone leave, Nico thought, as he seemed to every moment of every minute of every day, that he'd been behind bars far too long. Eight years too long after one of his men had turned informer. A hazard of his trade and a reason to rule his empire like Satan himself.

Johnny Milano had worked for him for over twenty years, but he'd squealed to the FBI like a sow on heat. And despite the fact he'd given Johnny his first break – had let him in to the heart of the Russo family and even paid for the cocksucker's wedding to some two-dollar stripper from Long Island – Johnny Milano had repaid him by telling the feds everything he knew about the drug deals, the money laundering, the illegal shipping, the prostitution, the smuggling, the whole goddamn lot.

But Nico had had a tip-off from someone on his payroll in the bureau and consequently managed to cover most of his tracks. The FBI couldn't find anything that was going to stand up in court relating to any illegal activity, but ironically what they *did* find was in connection to tax evasion linked to some of the family's *legal* businesses.

The IRS had thrown the book at him and he'd been given fifteen years, and it looked like he was going to have to serve all fifteen. The parole board didn't seem interested in letting the head of the Russo family back out on the streets.

Though he'd sure as hell made Johnny Milano pay. Johnny had thought the FBI witness protection would keep him safe, but there was no such thing as protection for rats. No hiding place. His men had searched and they'd found the whole of the Milano family. The mother, the grandmother, the children, even the pet rabbits, along with the two-dollar stripper from Long Island. No one escaped revenge. Revenge had been Johnny

Milano's executioner and it would be anyone else's who dared to cross him.

'Nico.'

Breaking his thoughts, Nico looked up to see Chris D'Amato, his cellmate – and a good friend – walk into the shower room. 'It's for you, Nico.'

He held out a mobile phone.

'Who is it?'

'She says her name's Alice Rose.'

Nico Russo whirled the pool of blood – yet to be cleaned up – with the tip of his boot. He leant against the tiled wall, feeling the damp go through his prison shirt. Of all the calls he'd imagined he'd have, this *certainly* wasn't one.

His voice was low, calm. Warm. 'Hello, Alice Rose, I've heard a lot about you.'

'Have you?'

'Yes, from Cabhan. Though I haven't seen him in a while.'

On the other end of the phone, Alice was eager. 'So do you work with him?'

Kicking Don Lombardi's severed tongue to the side and signal-ling to Chris to pick it up, Nico smiled. 'You could say that. Anyway, to what do I owe this pleasure?'

Feeling happier, Alice's tone was light. 'I don't know if Dad told you, but it's his birthday next week.'

'No, Alice, he didn't tell me.'

'Well, I was hoping to have a surprise party for him, do something nice, invite all his friends and work colleagues. Is that silly?'

'Why would it be? I don't think you ever get too old for a birthday party, do you? Well, I know I don't, I'd want a party even when I'm too old to blow out the candles.'

Delighted that Nico felt the same, Alice giggled. 'Obviously, he doesn't know I'm phoning you.'

'Obviously.'

33

'And I know this is a lot to ask, but I was wondering, *hoping*, you could come. I'm going to get as many people together as I can, and we'll have the party in the school hall. It's only small, but I'm going to make some decorations, so it'll look nice. I just want to make him happy. Will you come?'

As Alice held her breath in anticipation, Nico looked up at the clear blue sky through the thick prison bars. 'Alice, I'd love to, really I would, but the problem is, I'm a bit caught up here and won't be able to make it. I'm sorry.'

Disappointed, Alice said, 'And there's really no way?'

'I'm sorry, honey, no way at all, but I tell you what, I could get my brothers to come. Salvatore and Bobby. They'd like that. They work with your dad, too.'

'Do they?'

Using the tip of the bloodied scissors to pick out a crumb in his teeth, Nico nodded. 'Yeah. Your dad's like family to us. He's got a special place in all our hearts . . . You know, I'm so pleased you called me, Alice, this has *really* made my day. How did you get my number, by the way?'

There was a pause before Alice sheepishly admitted, 'Last time Dad came to see me, I took his phone so I could write down all the contacts. Is that really bad of me?'

Nico winked at Chris D'Amato as he watched him drag Don Lombardi up onto his feet.

'No, Alice, I wouldn't call that bad. Believe me, I've done a lot worse myself.'

'You have?'

Nico chuckled, his tone teasing. 'Oh yes, Alice, things so bad I'd be in a lot of trouble if I told you.'

Alice giggled again, enjoying the conversation.

Nico continued. 'That's better, it's good to laugh at ourselves, and besides, I'd say it was clever what you did. If you hadn't, well, you and I wouldn't be speaking now, would we? And I've got an idea you might like. Why don't you leave it to *me* to invite

34

the people your dad would want at his party? You don't want to have people there he doesn't get on with, do you?'

'No, of course not. Would you really do that?'

'Absolutely, I'd do anything for Cabhan. But you need to tell me where you are so I can tell my brothers and make all the arrangements.'

'Thank you, Nico, thank you so much! It's going to be brilliant. And you won't tell Dad anything about it, will you?'

'You have my word. *Lo prometto*. I promise. We wouldn't want to spoil the surprise, would we? We want to give him a birthday he'll never forget.'

6

Franny Doyle yawned as she made her way along the glass-panelled corridor of the Sheraton Hotel located in downtown Denver, Colorado. She was hot and tired after travelling for the past two days. It hadn't helped that her flight had been a particularly turbulent one, or that opposite her – in the usually staid business class – a very large, noisy Greek family had insisted on breaking into the occasional champagne-fuelled song. Then, to make matters worse, the cab driver who'd picked her up from the airport had, for some inexplicable reason, shouted at every passing car before refusing to make his way around the road-works, causing her to get out and walk the whole of the mile-long pedestrian strip in the searing Denver heat. Still, at least she was here, and ultimately that was all that mattered.

As she walked along the thick brown swirl carpet, grateful for the air conditioning that blasted out near sub-zero temperatures, she felt her phone buzz in her pocket, letting her know she had a voicemail.

She listened as she waited for the lift to make its way down from the twenty-second floor. It was Alfie . . . again:

Pick up, for God's sake! I don't know how many bleedin' messages I've left, but you can't keep ignoring me. For fuck's sake, Franny, why are you doing this to me, darlin'? Just call me and let's sort this out. I get that you could be mad at me. Maybe I didn't give you as much attention as I should've done, or maybe you think I don't tell you that I love you enough. But I do love ya. From the minute I knew ya, I started falling for ya. But Jesus, Fran, whatever it is I've done, don't take it out on our future. Vaughn's future. You want me to come and find you, Franny? Is that what you want, darlin'? To show you I care? Cos I do, but I just haven't got time for these fucking games at the moment! . . . Franny!

Stepping into the lift, Franny clicked off the phone, smiling sadly to herself as she fought hard not to feel the devastation and guilt of what she was doing to him, because there was no getting away from it, she loved Alfie with all her heart, he was her soul mate. But the fact was, she just couldn't afford to let her feelings for him change what she had to do, no matter how hard it was.

She knew he was hurting as well. The variety of messages from him since she'd texted him about the change of plan had ranged from calm to bewilderment then to anger before returning to calm in a merry-go-round of mystified emotions.

She didn't blame him. Not one little bit. How could she? She'd taken his and Vaughn's money, and the only explanation he'd had was a short, swift text. He deserved better, but she couldn't explain, mainly because he wouldn't understand. Yes, he'd appreciate the principle of it – caring and looking out for family – but she knew that Alfie saw this money as his one chance, his *last* chance at making it back on top, so there was no way, if he'd had his choice, he'd let her spend it on getting Cabhan out of trouble.

And of course, Alice Rose. Sweet Alice Rose whom Cabhan had only learnt of in the last couple of years.

Alice had been conceived following a brief affair Cabhan had

had during a short business trip to the States sixteen years ago. Although Alice's mother, Clara, and Cabhan had parted on good terms – friends even – and had kept in contact over the ensuing years, Clara had never told Cabhan *anything* about Alice until it'd been completely necessary for her to do so. And that had only been in the most extreme situation, when Clara had been diagnosed with a rapidly progressing form of multiple sclerosis.

Cabhan had been thrown into the deep end: he had only learnt he was the proud father of a beautiful young girl two months before Clara had died. Alice, of course, had been devastated. The other thing she had been was naïve for her age, having grown up in a tiny farm community in George County, Mississippi. Clara had not only protected her from the world, but had brought Alice up in a highly religious environment, which was certainly at odds with Cabhan.

Though not knowing how to get through to a teenager who had not only lost her mother but had been brought up as if God were her best friend, Cabhan had asked around and found a small and exclusive boarding school at a girls' convent – as nuns and the religious community were something Alice understood. Business allowing it, Cabhan had visited her every day, then after a while a smile had slowly returned to Alice's face.

What followed was the blossoming of a beautiful loving bond between Cabhan and Alice Rose. He loved Alice as Alice loved him. Completely and absolutely. In fact, Franny didn't know anyone who'd met Alice and hadn't fallen in love with the sweet, innocent, kind-hearted girl, who somehow had been shielded from the world turning upside down.

Suddenly, Franny shook herself out of her thoughts. She didn't want to start feeling sentimental, she had a job to do: somehow she had to get Cabhan out of the mess he'd found himself in, before the Russos began to point the finger of blame.

Quickly looking along the corridor, making sure no one was coming, Franny tapped lightly on door 493. 'Cab! Cab! It's me.'

It took less than thirty seconds for Franny to hear the locks of the hotel room unbolt. Then, looking stressed and tired, Cab opened the door, giving her a quick, grateful smile before his expression immediately turned pensive as he glanced up and down the hallway. 'You made sure no one followed you?'

Saying nothing, Franny nodded as she walked into the large Presidential suite, which looked out west across the city, over the Broncos' 'mile high' stadium to the snow-capped Rocky Mountain National Park.

She turned to Cabhan, who was pouring himself a large bourbon at the bar in the corner of the freshly decorated room, and gently spoke, her large emerald eyes imploring him and full of kindness. 'How about you leave that drink for a minute until you give me a hug . . . It's good to see you, Cab.'

With her mane of thick, glossy chestnut hair falling over her beautiful face, skin like a porcelain doll, she smiled at Cabhan, though it was tinged with sadness. For a long time now, he hadn't been himself. He'd been withdrawn, troubled, and each time they *had* spoken she'd also got the sense he was on edge. Nervous. She'd even go so far as to say he seemed afraid, and the man she'd known all her life had never been afraid of anything. But that was before. Before he'd started working for the Russo brothers.

She'd warned him. Begged him to think carefully about getting involved with them, because she knew, *knew* how dark and dangerous they were. Her father – who at one time had done business with the brothers – in the end refused to do so, which spoke volumes, because the game they were in was filled with sewer rats, scumbags, thugs, but the Russo brothers? They were on another level entirely. They had no moral code. *Anything* went. She'd heard the stories and wished she hadn't. Nico, Salvatore, Bobby. All three brothers as twisted and dark as each other.

But there'd been no telling Cabhan back then. After what had happened with her father, he'd retreated and put a whole ocean between them. It'd hurt her and she'd missed him, but although she'd never been happy with him heading off to America, she'd understood that was Cabhan's way of dealing with things. Though what she'd never grasped was why he'd gone to work with one of the most notorious families on the East Coast. The only reason she ever came up with was that it was some kind of self-imposed punishment, Cabhan's guilt over her father; though when she'd put that to him, Cabhan had simply laughed it off.

Now, however, he'd realised that he needed to come home, and nobody could've been more delighted than her. It was the right thing to do for everybody, but after what happened to Ally, to get Cabhan away from the Russos would be harder than ever.

Welling up with emotions, Cab's voice broke. 'Fran, I don't know what I would've done if you hadn't come. Thank you. I'm indebted. I—'

She cut in. 'Cab, stop. You don't owe me anything, and truthfully, there's nowhere I would rather be. Okay, maybe under different circumstances, but you, me and Dad, we were always a team, weren't we? So, me being here certainly doesn't need any thanks.'

Absentmindedly patting down his short, boxed Afro, Cab asked, 'What about Alfie? Was he all right about you coming?'

Franny's pause, although only a millisecond, was long enough for Cabhan, who knew her so well, to say, 'You haven't told him, have you? Franny, don't ignore me.'

Franny's tone was slightly irritated. 'I'm not a child, Cab.'

'That's right, so you can start off by telling me why Alfie's in the dark.'

Putting her bag down on the tangerine orange furniture, Franny decided to take a bourbon herself. 'Look, it's just best like this. The fewer people who know where you are, the better.'

Cabhan pulled on Franny's arm, turning her round to face him. His Irish accent was always more pronounced when he was passionate. 'Don't give me that, Franny Doyle. This is Alfie we're talking about. There's no way he'd say anything to anybody. We both know that. So, come on, tell me what's *really* going on.'

40

'Cab, I love you, but I know what I'm doing, so leave it, *please*. Besides, I think you've got more to worry about than what I do or don't choose to tell Alfie.'

Before Cabhan had time to reply, his phone – which was sitting on one of the dark wooden deck chairs on the balcony – began to ring.

Stepping outside, he gazed at it, his expression becoming strained again. 'It's Salvatore.'

'Have you spoken to him since the accident?'

Cabhan shook his head. 'No, you told me not to, but he knows about Ally. Actually, the whole of the American press seem to know. It was splashed across all the papers yesterday. The headlines all say the same thing: *notorious crime boss's daughter dies in accident*. The only reason I left my phone on was in case you needed to get hold of me, but Salvatore's been calling day and night. I haven't listened to the messages, I thought it was probably best not to, though I doubt he's wishing me well.'

'Give it to me.' Franny gestured with her hand, her manner and her authority reminding Cabhan of her father, Patrick. But then that wasn't surprising: Patrick had taught Franny everything he knew about the business they were in. He'd started her off young, knee-high, showing her everything from how to pick pockets like she was the Artful Dodger to cracking safes and locks. And when she was old enough he'd gone on to show her how to run large business empires built on handshakes with dangerous men and dangerous deals.

Taking the phone, Franny looked at Cab, then, giving a tight smile and taking a deep breath, she swiped the answer button.

'Salvatore. It's me. Franny Doyle. You need to listen to what I'm going to say, because there are a few things we have to talk about . . .'

7

Salvatore Russo, holding the phone, kicked away the naked teenage hooker who seemed to think helping herself to his best cocaine was part of their deal. Watching her sprawled on the floor, he glared angrily as he sat at his gold-leafed kitchen table in one of his palatial homes in Fort Collins, northern Colorado, in only his cream cotton boxer shorts, which were straining at the seams and sticking to him like glue. His diamond-encrusted medallion, given to him by his father, hung amidst the sweat-drenched hair on his chest, and the oozing perspiration trickled leisurely from between the creases of his twenty-inch neck.

It was hot. Too damn hot, added to which the maintenance guy had given him a whole heap of bullshit along with some prissy smirk about how he wasn't able to fix the air con until Monday. Two goddamn days away. Well, he'd teach the mother-fucker about how it wasn't possible to fix things. He'd make sure no doctor, no hospital, no surgeon could fix his goddamn legs and face once he'd finished with him and then he'd see who was smirking . . . Two goddamn days. The man was a jerk. And now, *now*, he had this *bitch*, this *ball-breaker* of a woman answering the phone like she was goddamn Capone.

Spitting at, but missing, the waste bin, Salvatore growled down the line as he gestured to the prostitute to leave the room.

'Put Cabhan on . . . *adesso*! Now! I wanna know what the fuck he's done with my coke.'

'He's not available to speak to you . . . but I am.' Franny stopped, then, with her tone dripping in sarcasm, added, 'And it's good to see you've got your priorities straight.'

Salvatore, shaking with fury, hissed through his teeth whilst he squeezed his phone in both hands. 'Fuck you!'

'No, fuck you, Sal. I would've thought you'd have asked about Ally first, but I forgot, you're a Russo.'

'There's nothing to ask, my niece is dead. Now if I were you, I'd go and sort your fucking period out and pass the phone to Cab. I don't deal with women.'

Another pause before Franny, coolly and matter-of-factly, said, 'That's not what I've heard, Sal. I hear you deal in women all the time.'

Flickers of white light appeared in front of Salvatore's eyes. Blind rage and fury surged through him as he felt his blood pressure go from baseline to sky-high. He pressed his muscular fingers onto his eyelids, massaging them, trying to find some relief from the stress.

'Bitches like you need to be put in their place.'

'And that's why I'm at the top of my game. I'm in my place . . . So, are we going to keep going round and round in circles, or are we going to talk business? But I do want you to know I am *genuinely* sorry about Ally. *Le mie condoglianze.*'

Standing up, Salvatore began to pace around the large, expansive kitchen. He laughed scornfully. 'Is that some kind of joke? I don't want your fucking condolences. I curse them. You hear me? Like I curse Cabhan. He murdered my niece, and he'll pay for that.'

Franny spoke firmly. 'Salvatore, we both know that it wasn't Cab who killed Ally. *She* was the one who was driving, not him.'

Mopping up the trickling sweat from his brow with the corner of a blue napkin, Salvatore opened the fridge and stuck his head inside for cool relief. 'Let me tell you something, if you were standing next to me right now, I'd blow your fucking head off. My niece is dead. She was *sixteen* years old, yet you think you can disrespect her when she's not even cold in the ground?'

'No, Sal. I'm not saying it was her fault, I'm saying it was an accident. A tragic one, but she was driving nevertheless. They are the facts.'

Salvatore raised his voice along with his head, banging it hard on one of the fridge shelves, sending cooked meat and salad along with his temper up in the air. 'Goddamn whore, pass me over to Cabhan! I wanna know what happened to my coke.'

'He got rid of it.'

It was Salvatore's turn to pause. 'What the fuck are you talking about?'

'Like I say, he got rid of it. Ripped the bags open and let it go.'

Incandescent with rage, Salvatore ran his arm along the breakfast bench, dragging and smashing the bowl of cut fruit along with bottles of olive oil and vinegar onto the marbled floor.

'So Cab thought it was a good idea to play snow globe with my coke, like it was Santa's fucking day out?'

'It was a good job he did, otherwise the police might've been wanting to talk to you.'

'Rat me out? That wouldn't be a smart idea, he knows exactly what happens to rats and their families.'

'No, he wouldn't have, but it would've been pretty easy for the police to work out who it was they needed to come and talk to. He did you a favour.'

Salvatore burst into menacing laughter. 'Some fucking favour. Do you know how much money I lost?'

'Not exactly, but I'm willing to compensate you. Every dollar. So, what do you say?'

Salvatore stared out of the large window of his house, which looked out across the lawn towards the ornate water fountain. 'I don't think so.'

'Problem is it's not your decision to make, is it, Sal? We both know who's really in charge.'

'Where you're concerned, I *am* in charge.'

'No, but you're not. I want to speak to your brother. I want to speak to Nico. Make it happen, otherwise the offer's off and you'll be out of pocket by about three million dollars.'

8

Back in the heart of Essex, Lola Harding sat in Janine Jennings' mansion worried sick. She'd had a sleepless night fretting about what she should do, about what she should think, and this morning she was still none the wiser.

Looking out of the bedroom window of the house, located just outside the pretty village of Wimbish, Lola groaned, the shot of rum she'd added to her morning coffee not helping. The problem was she classed herself as a close friend to both Alfie – Janine's ex-husband – and Franny, knowing them both for as long as she could remember.

When she'd been a tom in Soho, they'd been kind and looked out for her, making sure none of the pimps gave her a hard time. And when eventually she'd turned her back on the street, becoming the proud owner of a café, Alfie, the number-one face at the time, had made it known that *her* café and *her* café alone was the only place to go. Consequently, customers flocked in, not wanting to get onto the wrong side of the irrepressible Alfie Jennings.

But time had passed and Soho had changed. Most of the faces, including Alfie, had moved away, leaving her alone. With business bad and it becoming too much to run the café, she'd closed up and the life she'd loved, had cherished, vanished overnight. It'd made her feel like there'd been a death. Loneliness had engulfed her, strangled her, and the days and weeks had been passed in her small flat, which soared high above the city, not speaking to a soul.

They'd been awful days and she'd sunk into a dark depression, but out of the blue she'd bumped into Janine at a supermarket, or rather she'd watched from one of the aisles as Janine gave the manager a tongue-lashing. It had made her laugh, reminding her that *some* things never changed.

Although she knew Janine well through Alfie, they'd never been particularly close, but that afternoon they'd had a cup of tea and a chat and reminisced for hours. By the end of the day a miracle happened: Janine, with her loud, coarse mouth, and her busybodying, troublemaking ways, had asked her to come and stay and she'd never looked back. Not once, and she loved Janine for that.

Despite being fraught with fights and quarrels, Alfie and Vaughn had recently moved into the house. They had come back from Spain to set up their business and Janine was allowing them to stay whilst they got back on their feet and re-established themselves as faces to be reckoned with.

But now there was trouble. *Big trouble.* Franny, who'd been so good for Alfie, made him grow up, had taken none of his bullshit or his womanising ways, had done what she thought Franny would never do – she'd taken his money and disappeared. Just like that.

She was supposed to have joined Alfie back in England, but instead she'd cheated him out of his money. And Lola had to admit it hurt to think that's what Franny had done, because to her, Alfie and Fran were family, and family looked out for their own.

But the question she had to ask herself was *why*? Why would Franny do it?

Taking a sip of her coffee with the sun blazing through the window, Lola shook her head. She couldn't stand to see Alfie – whom she loved like a son – so torn apart. She had to do something, somehow try to sort it out. Both Alfie and Franny were too important to her and, even though he'd told her to stay right out of it, telling her not to breathe a word to anyone, she needed to follow her instincts and do what was right.

Sliding out her phone from the pocket of her pink towelling dressing gown, Lola dialled a number. She moved across to her bed in the corner of the grey velvet room, listening to check no one was coming.

The phone rang several times before it was eventually answered by a sleepy voice.

'Hello?'

'Franny, it's me, Lola.'

There was silence on the phone before Franny spoke again. 'Hello, Lola. It's good to hear your voice.'

'You might not think that after I've said what I need to. I'll get right down to the bones of it: I want to know what the hell's going on. Alfie's in a real state. His head's all over the place. How could you do it to him? I thought you loved him. I thought you were different, and to tell you the truth, Fran, I'm shocked. I keep telling myself there must be a good explanation, a reason why you robbed him blind, but for the life of me I can't think of one.'

Sighing, Franny quietly but firmly said, 'Lola, I love you, you know I do, but this isn't anything to do with you.'

Not remembering a time when she'd ever raised her voice to Franny, Lola, upset by her coldness, shrieked down the phone. 'But that's where you're wrong, darlin'. It *is* to do with me, because I thought we were family and family don't do this to each other. What is it? Have you met someone else? Want to set up shop on your own? Or is it some kind of payback that you've been planning all along?'

'Lola, that's not what happened. You've got it all wrong. Look, I'm tired, it's the middle of the nigh—'

Franny stopped, realising what she was about to say.

Frowning, Lola asked, 'What do you mean? You were going to say middle of the night, weren't you? For God's sake, Fran, tell me where you are. Are you in trouble? Is that it? Cos I know you, my Franny wouldn't do anything like this.'

'Lola, please, you trust me, don't you?'

Lola sniffed, her body stiffening as she sat on the silky grey covers. 'I did. I thought you were the most trustworthy person I ever met.'

'I still am.'

Forcing back the tears, Lola closed her eyes. 'Well, you've got a funny way of showing it. At least speak to Alfie, sort this out with him before it's too late. He's devastated, sweetheart, and not just because he needed that money for his business deal – which thanks to you looks like it's now going to fall through – but because he loves you. He'd never loved anyone in his life before he met you. You've broken his heart, not to mention mine.'

'Lola, I have to go. I'm sorry. Just know that if there was any other way, I would've chosen it. Look after Alfie for me, won't you? I hope that one day I'll be able to explain.'

'Franny, listen to me—'

Lola sat looking at the phone as Franny cut it off.

'Who was that?'

She jumped, not realising anybody had come into the room. It was Alfie. His handsome face stern and suspicious.

'No one.'

Pushing back his black hair away from his eyes, Alfie walked across to Lola. Standing over her, his six-foot-plus muscular frame dwarfing her, he said, 'You weren't speaking to no one, you were speaking to someone and I want to know *who* that someone was.'

Fidgeting with the phone, Lola smiled, assuming innocence.

'When I say no one, I mean it was no one important. You know, one of those cold calls.'

Alfie bent down towards her, his nose inches away from Lola's. 'You're lying to me. I always know when you're lying. Don't go behind me back, Lola, otherwise you and I are going to fall out, *big time*.'

Feeling guilty, Lola looked Alfie straight in the eye. 'And why would I want to do that, hey? Listen, I know you're having a hard time, Alfie, but there's no need to get paranoid. Look, lovely, why don't I make us a coffee, this one's gone cold. I'll make you and Vaughn a bit of breakfast, what do you say? Look, darlin', I am so sorry that you're hurting. I hate to see you like this.'

Alfie shook his head, feeling the shame creeping over him. 'No, I'm the one who's sorry; I shouldn't take it out on you. This thing with Franny is eating me up. If only I could get to speak to her, you know?'

Lola gave a tight smile but said nothing as she continued to listen to Alfie. 'But I guess her message is loud and clear. It's pretty obvious how she feels, cos she won't even answer my calls, so I'm left here not knowing what I've *fucking* done. Have you any idea what that feels like? I should've known though, shouldn't I? Look at her father and Cabhan: gangsters, faces, and they taught her everything she knows. What do they say? The apple doesn't fall far from the tree.'

'Alfie . . .'

Kicking the bedside table, Alfie glared and pointed at Lola. 'What? You think I'm being a hypocrite? Well, I'm *not*, the difference is I may be all those things her father was, but I'd never screw over my own. I'm not the bad guy here for once.'

Standing up, Lola tried to calm a pacing Alfie. 'Sweetheart, I'm sure it'll work out. I know it hurts.'

Alfie glared. 'Oh, it ain't hurting me, it's screwing me over. Fucked me financially, like I've got me bollocks caught in a vice,

50

and to tell you the truth, I wouldn't want to sort it out now even if I could.'

'You don't mean that.'

Alfie's handsome face reddened. 'Oh, I do, and if she were here right now, Lola, do you know what I'd do? . . . I'd fucking kill her.'

And with that, Alfie Jennings stormed out of the room, leaving Lola standing there, a deep sense of unease beginning to creep over her.

9

The hot Colorado air whirled through the prison window bars in the visitors' room. It was empty save the two armed guards who stood by the door waiting to be relieved from their lunchtime shift. They nodded a respectful greeting, first to Officer Johnstone and then to Nico as they walked in, making sure the latter's greeting was clearly seen by the recipient. No one wanted repercussions from a Russo.

Striding across the magnolia-and-steel-blue-painted room, and deciding that for the time being he wouldn't mention anything about the call from Alice, Nico hugged his brother. It was the first time they'd seen each other since the accident, though they'd spoken briefly on the phone.

'Nico, I'm *so* sorry for your loss. *Mi si spezza il cuore.* My heart breaks.'

Breaking away from the hug, Nico pushed the thought of his daughter, Ally, out of his mind. They weren't here to talk like women. They were here to talk business. That was all, and that was the way it should be.

He'd already learnt about his daughter's passing, so there wasn't much to discuss. Yes, it'd been a waste of a young life. The girl was only sixteen. But that was what she was, a girl. Losing a son, well, that would've been different. He knew if that had happened he'd be inconsolable with grief, but a girl, there was only so much sadness he could feel. He hadn't built his fortunes on weeping beside gravesides for the women in his life.

His father had always taught him that for the right money a man would kill his own mother. Well, he hadn't needed money, he'd been happy to do it for free. She'd been a whore, though he could've forgiven her for that; in one way or another all women were whores. What he couldn't forgive was the fact that to save her own ass, not wanting to do a stretch inside for handling dirty money, she'd ratted him, Bobby and Salvatore to the cops.

They'd all been given six years whilst she'd walked free and just got on with her life. That had been twenty years ago, but on the day he'd been released, unlike his brothers, he hadn't gone looking for his favourite meals of passatelli and pussy, he'd gone looking for her. For his mother. And, like Johnny Milano, he had made her pay.

It'd only taken a few hours to find her, grilling peppered swordfish on a barbecue for his cousin's engagement party, and right there and then he'd held down both of her hands on the grill bars, and when he'd got bored of listening to her screams? Well, he'd put a gun in her mouth and blown her clean away.

But of course, out of respect for his cousin's engagement, he'd paid for another party, only bigger and better, and out of respect for Italian custom – something very important to him – he'd gone to his mother's funeral, laying a wreath made up of white lilies and yellow roses – her favourite flowers – at her gravestone.

'Thank you, Sal,' he said eventually, his thoughts returning to Ally and Salvatore. 'She would've made somebody a good wife. However, let's get down to business and why you're here.'

Salvatore nodded, taking a seat in the deserted visitors'

room. He spoke respectfully, although what he was about to say he knew was the last thing that Nico would want to hear. But what choice did he have? Franny certainly hadn't given him one and being out of pocket by a couple of million dollars was a sting, and there'd be no hiding that. He chose his words carefully.

'Nico, as I said when I spoke to you, we've a problem. There was coke in Ally's car ready to be shipped out along the coast, but after the accident, it had to be disposed of by Cabhan.'

Salvatore stopped to stare at his brother. He could see the vein on the side of his head pulsating.

Coldly and simply, Nico said, 'Go on.'

'Given the circumstances, Cabhan felt it was the right thing to do. He couldn't call the cops without them discovering what was in the car, and even if he'd never called anyone, he would've been stuck there and we would've still been out of pocket anyway. There was no way he could've got off that ledge without help. Maybe getting rid of the coke was the only thing he could've done.'

'How much coke are we actually talking about?'

'Just over two million dollars.'

Nico nodded again, saying nothing. Giving away nothing. His face void of emotion.

After a couple of minutes, Nico said, 'Tell me, Salvatore, why didn't I know about the coke before? Why hadn't you asked my permission before you went ahead with this?'

'I'm telling you now.'

Slowly and menacingly, Nico leant across the table to his brother. '*Ora non è prima*. Now is not before. Do I need to remind you about respect, Salvatore?'

'Nico, I'm sorry. I didn't mean it to sound like I was disrespecting you. I meant this is the first opportunity I have had to tell you.'

'But if the accident hadn't happened, and you hadn't lost all that money, you wouldn't have told me about this shipment, huh? Maybe you're pleased I'm in here. So you can run things without telling me, is that it, Sal?'

Sal stared at his brother. 'No . . . No, of course not.'

'Do you think this is something I should worry about? That my little brother is trying to take over the family business behind my back?'

Salvatore pleaded with his brother, kissing Nico's hand. 'Nico, Nico. *Please*, it's not like that. Sometimes I want to get ahead. Make decisions without running them past you, because I don't want to disturb you all the time.'

Nico's face darkened as his voice rose. He gestured with his arm. 'Disturb me from what, Salvatore? Does this place look like an opera house to you? Like you're disturbing me from the opening act of *La Traviata*?'

'No, Nico.'

'No, because I'm in this fucking hellhole night and day. I was the one who took the rap, not you, but I did it for *you* and you repay me by going behind my back . . . Tell me something, Sal, should I be blaming you for the accident?'

Salvatore's face blanched. 'What?'

'Ally was your niece, it was your job, whilst I was in here, to look after her like a father.'

'I did.'

'No, because if you had she wouldn't be dead. Why didn't you drive her home that night?'

'She insisted on driving and wanted to go with Cabhan.'

Nico slammed both his fists down, his voice rising. 'And *you* let her?'

'I didn't see it as a problem. Ally drove that car so many times . . .' Salvatore trailed off.

'So who should I be blaming, Sal, if it's not you? Ally? Cabhan? Who?'

Under pressure, Salvatore's eyes darted around the room.

'Maybe . . . I don't know. Perhaps there isn't anyone to blame apart from the accident itself . . . Look, I'm sorry. I'm sorry about all of it, and from now on *everything* will be run past you as it always was.'

Though Nico's tone was warmer, his stare was so hard and so even, Salvatore couldn't look at him.

'What is this? You're going soft on me, Sal? Either pussy must be good or business must be. So good that you're okay with losing our money . . .'

Reaching across the table, Nico clipped his younger brother across the side of his head, like he had done when they were kids. 'Huh? I'm right, aren't I? You've got some pussy you haven't told me about.'

Laughing, Salvatore leant back on the plastic chair. 'No, it's just that there's an answer to this problem.'

Nico's voice was full of interest. '*Sto ascoltando.* I'm listening.'

'Franny Doyle. Patrick's daughter.'

Looking surprised, Nico thought back. He remembered her name, mainly from her father and how much he'd talked about her. He was as proud of her as any man would've been about a son. She'd been his driving force. Everything he did, he'd done for her. And Cabhan had been the same, idolising Franny as if she were his own kid. Though the couple of times he *had* met Franny, the only thing that stuck in his mind was that she'd been a ball-breaker with too much of a smart mouth.

'You're making no sense, Sal.'

'Franny wants to compensate us for the money. Although she says that Cabhan acted with our best interests in mind, she still wants to show her respect by paying for what was lost . . . She's insisting on seeing you in person.'

Nico Russo contemplated this thought and, intrigued by meeting this woman again, he answered simply, 'Okay. When?'

'She's here now, Nico, with Cabhan. I'm sorry, but she gave me no choice.'

Picking a crumb of food out of his teeth, Nico looked at his brother scornfully. 'How can a woman give you no choice?'

Humiliated, Salvatore flushed. 'I'm sorry. What shall I tell her?'

'Show her in. What sort of host would I be if I turned my guests away?'

10

Ten minutes later, with the prison officers having been left to stand outside on Nico's orders, Franny and Cabhan sat opposite him. Franny spoke calmly and firmly, showing great respect towards Nico, despite feeling none. She knew that this might be their best opportunity to get Cabhan back home to England.

'Both Cab and I are extremely saddened about Ally.'

Cabhan nodded, his expression of remorse genuine. 'I keep going over it in my head, Nico. The car, it just—'

Nico put up his hand to stop him from saying any more. 'No more talk of it, *please*. Salvatore tells me there isn't anyone to blame, it was just an accident. Tragic things happen . . . Which reminds me, how is your daughter . . .?' Nico paused to feign ignorance as Cabhan shuffled uncomfortably in his seat. 'I'm sorry, her name escapes me.'

Cabhan's voice was strained. 'Alice. Alice Rose.'

'Ah, that's right . . . Is she well?'

'She's very well, thank you.'

Nico smiled, his eyes darkening. '*Bene*. Good. We need to look after our families. Hold them close. You never know when something may happen. Life's too short, wouldn't you agree, Cab?'

'I would.'

There was a tense silence before Nico clapped his hands. 'Enough of this talk. Why don't we just get on with business?'

Giving a quick side glance to Cabhan, Franny, knowing he wanted to get this over and done with as much as she did, took Nico's cue, her voice cold and hard. 'Okay. So how much are we talking about, Nico? How much did you lose?'

Nico watched Franny evenly. He'd forgotten how much like an Italian goddess she looked, but that didn't stop him having an aversion to her. Mouthy broads who thought they were men, in his experience, always came to a very bad end.

'About two and a half million dollars.'

Franny nodded calmly, rivalling the outwardly composed Nico. 'Which is about one point eight million pounds, but as a goodwill gesture, to show there's no hard feelings between us, I'm willing to give you two million in British sterling, that's as long as we can draw a line under it all.'

Nico Russo chewed down hard on the inside of his cheek, tasting blood, his expression once again not giving away any kind of emotion as he turned to Cabhan. 'You let women do men's business now?'

'It's not for me to let her, Franny does what she wants. She is her own woman and her own boss.'

'Then it's a shame it wasn't Franny who came to work for us instead of you. It seems like she's the one with the balls. Tell me something, Franny, where did you get the money from?'

Franny gave a smile, pushing Alfie out from the back of her mind, focusing only on the matter at hand. 'Nico, I get my money from the same place you do.'

Nico smiled back, genuine amusement in his eye. He put his hand out for Franny to shake.

'Okay, Franny, it seems we have a deal.'

Franny held Nico's hand as well as his stare just as hard, the Doyle strength pushing through. 'And you'll speak to the rest of the family about Cabhan coming home?'

'Yes.'

'So that's it, we're even?'

Nico nodded and smiled.

When Franny and Cabhan had left the visitors' room, Salvatore turned to Nico.

'I'll arrange for her to transfer the money today to one of our accounts in India, and then it's done.'

Nico's eyes turned dark and cold. 'No, Salvatore, it's only just beginning. Never forget that in life there's *always* somebody to blame and there's always a way to get revenge . . . An eye for an eye, a tooth for a tooth . . . a daughter for a daughter. Let's go and wish Cabhan a happy birthday with the sweet Alice Rose.'

11

Alice walked along with Sister Margaret, hardly able to contain herself. She'd spoken to Nico again and everything seemed to be under way. He'd been amazing, kind and caring, so in return what she'd done was make certain she'd said a prayer of thanks each morning in chapel for him. After all, she didn't want to take for granted any of the angels sent her way.

The party was all set for Saturday and she had a feeling it was going to be just perfect. She couldn't wait to see her dad's face. She loved him so much at times she thought she was going to burst.

'You seem distracted, Alice.'

'No, I'm just thinking, Sister Margaret.'

'Well, I hope your thoughts are full of godliness, Alice, rather than temptation. You know, every temptation is an opportunity to prove the Devil wrong, Alice Rose.'

Alice smiled warmly. 'Of course, Sister Margaret.'

'You know, if there *is* anything you want to tell me, you can. I don't . . .'

Wanting to say more but hearing the front gate bell ring, Sister Margaret turned to walk down the tree-lined driveway. She raised her hand to the waiting car.

'I'm coming . . . I'll be back in a minute Al—'

As she spoke, Alice suddenly saw Sister Margaret's cream robe turn crimson. Terror gripped her as she watched, not quite comprehending what was happening as the nun's head began to loll back, her body sinking to the ground, blood oozing as her eyes held Alice's stare.

Alice began to shake, her whole body trembling as her screams mixed with the warm winds. Hysterically, she ran towards Sister Margaret and threw herself on the ground. Desperately afraid and racked with terrified sobs, Alice cradled the nun's head in her arms. 'Don't die! Don't die! Sister Margaret . . . *Please . . . please . . . please*!'

Blood trickled out of the side of Sister Margaret's mouth as she tried to speak. 'Run, Alice. Run. Get help, and may God protect you . . .'

A sound at the gates made Alice look up. Cold sweat began to drip from her as she saw two cars driving through them. She knew she had to move or they'd see her, but it felt like her legs were made of stone, as if fear were holding her down.

Breathing out slowly, Alice closed her eyes, petrified to move and feeling her whole body go into spasms as Sister Margaret whispered up at her.

'Alice, go! Go, child . . . *Now*!'

Too frightened to speak, Alice nodded as she backed away slowly before breaking into a run, terror stopping her from turning around as she sprinted as fast as she could back through the meadows, heading for the white stone field shelter. She raced through the open archway to the relative safety of the dark, empty building, feeling like there were someone right behind her, feeling like she could almost feel their breath on the back of her neck.

Terrified, trying to stop herself from crying, unable to stop shaking, Alice peeked through the dusty window, sneaking the smallest of glances . . .

Over by Sister Margaret, the cars stopped. The doors flung

open and Bobby Russo – his face covered by a demonic clown mask – stepped out. Leaving the other men by the brand-new blacked-out Escalades, Bobby sauntered across to the nun, watching for signs of life.

Poking her with the nozzle of his semi-automatic, his voice was thick and nasal. 'Where's Alice Rose?'

Not getting a response, Bobby kicked Sister Margaret on the top of her thigh with the tip of his boot, causing her to moan out loud. He chuckled. 'So you are alive . . . I need to know where Alice Rose is.'

Through blood-covered lips, Sister Margaret rasped, 'God forgive you!'

From behind the mask, Bobby grinned, his voice mocking. 'Hey, Sis, I don't need your God to forgive me, I've already booked my place in hell. Front-row seats. So don't you go troubling yourself about me, just tell me where Alice is.'

Riddled with pain, Sister Margaret spat her answer. 'Never!'

'Oh, it's like that, is it? Going to be a ballsy broad? Fine, Sis, have it your own way.'

After taking off the safety catch, Bobby pointed the gun straight into the nun's face, pushing it down hard onto her forehead. 'Prepare to meet your Maker.'

'Bobby! Leave it! Come on!' Salvatore called, gesturing for his brother to join him.

Glancing down at the nun, Bobby shouted back, 'What about her?'

'Jesus, Bob, I said, *come on*!'

Shrugging and flicking the latch back on his gun, Bobby, whistling, walked across to Salvatore who, along with the other men, wore hideous, gruesome masks.

Giving out his orders, Salvatore, with cocaine and adrenalin rushing through his veins, spoke quickly. 'Spread out. We know she's here somewhere; the place isn't that big. And have fun, make noise, we're in the middle of nowhere, so no one's going to hear them scream. If anyone does manage to call for help, it'll be a hell of a long time before they get here.'

Bobby looked around the grounds of the convent through the small slits of his mask and glanced at his brother. 'Problem is, Sal, we don't know what the kid looks like.'

Salvatore sniffed, then said calmly, 'Then there's only one thing for us to do. We kill them all . . .'

'Alice . . . Alice . . . Come out, come out, wherever you are!'

Still hiding in the corner of the outhouse, Alice, hearing her name, whipped around, confusion mixing with fear.

Puzzled and scared, wet with sweat, she crept back across to the tiny window, taking another peep, freezing at the sight in front of her . . . There were nine, ten men, all standing in a row wearing clown masks, gruesome and deathly but worse still, they were looking her way. Heading towards her hideout.

She heard herself cry out, but she quickly slammed her hand over her mouth, not trusting herself not to make a sound as tears of terror ran down her face.

Taking a deep breath, Alice tried to calm herself and, not knowing what else to do, dropped to her knees, squeezing her eyes shut and clasping her hands together as she moved her lips in a silent prayer. But she felt no solace and the fear continued to flood over her, making her feel like she was drowning in a pool of horror.

Braving herself to peep with one eye, Alice could see the men were still there, and for the first time in her life she was scared her prayers weren't going to save her. Right then and there, she decided her mother had been right: the sin of forgetting to give thanks meant God would forsake her in her hour of need, like she'd forsaken him. And although she realised she'd been bad, she wished he'd give her a second chance, forgive her, because she was really terrified and had no idea what to do or where to run. All she wanted was to see her dad.

Shivering, Alice's thoughts began to rush. She couldn't think straight, her chest beginning to tighten, making it hard for her to breathe, and her tears were choking her, blocking her airways. It felt like she was going to die.

'Alice!'

She held her head in her hands, rocking backwards and forwards. Why were they calling her name? How did they know it? She just wanted them to go away.

'Alice, where are you?'

Swallowing hard, Alice nervously crept forward, craning her head round the open archway, pinning herself against the wall in the shadows. As she watched, she banged her hand over her mouth again, this time to stop herself from screaming. Horrified, she saw one of her schoolfriends running, her face marked with terror as she charged towards the flower-filled woods. But it was too late, one of the men had spotted her, aiming and firing his gun in quick succession until a fountain of blood spurted out of the back of the girl's head as it burst open, splitting into tiny pieces.

Waves of nausea overwhelmed Alice and she struggled not to faint. She vomited in the corner, trying desperately not to make any noise. She knew she had to get out and wiping her mouth, Alice headed for the back window of the outhouse, which faced towards the convent.

Glancing quickly behind her, panic-stricken, Alice clambered out, running frantically along the stone path, hoping to head towards the woods. At the corner of the outbuilding, hearing voices coming from the entrance of the school. Startled, Alice crouched down by the rose bushes, pushing herself as far back as possible.

As she waited, Alice looked down, suddenly feeling like she'd stepped into something warm. Wide-eyed, she stared as she watched her white canvas sneakers begin to turn red, soaking up the flow of blood oozing towards her.

Sick with fear, Alice's gaze followed the trail. She gasped in panic. There, lying only yards away, were the bodies of Sister Abby and Sister Mary along with three of her classmates. Furiously, Alice scrabbled back, tears blinding her vision as she fought her urge to scream whilst the sound of more gunshots made her jump.

She put her fingers in her ears, desperate to block out the cries of her friends as she stumbled along the path again, tripping over more bodies of her classmates as she began to run towards the side door of the convent; the smell of death mixing in the air with the sweet aroma of purple cornflowers and poppy mallows.

Nearly at the main building, Alice froze in horror as she saw an evil clown with bright red hair, terrifying teeth and a blood-stained mouth standing guard by the entrance of the school, a sub-machine gun in hand. As fear clutched her stomach, she swallowed her vomit back down, petrified she was going to be caught.

Trembling and about to go back the way she came, Alice heard men's voices behind her getting louder, getting nearer. Hiding again, but keeping her eyes on the clown by the door, Alice tried to work out what to do next . . . He hadn't seen her *yet*, but he would if she stayed where she was – though the problem was there was no way she could get to the side door *without* him spotting her, and turning back wasn't an option.

Then, suddenly, an idea came to mind and with a rush of renewed hope, Alice checked all around her, feeling her heart thump in her chest as she tiptoed along the wall, fixing her gaze firmly on the clown.

A few feet further, Alice came to a halt by the fire escape ladder fixed to the outer wall of the convent. If only she could manage to climb up to the roof, she could get in through the skylight and make her way through to the other side of the building, which would give her access to the woods. Then just maybe, *maybe* she stood a chance.

Looking up to the top of the five-storey building, Alice, who was terrified of heights, closed her eyes briefly, kissed the cross on her necklace and prayed for strength as she tried to push away her terror, to stop herself from shaking. Then, a moment later, Alice Rose began to climb.

12

Sister Margaret opened her eyes. The pain was unbearable but she needed to move and get help. Turning her head slowly to check no one was about, she winced in agony and, unable to stand, began to pull herself along the ground. She could feel herself losing blood, but she needed to get to the office before it was too late.

Exhausted, she dragged herself along, saying a prayer for every dead body she passed as she ignored her own suffering, focusing on getting to the building and listening out for any approaching footsteps.

After what seemed like forever, Sister Margaret finally made it to the small green door situated at the side of the convent's office block. Stretching up for the door handle, she struggled to reach high enough, as the excruciating pain from the bullet – which sat like a ticking time bomb in her chest – prevented her from doing so.

With her hands trembling and blood running down her arm, she tried again, fighting back frustrated tears. But it was no good, the pain acted like a barricade.

Panting, Sister Margaret leant against the door, closing her eyes in anguish. Then almost immediately she opened them, smiling to herself ruefully, admonishing herself for thinking her despair wouldn't be answered and guided.

She pulled her rosary beads from her robe pocket and held them in her hand before flicking them up in the air, only for them to fall back down on her lap. Undeterred, Sister Margaret tried again. This time they hooked over the silver door handle, creating a loop to hold onto.

Grabbing the large wooden cross on the end of the rosary, Sister Margaret drew herself up. The weight of her body on the beads – as she intended – pulled and released the door, giving her the opportunity, before they broke, to throw herself forward and tumble inside the hallway.

Still unable to stand, she heaved herself along the corridor, a trail of blood behind her. Drained and weak, feeling like time was running out, she summoned up the last of her strength as she began to cough up blood.

Making it to her office, Sister Margaret held onto the sides of the dark wooden furniture to drag herself along. At her desk she rested for a moment, trying to get her breath as she pulled at the phone wire, bringing books and letters along with the phone crashing down onto the floor.

Trembling, she yanked a slim black notebook out of her other robe pocket, the white pages in it turning red with her blood. She could feel herself starting to black out, the words and numbers on the pages blurring in and out of vision.

Punching out a number whilst grimacing at each movement and every pain wave, Sister Margaret cradled the phone in her arms as it rang.

'Hello?'

'Mr Morton, it's Sister Margaret.'

'Hello?'

The nun's voice was almost inaudible. 'Mr Morton, you've got to come. They're after Alice . . .'

'Hello? I'm sorry, I can't hear you.'

Sister Margaret fell forward, the phone dropping out of her hands as her face slammed down onto the hard parquet tiles. Her body smashing against the wood.

'Hello? Hello?'

In the corridor Alice, hearing a noise in Sister Margaret's office, stopped, her heart racing not only at the sound coming from inside the room, but also at the trail of blood snaking up the hall. She began to shake again as she listened, panic and dread overwhelming her. But there was silence. Nothing but silence. Then, breathing out to quieten her fear, Alice slowly moved forward and peeked through the crack of the open door.

Gawking in horror, feeling like she were in a waking nightmare, Alice saw the lifeless body of Sister Margaret sprawled across the floor. She ran into the room but immediately slipped on a pool of blood, which threw her forward to trip and fall on top of the nun.

Letting out a small scream, Alice, hysterical, pulled herself into a ball as she began to cry uncontrollably.

'Hello? Hello? Hello, are you there?'

Quivering and curled up tightly, Alice frowned, straining to hear. Then, almost too traumatised to move, she slowly turned her head towards the sound.

'Hello? Hello?'

Suddenly realising there was somebody on the other end of the phone, Alice crawled forward, picking up the receiver as her hands shook furiously and her voice trembled. She spoke through dry lips. 'Hello?'

'Alice?'

Overcome with emotion, she nodded, breaking down into silent tears as she heard her father's voice.

'Alice?'

Trying to talk quietly as she furiously began to hyperventilate, Alice only just managed to get the words out. 'Dad, Dad, you've got to help me!'

'Alice, Jesus Christ, what's happening?'

'Everyone's dead, they're dead.'

'What are you talking about?'

Alice began to rock, sobbing into the phone. 'Please, help me. Help me.'

'Alice, you're not making sense.'

'Sister Margaret, she's dead too. I think they all are.'

Cabhan's voice was urgent and full of fear. 'I don't know what's going on, but you've got to get out of there. You hear me?'

Alice shook her head, snot and tears running down her face. 'I can't, the clowns are everywhere . . .'

'Alice, you're frightening me. Look, we can be there in about an hour, maybe less. We're already in the area, but you need to . . .'

Cabhan's words were cut off as Alice, looking up, dropped the phone, suddenly beginning to scream as a gruesome masked figure at the window stood staring in at her. The man aimed his gun, but as the bullet shattered the glass, Alice Rose turned and ran.

13

'You saw her, but you thought it was okay to let her go?' Salvatore stared at Stefano Greco – an old schoolfriend who'd worked for his family for the past ten years – with unadulterated hatred.

'I didn't, Sal, I fired and then she ran off before I managed . . .'

Standing by the door of the tiny whitewashed chapel of the convent, Salvatore raised his voice, pacing agitatedly. 'She's a kid and you had a fucking semi-automatic in your hands. Do the math, Stefano . . . What did she look like?'

'Blonde . . . no, maybe brown hair . . . I dunno, Jesus. I didn't see her properly, Sal, but look around you, everyone's dead, *she* might be dead already, we don't even know if that girl was her.'

Salvatore smashed an iron bar into Stefano's face and listened to his piercing scream as one of his cheekbones splintered in two.

Panting, Salvatore crouched down level with the writhing figure on the floor. Fear knotted Stefano's insides, suddenly aware that he could easily lose control of his bodily functions, such was the terror he felt.

Salvatore snarled, 'But we don't know it *wasn't* either, do we? And now it might be too late. If it was her, we need to go and find her. My orders, Stef, were to kill everyone on sight.'

Stefano trembled in pain. 'Sal, *Mi dispiace*.'

'You're sorry?'

With fear dancing in his green eyes, Stefano nodded. '*Sì! Sì!*'

Licking his chapped lips, Salvatore picked up a taper and lit one of the candles in the rack outside the chapel. He made a sign of the cross before watching it burn along with the dozens of other tea lights flickering in the warm breeze. He smiled.

'Do you know what these are for, Stefano?'

Nervously, Stefano mumbled, '*Sì*, they are the candles for the dead.'

Salvatore drew his eyes away to look at Stefano. 'That's right, and I lit that one for you.' Then, without missing a beat, Salvatore whipped out the gun he had tucked away in his trouser waist and placed the nozzle onto Stefano's nicotine-stained teeth before casually pulling the trigger.

Wiping away the blood and pieces of flesh from the front of his clothes, still wearing his clown mask, Salvatore addressed his brother. 'Bobby, put his body in the car and clean up his mess, we don't want to leave the cops a calling card. Then take some men and search down by the river. I'll take the others and go up into the woods. If you see anything, even a fucking racoon, you shoot it dead. You hear me?'

He stopped to point his gun at the congregated men, adding, 'You understand me, guys? Whoever she was, you bring that girl's head back to me, unless of course you want to end up like our good friend Stefano. Now let's go!'

Racing through the trees and across the meadows, Alice tried to shut out the bloody images in her head. She tried to think of something good, like her mother, like her friend Isaiah, but it was impossible because she could still hear the screams, still smell the blood. The scent of death seeped out of her pores and she was scared, terrified and couldn't think straight.

Running as fast as she could, drenched with sweat and not knowing where she was going, she just knew she had to keep moving. Alice focused on getting away, but the problem was, even though she knew the area so well – had explored every corner of it – suddenly every tree, every bush, every pathway looked the same. She couldn't remember *anything*.

The lake house was on the top of the hill, she knew that, but which track to take she couldn't remember. She was lost and if she wasn't careful she'd end up back at the convent where the demonic clowns were. Where the blood was. The thought of it made her suddenly gasp and she could hardly catch her breath, but a noise from behind sent her scrabbling forward. Seeing a clump of bushes, Alice threw herself underneath it, squeezing her eyes shut as the tears rolled down her face again.

'Alice! Alice! It's no good hiding, honey. We just want to talk to you.'

The scrub was vast, allowing Alice to scramble backwards on her stomach, her skin snagging on sharp thorns and bushes, but she didn't make a noise. Ignoring the pain and blood trickling down her face, Alice saw six . . . seven . . . eight clowns all walking in her direction.

'Alice!'

Shaking, Alice glanced behind her. She looked across to one of the meadows, a thought coming to mind.

Creeping backwards, Alice kept low to the ground, watching out for any branches that might snap and make a sound. Nearing the fenced meadow, Alice nervously glanced about. Breathing deeply, she tried to steady her nerves and racing heart.

She burst out of the shrub, ran along the edge of the field and made her way to the small copse, whispering a name, quietly and softly so as not to spook him. 'Mac! Mac!' A few seconds later, the convent's retired pony ambled into sight.

'You're going to get us out of here, aren't you, boy?'

Opening the gate as silently as she could, Alice walked into

Mac's paddock and grabbed his head collar from a wooden post.

Wiping the sweat from her hands, she gently approached Mac and slid the noseband over his white muzzle, all the time talking softly as she guided it over his ears.

'There you go, boy, there you go.'

After making sure it was secure, Alice looped the rope over his head, tying it gently to both sides of the head collar. Not seeing anything she could climb on, she placed her left hand on Mac's withers, holding onto his mane, before jumping and swinging her leg energetically over his back.

With her voice trembling, Alice continued to speak to Mac, reassuring herself as much as him. 'Sshhh, boy, it's okay. It's okay. It's going to be okay.'

Holding the rope, Alice ducked down, avoiding the low-hanging trees as she moved Mac slowly forward. She stared at the horizon. Over by the far field she could see two of the clowns pointing towards the trees where she was hidden. Her heart began to race faster again and Mac, sensitive to fear, began to get edgy, backing up and circling around.

She needed to move, to get to the far corner, which she suddenly remembered would take her over the bridge and along the path to the road. She also needed to make sure she stayed on the far side of the meadow, but this could be her chance . . . perhaps her only chance.

Eagerly and with the tiniest glimmer of hope, Alice squeezed her legs to get Mac to move forward again. It'd been a long time since she'd ridden and it was certainly a long time since anybody had got on him. But if they could do it, if they could ride away, then she'd be able to get to the road and to help. The thought made her feel braver.

Taking a deep breath, Alice leant forward and whispered into Mac's ears as they hid in the shadows of the trees. Then, with one almighty kick, deciding it was now or never, she set off across the fields with Mac, who was so startled he immediately cantered before transitioning into a gallop, head down and looking like a horse ten years younger.

Alice was going at such speed tears were streaming down her cheeks, caused by the wind blowing hard in her face as well as her fear. She didn't dare to look back as she galloped towards the end of the meadow, through the long grass covered in daisies and towards the stream in the far corner.

A sound of guns firing had Alice clinging onto Mac's mane as she lost her balance for a moment, sliding to the side, but she could feel Mac giving it his best effort, sensing her terror.

'Come on, boy, come on! We're nearly there.'

Then, after jumping over the small stream and into the woods, Alice slowed Mac, giving him a chance to get his breath back before steeling herself to turn around.

In the distance she could see the clowns, but they were too far back to catch up. If she kept going up towards the road, which was a few miles along, she could hopefully flag someone over.

With tears of relief, full of determination, Alice ducked her head under the trees as Mac set off into a trot, heading up the hill to safety.

It felt to Alice like she'd been riding for hours, with the bushes and branches snatching and scratching on her skin, but finally she could see the road up ahead.

Exhausted, she guided Mac onto the lane, but a sense of dread engulfed her. Out of the trees she felt exposed and vulnerable on the wide tarmacked road, which wound and weaved through the hills. But there was no other route; the track she'd been on fell away, so the only means to get help was to continue along the lane.

As they walked along, Alice felt as if every noise and every movement of the trees was danger lying in wait. Then a sudden sound of a car behind them triggered Alice's panic. She trembled in terror, sweat pricking at her forehead. She didn't dare look back, even though the car was getting nearer and she could almost feel the heat from the engine. She tried to push Mac on to go faster, but the hard ground was too much for his unshod feet. Then Alice heard what she'd been dreading, the sound of the car door opening and feet running towards her.

A hand on her arm grabbed her, making her scream.

'Alice! Alice! Stop, stop, it's me.'

Covered in Sister Margaret's blood, Alice stared at Cabhan. Her voice was almost unrecognisable. 'Dad?'

'Yes, baby, it's me.'

Alice broke down in tears of relief as she leant forward, burying her face in Mac's mane. 'They killed her, Dad! They killed her! They just shot her and then . . . and then they began to call out my name.'

'What?' Cabhan's voice was sharp with concern, though his hands were still gentle as he held onto his precious daughter.

Alice nodded frantically, her nose and eyes streaming. 'Yeah, they kept calling out for me.'

'Okay, okay, honey. Alice, Sshhh, it's going to be okay, baby. Look who's here with me.'

Alice glanced up into the face of Franny.

'Hi, sweetheart,' Franny said, her voice full of warmth and tenderness. 'I'm so sorry you've been through all this, but we're going to get you out of here. Like your dad says, it's going to be all right, though we need to get you off this road and into the car.'

Distressed, Alice cried out, 'What about Mac? I can't leave him. He saved me.'

Franny smiled at Alice, speaking as gently as she could. 'He'll find his way home, the convent's over there. He'll be okay.'

Panic-stricken and wide-eyed, Alice cried as Franny glanced at Cabhan, 'But they're all dead, Franny.'

Wanting to, but not allowing herself to break down, Franny

knew that she had to stay calm and she spoke a little more firmly. 'Okay, baby, we'll call someone; we'll make sure they go and look after him. I promise you, he'll be all right, okay?'

Alice nodded, trembling as Franny continued to talk. 'But, Alice, we *really* need to get you off this road. I want to get you to a safer place.'

Franny turned to whisper to Cabhan as he lifted Alice off Mac, watching the woods.

'It's got to be them. It's *got* to be Salvatore. This isn't some random, crazed shooting. We need to get out of here before they find us and before the police get here. We need to disappear.'

Cabhan nodded, the full horror of the situation beginning to hit him as well. Why they'd thought it was some American-style school shooting, he didn't know. Why hadn't he just put two and two together, or maybe he had, maybe he just hadn't *wanted* to believe it was the Russos.

'Are you hurt?' he asked Alice, wiping away the nun's blood still covering her.

Alice shook her head against his chest, cradled in Cabhan's arms as he carried her towards the car. He kissed her, whispering words he knew in his heart were hollow. 'It's okay, it's okay. It's all over now. Everything's going to be all right.'

As Franny got in the car after quickly glancing back towards the woods, Cabhan gently placed Alice on the back seat, covering her with a blanket as she continued to shiver. And in the distance, in the shadow of the trees, stood Salvatore Russo, watching as Cabhan drove away at speed, and he smiled.

14

Nico Russo ruminated as he glanced out of the prison window. He sniffed the bitter espresso that he'd got one of the wardens to make, then took a sip. He sat watching his younger brothers, his expression as usual blank, the only giveaway sign of his seething and burning anger the muscles pulsating on his jaw line as he clenched his teeth, grinding them until they gave out a low screech.

Bobby, uncomfortable with the silence, which had hung in the air for the past five minutes, glanced around the empty visitors' waiting room, locking eyes with the prison officers in the corner before turning away contemptuously. Trying to keep his voice light, but still with respect, he leant across the table, touching Nico's hands.

'Nico, both Sal and I did everything we could to get the girl.'

Laughing scornfully, Nico pulled his hands away before burying his fist in Bobby's face, the force of the blow knocking him to the floor along with the coffee. Officer Johnstone went to make a move, but Nico raised his hand, indicating for him not to interfere.

'How dare you come in here to disrespect me! You think I'm stupid, Bobby?' Nico loomed over his brother, speaking dangerously low. 'First, Salvatore goes behind my back by not telling me about the cocaine shipment . . .' Nico paused as he stared at Salvatore angrily until he dropped his head as Bobby shot him a puzzled glance. 'Now, you think you can come and give me excuses whilst *I* sit and rot in this place. She's a kid. Sixteen. *Fucking* sixteen and she gave you two the runaround. I want her found, she's mine. I want her. I want you to bring me her heart. You understand me? No more excuses.'

Getting up slowly and sucking the blood from his lips, Bobby shook his head. 'Nico, it's not an excuse, I don't want you to think we didn't try.'

Raging, Nico growled out his words. 'This family was built on success, on honour, on men who could be counted on, but, in turn, this family will be destroyed by failure, by weakness, by motherfuckers like you. By my own brothers.'

'Nico—'

Nico flew at Salvatore, grabbing hold of his face, squeezing and crushing it between his gigantic, rough hands. He shook, trembling with rage as he spoke, his mouth touching his brother's cheeks. 'I love you, Sal, you're my own flesh and blood. You hurt, I hurt, whatever pains you, pains me, but I'll break your neck right here, right now, if you continue to disrespect me. Understand?'

Salvatore gave a tiny nod. '*Sì.*'

Then, taking a deep breath and exhaling noisily, Nico let go of his brother's face and placed a kiss on the top of his head. 'Good, good. I'm glad that we've got that sorted out . . . Now, give me your cell.'

Clearly relieved, Salvatore gave a small smile as he passed over his phone. Scrolling down the numbers, Nico came to the one he wanted, but just as he was about to click the call button, Officer Johnstone stood up.

'Nico, you can't have the phone in here. You're not supposed to have phones in prison, you know that, and this block picks up unauthorised mobile signals. Use it when you get back to your wing, or we'll both be in trouble.'

Nico walked over to the officer, his face twisted with rage. 'You think it's okay to speak to me like that in front of my family? What are you trying to do, embarrass me?' He stopped, then walked even closer to the warden and pressed his forehead against his. 'I know where you live, Officer Johnstone. I know where your mother lives and your children, so don't push me, because like that –' he clicked his fingers '– they could be gone.'

Officer Johnstone, alarmed, put his hands up, backing away slowly. 'Okay, Nico, okay, I was only saying, there's no need to do anything rash. We've got an agreement that we're going to stick to . . . I'm sorry.'

'And you'd do well to remember that. Now, get out of my fucking face. *Capito*?'

As the officer nodded in understanding, Nico turned and pressed call, waiting for it to ring before going straight to voice-mail. He paced as he talked.

'Hello, Cabhan, it's Nico. Happy birthday. I understand from my brothers that your girl got away, but I just wanted to call and tell you, there's no hiding place, nowhere we won't find you. Nowhere revenge won't touch you. I *will* find you, Cabhan . . . or rather, I'll find your little girl. Hide, Alice Rose, hide, because Nico's coming, ready or not.'

15

'Cab, it's been over four weeks, we can't stay here. Look at her. She's getting worse by the day. She's just a kid and I'm worried about her, I'm worried about all of us,' Franny whispered to Cabhan as they stood in the tiny motel room just outside Frenchtown in Montana.

When they'd found Alice, they'd driven through Iowa before hitting South Dakota, then finally reaching western Montana to hide out in the tiny, mostly unpopulated area, but not for one moment had she thought they'd still be holed up in the motel a month later. Not that either of them had a plan, and as each day went on it seemed less likely that Cabhan would come up with one. She'd never seen him like this before: he was struggling to cope, blaming himself, and the tension in the air was almost unbearable.

'So tell me, what the fuck *are* we supposed to do? What better ideas have you got? Nico's not playing when he says he's looking for us. You know what he's like, he won't stop until he's got Alice . . .'

'Look around you, Cab, there's nothing here for us. We have five hundred dollars to our name. That's it and it's going to run out soon and then what? We have nothing. The day we went to see Nico, I transferred all of the money. Alfie's money. And he's not happy. I've given up listening to his voicemails, but when I went through Evaro yesterday, I tried the bank cards and guess what? He's stopped them all, and I doubt the motel manager is going to be full of understanding if we tell him we can't pay for the room.'

Cabhan stared at Franny, hissing through his teeth, hating the fact that the bitter anger he felt towards Nico was being directed at her. 'What the fuck do you want *me* to do about it? I'm as screwed as you are. I can't use my account because they'll know where we are. And besides, my bank account is a business account set up by Salvatore to make sure he knows my every move.'

Franny glanced around the dark, grimy room. Two double beds, a bedside cabinet propped up by a Bible. A threadbare chair in the corner that had seen better days and an en-suite bathroom consisting of a toilet and shower, both barely working.

Refusing to be hurt by Cabhan offloading his stress onto her, Franny kept her voice quiet.

'Cab, I know this is tough, but we've got to think of something. Alice has been through a massive amount of trauma; we need to get her some help. She's a kid; she can't just lie there. She's hardly said a word for three whole weeks.'

'You don't think I can't see that? You don't think I'm worried about her? She's my daughter, Franny. Jesus Christ, I've only known her a couple of years and look what I've done to her life. I just can't think straight anymore. Every time there's a noise I think the Russos will come walking through that door.'

Overwhelmed by guilt, Cabhan turned away from Franny, not wanting her to see him breaking down. He continued to speak, his voice cracking on every word. 'I feel so helpless and I'm so fucking angry with myself. I'm ashamed to admit it, but I'm scared. I'm scared for Alice, because this isn't going to be over anytime soon.'

Franny grabbed hold of Cabhan's arm, pulling him towards

the door of the room, and gently pushed him outside into the warm Montana air.

Looking out towards the vast, rugged hillside, Franny smiled compassionately. 'Let's not talk in there, Cab, you don't want Alice to wake up and see you upset. And we don't want Alice to know *anything* about the Russos, you hear me?'

'So what are we going to tell her?'

Franny shrugged, her eyes darting around as she kept watch on the road. Although she'd never admit it, she felt the same air of unease as Cabhan did, but the last thing he needed was for her to crumple as well. The other thing she didn't really want to admit, not even to herself, was that she wished Alfie were here. She missed him so much, plus he would know what to do, because right now she didn't think she was doing such a great job of looking after Cabhan or Alice. Of course, she knew she *had* to be strong – the problem was she didn't feel very strong at all. 'I don't know, Cab. Why don't we tell her it was a robbery?'

'A robbery? More like a fucking homicidal maniac. Have you seen the news? Seen what they're saying about it? They're coming up with all sorts of ideas about how it happened. Cults, crazed killers, the other night they were even mentioning terrorists.'

'Then that's good, isn't it? It means they're not talking about Nico and they're *not* talking about us. So we don't have to tell Alice anything apart from it was a robbery, because nobody knows the truth and that's the way it's going to stay.'

Cabhan stared hard at Franny, his thoughts racing. 'You can be cold sometimes. Does nothing bother you, Fran? Are you really that hard? Just wipe it away like it never happened?'

A flicker of hurt crossed through Franny's eyes, which went unseen by Cabhan. 'That's not how it is.'

'Really? Because it seems like you're forgetting those kids, those nuns, are only dead because of me.'

'Because of Nico, not *you*.'

Cabhan shook his head as he kicked at the white dusty ground in angry bemusement. 'You're something else, you know that?'

'All I know is that we need to think about *now*, about Alice and about how we're going to get out of this mess. The last thing we want to do is start telling Alice any more than she needs to know.'

'So what you're saying is tell her nothing and get on with our lives, is that it?'

Feeling edgy as a car appeared in the distance, Franny nodded. 'If we can, that's exactly what we do. Look, Cab, someone has to be practical about this. I'm just trying to do what's best for Alice and if that makes me cold, that's totally fine with me.'

Emotional, unable to look at Franny, Cabhan continued to stare at the ground. 'I'm just so fucked off with myself. I mean, how did they know where she was? How did they find her? I was so careful, or I thought I was. I was a fool, Fran, to think that I could've walked away scot-free from killing Ally.'

'Cab, it was an accident, when will you get that into your head?'

Becoming angry again, Cabhan raised his voice. 'But the blood of so many people is on my hands. If it wasn't for me they'd all be alive. Have you any idea how that feels, Fran?'

Gently, Franny pulled Cabhan towards her. 'No, no, I don't, but you've got to give yourself a break. Stop beating yourself up. I know it sounds heartless, but it's happened now. There's *nothing* we can do, so we need to put all our energy into getting out of this mess. On keeping Alice safe.'

Lighting a cigarette, Cabhan nodded gratefully. 'I know you're right, but I've no idea how. I've never felt this useless since what happened to your dad. We're fucked, Fran.'

'No, Cab, we're not, I won't let that happen. Look, I think we should go back to England. To Essex. At least there we've got people around us, and I don't think they'll come looking for us there. Once I see Alfie face-to-face, I'm sure I can make him come around.'

Cabhan, knowing Alfie very well, raised his eyebrows.

'You sure about that? This is Alf we're talking about. Remember, he told me if I went to work for the Russos, I'd be on my own. He's made it very clear how he feels.'

Sounding just as unconvinced as she felt, Franny said, 'It'll be fine. At the moment he doesn't know why I took the money, but once he does he'll understand. Alfie is . . .' She trailed off, not wanting to think about his reaction, especially after his last message yesterday, which was full of threats and anger. But underneath it all she could also hear his hurt, which sliced at her heart . . . Quickly wanting to change her train of thought because it felt too raw, too painful, Franny continued, 'Anyway . . . look, we've got our passports and I've checked the flights. We can get one in four days' time from Missoula International, then get connecting flights from there. And then it's back to Essex.'

Taking a deep drag and letting the smoke slowly ebb out of his nose, Cab tried not to sound frustrated. 'Hate to say it, Fran, aren't you forgetting one thing? Money. We need money.'

Franny rested her head on Cabhan's shoulder and sighed. 'Look, don't worry about that. Trust me. I've got an idea.'

16

'Alfie, are you all right? I was just wanting to have a chat, run something by you, but I can leave you to it if you like.'

Back in Essex, Bree Dwyer stood in the bedroom doorway looking at Alfie as he threw his phone angrily across the room.

Not realising anyone was there and feeling startled, Alfie snapped, 'No, I'm fine, darlin', why wouldn't I be?'

She walked in, her long blonde hair tumbling over her shoulders as she bent down to pick up his phone. 'Maybe because most people who are actually fine don't usually fling their phone away.'

Alfie gave her a half-smile, his handsome face lighting up. He shrugged. 'You got me bang to rights there . . . Look, it's just business. It pisses me off sometimes and now, with Vaughn away in Portugal trying to sort out some new contacts, I'm left to deal with everything on me own. Who knew that setting up a bookie business would be so stressful? Still, once we do it'll all have been worth it, and some bird fucking off with my money will be just a distant memory . . . Listen, just ignore me, I get like this when I have me work head on.'

Passing the phone back to Alfie, Bree caught sight of the last number he'd dialled. Although she tried to stop herself, her voice edged on the accusatory. 'Franny? She's business now?'

Always hating being pushed on something he hadn't been completely honest about, Alfie snarled, 'What is this, have I suddenly found meself in Court Number One of the Old Bailey? What is it with you women, hey? It's like you're always looking for trouble. You can't just be happy with the way things are.'

Bree stared at Alfie, her green eyes pools of hurt. 'I think you're overreacting a bit, Alf, I only—'

Alfie cut in, guilt and frustration plaguing him. 'Am I? Really? *I'm* overreacting? Oh, so it was me who picked up the phone and started throwing accusations about, is it?'

'Alf, I haven't accused you of anything.'

Pacing, unable to stop how unreasonable he was being, Alfie pointed at her. 'That's not what it sounded like to me. It sounds like you think I'm going behind your back and somehow playing you against Franny.'

Bree gave a sad smile. Even though it was only very recently she had met back up with Alfie after years of not seeing him, she knew exactly what he could be like. 'Well, are you? Cos I'd understand if you were unsure about *us*. Maybe this is all just a rebound, maybe I'm your rebound.'

Raging but not quite sure why, Alfie raised his voice. 'This ain't a game of basketball, Bree. I'm a grown man who knows my own mind. Franny's screwed me over, it's as simple as that. She took all my money and left me. Disappeared without even looking back.' As Alfie said the words, a sharp pain came into his chest, a wave of feeling he didn't, wouldn't, couldn't, he'd be damned if he acknowledge. *Shit*.

Bree spoke quietly. 'But that's what she did to you, not what she *means* to you.'

'Look, she means nothing to me. It's been over for . . .' He stopped, knowing what he was about to say was a blatant lie but seeing it as an essential one. 'For months. Me and Franny have been over for months, so you ain't got nothing to worry about.'

Wanting to believe him but her gut telling her otherwise, Bree said, 'That's not what Lola said.'

Fuming, Alfie shook his head, making a mental note to speak to Lola later. 'Oh, so now she knows more about my relationships than me, does she? She was the one sharing the bed with Franny now, was she?'

'Alfie, listen . . .'

'I don't want to listen. You seem to have all the answers, so why bother asking?'

Bree looked at Alfie, a mixture of sadness and unease. They went back a long way, back to when she'd been a kid. Alfie had been the first person she'd ever loved and to this day she still loved him.

They'd first met when she'd been friends at school with Sandra, his little sister, and back then they'd all felt like family, especially as she didn't have family of her own, having been placed in foster care when she was only three.

Each day when Alfie had collected Sandra from the school gates, he'd let Bree – who didn't want to return to the abusive foster home and had nowhere else to go – tag along with them. And even though Alfie was older and had already started out in his life of crime, he'd bothered, he'd looked out for her, and she'd been grateful.

At first she'd been shy, blushing and embarrassed when he'd talked to her, but eventually she'd not only started to feel comfortable, but she'd also begun to trust him, something she'd thought she would never be able to do when it came to people.

He'd looked after her so well, caring for her, feeding her, even buying her clothes. Then one day, without warning, without giving her time to let Alfie know, the social workers had moved her away, placing her in another foster home, and she'd been devastated. It'd broken her heart. But he'd tracked her down, checking she was all right as well as getting Sandra to keep in touch; though, over time, everyone began to get on with their lives and they'd lost contact.

But things had been difficult for her, things had gone badly wrong, and she found herself trapped in a life she couldn't escape. Until she bumped into Alfie again a short while ago and, like all those years ago, he had saved her.

The past few months of her life had been so difficult, so traumatic, and everything had begun to feel like a haze, but Alfie had let her stay with him at the house and it'd made her feel better. They'd become closer, closer than she'd ever thought possible, and he'd told her she was just what he needed, explaining that he and Franny were long over – except the more she discovered, the more she realised that things weren't quite what they'd seemed. 'Long over' seemed to be turning out to be a matter of a few weeks, and although he'd insisted that Franny was in the past, she doubted it was the case.

Alfie had truly been her everything when she was a kid. Always so kind, so strong, so funny and God, how she'd loved him as she did now. And that was the problem. She never wanted to let him go again but it felt like she might have to, because she needed to know he was sure about what he wanted. The last thing she wanted, no matter how much she loved him, was for Alfie to jump into a relationship with her if his heart wasn't in it. That she couldn't take.

'Bree, I ain't bullshitting you, you mean the world to me, you always have. You make me feel good about myself. I'm angry at Franny, that's all, and it's true that she hurt me but it ain't true that I want to be with her. It's you who's here, not her. She's long gone. So please stop worrying, you ain't any kind of rebound. Franny's in the past, she ain't coming back.'

Alfie smiled at Bree, though a sense of uncertainty filled his being that he tried to push aside. He refused to think he had rushed into anything, because Franny had just cut him out of her life like he meant nothing to her. And what difference did it make if he told Bree it'd been over for months rather than a matter of a few weeks, because ultimately the outcome was the same, wasn't it? Franny didn't want to be with him, so he'd do what he'd always done. He'd get on with his life and not look back. 'So come on, what was it that you wanted to have a chat about?'

Bree shrugged, hoping that she sounded nonchalant. 'Nothing. I can't even remember now. Can't have been important.'

Alfie stared back into Bree's face, so warm and so beautiful. He smiled. 'I know I'm hot-headed, Bree, but I don't mean anything by it. You do know that you can tell me anything, right?'

'Right.' Smiling back, Bree sighed. Alfie was right, she could tell him anything – well, almost anything . . .

17

Alice Rose felt the warm breeze and the sun on her face as she sat on the white plastic chair outside the motel by the edge of a deserted road. With her legs tucked underneath her, she gazed out towards the mountaintops wondering why she hadn't done what her mother had taught her. Why she hadn't prayed hard enough, given enough thanks, and why had she lied? It was because of this that Sister Margaret was dead. *Everyone* was dead.

Closing her eyes to try to stop the tears from falling, she remembered the verse in the Bible from Deuteronomy, remembering her mother standing over her bed reciting the words. She could hear them now:

The Lord will send on you curses in everything you put your hand to, until you are destroyed because of the evil you have done in forsaking him. The Lord will cause you to be defeated before your enemies. The terror that will fill your heart and the sights that your eyes will see will afflict you with madness, blindness, with no one to rescue you from your enemies and they will pursue you until you are destroyed.

Putting her hands over her ears, she squeezed her eyes closed but immediately saw the images of her dead friends in her mind. She began to cry deep, painful tears. 'I'm sorry, I'm sorry. I'm so sorry.'

As she sat, rocking in her chair, she felt her phone ring. She ignored it but it rang again, then again before finally, wiping her running nose, Alice pressed the green button on her mobile.

'Alice?'

'Yes?'

'It's Nico . . . I hadn't heard from you and I was wondering if perhaps your dad had said anything about me, talked about me at all, and that's why you hadn't called.'

Alice swivelled round, checking that Franny and Cabhan were in the motel room. They'd asked her not to speak to anyone, tell anyone where she was, though when Franny had gone to do the laundry she *had* managed to sneak a call to her friend, Isaiah. He'd been away at Bible camp though and unable to talk. But since then it felt like Cabhan and Franny were watching her every move, she just wasn't sure why, and when she had tried to ask them, they had just changed the subject.

'Like what, Nico? What would he have said?'

Nico smiled to himself and said gently, 'Oh, I don't know, maybe he was cross we didn't come to his party.'

Alice gasped. 'You don't know, do you?'

'Don't know what, Alice? Is everything all right? You sound like you've been crying, have you?' Bursting into tears again, Alice explained the story as Nico lay on his prison bed listening quietly. She told him all about Sister Margaret and the clowns who'd terrified her, about hiding out in the field shelter and what had happened to her friends, and when she'd finally finished, feeling sick and scared at the thought of it all, she said, '. . . So you see, that's why I didn't call, and my phone's been turned off most of the time. I haven't even been able to speak to Isaiah, not that they'd let me if they knew I was trying. The only reason they haven't taken the phone is because they trust me, or they say they do, but I don't think that can be true, otherwise they'd tell me what was really going on.'

Playing with a toothpick between his teeth, Nico covered his yawn. 'You poor thing, Alice, I'm so sorry, but such a brave girl. It must've been so traumatic for you.'

Grateful for his understanding, Alice answered softly, wishing she could feel braver than she did. 'It was.'

'I don't know if your dad told you, but my daughter died just recently in an accident. I was devastated, Alice. Worst day of my life.' He paused and, using what he knew about her from what Cabhan had told him, Nico calculatingly added, 'But do you know what I did, Alice? I prayed.'

Again, Alice gasped.

'Everything all right? Have I upset you?'

Feeling the sun on her face and giving a tiny smile, Alice nodded as she spoke down the phone. Her heart raced as she spoke eagerly. 'No. No, the opposite. I just didn't know you were like me.'

'Like you?'

'That you believed.'

'Oh, I do, Alice. I don't know where I'd be without my belief. I'd be lost. You know, maybe . . . Oh, it doesn't matter.'

Suddenly feeling better than she had for the last few weeks, Alice urged Nico on. 'No, please, finish what you were going to say.'

'Okay, perhaps it's silly but it sounds like we've both been through such a difficult time lately, so I thought it would be nice to say a prayer together.'

Genuine delight and relief rushed through Alice as she fought back the tears. Speaking quickly, her words tumbled out of her mouth. 'I'd like that, Nico, and you're right, it's been so hard, and I don't feel I can talk to Dad at the moment, he's so upset and won't tell me anything. I don't even know why we're here. I don't understand what's going on. And what happened at the convent, I know that somehow it was my fault. I just know it . . . They were even calling my name, Nico. How did they know my name?'

Nico purred out his words as he stood up and looked out of the tiny barred window of his prison cell. 'Alice. Sweet, sweet Alice, try not to get upset. Maybe these people heard someone call your name. That nun you mentioned, perhaps she told them your name. It'll be a simple explanation. You shouldn't blame yourself.'

Remembering her mother's words, Alice chewed on her lip tentatively as a sinking feeling hit the pit of her stomach. 'Really? You don't think it's because I've sinned that evil found me?'

'Alice, it hasn't found you yet, and trust me, when you see evil you'll know it. It'll peel your skin away, leaving only your flesh, and burn out your eyes. So no, Alice, evil hasn't found you . . . yet.'

Alice's voice shook. 'Thank you, Nico.'

'For what?'

'For listening. You're so easy to talk to. You remind me so much of my friend, Isaiah. He was easy to talk to as well. I miss him.'

'Well, that's why *we* need to stay in touch, then you'll have someone to talk to. I'm thinking maybe I should talk to your dad, find out what's going on. Perhaps somehow I can help.'

Standing up and crossing over the wide, empty road that stretched further than the eye could see, Alice walked away from the motel, making double sure no one would hear her. Even though she barely knew Nico, he felt like her saviour, like he had been sent to her.

'Would you? Would you help me? Because I'm so worried about him. I just don't know what to do and I love my dad so much.'

'Of course. But I think it'll probably be better if I can talk to

95

him face-to-face. It sounds like he could do with a friend. Maybe you can tell me where you are and I can drive on up, sort whatever's going on. Though it's probably best not to tell him I'm coming. Your dad can be a proud man and sometimes he doesn't always know what's good for him. So, what do you say, Alice? You think it's a good idea?'

And without hesitation, Alice Rose, feeling at peace, began to give Nico the address.

18

Deep in thought, Franny Doyle tried to calm her nerves, standing outside the small liquor store on the isolated road. She'd asked Cabhan to wait in the car for her whilst she popped in to get a few groceries, but that was only half the story.

Glancing towards the car parked a couple of hundred yards away, Franny's heart pounded as she pulled her scarf up over her face, leaving only her eyes exposed. Tugging down her hoody and feeling more out of her comfort zone than she'd ever felt in her life, Franny, taking a deep breath and, knowing that this was the only way, pushed open the door.

The bell above the store entrance rang as she edged in and made her way along the aisle, past the bottles of beer, past the cereal boxes and the giant packs of kitchen rolls, to the front of the store.

From behind her scarf, Franny's mouth became dry. *Shit.* A grey-haired man, bent double, shuffled out from the back room and, with a smile along with a soft Montana lilt, said, 'Hey, ma'am, can I help you?'

Of all the people she didn't want it to be, an old man was right there at the top of her list. Hating herself, she slowly pulled Cabhan's gun out of her pocket, all the time focusing on the reason she was going to such extreme measures: Alice.

Stretching her arm out, she expertly pointed the gun level with the old man's eyes.

'Give me all your money. Give me whatever you've got in the till and what you've got in the safe. And whether you believe it or not, I will make sure I return all of it. Every single cent.'

The old man's stare locked with hers, contempt rather than fear pouring out of his eyes. 'There ain't nothing in the till, so you've had a wasted journey, *ma'am*.'

'Show me . . . Go on. I said, show me!' she repeated firmly, trying to keep her emotions in check.

The man chewed on his gum, hostility oozing out of him. 'And if I don't, what then?'

Knowing she was being tested, Franny, aware of time and realising that there couldn't be any mistakes, snapped her reply. 'Do yourself a favour, don't ask questions because I don't think you'd want to know the answer. Now, just give me the money and this can be over really quickly.'

With his gaze on the gun, the old man tapped on the till, springing open the drawer. Inside were a number of ten- and twenty-dollar bills.

'Give it to me! All of it. Hurry up!'

Seeing the man was not going to cooperate, Franny, desperate to get out of there, leant across the counter and grabbed the cash. 'Now, where's the safe?'

'We don't have one.'

Quickly clicking off the gun's safety catch, Franny raised her voice, feeling agitation beginning to creep over her.

'I haven't got time for this, so just show me where the *fucking* safe is.'

Full of hatred, the old man gestured with his head. 'It's through there.'

Rushing behind the counter, Franny, her forehead covered with sweat, ran into the room, but as she did so she heard the door shut behind her. Panicked, she began to bang on the door as the old man hurriedly turned the key.

'Open the door! Open it! Fuck! Fuck! Fuck!'

'Hello, 911? There's a robbery taking place . . .'

From the other side of the door, Franny could hear the old man on the phone. Angrily, she kicked the wall hard. Jesus, how had she been so stupid? It was a number-one schoolboy error. Her father had taught her *so* much better than this. *Fuck. Fuck. Fuck.* What was she supposed to do now? More to the point, what were Alice and Cabhan supposed to do? She had let them down, big time.

She hammered on the door again with the end of her gun, trying to make her voice sound hard and authoritative. 'Let me out! You hear me? Let me out of this room.'

In frustration, Franny twirled the chamber of the gun. Not one single bullet in it. She'd taken them out as a precaution, never intending to shoot anyone and never wanting to hurt anybody either. But now look, she was screwed and it was all her own doing.

She fought back tears as the old man spoke to her through the door, a satisfied tone in his voice.

'They'll be here in a minute, lady, and then let's see what you've got to say for yourself.'

'Just open the door. You hear me! *Please*.'

'Not so bold now, are we?'

'Just let me go. This isn't what it seems. I was never going to hurt you. I was desperate, that's all.'

'Tell that to somebody who cares.'

With anxiety rushing through her and beads of sweat running down her face, Franny looked around the room. There was nothing. No window to climb out of, no chairs to break the door down, no sharp objects to prise the door open with, but then she stopped, her gaze going to the corner of the room. There was one thing that she did see. In the corner there was the safe.

A mechanical dial safe. One of the first ones her father had taught her to crack.

Rushing across to it, Franny did what her father had always taught her – make use of any time, *whatever* the situation.

Hurriedly bending down, Franny pressed her ear against the safe and began to turn the dial slowly to listen, trying to determine the contact point of the lock, hoping to hear the lever make its connection with the notch . . . She gasped. There it was, the small click that would allow her to work out which numbers on the dial face corresponded to the left and right.

Putting her finger in her ear to block out the old man's shouts, Franny continued to work on the combination, each time starting the process from a different position before skilfully turning the dial to the left, then to the right, listening and pausing, mentally remembering the numbers as she re-engaged the dial cam, finding the point of zero.

'. . . Ten years you'll get for this. Don't know who you think you are, coming into my goddamn shop.'

Down the road, Cabhan sat in the car, checking his watch for the fourth time. He had no idea what was taking Franny so long. He glanced up and, not seeing anybody, decided to get out to see if Franny needed any help with the groceries.

'Wait here, Alice, but make sure you keep the doors locked, you hear me? I'm just going to see if Franny needs any help. I'm going to get myself a Dr Pepper. You want anything?'

Giving a small smile, Alice sleepily shook her head before drifting off again.

Walking to the store along the dusty road, keeping the car in sight, Cabhan was grateful to get out of the Montana heat. He opened the door, heard the bell ring and immediately was greeted by an old man, waving frantically and shuffling over.

'I've called the police. The cops are on their way.'

Not understanding, Cabhan frowned. 'Cops?'

'Yes, sir, we got a robbery in here. Ain't the first time and I doubt it'll be the last time. Anyway, I got them locked in there. Hopefully, the police will be here any moment now.'

Concerned, Cabhan looked towards the door then back at the man. 'Are you okay?'

'Yeah, she had a gun but—'

Cabhan cut in. '*She*?'

'Yes, sir, probably a crackhead taking a chance. You wouldn't believe the kind of folk you get out here.'

Tentatively, Cabhan walked towards the door as the old man called after him, 'I wouldn't do that, sir. Like I say, she got a gun. Don't think she'll use it though, but you never know, desperate is as desperate does.' The old man stopped to take a breath before raising his voice, shouting furiously, 'Think it's okay to go around scaring folk, do you? Well, let me tell you something, I'm going to make sure you pay for this.'

'Just let me out!'

Startled at the familiar voice, Cabhan's thoughts began to race. He glanced at the man, who was staring at him. 'How long did the cops say they'll be?'

The man hobbled towards Cabhan, adjusting his hearing aid. 'They didn't. Round here it could take hours, but then again, they could be pulling up now. But it took the cops over two hours to get to Mrs Jones from—'

Cabhan interrupted, not wanting to hear any more. 'Are you sure it's a good idea to keep her in there? What if she has an accomplice waiting nearby and they decide to come looking for her? What then? Maybe you should just let her go.'

For a moment the man looked worried, but quickly his resolve returned as he heaved from underneath the counter a shotgun, dropped two bullets into it and snapped it closed.

'Nope, I'm not going to let these scumbags from the city get away with it. Round these parts you've got to look out for each other. Anyone else comes, they'll have me to worry about.'

Panicked, Cabhan tried to think quickly. 'Okay, well, maybe, maybe we should look outside, make sure there isn't anyone there. Why don't you go and I'll wait here? Make sure she doesn't get out.'

The man looked at Cabhan strangely, uncertainty coming into his eyes. 'I know that's an Irish accent you've got there, but you're not from around these parts, are you?'

Picking up on the man's unease, Cabhan tried to reassure him whilst glancing out of the shop window, desperate not to see a police car rolling up. 'No, I've come up from New York. I've always fancied coming to see Montana and it hasn't disappointed. I wouldn't mind getting myself a cabin up in the mountains.'

The man continued to stare, his fingers tightening around the gun.

Trying again, Cabhan smiled to give himself an air of calm. 'I'm here with my daughter. In fact, she's in the car outside. Look.' He walked towards the door and opened it up to the deserted street before pointing down the road to a sleeping Alice. 'There she is, she's fast asleep, but you can just see her.'

The old man squinted towards the parked vehicle and on catching a glimpse of Alice, he visibly relaxed. Smiling, he shuffled over to the counter and picked up a packet of sweets with an image of a mountain printed on it. 'Here, take this for her. Montana candy.'

Cabhan narrowed his gaze, acutely aware that time wasn't on their side, vaguely replying, 'Is there such a thing?'

The man cackled, his badly fitted false teeth dropping down from the roof of his mouth. Pushing them back up, he shook his head. 'No, but it sounds good. These things were made in China, I think.'

He paused, moving closer in to peer at the tiny writing on the back of the sweet packet. Unable to see in the dim light, he moved towards the window and placed the shotgun down on the counter.

Without a moment's hesitation, and seeing this could be his only chance, Cabhan jumped forward and grabbed the gun. Swivelling round, he pointed it at the man and spoke firmly, without malice. 'I'm sorry, I really am, and don't worry, I'm not going to hurt you if you do what I say, okay? I just need you to let her out.'

The old man glanced from the gun to Cabhan. 'How can you live with yourself?'

'*Please*, just open it. I wouldn't do this if I didn't have to . . . I said, open it. *Now*!'

Taking the bunch of keys out of his pocket, he threw them hard at Cabhan. 'Keep telling yourself that you don't have a choice. I hope you rot in hell.'

Not answering, Cabhan rushed over to the door, unlocking it as quickly as he could. He swung it open and came face-to-face with Franny. The scarf was still pulled up over her face, but her eyes showed her shock.

Angrily, Cabhan bellowed at Franny. 'We need to get out of here! Let's go!' Then, turning to the old man, he gestured with the shotgun. 'Get in. Get inside.'

As the old man shuffled into the room, Cabhan threw a couple of bottles of water and a chocolate bar inside. 'I'm sure the police will be here soon; you won't be in there for long. You got your phone?'

The man nodded, patting his pocket.

'Good, and I'm sorry that I had to do this.'

Then Cabhan pulled the door shut and locked it before turning to stare furiously at Franny. He hissed at her, 'You've got a lot of explaining to do, but right now we've got to get the hell out of here.'

19

Half an hour later, driving past the creeks and gullies of Montana, down endlessly long back roads surrounded by flower-covered hillsides, Cabhan screamed at Franny, banging his fist on the dash. 'Pull over! Pull the fuck over! Now!'

From the back seat, Alice awoke, startled, and sat up. 'What's happening? What's going on?'

Turning around and annoyed at himself for not being able to hold onto his rage any longer, Cabhan smiled at his daughter, feeding her with a lie. 'Sorry, sweetheart. I need Franny to pull over because I think we might've hit something.'

Alice spun round, looking back at the road. 'What do you think it was?'

'Perhaps a deer. Look, you stay in the car. If we did hit something, I don't want you to see anything that might upset you. Franny can come with me, *can't* you, Franny?'

Without waiting for an answer, Cabhan jumped out of the car. After going round to the driver's door, he pulled it open, grabbed Franny's arm and hauled her out whilst keeping a fixed smile on his face for Alice's benefit.

Whispering under his breath and ignoring her half-hearted protests, he dragged Franny away. 'Keep moving, you and I need to talk.'

Underneath the achingly vast blue sky, Cabhan, well out of sight of Alice, pushed Franny against the trunk of a gnarled pine tree. 'Come on then, tell me. Tell me what the hell you thought you were doing back there. Because now not only will the Russos be looking for us, but we'll have the goddamn cops as well. It's hardly a win-win situation, is it? Well done for that.'

Furious with Cabhan's attitude and still feeling guilty for her actions, Franny pushed him back, her beautiful face twisted in anger as her eyes darted back to the road, ever vigilant. 'I was doing what *you* didn't.'

'Oh, really, and what was that, hey?'

'What was needed to get out of here. You know as well as I do the Russos will be looking for us even as we speak. We need to get back to Essex, because at least there we might have a chance. Here, we're just sitting targets. So I did what needed to be done.'

'Without telling me?'

Franny held Cabhan's stare. 'Yes, Cab, because I know what you would've said.'

'That's right, I would've said *no*, because from where I was standing all that you managed to achieve was needing my help to get *you* out of a situation that had gone very badly wrong.'

Not fully meaning her words, but hurt and annoyed with herself for feeling so emotional, Franny pointed her finger accusingly at Cabhan.

'Whatever, Cabhan. I know I was doing the right thing. So, no matter what you say or think, I was actually sorting out our problem instead of just sitting there feeling sorry for myself, which is what you've been doing for the past few weeks.'

Incandescent with rage, Cabhan stepped towards her. 'Seriously, that's what you think I've been doing? Not grieving for all those kids who were murdered, not worried about Alice, not devastated about Ally, not terrified what the Russos will do next, but feeling sorry for myself. Well, *fuck* you, Fran, and your coldness, because some of us care.'

Franny stared at Cabhan, wanting to say so much but not being able to find the right words. She had been brought up by her father and Cabhan after her mother had killed herself when she was just a baby. And against all odds, Patrick and Cabhan had raised her in a household not only full of love and warmth, but also one where weakness wasn't an option and personal emotions were often seen as the enemy.

Her father, a number-one face and successful businessman, had expected her to follow in his footsteps, and she had. Wanting to please him, always looking for his approval because she had loved him so much. But it had also been hard trying to live up to his expectations whilst at the same time wanting to find her own way. It didn't help that her own moral compass didn't always tally with her father's.

How far he would go and what he would do to get and stay on top of his game was further than she had wanted to go. Violence and murder were not things she had wanted to be part of, yet they surrounded her as far back as she could remember. So, to cope, she had done what she had been taught to do: put up an emotional wall, feel as little as she could and not let her emotions be her guide. And, up to a point, living that way had served her well, allowing her to run her father's business empire and still sleep at night. But it had come at a price. She had learnt to suppress her emotions so much that at times it was hard to show how she really felt, how she *did* love, how she *did* get afraid, how she *did* feel pain as much as the next person, and so it often felt like she was in a very lonely place.

Kicking the pine cones on the ground and feeling her temper, mixed with the hurt that she was usually able to keep under control, rush through her body, Franny spat out her words. 'I care. *I care.* You hear me, Cab? Why the hell else do you think I was in that store? You think it made me feel good that I was holding a gun up to that old man? Well, do you? Because you know me and that's not what I'm about. Never did I think I'd do something as sickening as that, but I did, and I did it for Alice and I did it for you. After all, none of this, none of it is about me. The Russos weren't after me before, but they are now. Alfie didn't hate me before, but he does now. So, don't you fucking dare say I'm cold when I did all this because I love you and I love Alice.'

Too stressed to allow himself to be drawn in by Franny's emotional speech, Cabhan was unusually brutal. 'Don't kid yourself, Fran, you're as hard as they come. Like a fucking iron bar. And I'm not saying that you don't love us, I know you do, but don't forget it was me and your dad who brought you up. Taught you everything you know, taught you how to stand on your own two feet, stand up to any face or gangster out there. Your dad taught you to be the best, and in the world we're in you don't become the best without having balls of fucking steel, and you, Franny Doyle, come with two pairs.'

Hurt, but now managing to hold her emotions in, Franny spoke in a voice like ice. 'Maybe you're right, Cab, maybe I am just cold, but it's a good job I am, because otherwise we wouldn't have this.'

Out of her hooded grey top's oversized pockets, Franny pulled three large bundles of fifty-dollar bills and threw them at Cabhan, who bent to pick them up.

Puzzled, he looked at Franny. 'You got this from the store?'

Franny's tone dripped with sarcasm. 'That's right, Cab, you taught me well, so whatever it is you think of me, whatever cold bitch you think I am, at least now we have enough money so we can all go home.'

Back in the car, Franny once again pushed down her emotions as she took a deep breath and pressed send, rereading her text as it sent:

Alfie, I know you're probably angry with me, but like I said b4, I had something I needed to do that I couldn't tell you about. But I want to explain now. But I'm going to come and do it face-to-face. I'll be home next week or so . . . And Alfie, I love you. I hope you can forgive me. F x

Part Two

PRESENT DAY

20

It was over a week since Franny, Cabhan and Alice had headed towards Missoula airport, and Franny had never been so pleased to see the white sign welcoming her to Essex; nor had she been this pleased to feel the light summer rain on her face. The one thing she *wasn't* so pleased about was catching a glimpse of Janine's mansion looming in front of her, because it meant only one thing. It was the moment of truth.

Sitting in the car as dusk closed in, putting off the inevitable, Franny stared at the house, imagining and wondering what Alfie was doing inside. She'd left Cabhan and Alice at her friend's house; she knew she needed to sort this out on her own.

For the past few weeks she hadn't let herself think of him, only about the money she'd taken and how eventually she was going to explain it. All she'd been focused on, *had* to be focused on, was Cabhan and Alice. But now as she sat outside, minutes before she was about to come face-to-face with him again, she finally allowed herself to admit how much she'd missed him, how much her heart had ached for him. How much she loved him.

Puffing her cheeks out, Franny exhaled hard, trying to calm her nerves and ignore her fear that there was a strong possibility

Alfie just *wouldn't* forgive her. Although she hadn't spoken to Lola again, she had received a voice message from her. She'd only been able to understand half of it, partly because of the bad signal but mostly from Lola being so inconsolable it was hard to hear what she was saying. There was one sentence she had heard clearly from the message: 'Alfie, he's so angry, he says he wants to kill you.'

With her stomach in knots, Franny stepped out of the car, walked towards the gates and tapped in the security number. It'd been a while since they'd seen each other properly. Before Alfie had left Spain to come back to Essex, he hadn't seen her for about a month whilst he and Vaughn worked on getting the money together to buy into their new business. Then when they had met up, it'd only been for less than five minutes, when he'd handed the two million pounds over to her. The two million she'd given to the Russo brothers.

Counting down from ten, Franny knocked on the wooden door, Lola's warning ringing in her ears. Waiting and listening.

A few minutes later, the door was swung wide open.

'Alfie, it's good to see you. Can we talk?' Franny said calmly as she pointed her gun straight at him. 'You're looking well, by the way. Aren't you going to invite me in? I know you weren't expecting me, but I did send you a text.'

Alfie Jennings stared at Franny, his thoughts racing, his heart thumping, before he glanced at the gun in shock and disbelief, a look of bemusement on his handsome, chiselled face. His voice dripped with bitterness. 'So first you steal my money and then you turn up on the doorstep with a gun halfway up me nose. Welcome home, Fran, you really are your father's daughter, ain't you?'

'Leave my dad out of it, Alfie. I'm here to talk. Explain.'

'Talk, with that thing in my face? Are you having a laugh?'

'No, far from it. I thought I might need it, I know what you can be like.'

Alfie shook his head as he growled out his words. 'So, are you planning on using it then?'

Franny held Alfie's stare, her beautiful eyes hard and steely. 'If I have to. I've heard your messages, Alf – they weren't very nice – and I also understand from . . .' Franny suddenly stopped; something told her it probably wouldn't be the wisest move to tell Alfie Lola had been in touch warning her against him.

Alfie narrowed his eyes suspiciously. '*Understand* what?'

Franny tried to sound casual. 'Nothing . . . I . . . I just understand you, that's all. So, let's just call this a precaution.'

Hissing at her, Alfie said, 'You really are a cold cow, ain't you?'

Franny took a deep breath. All she really wanted to do was tell Alfie she loved him, tell him that she'd missed him and it'd hurt so much them being apart, but she didn't know how to. She just didn't know how to say it, so instead she did what she knew – she looked at him coolly and spoke in a firm, detached way. 'I understand you're upset, Alf, and I'm sorry.'

Giving a dark half-smile, Alfie raised his voice to the roof. 'Upset, upset? No, darlin', I'm not upset. Shall I tell you what upset is? Upset is when I bang my toe on the side of the bath, or when I realise I've got a flat tyre on my new car. What *I am* is fucking *murderous* that the person I loved, *trusted*, made off with two million quid. The money for our future. The only money I had in the world. So therefore, you cheeky fucking cow, I think what you need to do is pass me that gun so I can point it at the right person.'

'Alfie, this is difficult for both of us.'

Exasperated, Alfie threw his arms in the air. 'There you go again. The ice queen cometh. You're talking like somehow you're the hard done one. Well, I'm sorry, Fran, it was you who ripped me off, not the other way round, and without even an explanation. Face it, darlin', you don't give a shit about anything, let alone me and you.'

She could feel the tightness burning in her chest. She wanted

113

to scream that being with him was one of *the* most important things in her life. She wanted him to sweep her up in his arms and forgive her, telling her they'd spend the rest of their lives together, but it always came down to the same problem: she just didn't know how to access that part of her. So again, unable to do anything else, she answered matter-of-factly.

'I didn't rip you off.'

Alfie tipped his head to one side, his tone sarcastic. 'Really? Are you sure about that? So then I take it you've brought my money back.'

Slowly, Franny shook her head, the sadness inside her making her feel like she were drowning in it. The strange thing was, looking at him now, she felt further away from him than she had ever done before. 'No. But I've brought Alice and Cabhan.'

The laughter that came from Alfie was harsh and hostile. 'What is this, your version of Jack and the fucking Beanstalk? I give you two million quid and all you bring me back is them? Jesus Christ, why don't you just give me the beans and cut to the fucking chase? Or are you going to tell me it's too late, because the giant ogre's already coming after us?'

Ruefully, Franny said, 'If only that's all it was.'

'What are you talking about now?'

'I took your money because of the Russos.'

Alfie's face blanched. 'Jesus Christ, Fran.'

'They were going to kill Cabhan and they came after Alice, too.'

Alfie sounded shocked as he pulled the door open wider. 'You should've told me. Look, for Christ's sake, just put that gun down and come inside. I need to hear this.'

Half an hour later, Franny sat tensely on the big green Chesterfield in the lounge, waiting as she had done for the past few minutes for Alfie's response to the story. But instead of talking, Alfie paced in silence, lighting up a cigarette and dragging on it deeply.

Giving up that Alfie was ever going to speak first, Franny said, 'So, you can see that I didn't have any other choice.'

Alfie leapt towards Franny, his face inches away from hers as fury seeped out of him.

'You had so many other choices, but the problem was you thought you could just go in with your magic wand, like you always do, and hey presto, everyone's happy again. But it don't fucking work like that, Fran, and it certainly doesn't work like that with the Russo family. What possessed you? How could you think going to see Nico in prison would do anything apart from giving him a boner? He plays games with people's lives, you know that. He's a psycho and he's got those two crazy brothers swimming around like sharks looking for blood.'

'I had to help Cabhan.'

In frustration, Alfie threw his cigarette in the fireplace, grabbed hold of Franny's top and shook her hard. 'No, you didn't, Fran! No, you didn't! I told you, and I told him, that if he went to work for the Russo brothers he's on his own. He knew that, but he still went to work for them and now look. I knew this would happen. This is what I was afraid of.'

Pushing Alfie's hands off her and smoothing down her grey marl top, Franny stood up angrily. 'There was no way any of us could've known that Ally was going to get killed in a car crash.'

'No, you're right, but if it wasn't that, it would've been something else. You knew as well as I do, the Russos were never going to let him come home without some sort of retribution, and guess what? You've just gone and made it all worse.'

'How do you make that out?'

'You ran. You ran and hid and Nico's favourite game is hide-and-seek.'

Frustrated, Franny looked at Alfie in bewilderment. 'You expected us to stay?'

'No, not you. You should've left Cabhan to it. You should've allowed him to take the hit.'

It was Franny's turn to hiss through her teeth. 'Have you any idea what you're saying?'

Hardly able to contain his fury, tension behind Alfie's eyes began to make them throb with pain. 'I know exactly what I'm saying, and I mean it. This business ain't for the faint-hearted and there's got to be sacrifices. Cabhan knows that. He shouldn't have accepted your help. He should've just taken the consequences.'

'And Alice? What about her?'

'He should've sent her over here a long time ago, but now? *Now* you're bringing the Devil to our door, asking me to let Alice and Cabhan stay here. It's a death wish.'

Not sounding as confident as she did before, Franny replied, 'They've got nowhere else to go. They're family and we stick together, no matter how tough. Besides, it'll be fine . . . for now, anyway. Especially if we lie low. Don't look like that. I'm telling you, Alfie, it'll be okay.'

Slowly and precisely, Alfie said, '*Will. It. Fuck*! When have you ever known Nico to give up?'

Not being able to hold Alfie's glare, Franny shrugged as she turned away. 'They don't know where we are.'

Enraged at Franny's seemingly casual response, Alfie grabbed hold of her face and turned it towards him gently. 'But for how long though, Fran? For how long? They know Cabhan is in touch with you, they know you have a base here – come off it. This is a game for Nico, and he *will* seek you out and then there will be blood.'

'Alfie, look, can I talk to you? I need to tell you something. I've been putting it off too long, I . . .'

Bree Dwyer, full of determination, walked through the door as she spoke, but on seeing Franny and Alfie she trailed off, her long blonde hair tumbling over her shoulders. As she turned to Alfie, her green eyes twinkled warmly despite her obvious confusion.

'Sorry, I didn't know you were with anyone. I'm Bree.'

Franny looked quizzically at Alfie, then back to Bree. 'Hello, Bree, I'm Franny.' Turning to Alfie, she added, 'Care to explain?'

To which Alfie, with a tight smile, simply said, 'It's complicated.'

Franny nodded as the truth hit her, unable to say anything as waves of nausea rushed over her. The room seemed like it were spinning and a sudden pain in her stomach stabbed at her like a cramp. If she could just get to the door then she'd be all right, and from there if she could just make her way to her bedroom, she'd be fine. But suddenly the door seemed so far away, the room so wide, and as she took a step towards it, her legs began to give way, trembling as she went.

'Franny!'

She couldn't turn around. She just couldn't turn around. Just head for the door. That's all she needed to do, head for the door. *Nearly there. Nearly there.*

'Franny!'

Alfie's voice sounded again, cutting right through her as she walked through the door and along the corridor, swaying and holding onto the wall as she went. Stumbling up the stairs, she felt like she were in a trance.

She stared at the guest bedroom door for a moment before slowly pushing it open and stepping inside. Franny immediately felt a rush of emotions hit her like a sledgehammer, taking the breath out of her as she gasped for air. In agony, she wrapped her arms around her middle, collapsing to the floor. And in the darkness, with tears streaming down her face, Franny Doyle curled up into a tight ball, the pain sweeping through her body as if she'd been in a car crash.

21

'*It's complicated.*' Alfie played over the words in his head like they were on repeat. Who the hell said that? But then what was he supposed to say? Because it *was* complicated. And as much as it seemed strange, in the shock of Franny turning up he'd forgotten all about Bree. And now his head was wrecked. How was he to explain? He couldn't even explain to himself. No wonder Franny had just got up without another word and gone to one of the spare guest rooms, if that was the only explanation he could come up with.

But she'd be all right, he was sure of it. She was a hard cow when she wanted to be and anyway, how much could she really care? After all, look at what she had done to him – that was much worse, wasn't it? Taking two million pounds and disappearing into thin air without as much as a by-your-leave, that was worse than what he'd done. Though the look on Franny's face hadn't said that. Hurt. That was what he'd seen . . . She'd looked ill . . . No, no way, he wasn't going to let himself think like that or feel guilty. *Fuck it.* She had wronged *him.* He didn't know if she was coming back. He didn't know she hadn't just done a runner with some Spanish bloke . . . Or maybe he did. Maybe underneath he knew she wasn't really like that . . . *Shit.*

He couldn't think clearly and now he had more explaining to do.

'Listen, Bree, I know you said you want to talk to me, but I need to tell you this—'

'Alf—'

'No, let me say this first, otherwise I may never say it. Look, maybe I wasn't as straight with you as I should've been, you know, about how long me and her have been separated, and maybe I haven't told you everything I should've done about Franny and the way I feel. I dunno. Don't get me wrong, I never lied to you, not really, but I thought it was over. I thought Franny wasn't coming back.'

Nervously, Bree chewed on her lip. She was still in shock. She hadn't, in a million years, thought that Franny would turn up – not from the way Alfie had been talking anyway – and her heart had gone out to her. It was clear from the look on Franny's face that she still felt something for Alfie, but the question was, what was it that Alfie felt for Franny? In truth, she was scared to hear the answer.

'So what are you trying to say, Alfie?'

Alfie stood by the green Chesterfield couch, hating to hear the hurt in Bree's voice, and it didn't help that he couldn't think of the right words to make her feel better. He tried to ignore how beautiful she looked, playing down what had happened between them in the past couple of months by *telling* himself and wanting to believe what he and Bree had was like a holiday romance. Because when he saw Franny, even though he was angry, though he hated her and wanted her to feel the same kind of pain he had felt, even after all that, he still loved her, fully and completely. But then standing here with Bree, it felt like he loved her too. *Shit*.

Walking up to her, Alfie pushed Bree's long blonde hair out of her face. 'Bree, look, I never knew she was going to turn up. I would've never strung you along if I'd thought that me and her . . . well, not that I strung you along . . . You mean a lot to me, you always have done. But seeing Franny . . .' Alfie trailed off, but then added quickly, 'But what me and you had was real though.'

Bree felt the pain tighten in her chest. '*Had*?'

Irritated that this wasn't going as smoothly as he'd like – in fact, it wasn't going well at all – Alfie snapped, 'No, I don't mean *had*, I mean what we *have*. It's real, of course it is, but if you don't mind, I'd like to maybe, well, maybe we could play it down for Franny's sake and have a chance to work out what's going on.'

'You mean you want me to lie to her?'

Never having been any good at feeling guilty or dealing with women's emotions, Alfie resorted to being hard and uncaring. 'I never said lie, did I? I mean, after all, nothing with us was official, was it? It was just a casual arrangement between two consenting adults.'

Alfie turned away, not only knowing he was being unfair, but also knowing this way seemed easier; making a woman hate him was simple, over the years he'd become an expert at it. Get a woman to hate you and it saved all the pain and hurt, but, more to the point, it saved him from dealing with emotions he was scared of.

He knew it was a joke really, because he'd be prepared to face the hardest of men, go up against any kind of problem, no matter what. Nothing really frightened him, nothing except love that is, because love had a way of ripping his very heart out. That kind of pain he didn't want to deal with, he never wanted to go through that again.

When he was just a boy he had found his mother – whom he had adored and who had loved him utterly – covered in blood with a pair of garden shears sticking into her neck after she'd taken her own life. The pain of one minute having her love in his life and the next minute having it snatched away from him had been an unbearable agony. So, love was fine whilst it was fine, but the minute it started to go wrong it was easier for him to get out and not look back rather than deal with the pain of what might come.

'Alfie, why are you doing this?' Bree asked quietly, reaching out to touch his shoulder softly. 'Look at me?'

'Bree, *please*, don't make this harder than it has to be, darlin'.'

Angry now, Bree snatched her hand away and snapped at Alfie. 'Harder for who, Alf? It was only last week you were saying to me that you and Franny were over. You gave me all the chat about how she'd hurt you, that you didn't have any feelings for her. And you know what, more fool me because I believed you. What a fool I was to think we could have a happy ever after.'

With guilt making him rage, Alfie replied harshly, 'Jesus Christ, Bree, I never promised you anything. You're making it out like I've been down on one knee begging you to be my missus.'

Bree's green eyes flashed with anger, though it was hurt she was feeling. Hurt and humiliation. 'You can be a real idiot, Alf. I'd forgotten that side of you. You might not have promised me anything—'

Alfie cut in. 'Well, there you go then, what's the problem?'

Fighting back tears, Bree shook her head. She hadn't known what to expect when they'd got together, but she certainly hadn't expected this. 'The problem is, Alfie, it wasn't just about making a promise. It's about all the other things you said, the things you did. I really thought you cared.'

'I do, but—'

Trying to be strong, Bree pushed further. 'No, Alf, what you're doing is trying to dig yourself out of a hole.'

Alfie rubbed his head, unable to look at Bree directly. 'I just don't want any grief with Franny.'

Staring at Alfie in bemusement, Bree, feeling like she'd been sucker-punched, sat down on the couch. 'How can you get me so wrong? Don't you get it, Alfie? For me, it's not about Franny, it never has been. I genuinely thought it was over, so I haven't got an argument with her, she hasn't done anything.'

Alfie scowled. 'Really? You think taking two million quid from someone isn't doing anything wrong?'

'For God's sake, Alfie, we ain't talking about money, we're talking about loving someone. She's out there hurting, probably not understanding, any more than I do, quite how it came to this. Face it, Alfie, you're the one who hasn't been straight here.'

Fuming and red-faced, Alfie raised his voice. 'Bree, will you just fucking listen. How many times do I have to tell you, I didn't know she was coming back.'

'Maybe not, but you *did* know you had feelings for her.'

The two of them stared at each other in the echoing silence, both deep in their own thoughts.

Eventually, Alfie said, 'Anyway, what was it you wanted to say to me? When you came into the room, you said you had to tell me something.'

Bree just shrugged. How could she tell him now? How could she tell him she was pregnant? It was all a mess. *Especially* as she didn't know if the baby was Alfie's or her ex-husband's; though she had a feeling, or perhaps it was just a hope, it was Alfie's.

Nevertheless, she had hoped they might talk about it, because after the past few years and everything she had gone through she didn't trust herself to make the right decisions, the right choices. Secretly, she wasn't sure if she was good enough to be a mother again. She had messed up big time in the past and she was scared she might do that again, so she'd needed to speak to Alfie about it. But now Franny had come back, now she *knew* Franny meant something to him, there was no way she wanted to make it more difficult for anyone. Even though it felt like the happiness she'd finally found had been swept away all too soon, she owed him that. Owed him to keep her mouth shut. Because if she *really* did love him, no matter how much it hurt, she would let him go.

'Nothing, well, nothing important anyway, only that I don't really fancy going to London tomorrow. I hope you don't mind.'

Strained, Alfie lit a cigarette. 'No, of course not, I was going to say the same thing myself. I don't think it's really the right time for us to go and live it large.'

Bree sat stony-faced. 'Absolutely.'

'There's one more thing . . . I don't think it's a good idea for us to share a room anymore. Is that okay? I'll sleep in one of the spare bedrooms and I'll get my things out of your room tomorrow, I don't have to worry you tonight.'

Wanting to burst into tears but instead just giving a small, tight smile, Bree, almost unable to get the words out, nodded. 'Fine, whatever you say. I understand.'

Alfie nodded. Guilt and shame were running through him, knowing that Bree was hurting, but he chose instead to follow her words. He winked at her. 'I knew it, I knew you'd understand. That's my girl.'

And with that, Alfie Jennings walked away, leaving Bree with her heart breaking.

22

It was just before 7am as Alfie Jennings sat having a cigarette in the large white kitchen watching Cabhan and Alice approaching the security gates on the CCTV. He clenched his jaw, not in the mood to speak to Cabhan, especially in front of Alice. What he had to say might not go down very well.

He'd thought he'd been angry last night when Franny had told him the story, but the more he mulled it over, the more he'd wound himself up. Now, he wanted to do somebody some serious damage. It didn't help that he had missed lying next to Bree last night or that his heart still beat for Franny. *Shit*.

Having buzzed Alice and Cabhan in, Alfie walked along the hallway to open the imposing wooden front door.

On seeing Alice, Alfie grinned, bringing her into a strong, warm embrace. 'Hello, darlin', it is *so* good to see you. It's a shame it's under these circumstances, though. Franny tells me what a brave girl you were, that you used your head, not many people would've been able to think straight if the Rus—'

'Robbery. If a robbery happened. Because that's what it was, just a robbery.' Cabhan, having cut in, gave Alfie a warning stare.

Not appreciating this knock-down, Alfie seethed inwardly. 'Listen, Alice, I need to have a quick word with Cabhan. You've had a major journey, so why don't you go upstairs and get settled. The second room on the right will be your bedroom.'

Alice smiled. She'd always loved Alfie from the first time she'd met him. He'd always been so kind and gentle towards her, so she stayed in his embrace a little while longer, feeling the safety she'd been craving since what happened at school. 'Thank you so much, Alfie. It's lovely that you're going to let Dad and me stay.'

'Of course! I'm looking forward to getting to know you more. It'll be a pleasure, and Lola can't wait to see you later. I know it's been tough on you these past few weeks, but we'll get through this together, right? Now off you go and get yourself settled in.'

Nodding, Alice skipped off and ran up the stairs towards her new room.

'Hold up, Alice, we need to talk. Wait there for me,' Cabhan shouted after his daughter.

But as he turned to follow her, Alfie grabbed his arm, whispering furiously, 'No, Cab, *we* need to talk, and now!'

'We do, but it can wait, I've got to make sure my daughter's okay.'

'It's a bit late to start worrying about that now, ain't it? I just want to know what the fuck you're playing at getting Franny and Alice involved in your shit. You needed to sort this out with the Russos on your own.'

'It's sorted.'

Alfie scowled at Cabhan. 'How? Because you've come here? Do me a favour. You and I both know it's not over yet. These are the Russos we're talking about.'

Cabhan pulled away. 'Look, Alf, I never wanted to involve anyone else in this, but I am handling it my way. So I'd appreciate it if you could keep your mouth shut about the Russos. Alice knows nothing and I want to keep it that way.'

'And how long will that last? She's going to find out soon enough, she's not stupid. So, the sooner you tell her, the better.'

'You're right on one thing, she's not stupid, but what Alice is is *different*. She's . . . she's innocent. She's been sheltered. The girl even thinks I work in insurance.'

Alfie stared at Cabhan with disdain. 'You mean you can tell her anything and she'll believe it.'

'I didn't say that.'

'No, you didn't have to, but let me tell *you*, you're playing a dangerous game with that, Cab, and it'll come back to bite you. I should know.'

Ignoring Alfie's warning, Cabhan turned and ran up the stairs two at a time to catch up with his daughter.

'Hey, baby, sorry about that.'

Smiling, she turned around, her corkscrew hair tumbling over her face as she waited on the wooden landing for her father.

Just then, hearing Cabhan and Alice, Franny came out of her room, looking tired and pensive.

Slightly out of breath, Cabhan smiled back, but he couldn't hide the tension in his body and behind his eyes. The overwhelming pressure and guilt sitting on his shoulders like a dead weight.

'I know it's been a bit of a whirlwind these past few days, and I know we didn't have a chance to talk last night, but, for the time being, *this* is where we're going to stay. This will be your home until we decide exactly what we're going to do, so we need to get you settled in. I want you to be happy, Alice, that's the main thing.'

Sadness poured out of Alice's eyes. 'I'm fine, Dad. I don't want you to worry about me.'

Sensing a stress headache coming on, Cabhan massaged his temples as he stared at his daughter. 'I don't think you are. You haven't told Franny or me *anything* about what's going on with you. Alice, you've had a terrible time and seen some awful stuff, but it's no good bottling it up. I know what it's like to have people close to you die violently and all the feelings that come with it, so one of the first things we need to do is get you some kind of help.'

'Like I say, Dad, I'm fine. Really. I don't need to see someone, I just wish . . .' Alice trailed off.

'You wish what?'

'I just wish you'd talk to me. I don't understand what's happening. I don't get why we came here like we did. Everything seems so difficult right now. And the convent, I—'

Cabhan jumped in, his stress turning into anger. 'It was a robbery, Alice, you know that, we've already told you.'

'I know, but—'

'But nothing. That's all there is to it. What else do you want from me, Alice?'

Not understanding why her dad was so cross, and not able to find the words she wanted to say, in turmoil and desperation, Alice quickly replied, 'What I want, what might help me, what might help all of us, is if we pray. You, me and Franny. I'd really like that, Dad. I think that could help me, it could help you. Why don't you just try it, Dad?'

Cabhan stiffened. He glanced over to Franny before looking back at his daughter. 'That isn't going to help me. It's never helped me and it's not going to help me now.'

Hoping to calm him down, Franny put her hand on Cabhan's arm. 'Cab, come on. Alice doesn't mean any harm. This is tough for all of us. Calm down, okay?'

Realising he was bringing to the present his own childhood memories of the abuse he'd suffered under the hands of priests, Cabhan nodded. He tried to smile reassuringly at Alice and softened his voice, his Irish lilt lulling. 'Look, I'm glad you can find comfort in that stuff, and I know it's how your mum brought you up, but whether you like it or not, I'm going to take you to see somebody. You've been traumatised. You need *proper* help.'

Wide-eyed and bewildered, Alice felt distraught. 'But it is

proper help, Dad. It can make everything better, but we have to do it together.'

Trying not to but failing, Cabhan shouted, 'For goodness' sake, Alice, where was your God when your mum died or when those kids and nuns got slaughtered? Where was he then? You're in the real world now, not fantasy land or whatever commune you were brought up on, so, sweetheart, get used to it, and I want to hear no more talk of that crap!'

As Alice turned to run, Franny grabbed her, bringing her into a tight embrace as Alice wept through her words, shaking. 'Franny, *please*, tell Dad he's wrong.'

Giving Cabhan a hard, cold stare over Alice's shoulder, Franny, furious with his attitude, said, 'What harm can it do, Cab? This is what Alice does, it's what she knows, all she knows. It's who she is. Give her a break.'

Enraged at what he saw as Franny going against him, Cabhan spoke through gritted teeth. 'I'd appreciate it if you'd leave the decisions of what's best for my daughter down to me.'

Amazed by Cabhan's behaviour and feeling wretched herself from the events of last night, Franny shook her head. 'What has got into you, Cab? I was only saying.'

'Well don't,' he snapped.

Turning her attention to Alice instead, Franny drew the girl away from her and smiled warmly into her tear-filled eyes. 'So, are you excited about being in England? I know it's been a long time coming, but it's a new beginning.'

'Is it?'

Franny nodded, hoping that she sounded sincere. 'Yeah, of course. We can all start afresh.'

Alice, feeling miserable, shrugged. 'I don't think we should've come.'

'Why not, honey?'

Alice looked past Franny to her dad. She was *so* worried about him and nothing made sense anymore. The only time it had in the past few weeks was when she'd spoken to Nico. He'd understood everything she'd said, *and* he hadn't got angry with her or made her feel stupid when she'd talked about her beliefs. But the best part about her conversations with him was that he'd made her feel like everything was all going to be fine. He'd made her feel safe.

'It just seems such a rush. I didn't mind the motel; I would've been happy to stay a while longer.'

Franny, puzzled, smiled again. 'If you liked it back there, Alice, you'll love Essex. There's so much for you to do here. I can't wait to show you around. I know it's been tough, it's been awful for you, but I'm sure eventually you'll see this is the right thing to do.'

Grateful for Franny's care and not wanting to upset her, Alice nodded sadly, saying nothing. Overcome with emotion, Alice walked to her room, leaving Franny and Cabhan standing there in tense silence.

As Alice closed the door behind her, relieved to be alone, she felt her phone buzz in her pocket. Walking across to the window seat that overlooked the garden, she answered.

'Hello?'

'Alice, it's me. What happened, Alice?'

Alice's eyes darted to the closed bedroom door. 'Hold on a moment.' After tiptoeing across the room, she opened the door a crack, checking that Cabhan and Franny were no longer in the hallway, then quietly closed the bedroom door again and returned to the phone.

'Nico?'

'Who else?'

23

Sitting on the window bench watching Alfie and Cabhan walk into the garden having a heated discussion, her dad animated and angry, Alice sighed with relief to hear Nico's voice.

'I'm so glad you called.'

Nico's tone was soft and low as he hummed his words. 'Are you, Alice, are you really? Because I didn't know if you would be. You see, I thought we had an arrangement. I thought you wanted me to talk to your dad, help him work out his problems.'

Fear rushed through Alice. 'I do! I do! I'm so worried about him; I've never seen him so stressed. He's trying to hide it but . . .'

'Well, you've got a funny way of showing it, Alice. We paid you a visit at the motel like you wanted, and guess what, you'd checked out. I hope you're not playing games with me.'

Taken aback by his harsh tone, Alice shook her head and cupped her mobile in her hands. 'No, no, I would never do that. I want you to talk to my dad, because I don't know what to do. He won't listen to me and he looks really ill. I just can't talk to him . . . well, not the way I can talk to you, so I really *am* glad you called.'

'You sound upset, Alice.'

'I am a bit. I was so nervous you wouldn't phone me.'

Nico smiled to himself, playing with the toothpick in his mouth. 'Do not fear, for I am with you.'

Alice burst into tears of delight, her emotions overwhelming her. She spoke breathily. 'That's from the book of Isaiah! I knew you understood. I *knew* it. I think you're the only person who does . . . Nico, I tried, I really *did* try to call you, but I couldn't get through.'

Nico sat on the bed in the cell of one of the other prisoners, watching Chris D'Amato force a gag down the man's throat to keep him quiet; the man who'd thought it was a good idea to challenge *his* authority amongst the other prisoners. 'Alice, you wouldn't lie to me, would you?'

Alice wiped away her tears, hating the fact that Nico was doubting her. 'Of course not, Nico! I really did try to call you.'

'You see, that's the odd thing, Alice, because my phone's been working. Other people have managed to get through and look, here I am calling you, getting through to you without a problem.'

Hearing Nico's disappointment in her, Alice's mood dropped even further. 'I'm so sorry, Nico. When we landed, my phone just didn't seem to work. I know I should've called you sooner, maybe I need to ask—'

Spitting out the toothpick and grinding his teeth, Nico cut in, twirling a coin in between his fingers. 'Landed? What are you talking about, Alice?'

'We left. Dad and Franny thought it was a good idea to come back to England . . . I just don't know what's going on.'

Staring ahead, Nico's jaw pulsated, fury rushing through his veins.

'Nico? Nico, are you still there?'

'Oh yes, Alice, I'm still here, I'm not going anywhere. *Ever . . .* Tell me, Alice, what does the Bible say about keeping secrets?'

Alice frowned nervously, but after a moment she quietly said, '*For everything that is hidden will eventually be brought*

131

into the open, and every secret will be brought to light . . . Mark 4, chapter 22.'

Nico spoke firmly, making sure that Alice could feel his displeasure. 'That's right, Alice, but you thought it was okay not to tell me something really important. I thought we were friends. I was the one who was going to talk to your dad, arrange his birthday party.'

'I know.'

'Alice, there's not many people I would trust to share my prayers with. I thought that was special. I thought we had a connection. I was stupid to think our belief joins us somehow.'

Panic rushed over her. 'It was, it does! You're the only person who understands. You have no idea how great it was to talk to you last week, since Mum and Sister Margaret . . .' She trailed off, trying to block the images of the convent from hijacking her thoughts. Then, taking a deep breath, Alice continued, 'And we are friends, Nico, it wasn't like how you think it was, I promise.'

'But how am I supposed to help your dad now? Now that you're gone.'

'You could call him.'

Nico slammed down his fist on the thin prison mattress, dust and crumbs jumping from it.

'You know that won't work. We already discussed that, didn't we, Alice?'

Alice nodded her head robotically as Nico added dramatically, 'I tell you what, Alice, and this is something I wouldn't normally do for anybody, but I could make a special trip, seeing as it's you.'

Alice whirled round, hugging the phone. This was just what her dad needed. She knew that she couldn't help him, so the perfect person would be Nico. 'Would you? Would you really?'

'Yes, but no more secrets, not from me. Understand?'

Alice's heart soared. Nico seemed just to understand. The same way she thought, *he* thought. Her dad would be so pleased, and maybe he'd see that believing *did* bring angels. 'I promise.'

As he spoke, Nico stared at the man in his cell, a saccharine tone oozing out of him. 'But of course, we can't tell your dad I'm coming, can we? But that's not keeping secrets, is it? It's just doing what's best. Right, now we've got that sorted out, I need *you* to help *me*, would you do that?'

Alice sounded surprised. 'Of course, anything, Nico.'

'Well, I need to decide something. I can't quite make my mind up what to do. So, I thought I might flick a coin, but you need to call it out. Heads or tails. Heads, it's over and tails, it's just not over now.'

Alice giggled, not understanding, but having fun nevertheless. 'That's strange, but I guess I'm going to choose heads, because sometimes it's nice to have things over with.'

Nico flicked up the coin in the air, letting it drop on the cell floor. He stared at it and a large grin spread across his face. 'Heads it is, Alice. Just hold the line a minute.'

Putting the phone down, Nico stood up and walked towards the prisoner Chris held in a tight grip. Nico smiled as he leant into the man's face. 'Heads it's over . . . blame Alice.'

Then, placing the bed sheet in a noose around the man's neck and throwing the other end up through the bars across the window, Nico, with a surge of strength, yanked at the sheet, tugging the prisoner off the ground.

The man's eyes bulged and he began to choke, his fingers pulling at the ever-tightening sheet, his legs flapping in panic as he gurgled out a horrifying noise. Nico yawned, waiting for the man to stop moving, and once he did, Nico picked up the phone again.

'Sorry about that, Alice.'

'What was that noise?'

Nico stifled a yawn. 'It was just somebody hanging around.'

'Alice! You coming down? Lola wants to say hello!'

Hearing Franny call from downstairs, Alice hurriedly said, 'Nico, I have to go now.'

'All right, but text me your address.'

'When will you come?'

'Just wait and see – the best surprises are when you're least expecting them.'

24

In the garden, Alfie – having seen Alice take a quick glance out of her bedroom window – led Cabhan to the secluded copse, out of view from the house.

Without warning, he spun around and swung his clenched fist hard into Cabhan's face.

As Cabhan's lip bled, Alfie said, 'Right, now I've got that out of me system, maybe we can have a decent conversation. And hopefully, once we have done, we can put our differences aside and concentrate on what the hell we're going to do about the Russos.'

Fuming, his black skin mottled with angry red blotches, Cabhan reached up to touch his mouth tentatively.

'You're lucky I don't decide to take one of them bits of wood to your head, Alf. The last man who thought he could take a swipe at me ended up in a very sorry state.'

With the sun shining brightly through the trees, Alfie stared at Cabhan in contempt. 'Oh, so you're the hardman now, are you? Shame that wasn't the case when the Russos came along or when you begged Franny for me money.'

'There wasn't any begging. She offered.'

Alfie, tempted to throw another punch at Cabhan, replied,

'You didn't have to take it though, did you? But now you have, you owe me two million quid.'

Cabhan Morton burst out into bitter laughter. 'You're joking.'

'No, mate, I'm not. And neither will Vaughn once I've told him what happened to his money. He won't be best pleased. You're lucky I haven't called him to tell him that the runt who took our money is tucked up here in the house. So you better sort it before I do make that phone call, because the mood Vaughn was in, well, I don't think he'll play as nice as me.'

'You know I haven't got that sort of money.'

Alfie lit a cigarette to try to stop his anger bubbling over and took a deep drag. 'You see, that's one of the problems right there. If you had no means of paying it back, then why the fuck did you take it in the first place? You know how much I needed that money. That money was for our business, so Vaughn and I could get back on our feet.'

Cabhan stared at Alfie angrily. He didn't care for Alfie's tone; in fact, he didn't care for him at all. Snarling, he said, 'Yeah, but according to Franny, or rather the messages you left her, you managed to sort out some other money, so you didn't *actually* lose your business deal, did you?'

Lurching forward, Alfie grabbed Cabhan's shirt. 'That's not the fucking point. I had to put my neck on the line to get it and the fact is, I'm still out of pocket by two million because *you* decided to be a pussy and drag Fran into your mess.'

'What was I supposed to do?'

Alfie stared at Cabhan, not trusting himself to move, because right now he felt like breaking his neck. Yes, Cabhan was right in so far as he and Vaughn had managed to scrape the money they'd needed together to buy Reginald Reynolds' bookmaker business, but it hadn't been easy; in fact, it had gone right up to the wire.

Reginald had been Essex kingpin, number-one face and an old trusted friend, who'd got in contact wanting to sell his business – which included not only the best legal pitches at racetracks like Cheltenham and Newmarket, but also the monopoly on the illegal betting market in the East of England. And when Reggie had offered it to Vaughn and him, they'd bitten his hand off, knowing it was a proper touch.

So it was not only the reason they'd been looking for to come back home to Essex after their investments in Spain had all gone bust, but it was also a licence to print money, for him to get back on his feet and reclaim the crown of number-one face. And all for just two million big ones. It'd felt like such an easy deal. Both Vaughn and he had sold up in Spain, getting the money that they needed and knowing Reggie and his family only dealt in cash. It was then decided that Vaughn and he would travel to England first, and Franny, who could stay below the radar, would follow later with the cash on the boat of an old associate of theirs. And that's where it all went wrong. *Shit.*

'Alf? I *said*, what was I supposed to do?'

Snapping out of his thoughts and now angrier than before, Alfie, who *had* begun the conversation wanting to put their differences aside so they could concentrate on the Russos, raised his voice, fury coursing through him. 'You should've taken the bullet and it's a shame you didn't, because it would've saved me the trouble of wanting to do it myself.'

In the prettily decorated kitchen, grateful she'd managed to avoid Alfie so far, Franny poured herself a glass of iced water from the fridge.

'Hello, darlin', it's so good to see you.'

Franny turned to see it was Lola. Pushing their argument on the phone aside, Franny ran up to her and gave her a big hug, feeling a huge wave of relief rushing over her. 'Lola! Oh my God, it's so good to see you, too. I've really missed you. Listen, about the phone call, I'm sorry, it was just really difficult to explain.'

'I still don't know what's happened, Alfie didn't say when I saw him this morning, but don't worry about it now, you can fill me in later, it's just so good to see you. And you'll be pleased to know Janine won't be about for a couple of weeks or so, she's taken Molly . . .'

Franny frowned as Lola stopped what she was about to say.

'Go on, Lola. Who's Molly?'

Not knowing what Alfie had told her yet, Lola shrugged, playing it as casual as possible.

'Molly, oh, she's just a friend's daughter.'

Franny stared at Lola, hating the fact that her heart was suddenly beating harder. 'Why are you looking so suspicious?'

Trying to brush it off, but knowing Franny knew her too well, Lola waved her away. 'Me? Don't be silly. Why would I look suspicious?'

'Well, that's what I want to know. So, come on, tell me who Molly is.'

Swallowing hard and feeling like she was being cross-examined, Lola said, 'You've been hanging around with those men too much. You've become hard, Franny. I thought Alfie could be bad.'

A flash of hurt ripped through Franny, but she ignored it as she stared at Lola. 'Lola! Don't you see I'm trying to keep it together here? People think they can keep on telling me what a hard cow I am, and that's fine, but I seriously don't need that from *you* as well. So why don't you just make it that tad easier for me and *tell me* who the *hell* Molly is!'

Slumping on the chair, Lola conceded. 'All right, all right. Molly is Bree's daughter . . . Fran, it's nothing, don't read anything into it. Surprisingly enough, it was Janine's idea. She wanted to take her to Florida. Disneyland. Alfie had nothing to do with it. Look, love, Bree and Alfie, well, they haven't got what you and he have.'

Floored by her words, Franny held onto the kitchen bench, feeling like she'd had yet another slap in the face. 'So they *have* got something, then?'

138

'Franny, darlin', I don't know what to say. I feel terrible for you, but you have been away for a couple of months. What was Alfie supposed to think, to do? I can see how it looks like he's rushed into it, and maybe it was a bit of a rebound, you know, to make himself feel better. But seriously, Fran, it seemed like you'd just dumped Alfie and run.'

Franny sounded flat. 'I texted him.'

'Yeah, to tell him you weren't coming back, *and* you'd taken his money! Put yourself in his shoes. He couldn't understand any of it. He was lost, love.'

Pulling her long chestnut hair up and clipping it into a messy bun, Franny snapped, not showing the pain she felt. 'Not lost enough that he couldn't find his way into another woman's bed.'

Lola's lined face wrinkled as she tried to appeal to Franny. 'Don't be angry with him, he was gutted, and him copping off with Bree, that's just men's ways, ain't it? It's certainly Alfie's, he's always been like that.'

Pouring herself another drink, Franny felt her hurt turn to anger. 'Jesus, Lola, what century are you living in? I can't believe you sometimes. Why is it that you always make out that Alfie's this sweet, innocent boy? You've done that for as long as I've known you. If he loved me like he said he did, then he would *never* have set up home with the first woman he came across.'

'He's known Bree for a long time,' Lola said hesitantly before changing her mind. 'But look, that's another story for another day, because as things stand, the same can be said of yourself, Fran. Don't be a hypocrite, darlin'.'

Fuming, Franny looked at Lola in bewilderment. 'What are you talking about?'

'Well, if you loved Alfie the way you say you do, how could *you* not tell him what was going on?'

Exasperated, Franny pointed at Lola. 'Ditto, Lola. Because if *you* loved me like you say you do, how could you keep the fact that Alfie was playing happy fucking families from me? I've only been away for a few weeks!'

'Just calm down, Fran! We're going around in circles here. A lot has happened but no one's happier to see you back home than me and Alfie. This Bree, she ain't bad, she ain't the enemy. Give her a chance.'

Throwing her glass into the sink and hearing it smash into tiny pieces, Franny raised her voice again. 'So now there's polygamy in Essex, who'd have thought?'

Munching down on the Smarties Molly had left in a bowl, Lola sank deeper into one of the white leather kitchen chairs and shook her head in despair. 'It ain't like that, Fran. I know it's hard on you, but think of how Bree must feel.'

Red-faced, Franny couldn't believe what she was hearing. 'Bree? Bree? Are you being serious?'

'Yes, because let's face it, we're talking about Alfie here. Who knows what he told Bree about you. And like I say, he genuinely thought it was over. So, on paper he hasn't really done anything wrong. You're more of a threat to Bree than she is to you.'

With her eyes steely, Franny hissed her words. 'Listen, I've never competed over a man and I'm not going to start now. She's welcome to him.'

'That hard head of yours can sometimes be your downfall.'

Before Franny could say anything, the door opened and Bree, dressed casually in jeans and a striped sweater, walked in; though on seeing Franny, she immediately turned to go. Embarrassed, she mumbled her apologies. 'Sorry, sorry, I didn't know you were in here.'

'It's becoming a bit of a habit with you.'

Bree looked at Franny oddly, noticing properly how beautiful she was, which she had to admit didn't make her feel particularly better. 'I don't know what you mean.'

'Walking into rooms and not knowing anybody's there. You did the same last night.'

Uncomfortable and not sure if Franny was joking or not, Bree gave a small smile. 'Yeah, I did, didn't I. Listen, I'll leave you to it.'

Franny shook her head, intrigued by how seemingly shy Bree was. She could certainly see how Alfie had fallen for her. She spoke coolly, trying to sound as casual as possible. 'Don't go on my account, Bree, I was just leaving. I've got a few things to sort out with Cabhan.'

As Franny went to walk through the door, Bree began to stretch out her hand to stop her but decided it might not be a great idea and just said, 'I didn't know about you. Not really. I thought you and Alfie were over, I swear. I'm so sorry.'

Franny, a good few inches taller than Bree, turned her gaze to her, steady and even. A firmness in her voice. 'Why are you sorry?'

'I . . . I . . .'

'Look, Bree, my problem isn't with you. I know what Alfie is like, but you can appreciate this is hard for me, so I'm going to stay out of your way for now and maybe it'd be best for you to stay out of mine. But it's not personal.'

Bree scrambled for words. 'Franny, there's nothing between Alfie and I. We're just friends, that's all.'

With a cold stare, Franny leant in to Bree's face. She spoke quietly but powerfully, a warning tone in her voice. 'Did Alfie tell you to say that?'

Thrown and hoping she hadn't just made anything worse, Bree stammered, 'What . . . I . . . I . . .'

'Listen to me, Bree, one thing you need to know about me is that I don't need to be wrapped up in cotton wool. I like the truth. The other thing you need to know about me is I don't like games. I don't like lies, so if you want to stay on the right side of me, a word of advice, don't mess with me, and then, Bree, you and me will be just fine.'

141

25

'Oh, so you're still saying it's my fault, are you? That's rich coming from you. Who was the one who mugged me off, pocketed me money? It was you, Fran, you! So don't start giving it the holy treatment, like butter wouldn't melt.'

'The point is it hardly took you long to fall into bed with someone. How do you think that makes me feel, Alf? God knows how long it would've taken you to sleep with someone if I'd died. Knowing you, you probably would've picked up someone at my wake and had them in your bed before the priest could say dust to dust.'

'Turn it in, Fran, now you're being stupid, and for your information, it wasn't about the sex.'

'Oh, so if it wasn't about the sex, it was to do with how you feel. Finally, you're admitting that you have feelings for her.'

'Stop putting words into my mouth. You can be a hard bitch to deal with sometimes and anyway, I thought we were going to try to put this aside for the time being, at least until we sort this mess out that you've got us in . . .'

In the darkness of her bedroom, Alice listened to Alfie and Franny have yet another argument, the sound of their voices coming through the walls. She sighed as she knelt down, hoping her prayers might be answered and somehow she would then feel and think the way she used to. Because right now, right here, everything seemed so confusing, and she hadn't felt this lost since her mother had died.

Thinking of her mother made the tightness in her chest feel worse. She squeezed her eyes together, but her thoughts, as usual, were clouded, hazy, and all she could see was the face of Sister Margaret covered in blood and the sounds of her classmates being gunned down.

Scared and feeling no peace, Alice pulled her phone from her pocket and began to dial a familiar number.

Nico Russo stood alone in his cell. The moonlight shining through the small window. He closed his eyes, feeling the light, warm breeze coming through the bars. He breathed in deeply, taking the air through his nostrils, imagining Alice, sweet Alice Rose. His body stirred as he thought of her, thinking of what he would do if they were alone. Just her and him. Thinking of the way she would scream.

Nico's eyes glanced to the phone on his locker lighting up as it buzzed. He smiled as he picked it up.

'Alice. I was just thinking of you.'

'Were you?'

Nico spoke softly as he took off his clothes, feeling the cool of the night on his naked body.

'Yes, I was thinking how nice it would be to be able to share what I've learnt with you.'

'That sounds nice.'

Gently, Nico said, 'Oh yes, Alice, and I'm sure once I'd finished, you'd pray like you'd never prayed before, like your life depended on it.'

Alice tucked her knees up underneath her as she sat on the thick cream carpet in the darkness. Innocently, she said, 'Would I?'

'Trust me, that's all you'd be doing.'

Closing her eyes and not wanting anyone in the house to hear her, Alice whispered, 'That would be lovely, Nico, because right now I can't focus on anything, it's like . . .'

'Go on, Alice.'

'No, I can't say it.'

Caressing his chest, Nico crooned warmly to her. 'We're friends, Alice, you can tell me anything.'

'I'm afraid you might think less of me.'

'Whatever it is, I wouldn't judge you, that's not my place, and remember what we said about how keeping secrets was a sin.'

Alice took a deep breath and held back her tears as her words rushed out. 'It's just, I feel like I can't connect anymore. That my belief has left me. All I can see when I close my eyes is blood. Blood everywhere, and sometimes I'm sure I can even smell it.'

Smiling to himself, Nico purred, 'Poor, poor Alice. Have you told anyone else about this?'

In the darkness, Alice shook her head. 'No, I don't want to upset Dad anymore and he wouldn't understand anyway, no one would.'

'Except me, Alice.'

'Yes, except you.'

Lying down on his prison bed, imagining what she would smell like, Nico stifled his groans, then, getting himself under control, he asked, 'Alice, would you like me to pray for you? I could do that and maybe that would help you in your time of need.'

Alice, overwhelmed by relief, let out a long sigh. 'Would you really?'

'Of course, but the one thing I think may help is to actually see you. When I pray for someone I like to have a photo of who I am praying for. When my daughter died, I knelt in front of the photo and it brought me peace. It still brings me peace, I'm looking at her now.'

144

Nico turned to the blank wall devoid of any pictures or photographs. 'I'll put your photograph next to hers, then I won't just have to imagine what you look like, I'll be able to see you.'

Full of innocence and warmth, Alice smiled, feeling slightly happier than before. 'That's so kind, Nico. I can send you a photo from my phone straightaway. And Nico, when are you coming?'

'Soon, very soon. Now goodnight, Alice Rose, sleep well.'

A few minutes later, Nico's phone buzzed again. He opened the photo message and smiled as he studied the picture. 'There you are, Alice, there you are. Daddy's looking forward to hearing you scream.'

Having successfully avoided both Franny and Bree for the past couple of days, Alfie walked into the kitchen and right away wanted to run. Standing by the far side of the room preparing freshly squeezed orange juice was Franny, and on the other side, trying to seem busy but looking as awkward as he felt, was Bree.

Realising he wouldn't be able to do an about-turn and sneak away without being seen, Alfie once again said the first words that came to mind. 'Nice to see you two girls getting on.'

'Excuse me?' It was Franny who spoke *and* glared.

Shit. What was it about Franny that when she decided to put him under the spotlight it made him feel like some kid being reprimanded, like he was on some kind of hook? She'd always been like that. Too damn tough for her own good, too much her own woman. Independent and strong. Compassionate but feisty. Not a recipe for an easy life. But wasn't that why he loved her? Wasn't that why they had got together in the first place? Christ, he couldn't think straight. Everything was a mess. Life had been so much easier when all he had to deal with was staying on top of his game, being a number-one face, no women to worry about, no emotions to have to deal with. *Shit.* Okay, so he knew that he *should* be trying to sort it out with Franny and Bree, but all he could really think of was the Russos. He could see Franny was worried too, not that she'd admit it, not that she'd admit anything for that matter. Not how she felt and certainly not what she was up to.

Irritated by this thought, Alfie turned his attention back to answering Franny.

'I'm just saying, it's nice to see you two—'

Franny cut in. 'Don't bother repeating it, Alf. We're grown women, what did you think we were going to do, scratch each other's eyes out over you?'

Alfie smarted. 'No, I . . .'

'I don't think he meant anything by it, Fran.'

Franny turned to stare at Bree, slowly and deliberately. 'First, my name's Franny, and secondly, I think I've known Alfie long enough to know *exactly* what he meant. I'm not a teenage girl about to start some kind of catfight because her ex had his end away the minute she turned her back. But thank you, *Bree*, for your concern. *Noted*.'

Sensing this might not end well, Alfie tried to break the tension. 'Look, girls—'

Franny, stressed and still very confused, raged, 'Girls? What *is* wrong with you, Alf? Bree and I aren't your bits of play fluff. We're women, and what we don't like is to be lied to and put in a compromising position because you decided not to tell the truth.'

Fuming, Alfie barked at Franny, 'When you've quite finished, Emily Pankhurst, let me remind you that it was *you* who put *me* in a compromising position in the first place, when you ran off with my money. If it wasn't for you, I wouldn't have ended up having a thing with her . . . Shit, Bree, I didn't mean that. Wait, don't go.'

Bree Dwyer shook her head at Alfie as she headed for the door. 'Yes, you did, we both know that. Look, maybe it's best if I moved out. I never wanted to cause any trouble.'

Alfie glared at Franny as he pointed at her. 'See what you've done now, Fran?'

'Me? Are you having a laugh? You must be, because for one minute there I thought you were blaming me for this mess.'

Lighting a cigarette at the corner of his mouth, Alfie said, 'I am. One hundred fucking per cent of it, because whether you want to believe it or not, I didn't think you were coming back. I didn't think you loved me anymore and Lola was right, I was gutted. It felt like someone had put a spike through me chest.'

Just as Franny was about to open her mouth to reply, the kitchen door closed gently as Bree walked out. Franny went to follow her.

'Leave her, Fran, she's right, it's probably for the best.'

Giving Alfie a disdainful stare, Franny took the last sip of her orange juice. 'For who?'

'For us.'

'Grow up, Alfie. There *is* no *us*. Bree leaving isn't suddenly going to put things right. It's obvious no matter what you say that you've got feelings for her and that hurts, it cuts me so deeply, but I'm not going to get back together with someone who doesn't know where their heart lies.'

Struggling to find the right words, Alfie stuttered and mumbled, 'It . . . it lies with you, Fran. It always has. I love you. I mean I might be angry with you for what you and Cabhan did, but . . . but, Jesus, I can't imagine not being with you.'

'Look, I don't want to do this. In case you've forgotten, we've got the Russos to think about and what exactly it is we're going to do about them.'

'Don't you think I know that? But I also know you, Fran, you'll do anything rather than talk about us.'

With Alfie's words hitting a nerve, Franny bit back. 'Fine, you want to talk about us, then why don't we talk about Bree? Come on, tell me how you really feel about her.'

'Jesus, Fran, why are you doing this? The thing is . . .' Alfie stopped, unable to admit to Franny how he felt about Bree, because however much he wanted to write Bree off in his heart, he couldn't quite manage it. So, if Bree *did* leave the house, that made it simpler; it was *her* leaving him. 'Look, do you want me to choose, is that it, Franny? Do you want me to show you how much I care and say you're the one, because—'

'I'm not asking that, but you couldn't anyway. Admit it, Alfie, just admit that you care for her as well.'

'Fran . . .' Alfie trailed off again, truly stuck for words.

How the hell he'd got himself in this mess he didn't know. Jesus, he hadn't been faithful to anyone his entire life, not until Fran, and he'd been happy to do the whole one man, one woman bit because she really *had* been his everything, until overnight she'd just cut him off. And it'd hurt, hurt so badly he'd been open to anything that had made him feel better, and that anything had been Bree. Though, in truth, he'd *really* thought it would be a couple of mates getting reacquainted again, going down memory lane. Then bang, the next thing he knew he and Bree had become much more than friends, and as a result his head and heart were all messed up. *Shit.*

Angrily, picking up his thread, Alfie said, 'This mess is all down to you, Franny. You burnt out my heart when you said you weren't coming back . . . Wait! Where are you going?'

With sadness now filling her rather than anger, Franny shrugged, uncomfortable at showing Alfie any vulnerability. 'I thought you'd changed, that the old Alfie who went around hurting people and playing games had gone, but hello, here he is, standing in front of me in all his glory. You make me sick, and if you won't go and see if Bree's all right, I will.'

'Fran! Come on, sweetheart, *please.*'

At the door, Franny turned around to look at Alfie in pity. 'There's one thing I hate more than liars and that's cowards, and you, Alfie Jennings, are a coward.'

* * *

149

'Bree, what are you doing?' Franny stood at the bedroom door watching Bree, tears rolling down her cheeks as she threw her clothes into a large cream canvas zip bag.

As she continued to watch, she felt a pang of sympathy for Bree, knowing what it was like to be caught up in a situation that you had no control over. The other thing she felt was envy. It was strange, but she was envious that Bree could stand there and cry, letting out her feelings, connecting to her pain, being honest about how she felt. That was something Franny so wished she could do, because then she could tell Alfie that the thought of him being intimate with another woman sliced at her heart like a razor blade. That she'd missed him more than she thought was possible . . .

Still, she knew it wasn't Bree's fault, none of it, which just made it worse, because how much simpler would it be to blame her? It also didn't help that despite *everything*, she couldn't quite bring herself to dislike Bree. No, the only person at the moment she disliked was herself for causing all this. For hurting Alfie, which in turn had hurt Bree, so the least she could do, no matter how much she'd like it all to disappear, was to sort it out.

Without looking up, Bree eventually answered. 'What does it look like?'

'It looks like you're running away.'

Whirling round to look at Franny, Bree's expression held confusion. 'Just leave me alone. What do you want from me, Franny? I don't belong here. The sooner I'm gone, the better.'

'And what about your daughter?'

'She won't be in your way, if that's what you mean. I'll come and collect her when she's back from holiday.'

'Bree, you know that's not what I meant.'

Bree stared at Franny, unsure quite what her intentions were. 'Just let me get on, okay?'

'No, not until we have it out.'

Confused and upset, Bree stood with her hands on her hips. 'What is there to say? You've come back and that's the end of it.'

Franny grabbed hold of Bree's arm. 'There's a lot to say! I want to know what Alfie said to you, how you feel about him, how you feel about me turning up.'

'That's a joke from you. You haven't shown any emotion since you found out about me. I don't know you, Franny, but I do know you're going around making out that you don't care, that you don't feel anything, but that's not true, is it? But I guess if you do that and act that way it'll keep everyone at a distance.'

Pulling back, Franny coolly said, 'Don't you worry about me, Bree, I'm fine. I'm not the enemy here; this is messed up and I'm just trying to find a way through this, for all of us.'

Bree pushed her long hair behind her ears. 'Like I said, I'm not wanting any trouble, I've had enough of that in my time. I just want a peaceful life.'

'Is there such a thing, Bree?'

Zipping and picking up the bag, Bree walked into the hallway, making her way down the oak-panelled staircase with Franny a few steps behind.

'I don't know, but I'm not going to find it here, am I?'

'Bree, please don't go . . . I . . . I feel bad. I feel responsible.'

'I'm not looking for you to feel guilty, I'm just looking to get out of this before it becomes too painful.'

Talking quickly, Franny said, 'So where are you going to go?'

'I don't know, Franny. I'll find somewhere, though. Look, I'm grateful for your concern, but you don't have to worry. I might not come across as tough as you, but I'm a survivor, I always have been.'

Following Bree out into the sunshine and along the white gravelled driveway to the large, imposing gates, Franny broke into a jog to run in front of her. Irritation rising in her.

'Why does everyone assume I'm tough?'

Bree looked at Franny kindly. 'Come on, Franny, why do you think?'

'What? Because I work in the business I do? Because I'm my

151

father's daughter? Or because I don't cry in movies when the guy loses the girl?'

'Yes, for all those reasons, but it isn't a bad thing, it's just who you are.'

Franny's chestnut hair blew across her face in the warm wind and, surprised at the sudden wave of emotions welling up inside her, she said, 'You're wrong, it's what I've had to become, but I still have a heart. I still hurt like you do, but I just don't show it in the same way . . . Look, Bree, just think a minute. There's no need to rush off like this, you don't have to go. And as hard as this might be for me to admit, I get it. I get why Alfie got together with you in the first place. I know Alfie. What I did would've hurt him *really* badly and I never wanted that, *ever*. It's just that I had to think of Cabhan and Alice, I had to try to do something, and Alfie was a sacrifice I had to make and that's a tough one to accept. So . . . and I can't believe I'm saying this, but I'm pleased he had you. I'm pleased that being with you stopped him hurting too much.'

For the next few minutes Bree said nothing as she continued to walk with Franny at her side. They turned down the small country lane, past the small woodland and distant farmhouse.

'They were right, you are special.'

Franny frowned, 'What?'

'I heard Lola and Alfie talking about you. They both said it, and you know something, I agree.'

Taken aback by the sentiment and not good at receiving such compliments, Franny joked as she deflected the conversation. 'Bree, I'm not being funny, but I'm a city girl, I really don't do the long country walks bit. Come on, why don't we just turn back home . . . *Please*, come back to the house.'

Spreading her arms out as she stood in the middle of the road, Bree looked at Franny warmly. 'I appreciate the chat, but it doesn't change anything. Franny, don't you understand, I want you to have your happiness with Alfie. I'll be fine, I always have been.'

Exasperated, Franny snapped, 'For God's sake, Bree, just come back.'

'Why? What for? It's you Alfie wants. I just know it. I'm not going to kid myself.'

Quickly pulling Bree towards her and back onto the grass verge to let a speeding truck past, Franny grinned. 'You're going to get us both killed if you're not careful, though maybe Alfie would like that, save him the headache of two women!'

They both burst into laughter before Franny said seriously, 'Bree, I know Alfie, and I know he cares about you.' She stopped to put out her hand and added, 'Please, come on, what do you say? Let's go back to the house, sort this out properly.'

'I can't, Franny, because, to quote Alfie, *it's complicated*.'

'How complicated can it be?'

Bree rubbed her head. She spoke quickly, her emotions getting the better of her as tears ran down her face. 'Look, Franny, I know you mean well, but I'd rather you just leave it. I don't want to get into this. It's all a mess and I thought – well, what I mean is sometimes loving someone isn't enough and you just have to accept that things don't always work out. And truthfully, it doesn't help that you're being so nice to me or that I really like you, and it certainly doesn't frigging help that I'm—' About to say something she shouldn't, Bree snapped closed her mouth quickly.

'What? What were you going to say, Bree?'

'No, nothing.'

Franny narrowed her eyes, her voice firm. 'I've been around a lot of bullshitters, Alfie being one of them, and I know when somebody is giving me the brush-off. Tell me what you were going to say, Bree, because I can be as stubborn as Alfie and I ain't going anywhere until you tell me.'

'Please, just go, go home, Franny. Go back to Alfie.'

'Tell me!'

Frustrated and full of tears, Bree shouted back, 'Why won't you just leave it?'

Franny grabbed Bree's arm and held it. 'I said, tell me! Tell me, Bree!'

'I can't!'

'Just *fucking* tell me!'

'Okay, fine! I'm pregnant . . . I'm pregnant.'

Franny felt it like a slap. A hard, sobering slap. Everything in that moment felt unreal, and a heavy pain descended on her. Reeling, she said quietly, 'Is it Alfie's?'

'I . . . I . . ?'

Agitated, Franny raised her voice, desperate to hear the answer but terrified at the same time. 'I *said*, is it Alfie's?'

'I don't know. I think so, but there's a chance it could be my ex-husband's . . . Franny, I'm so sorry, none of this was supposed to happen.'

It took over a minute for Franny to trust herself to speak as she steadied herself on her feet, willing herself to be strong. Swallowing hard to stop the nausea from overwhelming her, it felt like Alfie was slipping even further away from her.

Once she had herself under control, she said, with a deep sadness, 'It's times like these I wish I could feel like other people do. You know, I wish I could scream and shout and tell you how much I hate you, tell you how much it hurts, but I can't. It leaves me feeling like I've got a big inflated balloon inside me that won't pop. When anything's too difficult, I become numb, tougher. Alfie calls it cold, and maybe it is, but it's the way I was brought up.'

Franny stopped to mimic an Irish accent. 'Don't let anything pull you down, Franny Doyle. Don't ever let me see you fall down on your knees. Don't let others ever see your weakness. Learn to hide your emotions, learn to cut yourself off from pain and that way you'll survive. That way, Franny, you'll always be on top.' She smiled sadly. 'But it's not true, is it?'

'Franny, I'm sorry . . . I—'

'This isn't your fault, you don't need to apologise, Bree.'

'But I do, I . . .'

Franny shook her head. 'No, you don't . . . I take it Alfie doesn't know.'

Kicking at the few daisies amongst the weeds, Bree glanced up at Franny. 'I couldn't tell him. I was going to but . . . but . . . Do you hate me?'

'Like I say, I can't hate you. I don't think I'd want to anyway. Maybe that would be easier, but I actually like you. Look, let's go back and sort this out.' Franny stopped and winked, her eyes suddenly filled with warmth and mischief as she gave Bree a genuine smile. 'Failing that, let's go home and give Alfie some grief.'

Alfie paced about the kitchen. He was a fool; he should've kept his mouth shut. Moreover, he should've stopped Bree from going instead of letting Franny run after her, or maybe he shouldn't. Oh shit, he didn't know. But what he did know was that he didn't understand women. Not one little bit. Women talked about men playing games, but you only had to look at Franny and Bree. First, Franny was playing it cool towards Bree, and then the next thing he knew, she was running after Bree as if they were best friends. His number-one rule from now on was never get on the wrong side of a woman, and certainly never get on the wrong side of *two* women.

He had to think how to handle it, so it wouldn't kick off again. If Franny came back on her own then he would make sure she knew how . . . *Oh shit*. That was the front door. Too late. Play it cool, he had to play it cool.

Going through into the hallway, Alfie readied himself for his half-prepared speech, but he suddenly stopped dead. The front door was open and his blood ran cold . . . Standing in front of him were four men wearing demonic clown masks and holding guns. A deathly silence hanging in the air as the men stared at him. He could hear his own ragged breathing as he took a step

155

back, edging backwards towards the lounge, his mind racing as the men continued to stare, dark eyes through the slits of their masks. But a sudden sound above him made him turn and, with horror, he watched Alice begin to walk down the stairs. The only words that came out of his mouth were, 'Run, Alice, run!' before a blow to his head knocked him out.

27

As Alice heard Alfie cry out in pain – too scared to think about what might've happened to him – she charged along the top landing, fear pushing her faster as she shouted in terror at the top of her voice. 'Dad! Dad! Dad! Help me! Dad!'

Panic shot through her as she ran towards Cabhan's room, her body shaking as she heard the sound of running feet getting closer.

The door of Cabhan's room swung open, but on seeing the masked men only a few feet behind Alice, Cabhan grabbed her, pulling her into the room, slamming and locking the door.

Alarmed, he yelled at his daughter. 'Help me with this! Quick!'

Alice nodded as she helped Cabhan haul the large black mirrored wardrobe in front of the door to barricade them in as the intruders pounded on it. Cabhan, his face drained and fearful for his daughter, spoke hurriedly, beads of sweat beginning to drip from him.

'We haven't got much time. You've got to get out of here, they're after *you*, Alice.'

Trembling, Alice's face held a picture of confusion and fear. She could barely utter the words as she stared at Cabhan in shock, her voice the tiniest of whispers. 'Me? They're after me?'

'Look, I'll explain later . . . Get down!'

Suddenly, Cabhan threw her onto the floor as shots were fired and a gruff American voice growled out from the other side of the door.

'Do yourself a fucking favour and give it up now, give *her* up, Cabhan, there's nowhere for her to hide.'

Although the mask muffled the voice, Cabhan immediately recognised it, and an icy chill ran through him. Salvatore Russo. Questions of how they found them so quickly ran through his head, but he turned back to Alice, dragging her upright as he began to bundle her towards the window. He spoke quietly as he unlocked it, his hands shaking. 'You've got to get out this way. It's your only chance. You haven't got much time.'

In a state of terror, Alice felt she couldn't breathe. She gasped, 'They were at my school! Dad, they were the same people at my school! Who are they? Why do they want me?'

Cabhan held Alice's arm tightly, frantically pushing her even closer to the open window.

'Alice, you've got to go! Go!'

Suddenly understanding what it was her father wanted her to do, Alice's eyes flitted to the door and then to the window and the sheer drop below. Petrified, she shook her head as hysteria began to overwhelm her. She spoke quickly, her voice beginning to rise in panic. 'I can't! Daddy, please, I can't! I can't, I'll fall. And what about you? What about Alfie? He was in the hallway! We've got to go and make sure he's all right. Dad, we've got to go and find Alfie. Dad!'

Tears pricked Cabhan's eyes as, panicked, he slapped her hard across the face. 'Alice, for God's sake, just shut up and go! *Please*, it's your only chance. If they find you in here, they'll kill you, but before they do they'll . . .' Wiping the cold sweat from his brow, Cabhan stopped, unable to contemplate the horrific torture she'd go through before they actually killed her.

More fearful than she'd ever felt in her life, Alice trembled,

her legs shaking so hard they bounced off each other. 'Dad . . .
Please . . . Dad . . .'

A loud bang on the door triggered Cabhan to pick Alice
roughly up and start pushing her through the window.

'No, Dad! No! You'll kill me, please! Stop! Stop!' she screamed,
clinging and holding onto the sides of the painted window frame,
kicking and trying to push backwards as Cabhan shook her,
trying to release her grip.

'Let go, Alice, let go. Just fucking do as you're told.'

'I don't understand. Dad, whatever it is I've done, I'm sorry,
I'm sorry!'

The agony and horror of what he was doing to his daughter
was overshadowed by the knowledge of what would happen if
he didn't. He cried out in despair, his words jumbled with Alice's
sobs of terror. 'I love you, Alice, I love you!'

And with that, Cabhan shoved Alice out of the window and
onto the wide ledge, preferring her to die from her fall rather
than at the hands of the Russos.

Cabhan slammed the window shut, locked it quickly and
threw the key up onto one of the bookshelves before quickly
pulling down the wooden blinds.

Suddenly, there was a massive crash as the wardrobe collapsed
from the gunfire, mirrored glass shattering everywhere as the
Russos and their men shot their way in.

From behind his mask, Salvatore grinned. 'Cabhan, *Ciao*! It's
good to see you, my friend. I take it you were expecting us? We
did tell you there's no place to hide. So come on, where is she?
Under the bed? In the bathroom?' He gestured his head towards
the en suite.

'Go to hell, Salvatore.'

'Now that's not nice. I came all this way to see you and this
is how you treat me. Does our friendship mean nothing to you?'
Salvatore aimed his gun, firing and shooting off Cabhan's left
hand.

Cabhan, dropping to the floor, screamed in agony. Blood poured out, turning the cream carpet red as flesh and tendons hung out from the stump of his arm.

Stepping forward, Salvatore towered over Cabhan. He smiled as he spoke. 'I always like things to come in pairs, seems a bit tidier, doesn't it?'

Whereupon Salvatore Russo shot off Cabhan's other hand. A moment later Cabhan blacked out. His last thoughts were of Alice.

28

In the same moment that Salvatore and his men shot their way into Cabhan's bedroom, Alice, feeling like she was going to be sick, tried to stop herself from screaming as she balanced on the wide window ledge, pinning her body against the rough bricks of the house, afraid to look down. Too terrified to make a move, to turn her head, to blink, to breathe, she was certain that any movement would send her falling to her death.

As she continued to shake, nervous of losing her balance, above her Alice could see a cast-iron window box full of pink and white flowers cascading down the wall. From where she was she could see it was bolted to the bricks, and an idea struck her: if she was careful, really careful, she might manage to reach up and grab a hold.

Taking a deep breath to settle herself, Alice, saying a silent prayer and feeling the warm wind on her face, tried to stretch one hand up, but as she did so it felt like her whole body was tipping forward, sliding off the ledge to the hard ground below. Swallowing a terrified scream, she slammed back, pressing herself against the wall, pulling her stomach in to hold herself steady.

Closing her eyes, Alice heard voices from inside and knew she had to try again before it was too late. Shuffling as far back as she could with her legs still dangling over the ledge, inch by inch she slowly raised her right arm, despite her body trembling as she drove all her weight towards her spine.

With her hands shaking, she felt her fingertips brush against metal, millimetres away from the bar of the window box, but she couldn't quite reach, couldn't quite stretch high enough. The only way for her to grab onto the bar would be to push herself up onto one knee first.

Petrified, but not allowing herself to cry, Alice felt dizzy with her hand still up in the air and didn't trust herself to bring it back down again. Preparing herself, her left hand on the ledge, her fingers spread wide taking the tension, taking the weight of her body, she built up the courage to push herself up.

She counted down slowly.

Three

Two

One . . .

Then Alice pushed, pulling her knee underneath her, but almost immediately she found herself sliding forward again. Desperately, she frantically snatched at the bar as her body swung round, tipping her sideways off the ledge, her shoulder burning in pain as she tried to hold on, as she wildly struggled to reach up with her other hand, letting out a panicked, muffled cry.

Alfie Jennings staggered along the path along the side of the house, the blow to his head making him dizzy. Hearing a sound, he stopped suddenly and jumped into the shadows. There it was again. Trying to figure out where the noise had come from, he looked around and saw nothing as he pushed himself against the wall. Then, cautiously looking up, he froze, stunned. Alice! Jesus Christ, Alice! His eyes darted around the large garden and although he couldn't see anybody, he didn't want to risk calling up to her in case anyone heard.

Without letting Alice know he'd seen her, Alfie hurriedly made his way round to one of the side doors to the stone backstairs, which took him directly into Janine's dressing room, trying to stay calm and keep the panic at bay.

With blood running down his head, silently Alfie crept through the interconnecting doors to Janine's bedroom, tiptoeing over to the main door to lock it before running over to the window. Carefully, not wanting to give Alice a fright, Alfie gently pulled it open. He whispered, 'Alice! Alice! It's me!'

Terror was etched into Alice's face as sweat ran down it. 'Alfie, help me! Help me! I can't hold on any longer!'

The ledge where Alice was balanced was just over an arm's reach from Alfie and pushing his fear for her aside, he spoke firmly and quickly, knowing that time wasn't on her side. 'Sshhh, Alice, don't shout, baby, they'll hear you. Look, you've got to swing towards me. Throw yourself forward and I'll grab your hand. Come on, Alice, come on!'

Alice stared into Alfie's eyes, her whole body trembling. Her voice the tiniest of whispers. 'I can't.'

'Alice, for God's sake, come on!'

Crying, Alice shook her head. 'I can't! I can't, Alfie!'

'You can, baby, you can, just keep looking at me. Don't look down, Alice! That's it, girl, that's it. Now you're just going to throw yourself forward. I promise I'll catch you.'

Traumatised and still clinging onto the bar, Alice began to cry harder. 'Alfie, no, it's too far.'

Alfie glanced down, as unsure as Alice if he'd be able to do what he promised. He chose his words carefully, somehow trying to get Alice to trust him. 'Listen, darlin', I know how brave you are, and I need you to be brave now, sweetheart. If you don't do it now, any minute, those men in there will come out and find you. Trust me, Alice, I'll catch you. I swear on the Bible I will.'

Triggered by his words, a sudden hope flickered in Alice's eyes. 'You'll catch me?'

'Yes, baby. On my life.'

Pausing only for a moment, Alice nodded then, taking a deep breath and quickly closing her eyes, she leapt forward, feeling nothing but air, her legs scrambling, her arms flying in nothingness, fear rushing through her . . . before she felt the hard tug of Alfie's hold pulling her up.

Alfie leant back, his feet jammed against the wall for support as he desperately tried to pull Alice up, frantically trying to maintain his grip.

'Don't let me fall, Alfie, don't let me fall!'

Alice clung onto Alfie, but she could feel her grasp slipping as Alfie, wet with perspiration, hissed through gritted teeth and with sheer determination kept trying to lift her. 'Keep still, Alice!'

'I'm falling, Alfie, I'm falling!'

Refusing to give in, digging deeper than he'd ever done in his life and unaware he was biting down on his tongue, Alfie used every muscle in his body to gather the brutal strength he needed to haul Alice up and through the window. As he felt her body beginning to pull towards him, Alfie – red-faced, with a trail of blood dripping from his tongue down to his chin – tugged her back, ignoring the burning pain in his arms and feeling like his elbows were being ripped out of their sockets. He panted through his exertion as she finally fell into his arms. With tears of relief cracking his voice, he held her close.

'I got you, baby, I got you, Alice Rose!'

Next door in Cabhan's bedroom, Salvatore called to his brother Bobby. 'Try in there. She's got to be in here somewhere.'

Bobby ran to the walk-in closet, flung open all the doors and checked behind the immaculate colour-coordinated suits and clothes. He turned back to Salvatore, shaking his head. 'No sign.'

'She's got to be here somewhere. Look again, we saw her come in.'

Bobby shrugged, incensing Salvatore enough to strike his

brother hard around the face with the butt of his gun, the mask taking some of the impact.

'Who the fuck do you think you are, Bobby? I want her found, understand me?'

Enraged, Salvatore turned away, but as he did, he noticed the window and a sudden thought crossed his mind. He pulled up the blinds and tried to open the window. It was locked.

Quickly, he picked up the little stool by the dresser and threw it squarely at the window, smashing the glass. Then carefully, he poked his head through the jagged pane and looked down. Seeing nothing, Salvatore glanced to the side, catching a glimpse of Alice's feet scrabbling through the window next door.

'She's there! Come on!' Salvatore pulled back, running out of the bedroom just as Alfie and Alice headed out onto the landing.

Seeing the men, Alfie raced back into the room dragging Alice and locked the door behind them. They ran through the inter-connecting closet, back down the stone stairs, hurtling along with the men not far behind. Alfie kept pulling Alice on through the tiled hallway until they reached the side door of the mansion.

As they made their way out, Alfie, out of breath and in pain, felt Alice tug on him. He spoke quickly, his eyes on the house, knowing any minute the men would appear. 'Come, Alice, keep going, darlin', we've got to keep going!'

Drained of colour and wide-eyed, Alice shook her head. Her voice shook with fear. 'What about Dad?'

Swiping the blood that dripped from his head and mouth, Alfie tried to pull Alice away from the house, but she was rooted to the spot, staring hard at him.

'Alice, we ain't got time for this, we've just got to leave him. Come on, before it's too late!'

'We can't just go. I heard gunshots, he might be injured.'

Raging and beginning to panic, Alfie kept his eye on the door. 'And so will we if we don't get out of here. Your dad knows what he's doing; he'd want us to leave him. We'll call an ambulance, police, whatever you want once we're out of here.'

'No, Alfie, he'll be scared on his own. Let's go back to Dad. I saw what they did to Sister Margaret. *Please* let's go back!' Verging on the hysterical, Alice trembled, her face red and puffy from crying.

'No way, darlin'. Come on, we need to go.'

Distraught, Alice covered her face and speaking through her hands, Alfie could see her tears seeping through her fingers.

'Why are you doing this, Alfie? Why won't you help him?'

Still trying to drag Alice, and with his vision slightly blurred from the bang on his head and the throbbing in his arms still causing him pain, Alfie snarled, seething inwardly at Cabhan. 'For fuck sake, this is *his* doing, don't you get it? And any minute now, you're going to be next. Now move it . . . I said, move it! . . . Fine, Alice, then you ain't given me much choice.'

And with that Alfie grabbed Alice, threw her over his shoulder and ran for the woods without looking back.

'Sal! Sal! They're getting away!'

The masked men ran out of the front door and into their truck as they saw Alfie and Alice disappear into the distance. Salvatore slammed on the accelerator, taking the corner at speed, punching the steering wheel as he turned into the deserted country lane.

'Shit! Fuck! Fuck!' He turned to two of the men in the back, barking out his orders. 'You get out here and search on foot. Me and Bobby, we'll drive around and look for them, okay?'

Almost before the two men managed to jump out, Salvatore punched the accelerator again and drove along the tree-lined lane, his eyes narrowed as he gazed across the fields. Suddenly, a grin spread over his face.

'There! Over there! I think it's going be our lucky day after all.'

29

From behind the trees Alfie spotted two masked men, armed and heading towards their hiding place. Knowing the area well, Alfie didn't doubt for a moment that if they stayed where they were they'd be spotted in a couple of minutes.

'Alice, come on! It ain't over yet!'

Giving her no choice and ignoring her protests, Alfie, his heart pounding, gripped her hard by the wrist and dragged her along, through the bushes and vast scrubland as fast as he could. As they scrambled over the gnarled roots of the blossoming oak trees they finally came to a small copse.

Breathing hard and looking agitated, Alfie stared at Alice. He grasped her by the shoulders, bending down so he could look directly into her face.

'Alice, you trust me?'

Panting, Alice whispered her reply. 'Yes, of course.'

'Then give me your hand.'

Puzzled, Alice slowly held out her hand to Alfie, who gripped it hard as he led her through a tiny thicket into a small clearing. Immediately, Alice began to shake her head. She pulled back as hard as she could, but her strength was no match for Alfie's.

'Alice, come on! We've got this far, we're nearly there now.'

'You're crazy. We'll die!' Alice trembled, her eyes resting on the abandoned quarry, Alfie was pulling her towards it, with its hundred-foot sheer drop and a pool of dark green water sitting ominously in the pit of it.

'I thought you said you trusted me,' Alfie said hurriedly but gently.

'I do but . . .'

'Then let me get you out of here. You and me are a team now, we've got to look out for each other and from what I see, you're a cat, Alice, you've got nine lives. And I reckon this geezer, this God you believe in, is probably going to protect you, cos he has so far and with any luck, he'll protect me as well. So, what do you say?'

Then, without waiting for Alice's answer, Alfie ran forward, holding Alice tightly as he jumped off the quarry cliff, the girl screaming helplessly as they hurtled down to the waters below.

Alfie, having lost hold of his grip on Alice's hand, yelled out as his feet broke the surface of the water, hitting a large rock, sending a searing wave of agony up his legs.

'Alfie, help me! Help me! I ca-n't sw-im.'

Alice bobbed beneath the surface, water rushing over her face and into her mouth as she cried out for help.

Wincing, Alfie swam over, a dark billowing cloud of blood blooming around him. 'I'm here, Alice. See, darlin', I told you you're a cat. It's okay, baby, I got you . . . I'm here . . . That's it, Alice, don't panic.'

Treading water, Alfie grabbed hold of Alice, gently turning her onto her back and holding his hand under her chin as he towed her to the side. Swimming slowly, he managed to get her to the bank. He dragged himself out and crawled towards the bottom of the cliff, out of view of anyone looking down from the top.

'Now, I need *you* to help *me*, baby. Can you do that?'

Alice nodded as she reached down and ripped open his torn trouser leg to reveal a badly lacerated and bleeding wound, gouged deep from below the knee to his ankle.

Seeing the look on Alice's face, Alfie forced a smile. 'It ain't that bad, darlin', it's just a scratch. Believe me, I've had worse.'

'Here.' Alice crouched down, pushing away her own fear as she wrapped the scrap of torn trouser leg around the deepest part of Alfie's wound, tying it tightly to try to stop the bleeding.

Through his pain Alfie gave Alice a small smile. 'A Girl Scout as well, you're pretty smart, ain't you? Tougher than you look.'

Grimacing from the pain, Alfie pulled his phone out of his pocket. He stared at it before banging his fist on the stony ground.

'Fuck, no signal! Damn it! Damn it!'

Overcome by exhaustion, Alice sat down amongst the wild weeds and cuckooflowers and began to cry low, racking sobs. His heart went out to her and an idea came to him. Picking up the phone again, Alfie pressed redial and turned slightly away from Alice so she wouldn't see he still couldn't get a signal.

'Hello, emergency, we need help . . .'

Pretending somebody was on the other end of the line, Alfie proceeded to give the address for both Cabhan and the quarry, smiling at Alice as he talked, hoping to reassure her, at least for now, that help was on its way.

Clicking off the phone, his hand shaking as he tried to hide from her the agony he was in, Alfie said reassuringly, 'See, everything's going to be all right. They're on their way. So you don't have to worry about your dad. Okay? It's going to be all right.'

There was a moment of silence before Alice said, 'What did you mean?'

Distracted by the throbbing in his leg, Alfie shrugged. 'What?'

Alice, her voice breaking under the strain, rubbed her arm as nettles stung her skin. 'What did you mean, Alfie?'

Massaging his head before flinching from the wound the

Russos had inflicted, Alfie leant back on the cold rocky stones taking in deep gulps of air to manage his pain.

He glanced at Alice and for the first time took in how young and vulnerable she looked, certainly younger than sixteen. Trying to muster up patience – something he was never usually good at – Alfie sighed heavily. 'Baby, what are you talking about?'

Alice's voice was quiet. 'You said this was his own doing. What did you mean by that? Why was *this* Dad's own doing?'

'Can we do this some other time? My leg's killing me.'

'Just *tell* me, Alfie.'

Alfie screwed up his face, his discomfort making him angry and irritable, though his focus of anger was mainly on Cabhan and Franny for the position they'd put Alice in, not to mention himself. It wasn't fair on the girl. She was innocent, or at least she had been before all the shit had gone down, and innocence was a rare quality, something to be cherished. Except now she'd seen and been through what most men he knew would've run from. But although there was a fragility about Alice, he could feel and see a strength shining through her. Christ, he didn't know many people who wouldn't have become a quivering basket case after dealing with what she had these past few weeks, yet here Alice was, trying her best, and there *he* was opening his big, fat mouth and making it worse.

'I don't know what I was talking about.'

'Back at the house you said all *this* was Dad's fault.'

Alfie shrugged his shoulders again. He reached over and lifted Alice's head up to wipe the tears away with the torn and bloodied cuff of his grey top.

'You must've heard wrong, darlin', and if I did say it, I didn't mean it. I was talking crap, more worried about keeping us alive than what was coming out of me mouth.' He winked at her, hoping now she would drop it.

'You did say it and I *know* you can remember. Please, tell me what you meant. I just want to know what's going on. I'm really scared, Alfie, and I don't know why we're here, why any of this has happened. I feel like I'm going crazy and if it wasn't for being able to talk to . . .' Alice stopped suddenly, changing her mind about what she had been going to say. 'Well, anyway, Franny's been great and so have you, but nobody's telling me anything. Please. Who are those people?'

Alfie gazed at Alice and saw the confusion in her eyes. 'Jesus, this ain't a good time right now. Talk to me later, when I'm not going out of me mind with this leg.'

'You'll just make more excuses.'

'Look, Alice, *it's complicated*, not everything is as it seems, not everything is so clear-cut, and a simple explanation doesn't always do it. Believe me, I know . . . Alice, for God's sake, where are you going? Come back here.'

Alice looked down at Alfie, anxiety rushing over her again. She couldn't think straight. It was like every adult was talking in riddles when all she wanted was straight answers. The only person who gave her the truth was Nico. Not even Franny had been honest with her, and she could see that Alfie was doing everything he could to avoid answering her.

'Not until you tell me.'

Alfie glared. Even though he felt for the kid, this shit he did not need, especially as he could hardly run after her and he was beginning to get pissed off. Teenage girls were *not* something he wanted to deal with when it felt like his leg was on fire. So, fuck it, maybe he should just tell her, not everything, but enough to shut her up.

'Look, your dad . . .' Oh Christ, how could he put it to her without frightening her off?

'My dad, what? What, Alfie?'

'Well, you know how people sometimes hide things to stop others from getting hurt? Well, that's what your dad did. He didn't want you to get hurt.'

'What does that mean?' Tears pooled in Alice's big almond

eyes, her voice brimming with fear. 'I don't get it, Alfie. I don't get it! Is it me? Have I done something? Why are they after me?'

A sharp pain ripped through Alfie's leg, making him lose his cool and spit out his words angrily. 'Jesus, Alice, you don't take any prisoners, do you? For fuck's sake, we don't need to do this. Your dad loves you and that's all you really need to know. If you insist, fine, I'll tell you, but don't say I didn't warn you. Your dad is not what he says he is. Come to think of it, neither am I. I'm not saying I'm ashamed of it, but sometimes I ain't exactly proud of it either.'

'Alfie!' Alice yelled, tears streaming down her face.

Realising he still wasn't saying what he should, Alfie held up his hands. 'I'll tell you but just keep your voice down, they'll hear us . . . Look, your dad's a face, or he was, now he's—'

'Face?'

'Gangster. Your dad's a gangster and—'

'And that's why those people are after him?' Alice, hysterical, scrambled to her feet.

'I said be quiet! But yeah, they're bad people, Alice.'

'And what, my dad isn't?'

Sensing the conversation was not going the way he'd hoped, Alfie tried but failed to stand up. 'Alice, hold up, he ain't bad, not like them.'

'How could he not be, you just . . .' Alice stopped, a look of horror on her face. 'Is that why Sister Margaret was killed, because of Dad?'

'Alice.'

Alice screamed at the top of her voice, fury and pain and confusion soaring into the air. 'Is it?'

'Yes. Fuck! Fuck! Yes,' Alfie said, trying to quieten her, 'but it wasn't as if it was his fault, not really.'

'Is that what you are?' Alice asked, shaking her head. 'A gangster?'

For some reason Alfie felt embarrassed. 'Yes.'

Almost unable to say it, Alice murmured the words, 'And Franny, please tell me that she isn't part of it.'

Alfie opened his arms. 'Darlin', listen to me—'

'Oh my God, she is, isn't she?' Alice gasped, her eyes wide. 'None of you are who you say you are. What is this? Who are you?'

'We're still us, Alice.'

Alice shook her head, backing away from him. 'No, no, you're not. Everything's a lie. I just want to go home.'

'This is your home now.'

'No, no, it's not. I don't care; I don't want to be here. I'll go and stay with my friend, Isaiah, if I have to. I don't want anything to do with you. I hate you!' Alice spat out.

Alice continued to back away, when Alfie suddenly leant up and grabbed her.

'Get off me!' she screamed as Alfie put his hand over her mouth to muffle her.

Alfie struggled to hold onto Alice as she squirmed. 'You can't go, I won't let you. Those men will kill you if they find you! Do you understand what I'm saying?'

Without hesitation, Alice bit down hard on Alfie's hand. Yelping, he released his grip, giving Alice the opportunity to push away from him and out of their hiding place.

'Fuck! Alice, come back! Alice! For fuck's sake, if they find you they're going to kill you, Alice! Alice!'

Watching Alice disappear, Alfie crawled along the side of the cliff, staggering and dragging himself until a few minutes later he heard his phone beep – he had signal. He dialled a number, which rang and then clicked to voicemail.

'Fran, I need your help. It's a disaster. A fucking disaster, and you need to call Alice, *now*!'

30

'What did they say? What did they say about Cabhan?' Lola Harding's hard stare bored into Alfie.

'What did who fucking say, Lola? I ain't got time for waffle. Alice is missing and I can't get hold of Franny, and Bree ain't picking up either. As for Cabhan, all I did was call for an ambulance. I didn't give me name or hang around for a chat, so I don't know anything more. My head's wrecked enough, so the last thing I want is you chewing me ear off whilst I wait for some poxy nurse to sort me leg out.'

Lola, deciding not to retaliate, stood in the corridor of the A&E department of Addenbrooke's Hospital in Cambridge, the strong smell of bleach overpowering as Alfie continued his rant.

'She could be anywhere. You should've seen the way she went off – she was in a right mess, Lo. I can't blame her; everybody should've been straight with her from the start. She ain't got her phone on her either and . . . Oi! Oi!' Alfie hailed the stern-looking casualty nurse who marched purposefully through the A&E. 'Listen, darlin', the only reason I'm here is cos I can't walk, not so I could camp out amongst the walking wounded. I've got something *really* important to do, therefore what I need *you* to do is stitch me up and do what you girls do, then I can be on me way.'

The nurse stared at Alfie with as much hostility as she could muster. 'I'm sorry but there are people in front of you. We can give you some painkillers whilst you wait.'

Beckoning her closer with his index finger, Alfie barked, 'I don't want painkillers, I want me leg *sorted* and just so it's clear, I don't give a fuck if everybody's been waiting here since the millennium, because they ain't got a sixteen-year-old girl wandering about in trouble. Now, do us all a favour and get me leg fixed, or should I fix it me-fucking-self? Give me the needle and cotton and it'll be happy days.'

'Sir, if you continue to be aggressive I'll have to get security.'

Alfie's face turned red as he laughed bitterly. 'To do what? Throw me out when I've only got one poxy leg to stand on? I can see how the country's going downhill, maybe—'

Lola shouted him down. 'Alfie, enough! You can't take it out on her . . . I'm sorry, love, he's in a lot of pain and he's worried about someone, well, we all are . . . Have you any idea how long this might take?'

Glancing at Alfie then back to Lola, the Nigerian nurse pursed her lips before answering. 'I'll go and see what I can find out.'

Alfie watched the nurse walk away as he yanked his phone out of his pocket. 'Where the fuck is Franny? What is it about that woman? She always seems to do a disappearing act when you need her. And here's the real joke, her and Bree are suddenly bosom buddies.'

'That's good, ain't it?'

'Good? No, Lola, it ain't. Nothing good can come out of two women plotting, it's like a couple of sharks smelling blood.'

Before Lola had a chance to answer, Alfie snarled a message on Franny's voicemail. 'Fran, it's me. This is getting to be a *fucking* habit. Now, you need to pick up the phone and call me ASAP. Alice has gone missing and let me tell you—'

'Alf Jennings?'

Alfie looked up, clicking off the phone as a tall Indian doctor came to speak to him.

'I'm Dr Shah, shall we go into one of the cubicles and talk?'

'No, mate, I ain't dying, am I? So, let's just do it here and get it over and done with.'

Wearily, the doctor simply said, 'As you wish. Your X-ray shows a hairline fracture on the tibia, which will heal by itself, so there's no need for a cast and you'll be able to get around, though it might be painful, but we can provide crutches if you want as well as analgesics. As for the laceration to your leg, it's pretty much down to the muscle layer, so you'll need deep tension sutures and then stitches to close the skin; therefore, I'd like you to stay the night and let the plastic surgeons fix it in the morning.'

Alfie shook his head. 'No way. I need it done right now. As quick as.'

'Mr Jennings—'

'Save your breath, doc, I ain't changing me mind.'

Seeing he was not going to get anywhere with Alfie, the doctor said resignedly, 'Fine, I'll do it myself, though it won't be as pretty. It'll probably scar and you may have to wait a couple of hours before I can do the procedure.'

Distracted, Alfie muttered, 'Whatever.'

Through the glass A&E doors he spotted a trolley being pushed through at speed by four ambulance men. Lying on it was Cabhan screaming in pain. Shocked, Lola grabbed hold of Alfie as they watched Cabhan, his body covered in blood, his face covered by an oxygen mask and blood-soaked bandages on the end of his arms, which were hoisted up on drip stands, keeping them elevated.

Anxiously, Lola hurried after Dr Shah, pointing at Cabhan as the trolley passed by. 'Where are they taking him?'

'By the look of him, I suspect straight to theatre,' Dr Shah answered dispassionately, his tone pinched.

'Will he be all right?'

The doctor gave a jaded reply as he turned away. 'I have no idea. Now, if you'll excuse me I have patients to see.'

'You?' Alfie stared at Lola incredulously.

'Yeah.'

'You, go and look for Alice?'

'Got a problem with that?'

Still waiting for the procedure to his leg, Alfie cocked his head to one side. 'Actually, Lola, I have, because the last time you got in the driver's seat, darlin', was when there were horses and carts.'

Annoyed with how Alfie was behaving, Lola smacked him hard in his chest with the back of her hand. 'Don't be so bloody stupid, it was on George's fortieth birthday.'

Alfie, raising his voice, leant into Lola's face. 'Lola, George has been dead for twenty-five years.'

'So?' Lola shrugged.

'So, if you add it all together, the last time you took control of any motor was a fuck of a long time ago. Face it, you'll be a liability and there's been enough casualties today. And besides, whose car are you going to drive? You can't go back to the house, not now.'

Sitting down, her varicose veins troubling her, Lola said, 'I know that, I ain't stupid, but think about it, when Janine went to Florida she parked her motor at Stansted Airport in the long-term car park, remember? And I've got her spare set of keys. Look . . .' Lola stopped talking and proceeded to tip the entire contents of her bag onto the hospital floor. She rummaged amongst the packet of tissues, chewing gum, odd sock, money, wallet and torn-out pages of magazines until she finally produced a key. Triumphantly, she said, 'Here.'

'Yeah, but to get the car out you'll need a code.'

'I'll text Janine, that ain't a problem. And from here I can get a cab, which will get me there within half an hour and it's on the way home anyway. Then from Stansted we're only looking at twenty minutes or so to get back to the house, and Alice won't have gone far, will she? She ain't got no money and ain't got her phone. Hopefully, she'll keep her head down. She may be angry, but she's not stupid and she knows they're after her, but the longer she's out there on her own, the more likely it is the Russos . . .' Lola trailed off, unable to contemplate the idea that Salvatore and his brother might find Alice. 'Anyway, if I go now, I reckon I can be out there looking for her within the next hour or so.'

'You're forgetting one vital thing.'

Lola frowned as she absentmindedly watched a hospital porter push his mop and bucket along the corridor on a squeaking metal trolley. 'What?'

'Those ETAs you've just given me are for someone who can friggin' drive!'

Red-faced and getting to her feet, the incensed Lola wagged her finger at Alfie. 'What is it with you? You can be a pig sometimes, Alfie Jennings. I'm trying to help, I'm worried about the girl, and all you can do is mug me off with your comments. I'm the best bet you've got, I'm the only bet you've got, but instead of being thankful you have to try to make me look a fool. If it weren't for the fact that Alice is out there on her own, I'd leave you and your bloody leg to it. You know how to upset me, don't you?'

Hurt, she turned her back on him. Alfie opened his arms wide and spoke gently. 'Lo, you silly cow, you don't get it, do you? I don't want you to drive because I'm afraid something might happen, and I couldn't bear that. I'm sorry, I didn't mean to upset you, I appreciate you wanting to help, but I just don't think it's a good idea. Look at me, Lola.'

Lola turned back around, her eyes filled with love. 'Sweetheart, you and I both know that we can't risk the Russos getting hold of Alice and the longer she's out there, the more likely that will be. Look at the state of Cabhan and what they did to him, it makes me shiver to think what they'd do to her . . . We've got no other choice, there's no way you can drive until those doctors come back and sort out your leg, and who knows how long that will take. We've lost enough time already. Plus, I doubt you could drive anyway.'

Alfie rubbed his head. 'But have you seen Janine's car? It'll be like a rite of bleedin' passage and I don't know if that's a good thing.'

'Listen, I might not be Lewis Hamilton, but how hard can it really be?'

31

'Okay, I can do this. Like I said to Alfie, how hard can this be?'

Lola sat in the Ferrari F12 Berlinetta, shaking as she held the key. She tried to remember what Alfie had told her:

Unlike a lot of Ferraris, it has a traditional key, so just put it in the ignition like you did on George's Austin Metro.

Putting the key in, the car beeped and Lola took a quick intake of breath, nervously chewed her lip and then pressed the red button on the wheel marked 'engine start'. Immediately, the engine revved into action, making her feel like she were sitting on an explosion.

'Oh my Christ! Oh my Christ!'

Trembling, she looked for the gear lever then remembered there wasn't one.

There'll be three buttons: R, Auto and PS.

She'd no idea what the PS meant – the only time she'd seen that was at the bottom of a greetings card at Christmas time.

Once you press 'auto', gently use the footpads – not too hard, that car's like a beast.

As Lola pushed her foot down, the car let out a massive roar. She screamed, her false teeth coming loose as the Ferrari shot forward and picked up speed.

Remember, Lola, the car goes from zero to sixty-two in three seconds, which means be fucking careful.

'Oh my God! Oh my God!'

She slammed on the brake and the Ferrari juddered to a stop, throwing Lola against the padded steering wheel. For a few seconds, feeling useless, she held onto it, her head resting on the Ferrari emblem as her eyes filled with tears of frustration.

'Come on, get a grip, get a grip, think of Alice. You can do this.' Alone in the car her words seemed hollow, but refusing to let any vehicle beat her, Lola Harding pressed down on the pedal again – this time more carefully. The car cruised into a manageable, settled speed, the engine sounding like a heavy bassline.

Lola, it's got a V12 engine, which means . . . yeah, you got it, that thing's going to give you wings. With every stab of the throttle it'll make you feel like you're pouring fuel onto an open fire. Boom!

Looking down at the speedometer, Lola's eyes popped wide open. The dial said one hundred and three so, as gently as she could, she decelerated. The car jerked back and forward, then veered sharply to the right as she turned her head to look at a road sign.

Lola, with so much power it's easy to get oversteer, even if you make the smallest movement, so watch out for that, otherwise you'll end up tits up in a ditch. So take it slow and steady. It's a power train with a top speed of two hundred plus miles an hour, so do yourself a favour, darlin', and just stick to the speed limit!

After several stops and starts, Lola, more accustomed to the car, drove along relatively smoothly, making her way down the country lanes surrounding Wimbish village, a few miles away from the house. She squinted through the dark as she scanned the area, looking around for Alice.

She'd been driving about for over two hours now. She had contemplated getting out of the car, but she wasn't so steady on her feet when it came to walking through fields and on rough tracks, especially late at night. And the last thing anybody, and certainly Alfie, needed was for her to end up on her back with a twisted ankle when *she* was supposed to be the one looking out for Alice.

She felt desperately worried for Alice. She was terrified that the Russos had got to her first. She knew what they were like: they were animals, barbarians, specialising in pain. She had seen first-hand what they had done to Abel Gray's wife, Natalia. She had also seen the grief, the guilt and the torment Abel himself had gone through. The daily reminder of what Nico and his brothers had done to Natalia had changed him forever.

Deep in thought, Lola saw a figure out of the corner of her eye and suddenly slammed on the brake – or she thought it was the brake – until she found herself careering forward and skidding round and round as the car spun in a tight circle, picking up gravel and causing the tyres to burn and smoke. Screaming and letting go of the wheel, Lola stamped down again, this time managing to hit the brake, causing the car to come to a juddering, shuddering, abrupt halt.

With a cloud of tyre smoke surrounding the car, just for a moment Lola sat frozen in shock before she quickly pulled herself together. Opening the custom-made gull-wing doors of the Ferrari and somewhat undignifiedly crawling out, Lola ended up on all fours in the centre of the road. She called out to the person she'd seen running across the lane.

'Alice! Alice, it's me!'

Alice Rose turned around and stared at Lola in bewilderment.

Wiping her tears away, Lola, overwhelmed with relief at finding Alice safe and well, nodded. 'Don't just stand there like a lemon, come and help me up before I get run over.'

Alice gasped, feeling a wealth of emotion rush over her. As much as she didn't fully want to admit it to herself, seeing Lola was a relief. When she'd run away from Alfie, she hadn't thought about where she was going and she certainly hadn't thought about the masked men, until it had turned pitch-black and she'd found herself alone deep in the heart of the woods, where images of what had happened in the convent flashed through her mind and every sound felt to her as if the men in the gruesome masks were breathing down her neck.

'Lola?'

'I might be doing me best impression of a donkey, but who else do you think it is? Come on, love, hurry up,' Lola said warmly, smiling whilst very aware that they needed to get out of the area as soon as they could.

Alice, remembering the lies everyone had told her, shook her head. 'I'm not coming back.'

Irritated, Lola glanced up at Alice. 'I'm not being funny, darlin', but can we do this conversation when I'm actually standing up?'

Looking around nervously, Alice walked over and helped Lola up gently. Bemused, she pointed at the car. 'You're driving that?'

'Is that so hard to believe?'

Alice shrugged, feeling upset and confused again. 'To tell you the truth, Lola, everything's hard to believe at the moment . . . Anyway, I've got to go, will you be all right?'

Dusting off her hands, Lola sniffed, indignation flashing in her eyes. 'I will be once you get in that car.'

Sad and hurt, Alice just turned around and began to walk away. Nothing made sense anymore and she felt more lost than she'd ever done in her life. 'I already told you, I'm not going with you.'

In the middle of the lane, under the moonlit sky and surrounded by nothing but countryside, Lola felt the anger rise inside her. 'Are you being serious? I've just risked my life in that bloody car looking for you. Everyone's in a right mess and we're all so worried about you. Now get in that car before I get really mad.'

'No!' Alice shouted.

'Then where are you going?'

'Anywhere but here.'

Lola stepped forward, her hands on her hips. 'Is that right, young lady?'

Alice stared at Lola. 'Yes, it is!'

'How can you be so selfish when we're all out of our minds with worry for you? You ain't even going to ask about how Alfie is, are you?'

'Why should I?'

Blowing out her cheeks in annoyance, Lola wagged her finger at Alice. 'I know it feels like it, but this isn't just about you, Alice. A lot of people have been affected. There's your dad as well, aren't you going to ask about him either?'

With her heart telling her she wanted to know but her head telling her the opposite, Alice crossed her fingers behind her back.

'No, why should I? I don't care.'

Frustrated at the way Alice was behaving, but at the same time understanding how difficult it all must be for her, Lola's tone was firm but kind. 'Because, madam, not only do Alfie and Cabhan care and love you, but they also saved your life.'

With tears streaming down her face, Alice, having never felt more confused or hurt, raised her voice again. 'They wouldn't have had to save my life if they hadn't done what they did. It's all because of Dad that this has happened. If it weren't for *him*, Sister Margaret would be alive. I'll *never* forgive him for that! Ever!'

'Alice, please, your dad isn't a bad man.'

Distraught, Alice wiped her tears away. 'So everybody likes to tell me but I know different.'

Chilly in the night air, Lola wrapped her cardigan tightly around her, fighting back her terror that at any moment the Russos might appear. 'Do you think he wanted all this to happen, do you? Alice, he tried to protect you, not hurt you. He's been trying for months to get you back home, but they wouldn't let him.'

Anger flashed into Alice's eyes and, uncharacteristically, she screamed at the top of her voice, 'See, this is what I'm talking about. Who wouldn't let him? *Who*? Everybody round here just tells me half-stories.'

'You may be sixteen but that doesn't mean you need to know everything, young lady.'

Kicking the gravel with her pink lace pumps, Alice shrugged, swiping at her tears. 'But a bit of truth would be nice. Dad lied to me, Lola. He pretended that he was someone he's not. He never gave me the choice to make up my own mind about him. For these past couple of years, I've loved a person who didn't even exist, someone who isn't real.'

Overwhelmed herself now, Lola, trying but failing to be soothing, sounded cross. 'That's not true! The only thing that wasn't real was what he did for a living. Look, I ain't saying that they don't have their faults, and maybe it should've been handled in a different way, but Cabhan and Alfie care about you. Look at Alfie tonight. How many men do you know who would put their life on the line for some kid who isn't even kith and kin? And your dad, he did everything to keep you safe, *everything*, but now he's lying on an operating table as we speak – who knows if he'll even make it. That's the reality, Alice.'

It was like a sharp stab to Alice's stomach. She felt sick. Her face crumpled and her voice broke. 'What . . . what do you mean?'

'Oh, so you do care.'

Affronted, Alice restrained her feelings. She glared at Lola. 'I didn't say that, I said, *what do you mean*?'

'Alice Rose, has anyone told you what a feisty little mare you can be, not to mention stubborn? Maybe you should start thinking about other people and not just yourself.'

'That's what I have been doing, but I'm not going to do that anymore.'

Sighing, Lola's heart went out to her. 'Alice, lovie, don't lose yourself in this. This isn't you. The Alice I know is loving and caring, just like your dad and Franny and Alfie. Look around, look what you've got – you're lucky to have so many people who love you.'

Alice stalked towards Lola, her almond eyes brimming with fury, her stomach twisted in knots. 'I don't want to be around people like that.'

'None of us is perfect, Alice – doesn't that Bible of yours teach you that?'

Ignoring how cold it was getting, Alice gave an embittered smile. 'What do you know about it?'

'Enough. I know there's a story of how that Jesus bloke chatted away happy as Larry with them leopards and accepted them for what they were.'

'*Lepers*, not leopards. It's not *The Lion King*, Lola.'

Sniffing, Lola shrugged. 'Well, whatever, lions, leopards and tigers, they're all the same.' Alice rolled her eyes as Lola continued to talk. 'The fact is, Alice, you and I both know the whole point to all that religious stuff you go on about is to accept people no matter what they've done, how they look or who they are. You're supposed to love people regardless, darlin'.'

'Even gangsters?' Alice scoffed.

Lola sighed again, realising that winning Alice around was going to be trickier than she'd first imagined. 'Yeah, cos I ain't asking you to love what they do, but love who they are. Alfie, Cabhan and Franny are good people with good hearts, it's as simple as that. They saved me.'

Sitting on the bonnet of the Ferrari, Alice gazed at Lola coolly, slight ridicule in her voice. 'Are you going to tell me now that you were a gangster as well?'

Lola shook her head and took a deep breath. 'No, but I was on the game – a prostitute – for a long time, and if it wasn't for that lot, I might be still there now. So you see, all of us in one way or another have baggage.'

Staring in horror at Lola, Alice, her thoughts spinning, got up and moved away from the car. 'You . . . you were a prostitute. How could you?'

Taken aback, Lola shook her head. 'Alice, don't.'

'Don't what?'

'Don't look at me like that.'

'How else do you want me to look at you?'

With tears in her own eyes now, Lola spat out her words. 'Like I'm a human being. Like I still matter. Who are you to judge me, Alice Rose? You don't know my life, you don't know what I've been through, and believe me, sweetheart, you could never judge me more than I've judged myself over the years. Being out there on the streets, I lost everything. I lost me kids and I lost who I was, so don't you dare look at me like I've just crawled out from under a stone, because this is me, Alice, warts and all. This is who I am, but it's not *all* of who I am, and it certainly doesn't define me. So, do yourself a favour, darlin', and get off your high horse, stop being selfish and realise your life ain't so bad.'

Sobbing and wishing she were back in the safety of the convent, Alice blurted out her words. 'That's not true, it sucks, and you have no idea how unhappy I am, Lola. I can't stand it. I've never felt like this before and I don't know what to do. Mum's dead, Sister Margaret's dead and my dad isn't who I thought he was, and everyone lies about who they are apart from . . .'

Encouragingly, Lola spoke gently to Alice. 'Apart from who?'

For a moment, Alice thought about confiding in Lola about Nico, about the way he made her feel, the way he made her feel so special, but it was almost like she didn't want to share him, share what they had with someone who didn't think the way she and Nico did, so instead Alice said, 'Apart from you. You've told me the truth.'

Pleased, Lola smiled.

'But it doesn't change the fact that I'm stuck here, and all I want to do is go home and have life go back to the way it was.'

Alice slumped down in the middle of the lane weeping, her head on her knees as Lola gently cradled her. 'I know, sweetheart, I know. This has been so tough on you, don't think I don't understand that, but, Alice, as hard as it is, you've got to keep going, keep trying by finding the good in what you've got and the people around you. I ain't saying that's easy, but I'm saying like the sun will rise tomorrow, you too, Alice Rose, will rise.'

With Lola's words touching her heart, Alice smiled as she lifted her head, her eyes red and puffy. 'I'm so sorry, Lola, I didn't mean to be nasty; I didn't mean to judge you. I was just . . .'

Finishing off Alice's sentence, Lola cackled, 'Shocked that I was an old brass?'

'No! Gosh, no! Oh, Lola, I wasn't going to say that!'

'Alice, I'm just kidding. Oh, don't cry. Listen to me, I'm as tough as a pair of rain-weathered boots. My skin may look like I wash in milk and honey, but it's thick as an old rhino!' Lola burst out into laughter again, the deep lines on her face looking like ridges in the sand. 'Now come on, Alice, I need to get you out of here. We need to hurry, but if you're really lucky, I'll work out how to stop that car long enough to treat you to a Maccie D's on the way back. So come on, lovie, let's go.'

'How the fuck could you lose her? *How*?' Raging, Nico Russo upturned his bed in the small cell before sweeping everything off his side locker and kicking it over in fury. As it clattered to the floor, Nico stopped dead to stare at the only picture on the wall. The photo of Alice Rose. Her eyes staring back at him.

With shallow breaths, he walked up close and ran his fingers caressingly down the tiny photograph he'd got one of his men on the outside to print for him.

Closing his eyes, he imagined her, imaged her smell . . . her taste . . . her body . . . her blood.

'Where are you, Alice Rose, where did you go? Are you playing games with Daddy?'

Feeling both aroused and calmer, Nico picked the phone up again. 'Sal, are you still there?'

'*Sì*, Nico.'

'Good. I want you to find her, but I have an idea, a plan. I need you to do something . . .'

32

Alfie Jennings sat on the uncomfortable seats in Addenbrooke's Hospital waiting for Lola to pick him up. The relief of hearing that Alice was safe had nearly brought him to tears, and the pride and love he'd felt for Lola for finding her was immense.

Feeling his phone beep, he looked down at it. It was a text from Franny:

Who are you going to choose?

Seething, Alfie reread it, blowing out an exasperated lungful of air. He replied:

Maybe you should check your fucking voicemails before you start again with this stuff. I've been trying to get through to you for AGES!!!! WTF!

Alfie waited for the reply. It came in quickly:

I know you have. But you still haven't answered my question – who are you going to choose?

'Are you having a fucking bubble?' Alfie growled out loud as he read the text, just as Lola walked into A&E.

'Everything all right, Alf? Did the procedure go well? Alice is in the car. She's not keen on seeing you but I told her she ain't got much choice; though I doubt you'll get a word out of her. She's not happy, Alfie, though who can blame her? Anyway, I parked just outside in the disabled bay. Come on.' As Lola approached him she wiped her lips with a McDonald's napkin. 'You sure you're all right, Alf?'

'Do I look all right? And to answer your first question, everything isn't okay, it's so far from okay it ain't real. Can you believe I've just got a text from Franny and once again she's right up her own arse.'

As Alfie hobbled along next to Lola on the crutch the hospital had provided, heading for the door, she glanced sideways at him. 'What are you talking about now?'

'I'm talking about Franny not giving a fuck that Alice was missing or that Cabhan is in some induced coma or that I've got a poxy hairline fracture!' Alfie shouted the last part of his sentence.

'Calm down. Did she actually say that?'

'No, but she knows I was trying to get in contact with her and all she wants to know is who I choose?'

Standing in front of the Ferrari, Lola frowned. 'Who you choose?'

'Yes, just before all this happened, me and her, well, we were talking about Bree and . . .'

'Oh, she wants you to choose between her and Bree? Well, she's hurt, isn't she?'

Alfie raised his voice again. 'Hurt, no, I'm hurt. Cabhan's hurt. All she is is licking her wounds. She's crazy! We've got all this going on but all she cares about is all this shit between her and me.'

Clambering into the car, slightly out of breath, Lola panted, 'That's not true! Have a heart, Alfie.'

'Listen, Lola, my only concern is Alice and that's what hers should be as well.'

Trying to remember what button to push, Lola scanned the dash. 'Yeah, but—'

Before Lola had a chance to reply, another text beeped in:

Well, Alfie, who do you choose?

Alfie shoved the phone into Lola's hands. 'She's like a woman possessed. Only a few hours ago she told me that she didn't want me to choose and now, because Bree and her have had a mothers' meeting, she's putting the pressure on . . . Fuck it, I'm best off without either of them.'

'Come on, Alf, I know you've had one of the worst days, but I know you don't mean that.'

'Lola, look at my face – do I seem like I'm kidding?'

'She's clearly upset, Alf. Wouldn't you be if you came home and she'd got another bloke in her bed right in front of your nose? I admire her. I think she's shown enormous restraint. Most women I know would be tearing out Bree's hair. But not Franny, she's a proper lady . . . Did you tell her about Cabhan?'

Annoyed, Alfie tapped his fingers on the side panel. 'If you mean, did I leave a message for her, yes, I did.'

Lola quickly glanced over at Alfie. 'Well, there you go then, she obviously hasn't listened to the messages, otherwise she'd be on the phone like a shot. There's no way Franny would stay away just because of some domestic with you. Cabhan's like her second father and she'll be devastated once she finds out. Let's face it, I've been on the other end of your messages when you're on one, and they ain't exactly a book at bedtime. She's only just recovered from the last lot you left her. Once bitten, twice shy, and I don't blame her.'

Continuing to seethe, Alfie pulled a packet of cigarettes from his pocket. As he was about to light one, Lola snatched it out of his mouth. 'Not in the car. Alice is asleep, she's enough problems without having a lungful of smoke.'

Angrily, Alfie crumpled the cigarette up in his hand. 'Fine . . .' He stopped as he glanced at his phone again. Another two messages:

Well?
Choose.

Frowning, Alfie switched off his phone. He couldn't deal with Franny now. His focus had to be on Alice and what he was going to do, or rather how he was going to keep her safe. The Russos were ruthless – this was a game to them and there was no way they were going to let this go. The problem now was he had to make the decision about what to do with Alice on his own. Cabhan was off limits; they'd put him in an induced coma after his operation and who knew if he was even going to pull through. Jesus, what a mess.

With Alice squashed up asleep in the barely-there back seat of the Ferrari, Lola reversed out of the car park with a screech and a jolt as Alfie gazed out of the window.

'You know we can't go back to the house, don't you?' he said.
'I know.'

'You also know that wherever we go *has* to be somewhere that no one can ever find Alice, nowhere that anyone would think of looking for her.'

'Yeah, but where?'

'I think we should take her to stay with Abel. Abel Gray.'

Lola's eyes widened as she shook her head. 'Abel? Alfie, no, no, she can't go there, you can't take her there, that poor girl's been through enough already.'

'Lola, if there was any other way I'd take it, but what choice have we got?'

33

It had taken Lola over three hours to drive to Abel Gray's isolated thirty-acre country estate in South Hampshire, situated on top of a hill and tucked away within the New Forest with sweeping views of the coastline.

Although it was early morning, it was still dark and Alice had slept fitfully most of the journey.

Lola shivered as she stared into the dense woods surrounding Abel's imposing property, which was kept secure by great metal front gates locked with a heavy, rusty steel chain.

She whispered as if someone were listening, feeling ill at ease as a cold wind blew through the window and made a shrill noise around the car. 'Alf, I don't think this is a good idea, I think we should go. We can't leave Alice here, you know that. Alfie, see sense, *please*.'

With his heart pounding, Alfie also stared at the woods, which even in daylight blocked out the sun. 'Lola, my only concern is to try to keep Alice alive.'

'And you think leaving her with Abel is the way to do it?'

Alfie rubbed his head, knowing what Lola was saying was right. 'Look, maybe we should stay with Alice as well. That way we can make sure she's . . . well, that nothing happens with Abel.'

Lola shrank back into the car seat. 'No, none of us should stay here.'

'Where are we, Lola?' Alice's soft voice came from the back of the car.

Uneasy, Lola glanced at Alfie. 'We're just at a friend's house. But we're not staying.'

Alfie leant across and gripped Lola's hand tight. He gave her a hard stare as he hissed through his teeth, 'You ain't helping and I've already told you, this is the only way . . . Listen, Alice, I'll be back soon. I'm just going to sort this out with Abel first. He's not a great one for phone calls, so I couldn't let him know that we were coming.' Alfie turned to Lola and whispered, 'Lock the doors, do up the windows and whatever happens, don't open them under *any* circumstance.'

Lola held onto Alfie's hand. 'Please, Alfie! You're injured, you can't go. What about your leg?'

'It'll be fine, I'll see you soon.' And with that Alfie Jennings, trying to ignore his own doubts and pain, climbed out of the car, opened the boot of the Ferrari to take out a small black crowbar and headed towards Abel Gray's estate.

Limping around the outside of the grounds, using his crutch as an aid, Alfie noticed the twisted barbed wire on top of the ten-foot-high iron fence, like a thorn crown. Ivy and bristle grew high and thick, covering most of the estate wall.

It'd been a long time since Alfie had come here, maybe as far back as ten years ago when he'd watched Natalia be buried, and then he hadn't stayed long because after what had happened, Abel Gray was not a man who liked company and company certainly didn't like Abel Gray. Not that Alfie should've allowed that to keep him away, but what had happened had made it feel impossible for him to return. Until now. Until he'd had no other choice.

With difficulty, Alfie crouched down, feeling a shooting pain go through his leg. He stopped to take a deep breath, beads of sweat prickling on his forehead as he knelt by one of the old sycamore trees. He brushed the grassy earth away, uncovering an old stone floor.

Cautiously, he looked around, then he slipped the hook of the crowbar along the edge of one of the stone tiles and applied force to the opposite end of the bar. Strain masked his face as he pushed down hard, levering the stone tile until he felt it shift. With massive effort, Alfie moved the stone to one side, exposing a large hole in the ground leading to a dark secret passageway.

Manoeuvring himself to the edge of the hole, Alfie tried to remember how far down it went. He picked up a small pebble, dropped it into the hole and heard it hit the ground slightly before two seconds passed. *Shit*. It was further than he'd thought, and with his leg he knew it would be trickier than normal.

Throwing his crutch down the hole, hearing it clatter and echo as it disappeared into the darkness, Alfie prepared himself to jump and the inevitable pain that would come with it.

'Holy Christ! Holy Christ! Fuck! Fuck!'

In the dark passageway, Alfie rolled about on the damp cobblestone floor in agony, clutching his leg, which felt like it was going to explode. He gritted his teeth, squeezing his eyes shut as burning agony ripped through his shin and knee.

Curled up on his side, Alfie scrabbled in his pocket, pulled out the strong painkillers that the hospital had given him and popped them into his mouth from the foil blister like a starving man. From his other jacket pocket he pulled out his phone to light up the passageway.

With his hands shaking, Alfie switched it on. It took a moment for it to leap into life and as it did, it beeped – once, twice, five, six times – showing the number of text messages he had. They were all from Franny:

Alfie?
How hard can it be?

Too scared to choose?

Why no answer, Alfie?

Don't take too long, otherwise you might not be able to choose at all.

How's Alice?

Grimacing, Alfie stared at the messages, reading and rereading. He didn't even want to fill his head with them. His anger towards Franny would only cause a distraction. But as he lay on his back, waiting for the painkillers to kick in before he moved, he couldn't help sending off a quick text:

I can't deal with this right now. Why don't you just listen to your messages?

The reply came in quicker than Alfie had anticipated:

I have, but you still haven't chosen.

Not wanting to but furious with Franny, Alfie pressed dial, raging and feeling nothing but bitterness towards her. It rang and a moment later he heard her voice.

'Hello.'

Panting through the crippling spasms in his leg, Alfie snarled down the phone, 'Franny, what the fuck are you playing at? What is this? Get back at Alfie time? Why do this now? You're needed here, but instead you're playing silly fucking games. Right now I don't care whether your heart is torn out, because there's a kid who you say you love who needs our help.'

'I'm not interested, Alfie.'

'What? What the fuck?' Alfie's head was swimming. Everything in him wanted to scream down the phone, but he had to keep quiet; the passageway he was in ran underneath Abel's house and the echo travelled a long way. 'And Cabhan, what about him?'

197

'All I'm interested in is you choosing.'

Alfie hugged the phone angrily against his face, breathing heavily. 'Are you being fucking serious, Franny?'

'Bree or me, Alfie. It's that simple. Just make up your mind.'

The phone went dead and Alfie lay in shock, water dripping on him from the dark stone ceiling. His head was raging, but he couldn't let this affect him. He wouldn't let what Franny was doing mess him up – he had only one focus and that was Alice. She deserved better. Alfie pushed himself up from the cold floor and made his way along the tunnel, feeling more alone than he had done for a long time.

Franny clicked off the phone and closed her eyes before opening them to glance at Bree. She gave her a small smile.

'It'll be all right.'

'Are you sure about that?' Salvatore Russo grinned, pointing his gun at Franny as she passed back her phone, her hands tied together.

Salvatore crouched down, staring at Bree and Franny locked up like stray dogs in a steel cage. Although they hadn't found Alice when they'd been driving along, he'd seen Franny walking with her friend, and what a consolation prize that had been. It hadn't fully quelled Nico's disappointment in them not being able to find Alice – though they would, very soon – but at least it had been of some comfort to Nico, knowing that Franny Doyle was now part of his game.

Huddled up next to Bree and with her lip and eye swollen from the beating Bobby had given her, Franny held Salvatore's stare as he leant against the bars.

'Alfie will make the right decision; you're nothing to him. You'll never get Alice, you understand, *never*!'

Salvatore stood up and slammed the cage with his foot. 'Franny, don't ever underestimate us. That's why you're here in the first place, because you didn't think we would. The games are just beginning, the fun is about to start, and we may not have Alice *yet*, but baby, we got you.'

As Salvatore walked away, leaving the two women in the relative darkness of the warehouse they'd been brought to yesterday, Franny whispered, 'Bree, are you okay?'

'Yeah, I'm okay . . . You?' Bree answered quietly.

Feeling the rope dig and burn into her wrists, causing them to bleed, Franny shook her head, her mouth dry from not having had a drink for the past few hours. 'Not really but only because you being here is all my fault. I can't believe that you've been dragged into this – it was bad enough for Alfie, but you? I'm so sorry, Bree, and I know that won't help. The worst thing is I'm not sure how I'm going to get you out of this.'

Bree, her hair matted to her face with cold sweat, shuffled nearer to Franny so she could touch her fingers with her own. She was tired and cold, but her heart went out to Franny, since she could see the guilt in her eyes.

'This isn't your fault, and I don't want you to think it is, and it's not for you to get me out of here. We're in this together. You and me. Whatever happens, we've got each other.'

'I don't think you're getting it. You heard what Salvatore made me say, he wants Alfie to choose between us.' Franny gave Bree a rueful smile, the irony of it not being lost on her.

Kindly, Bree murmured, 'Then you'll be all right, Franny, because he'll choose you and that's the way it should be.'

'Bree, sweetheart, don't be silly, listen to what you're saying.' Franny's voice was urgent, firm. 'You know Alf, and he'll never be able to choose between us, he'll *never* do it. He couldn't even choose when it came down to his heart, let alone this. He'll never want either of our blood on his hands.'

Bree blanched at Franny's words, thinking of her daughter, Molly. She pulled her legs in towards her, as she heard the scurrying of rats close by. 'You . . . you think it'll come to that?'

Only just able to see Bree in the darkness, Franny nodded, fear for Bree creeping over her.

'Look around you, Bree, look where we are. I know the Russos and I know what they're like. Even if Alfie did choose, in reality there's no way Salvatore and Bobby are just going to let one of us go. This is a game for them, and you need to realise that unless a miracle happens, unless one of Alice's prayers comes true, the fact is, Bree, we're both going to die.'

34

It took Alfie more than half an hour to hobble down the stone passageway, which in normal circumstances would've taken him less than five minutes. But he'd made it and the fury he'd felt at Franny had pushed him onwards, working as a pain block better than any analgesics the hospital had given him.

The passageway led to a large, dark oak door, which slid open to reveal the back of a bookcase in the downstairs library of Abel's house. Pushing open the bookcase, Alfie stepped into the library and walked through to the great hall, panelled from floor to ceiling in dark wood. As the sun rose, Alfie could see layers of dust across every surface. He shook his head sadly as he noticed the walls, seeing a name scraped into the wood over and over again. 'Oh, Abel.'

His heart broke for the other man. It was clear that the torment of what happened with Natalia had never left him; in fact, as Alfie looked around, it seemed that, if anything, over the years it had just got worse. Everywhere he looked seemed neglected, the once smart home now falling into disrepair.

After Natalia's funeral, he had reached out to him, but Abel had never returned his calls, and the one time he had come down to see him, Abel hadn't let him in. And then, to his shame, he'd left it, and his once close friend had just become a distant memory.

Suddenly, a hard blow to the head had Alfie staggering forward, stumbling onto the grand wooden staircase. Above him, Abel Gray stood in the morning sunlight holding an axe in his hands as he stared, his eyes dark and wild, his hair unkempt and his pale face sunken, hollow and thin.

As Abel lifted the axe, the sharp steel blade glinting in the sunlight, Alfie held up his hand. 'Abel, Abel, it's me. It's Alfie.'

Staring hard at him, Abel leant forward, looking into Alfie's face. 'Alfie?'

'That's right, Abel. It's Alfie.'

Abel nodded, his eyes blank as he still clutched the axe, spinning it round in his hands as he continued to stare.

'Abel, mate, do me a favour and put that down, it makes me feel a bit uneasy.'

Without taking his eyes off Alfie, Abel lifted the axe above his head and swung it down hard, whistling it past and missing Alfie only by millimetres before it sliced into the wooden stair, splitting it in two.

'Get out, Alfie.'

Stunned, Alfie gaped at his friend, shocked at how his appearance had changed over the years. The Abel he knew had been a towering force, a handsome bulk of a man, one who always turned heads, a man who no one would mess with; but looking at him now, he couldn't even comprehend how this hunched, skinny man was the same person.

'Abel, please, I need you to listen to me.'

Abel's gravelly voice was hard and steely. 'Alfie, you're lucky it's you, otherwise that axe would've been in the middle of your nut. Now get out before I change my mind.'

'Abel, I need your help. There's a girl who's in trouble.'

As Abel bellowed, his voice filled the hallway. 'I said, get out! Get out! Get out!'

But Alfie didn't move. Slowly, Abel turned and walked away, striding along in worn handmade shoes and clothes that had once been tailor-fitted but now hung loosely from his skinny frame.

With his back to Alfie and his hand on the door leading to one of the large dining rooms, Abel said, 'I'll give you five minutes, Alfie, because you were a friend. If you're not gone by then, I'll kill you.'

'Then that's what you'll have to do because I ain't leaving.'

Abel answered matter-of-factly, his breathing short and shallow. 'Your choice.' He reached for the loaded shotgun by the side of the door, picked it up and swivelled it round to point it at Alfie before clicking off the safety catch. Without hesitation, Abel pulled the trigger.

But a split second before he did so, Alfie yelled, 'It's the Russos!'

The gun went off like a cannon, but Abel twisted it aside, managing to send the shot into an ornate glass table instead.

Closing his eyes in overwhelming relief, Alfie leant forward as he let out a long, deep breath. 'Oh fuck. Jesus, Abel.'

'Say it again. Say what you just said.' Abel's voice was emotionless.

Alfie glanced up. 'It's the Russos. I need your help. I need you to help keep Alice Rose safe.'

Abel Gray sat at the top end of the long oak table with his feet up, listening to Alfie, who stood by the diamond-patterned stained-glass window, tell his story.

'I don't know how long she'll need to be here, I ain't had time to think straight, but this is the only place I could bring her.'

'This house ain't suitable for a young girl, Alfie. You know that as well as I do. She can't stay here, it wouldn't be right,' Abel said, his gravelly voice echoing around the dining room.

'Abel, you know the Russos won't give up, not for now anyway.'

The muscles in Abel's once handsome face were drawn and

tense. 'Alfie, you're not hearing me. I know what I'm like and it's not good for the girl. It's better than it was, better than the last time you and Lola came here, but it ain't right.'

Alfie nodded, understanding what Abel was saying. He gazed out of the window and from where he was he was able to see the coastline. 'I know that, Abel, and if I had any other choice, like I told Lola, I wouldn't bring her here. But I ain't, so I thought I could stay with her, only for a while, to make sure she's all right . . . to make sure nothing happens to her.'

'It's a risk, Alfie.'

Alfie shook his head, still shocked by Abel's appearance. 'Not like the Russos. She doesn't know about them, by the way. Not fully – I promised Cabhan I wouldn't say anything to her – but what she does know sent her into some kind of meltdown.'

Abel fell silent as he mulled over the situation, then eventually he said, 'You'll keep her out of my way?'

Alfie gave Abel a half-smile as he gazed down, seeing the same name scratched over and over on the table's surface, like it had been in the hallway. He answered sadly, 'Yes, Abel, I'll do whatever it takes, but I want you to meet her. The girl's special, she even gives me a conscience, and I ain't had one of those since I were a kid.' He laughed as he continued. 'There's a side to her that seems so vulnerable, but at the same time she's strong, a fighter. A survivor. You'll like her.'

Abel rested back in the wooden chair padded with purple velvet cushions. 'I don't know, Alfie. I don't know if it's such a good idea to meet her.'

'It might help. Why don't I go and get them?'

Abel shook his head as he traced his fingers round the name he'd carved on the table. 'No, Alfie, not today – maybe I'll meet her tomorrow when I'm feeling more meself. We'll see.'

'But, Abel—'

Abel banged his fist on the table as he stood up to leave. 'I said, no! This ain't going to work if you don't listen. Look, we'll speak tomorrow, and for now you can all stay in the east wing, you know where it is, but, Alfie, make sure you keep Alice away from where I am, you hear me? I don't want her anywhere near.'

Before Alfie had a chance to answer, his phone rang. He answered as Abel watched him curiously.

'Hey.'

'Alfie, it's me.'

His voice was hard. 'I know who it is, darlin', I just don't know if I want to talk to you, Fran. There's a lot of shit going down and I can't deal with you right now, it's doing me head in. I can't cope with all the messages and calls, not now, not unless you're going to be here for Alice, because right now she needs you, and that's all that matters to me.'

Shivering, Franny sat in the cage with Bobby and Salvatore glaring at her from the other side of the bars. She knew exactly what she was supposed to say, they'd prepped her – apparently, it was a message from Nico, part of his sick game – but as they stared at her, she took her chance from the security of the cage and quickly blurted out something else. 'Alfie, just choose Bree, you've got to choose her, she's pregnant, but they've got us, Salvat—'

Salvatore Russo furiously pointed his gun at Bree, causing Franny to stop talking and to throw the phone back through the bars at him.

Picking it up, Salvatore growled. He snatched away the packet of biscuits he'd given them.

'You can forget about eating for now. Maybe next time you'll think twice about messing with me. I'll deal with *you* later, and don't think I won't. *Capito*?'

'Franny? Franny?'

'No, Alfie, it's Salvatore.'

Alfie reeled, his chair scraping along the dining-room floor as he staggered back. Feeling light-headed, he bent forward to keep his balance.

'Don't you hurt them, you hear me.'

'Oh, we'll do more than that, give us some credit.'

Alfie bellowed an incoherent sound before he took a deep breath as he struggled to talk. 'What do you want?'

'We want Alice.'

'You'll never get her.'

Salvatore chuckled darkly. 'How can you say that, Alfie, when I have two people here who you clearly care about? And now it turns out to be three, a baby as well, the more the merrier. Love is a strange thing – it causes you to make the wrong choices; that's why I gave up loving a long time ago. Life is easier that way.'

'Just . . . just tell me what you want.'

'I've already told you, we want Alice. After all, she is ours. Cabhan took our daughter and we'll take yours.'

Feeling physically sick, Alfie barked, 'And I've told you, you ain't having her.'

'For a clever man you're very stupid. Alice is just one person, Alfie, yet you're willing to sacrifice three other beings for her. *L'amore è fatale per gli sciocchi*, which means, love is fatal to fools . . . How old is Alice, by the way?'

Almost unable to speak, Alfie said, 'Sixteen.'

'Okay, so I'm going to give you sixteen days to decide what you're going to do. But to make sure that you take us seriously – to make it more fun – we're going to raise the stakes, we're going to get money involved. You find us one million within sixteen days, small change really, then *after* sixteen days, once we get the money you can choose which one of these women will walk free. If we don't have the money by then, both of them – and the baby – are dead. One million and Alice. Let's call the game, *sedici giorni di Alice*. Sixteen days of Alice . . . We'll be in touch.'

The line went dead and Alfie stared at Abel in shock. It took him a moment to utter the words. 'They've got them. The Russos have Franny and Bree.'

'I'll help you, I'll help you get them back.' Abel's voice shook with emotion and his dark eyes glittered in the dim morning light. 'But come with me first, I need to show you something.'

Alfie nodded, following Abel in a state of shock. Besides the fact that the Russos now had them, what spun in his head were Franny's words: Bree was pregnant. He couldn't think straight, there were so many questions in his head, but there was one he desperately needed answered: Was the baby his? He just couldn't believe it. Bree might be having *his* baby.

Suddenly it hit him. Bree had been trying to tell him something for a week or so – she'd been evasive and coy – so maybe *this* was what she'd been trying to tell him, that she was pregnant. Was he that difficult to talk to that she couldn't have told him straight? Though what had he done when she'd wanted to talk? Sweet FA! He'd been too absorbed in his own life, his own mess, even to worry about her, and now they were all paying a heavy price.

Coming to a door along the corridor, even though his mind was racing from the phone call, Alfie, limping in and trying to push Franny and Bree out of his thoughts, found himself standing with his mouth open, amazed at what he was looking at.

The rest of the house might sit lifeless and frozen in time, but this little room off the main corridor was a hub of information, a centre of activity. Alfie stared around in astonishment as he studied the walls, which were entirely covered with cuttings, printouts, photographs and documents, all about . . .

'The Russos.'

Abel nodded. 'I've spent years trying to find a way to bring them down. Waiting for them to make a mistake.'

Alfie, not usually stuck for words, shook his head. 'Abel, Jesus, it's—'

Suddenly, Abel, who'd been gazing up at a photograph of Nico Russo cut from a newspaper, snarled, 'What, Alfie, what is it?

That it ain't healthy, that it ain't good for me, that I should be focusing on other things? That I should be marvelling at me fucking roses?'

'Abel, you know I never meant that.'

Abel turned back to gaze at Alfie, his blue eyes piercing. 'What else have I got, Alf? What else do I deserve? Peace? Rest? How can I rest knowing that Nico, Salvatore and Bobby are out there whilst Natalia . . .' He stopped.

'But, Abel, look around you, all this stuff, all this—'

Angered by Alfie's seeming resistance to what he was being shown, Abel hit his chest, his eyes wild, burning rage pouring out of his voice as he ripped Nico's picture off the wall and banged it into Alfie's face. 'Don't tell me I shouldn't be doing this, don't tell me that I should be doing something else, cos this is my life now. *Him. Nico.* And it'll be the same for you, now that he's got Franny. It'll drive you crazy, you won't be able to think straight anymore, you won't be able to sleep, you won't be able to eat, and every second the thought of *him* will consume you.'

'I'm not saying that I'm—'

Abel cut in, bitterness twisting his whole being. 'You know what they did to her! But I, *me*, I had to *watch* them do it to her. To Natalia. I watched them like fucking animals raping her as she begged me to make them stop. She was calling *my* name, Alfie, do you know what that's like? Pleading with me to help her and I couldn't. They made sure of that by tying me to a fucking chair, so all I could do was watch and listen to her pleas . . . Sshhh. Sshhh. Can you hear that? Can you hear it, Alfie?'

'What, Abel? Hear what?'

Abel wandered around the room, staring up, staring round, staring at Alfie with a penetrating, tormented gaze. 'Her . . . There. There . . . Can you hear it? Can you hear her? You must be able to hear it. Hear Natalia.'

Sadly, Alfie shook his head. 'No, Abel, no, mate.'

Once again, Abel's eyes were wild and wide as he roared, raw emotion echoing around the house. He smashed the side of his head with his fist repeatedly. 'Well, I can! I can! That's all I hear.'

'Abel, come on. I know it tortures you, but you're not to blame. Nobody blamed you, she knew it wasn't your fault.'

Abel shook manically. 'You didn't see the way she looked at me.'

'I did, Abel, when you brought her back here, I saw it. She was ill, Abel, it wasn't you. What happened made her very ill. She never blamed you.'

Pacing about, Abel pointed at Alfie. 'Yes, yes, she did. She would ask me *why*, over and over again, *why* hadn't I helped her . . . *why* hadn't I told Nico where the money was . . . Well, I didn't know! I didn't fucking know, Alfie!'

Abel fell to his knees and, feeling inadequate, Alfie said, 'I know, mate, I know.'

'And now Nico is my oxygen and one day I *will* get my revenge. I told them a long time ago. *La mia vendetta* . . . I'll help you, Alfie, I'll do anything it takes to get Franny and Bree back . . . Now get out! Leave me alone! Go on, go!'

And as Alfie shut the door behind him, he looked at the name scrawled and carved everywhere in the corridor: *Natalia*.

35

In the darkness of the warehouse, Bree shuffled over to Franny in the tiny cage, sending the large black rat that had been nibbling crumbs off the ground scurrying.

It was cold, and hunger pains stabbed at her stomach. The only food they'd been given since they'd arrived three days ago consisted of a packet of biscuits, a half-eaten ham-and-cheese sandwich to share between them and the minimum amount of water.

She shivered, trying to push everything out of her mind as she had done when she'd been a virtual prisoner in her last marriage, tortured and brutalised by her ex-husband. Even there in the small trailer park where they'd lived, she'd found a way to shut off to survive, imagining herself to be in a place where no one could hurt her, and no one could find her.

And that's exactly what she'd tried to do now – shut off. But no matter how hard she tried, all she could think about was her daughter, Molly, Alfie, her baby growing inside her and Franny's haunting words: *we're going to die.* She took a sharp intake of air, the enormity of the situation hitting her; tasting the fear.

She wondered if the reason she wasn't able to separate herself from her surroundings was that in the last few weeks with Alfie happiness had touched her and she couldn't pretend to herself anymore that life wasn't precious. And now the terror she felt seemed to sit in her chest, weighing down on her with every breath she took.

But right now her concern was for Franny. She was worried about her because she knew, behind that tough exterior, Franny must be hurting and as scared as she was.

Bree shuffled even closer to Franny. Even in the darkness she could see her face, swollen and bruised from the beating that Bobby had given her for blurting out the truth to Alfie.

'Are you awake, Franny?' she whispered.

A moment passed before Franny's voice cut through the darkness. Franny winced as she spoke, her lip painful from being split by one of Bobby's punches. 'Yeah. Are you okay, Bree?'

'Yeah, I was just wondering how you were.'

Sitting up slightly to try to find a more comfortable position on the hard, wet concrete floor, Franny stared at Bree. Her tone defensive, she asked, 'What are you talking about?'

'I just want to make sure you're okay. I'm worried about you, you haven't said much for a while.'

Franny raised her eyebrows, seeing the strain on Bree's face. 'What is there to say? And like I told you before, I'm fine – worry about yourself, not me.'

'But—'

Hardening her tone even more, Franny snapped, 'Listen to me, Bree. I appreciate your concern, but talking like this won't help, it won't get us out of here, will it?'

Still keeping her voice in a whisper, Bree spoke warmly. 'I'm not saying it will, but it might—'

'Might make us feel better?' Franny cut in bitterly. 'Is that what you were going to say? Because if it was, don't bother. I'm not a child, so pretending all is frigging tickety-boo ain't going to work for me. The only thing that will work for me is to see you getting out of here alive. Now if you don't mind, Bree, I'd like to get some sleep.'

Feeling a sudden surge of loneliness at the loaded tension in the air, Bree hugged her knees close to her, wondering if this was really how she was going to spend her final days.

Alfie's face was whiter than white as he led Lola and Alice into the grand kitchen through what had been the servants' entrance. Although the sun outside was high in the sky and the day was bright, the minute they walked into Abel's house the darkness and gloom surrounded them.

Alfie's head was swimming as he tried to concentrate on Alice. He took her hand, but she pulled away, still not wanting to have anything to do with him. Hoping to make the atmosphere less tense, Lola asked, 'Are you all right, Alf?'

'I'm fine, Lola. I'll speak to you later.'

'Alf? You look terrible. Are you sure you're okay? Is it your leg, is it playing you up?'

Refusing to break down in front of Alice, Alfie answered tightly, 'Yeah, it's giving me a bit of jip, but can we leave it now. I . . .' He took a deep breath, unable to finish his sentence.

The thought of Franny and Bree with Salvatore made him feel ill. He had known Natalia and had seen what a mess they'd left her in and now, Jesus, now they were all pawns in the Russos' game.

He turned to Alice, just trying to get through the next half an hour. 'I'll take you to your bedrooms and I'm sorry, but for now you'll just have to keep on wearing the same clothes until we figure something out. But at least you'll be able to shower and wash all your stuff. And, Alice, you do know this ain't what I wanted for you, none of us did . . . I love you.'

Alice stared at Alfie oddly as Lola, sensing the strain, tried to sound cheery as she looked around the once splendid Elizabethan kitchen.

'I'm sure we'll be able to find something. Back in the day, Abel was one of the best-dressed people I know, him and Nat . . .'

Lola stopped, nervously looking at Alfie, worried by his expression she'd said too much.

Kicking the chair hard in anger as he walked past it and up towards the kitchen stairwell, Alfie snapped, 'For God's sake, Lola, why don't you just keep it fucking zipped, just shut it! For once in your life just shut it! Come on, I'll show you to your rooms.'

Alfie sat, head in hands, on the dark oak four-poster bed, the orange drapes around it faded and dusty. Glancing up, he looked out through the window to the wide sweeping views of the forest and sea.

His chest was tight and a sense of panic was rumbling through his veins. Only a short time ago all he had to worry about was which woman he wanted to be with. That was all. That was it. What a fucking luxury to have *that* as his only problem, *especially* as both women were such extraordinary human beings that it put him to shame. He hadn't seen it at the time, but now, *now* he knew that it hadn't been a problem at all, because *this*, this nightmare he'd somehow found himself in, *was* a problem. An unresolvable fucking problem. Choose between two women he loved, but by the way, Alf, choose which one will live and which one will die. *Fuck!*

Picking his phone up, Alfie stared at it for a couple of minutes then abruptly pressed call.

'Salvatore? It's Alfie.'

Salvatore's voice was slow but a hint of amusement danced in his words, emphasising his New Jersey twang. 'Can't stay away or are you phoning to let us know you've got our money already and you're keen to make your choice?'

Holding onto his anger, Alfie said, 'I want to speak to them.'

Salvatore laughed. 'Why?'

Taking a moment to fight his emotions, which seemed to cut like a razor at the back of his throat, Alfie squeezed his eyes shut

213

as he spoke, aware how much his hand was shaking as he held onto the phone. 'I need to make sure they're okay.'

'They're okay.'

Alfie smashed his fist against one of the wooden bedposts – the pain that shot through his arm making him feel better. 'Let's put it this way, Salvatore, I have no reason to trust you. I want to hear for myself.'

'Okay, Alfie, if that's what you want, but if you do, that will be a day down. Instead of sixteen days to get our money and give us Alice, you'll only have fifteen days. One day equals one conversation. Are you sure that's what you want?'

Alfie placed the phone on the bed. Pale, covered with a sudden cold sweat and feeling an intense throbbing in his leg, he got up and made his way into the cream-tiled en-suite bathroom, where he was promptly sick, retching up mucus and bile from his empty stomach, his nose blocking up with vomit. And then, for the first time in as long as he could remember, he began to cry, uncontrollable deep sobs, unable to stop the well of emotion drowning him.

Attempting to pull himself together, Alfie threw cold water on his face before going back to the phone. He let out a long sigh and then calmly said, 'Salvatore, are you still there?'

'Yes.'

'That's a deal, let me speak to them and you can make it fifteen days.'

'Are you sure?'

Not at all sure, but too afraid to question if he was doing the right thing, Alfie growled, 'Listen, you motherfucker, I've already said it's a deal, now just put them on the phone.'

Again, Salvatore broke into laughter. 'Alfie, we have a problem. You only get to speak to *one* of them, not both. Both of them was never the deal. Unless of course you want to make it fourteen days?'

Even though he wasn't fully able to think straight, Alfie knew that only having fourteen days was not an option – even fifteen days was really too little time to pull together that kind of money. Not that he had any idea what he was going to do; the sense of already being defeated hung over his head like Damocles' sword.

With hatred, he snarled, 'You'll pay for this, Salvatore.'

'I doubt it, Alfie, but if it makes you feel better to think that, knock yourself out. So, come on, who do you want to speak to? Who will it be?'

Taking long, deep breaths to try to calm the panic that was rising, Alfie rubbed the water off his face with his hand and opened his mouth to answer Salvatore. Then, changing his mind, he closed it. Jesus Christ, it was impossible. What he wanted maybe wouldn't be the right choice. If he chose Franny, what would he say to her? He knew she'd try to reassure him that she was fine, that she was strong, but he would also know that she was terrified, not that she would *ever* admit it. And if he chose Bree, how would Franny feel? And Christ, what would he say to her? He'd be able to hear the pain in her voice as she told him not to blame himself. She would tell him not to worry about her and to keep himself safe. And maybe he shouldn't be talking to them at all. Gambling one of the days away, for what? So *he* could speak to them, so it would make *him* feel better. But then he had to know, he wanted to know, and fuck, it was selfish, but he couldn't help himself.

'Bree. Put Bree on the phone.'

There was a pause before Salvatore said, 'Good choice, that would've been my choice as well. Mouthy women like Franny should be kept in their place, and besides, she probably wouldn't be able to talk very much, not with the fat lip Bobby gave her. Hold on.'

Alfie screamed down the phone, 'No! No! Salvatore, come back, what the fuck do you mean? Put Franny on instead, Salvatore!'

Then a soft voice came onto the line. 'Hello?'

It was like an ointment, a healing, soothing balm. 'Bree, it's me.'

Bree's voice was breathless. 'Alfie, are you all right?'

Although he was on his own, embarrassed, he wiped away his tears. 'Shouldn't that be me who says that to you? How's Franny? Can you tell her that I wasn't choosing you over her, I just . . . I just . . . How is she?'

Bree repeated Alfie's words out loud – 'How's Franny?' – at the same time as she glanced at her sitting huddled in the cage on the hard concrete floor, her face battered. Franny nodded, encouraging Bree to answer Alfie positively as Salvatore and Bobby stood above them, amused.

'She's fine, Alfie.'

'But Salvatore said—'

Bree cut in, speaking firmly. 'No, she's fine . . . I promise.'

'Good.' Alfie closed his eyes, knowing Bree was lying but too much of a coward to push it further – he didn't think he could cope with what he might hear. 'Good. I'm glad . . . Fuck sake, Bree, why didn't you tell me? Why didn't you tell me about the baby? Is it mine? Not that it matters, cos I love you anyway, and I know it's crazy cos I never said it to you before, but I do. But that don't mean I don't love Franny, cos she's my world, it's just . . . I, fuck, I'm being selfish, ain't I? I'm just a bit lost, a bit fucked up.'

'Alfie, it's okay.'

Alfie pressed his head against the intricate carved post of the bed. 'But it ain't, is it? And when it was okay, I messed up, I wronged you both . . . I . . .' He trailed off.

'Alfie, listen to me, and this is really important. I don't want you to choose me because of the baby.' She paused before adding, 'Cos I'm not going through with it anyway. I won't be going through with the pregnancy even if I get out of here.'

'What? Bree, look—'

'No, Alfie, I don't want another kid. So don't get sentimental,

Alf, I know what you're like. Now I've got to go . . . and, Alfie, we both love you too. Take good care of yourself.'

Bree clicked off the phone, unable to speak to Alfie any longer. She trembled as she handed it back through the bars to Salvatore, and in the darkness of the warehouse, Franny whispered, 'That wasn't true, was it, Bree? About the pregnancy, about you not wanting to go through with it, it's not true.'

Leaning on Franny's shoulder, with drops of water dripping on them from the leaking warehouse roof, Bree shook her head. 'No, it's not, but it might help him make the right decision. He may love me, but the difference is he not only loves you, but he *needs* you. He needs you, Franny. Problem is he doesn't even know it.'

36

Night drew in and Alice, having stayed in her room the whole afternoon, crept down the long airy corridor, trying not to make any of the wooden floorboards creak as she tiptoed along. In the darkness, with only the moonlight as her torch, she glanced behind her, shivering as she crept past the large gold-framed paintings of formidable-looking lords and ladies of bygone days, past the deer and boar heads covered in dust and cobwebs dotted around the wall, and past the brass suit of armour standing ominously at the end of the corridor, which felt to Alice as if it were watching her, stalking her from behind the eye slits in the helmet.

Alice came to a large wooden door and pushed herself into the shadows, making sure that no one was around. Looking up and down the hallway and certain that she was on her own, Alice turned the oversized brass handle as quietly as she could.

The room was pitch-black and a smell of musty cloth hit Alice's senses. There was silence apart from the soft murmur of Lola snoring in the large four-poster bed.

'Lola?' Alice whispered, not wanting to wake her but at the same time wanting to make sure that she was properly asleep.

Hearing no reply and unable to see in the darkness, her heart thumping, Alice crouched down to the wooden floor. She crawled along, feeling her way carefully, stretching her arms out to make sure she didn't bang into anything that would cause Lola to wake up.

Crawling further forward, Alice felt something soft under her fingertips. Still unable to see, she picked up the object and examined it. Quickly realising it was what she was looking for, Alice began to back away, but as she did her foot banged into the hearth, sending the fire grate crashing down.

'Hello? Who's there? Abel, is that you? Don't you come in here, Alfie's next door and I'll scream, don't you think I won't. You stay away from me, you hear? Abel? Abel?'

Alice stayed frozen, her thoughts confused. What was Lola talking about? And why did she sound so frightened? There was a huge part of her that wanted to make sure Lola was fine, but then Lola would want to know what *she* was doing in *her* room.

'Abel? Abel? I know that's you.'

Aware that Lola thought *she* was Abel, Alice, deciding to take her chance, stood up and ran out of the room, hoping to get to the door before Lola had the opportunity to switch on the light.

Slamming the bedroom door behind her, Alice stood in the corridor slightly out of breath. She leant her head on the door, hearing Lola's muffled, frightened cries. Ashamed of herself, but not wanting to waste any time, Alice quickly pulled herself together, ran along the hallway and through a set of double doors leading to the far end of the house.

'What are you doing here? Didn't they tell you to stay out of this side of the house?'

Alice jumped as a strange-looking man walked out of the shadows, his dark eyes wild, his face sunken and hollow, looking like a corpse in the moonlight.

'I . . . I . . .'

'I take it you're Alice.'

Abel's hand hovered over Alice's face. He turned his head to the side, staring at her strangely as she hid what she was holding behind her back. 'Do you know who I am?'

Alice breathed deeply, her face only inches away from his. 'You must be Abel.'

'I am.'

Terrified and unable to think of anything better to say, Alice, her voice shaking, said, 'It's nice to meet you.'

Abel Gray smiled, though it didn't show in his eyes. He whispered, his tone gravelly, 'I'm not sure about that, only time will tell . . . But you still haven't told me yet what you're doing in this side of the house.'

'I'm sorry, I didn't know I shouldn't be here.'

Abel nodded. 'Stay away, you understand?'

Alice answered quietly, her chest tight from fear. 'Yes, yes.'

Leaning even closer to Alice, Abel said, 'Can I ask you something?'

Backed up against the wall, Alice nodded. 'Of course.'

'Did they hurt you?'

'Who?'

Abel's blue eyes were void of emotion. It felt to Alice like she was looking into a deep, dark ocean.

'The men who are after you. Alfie's told me all about them, but he didn't tell me that. Did they hurt you in any way, Alice? Did they touch . . .' Abel stopped.

'No . . . no.'

Abel let out a deep sigh. His voice was strangled. Monotone. Devoid of sentiment. 'I'm glad, because if they did . . . if they did, Alice . . .' He paused, unable to speak of it anymore. 'Anyway, I bid you goodnight, and maybe it would be best if you went back to your room, locked the door behind you. It's for your own good.'

Alice, always curious and feeling slightly braver, asked, 'What do you mean?'

'I don't sleep very well and sometimes I have dreams, waking

220

dreams that seem to control me. It's strange, I know, and some-times when I do wake, I'm in places where I shouldn't be, and I wouldn't want to give you a fright . . . You know, I hear her, calling me.'

Still inches from his face, Alice stared at Abel. 'Who?' she whispered.

'Natalia. She calls me, and I have to go to her, make sure she's all right. I hear her voice.'

Not knowing who Natalia was, but intuitively knowing she must be someone special, Alice, losing her fear, smiled kindly. 'That's good then, isn't it?'

Surprise crossed through Abel's eyes before the light went out of them as suddenly as it had appeared. 'Yes, yes, yes, you're right, Alice, it is . . . Now goodnight. Sleep well.'

'Goodnight.'

As Abel walked down the corridor he spoke softly. 'And keep away from this side of the house, remember that.'

Alice didn't answer but watched Abel glide down the wooden hallway, waiting for him to disappear.

Once she was certain he had gone, Alice brought out Lola's bag from behind her back. Nervously, keeping an eye out, she rummaged in the bag, quickly finding what she was looking for . . . Lola's phone.

Leaving the bag in the shadows of the corridor, Alice slipped the mobile into her pocket, making her way carefully down the stairs to the pantry window she'd left open earlier on in the day.

Climbing out easily into the courtyard, Alice, jumpy and afraid, looked behind her and froze. Was there someone moving at the window on the top landing? She couldn't be sure. Maybe it was just a shadow, she couldn't tell.

For the next few minutes Alice remained still, her heart pounding as she made certain nobody was coming, assuming it must have been her imagination and trying to push down her fears. Then Alice started to run.

She darted along the side of the huge house. Though dismal in appearance, it hid a magnificence under the neglect. She sped through a courtyard, unkempt with weeds and grass growing between the large stone slabs, past outhouses that were once stables and summerhouses but were now derelict and hidden mostly by wind-bent trees and bushes. She noticed a lot of the windows of the house had been walled up, while others had rusting bars across them.

Uneasy, Alice checked behind her again as she hurried down the white gravel driveway, finding herself by a walled rose garden. She leant back against the wall, pulled Lola's phone out of her pocket, dialled a number off by heart and listened as it rang.

'Yes?'

'Nico, it's me, it's Alice.'

37

'Did you know? Did you know?' Alice was hysterical as she spoke into the phone, all her pent-up feelings and emotions pouring out.

'Alice, I think you'd better calm down.'

Ignoring what Nico was saying, Alice yelled, her voice accusatory and the feeling of betrayal rushing through her. 'I said, did you?'

'What are you talking about, Alice?' Nico snapped. 'First I don't hear from you and now you're calling to shout at me, is that how any friend behaves? I thought I meant something to you.'

Shaking, Alice paced along the wall of the rose garden as she wiped the tears from her eyes. She felt confused and blubbered out her words. 'You do mean something to me, of course you do, but I want to know if *you* knew about Dad. Everyone's been lying to me and I couldn't stand it if you'd been lying as well. Please, just tell me the truth, Nico, *please*.'

In his cell, Nico held onto a window bar as he looked out across the penitentiary yard. He thought for a moment, carefully working out what to say.

'Alice, Alice, calm down. Tell me exactly what you're talking about and then we can sort it out. That's what I'm here for, to talk, to help you deal with what's troubling you. Your problems are *my* problems. Come on, stop crying. I'm here now, Alice, so take a deep breath . . . That's right. Now just imagine I'm there next to you, holding your hand, comforting you. Imagine that I'm close to you, *really* close . . .' he purred down the phone.

Alice nodded, taking a deep breath as Nico had told her to do. Not wanting to disappoint him, she fought back her tears as she spoke. 'My dad, he's not what he says he is; everyone isn't who they say they are. I found out that my dad, he's . . . he's . . .'

'He's what, Alice?'

Embarrassed and ashamed, Alice quietly said, 'He's a gangster, he does bad things, and that's why all this has happened. What happened in the convent was because of him, and what happened back at the house, well, it's all because of Dad.'

'And you think I knew? Is that what you're saying?'

'Yes, no, I don't know, maybe. I just want you to tell me the truth. Are you a part of this as well, like Franny and Alfie are?'

There was silence, then Nico answered slowly, 'I think you'd better go, Alice. I have no wish to talk to you.'

'What? What! No! No! You can't go!'

Nico smiled to himself. 'Why not? What's the point? I thought you trusted me, I thought we understood each other when nobody else does. But it's clear I was wrong. How could you think that of me, Alice?'

Alice cupped the phone tightly, her tears running off the screen as she shook. 'I'm sorry, I'm sorry, Nico. I just feel so lost and I am scared. I just want to go home.'

'Look, Alice, maybe you're right. Maybe I *have* lied to you, but I was only doing it for your own good, trying to protect you. Look, let me explain and then you can be my judge. This is as much as I know . . . Your dad worked for me, insurance, do you remember me telling you?'

'Yes.'

'Okay, well, about a year ago he decided to leave the company. He told me he was after more money, he had to think about you, about your future, and I couldn't afford to give him a pay rise so I wished him well. Then I heard through the grapevine he was working for this thug, some criminal guy, and of course I was shocked, but what could I do? Then when you called me about his birthday party and it was clear you didn't know what he did, I wanted to protect you, so that's why I said he still worked for me. So, there you go, Alice, that's the truth, judge me if you like.'

Breathlessly, Alice whispered, speaking quickly, 'No, Nico I don't want to do that. *Judge not, that you be not judged. For with the judgment you pronounce you will be judged, and with the measure you use it will be measured to you. Why do you see the speck that is in your brother's eye, but do not notice the log that is in your own eye?* Matthew 7, chapter 1. Thank you, Nico, for caring . . . I love you.'

There was a pause before Nico smiled, his eyes narrowing darkly. 'I love you too, Alice, but you have to realise others won't understand.'

'I don't care.'

'Where are you, Alice? Tell me.'

Alice looked round the grounds. 'I don't know, not exactly. There's a guy called Abel we're staying with.'

The pause, the tension, the hatred from Nico was palpable. He could barely say the name.

'*Abel?*'

'What are you doing?'

Alice spun round, clicking off the phone. Her face drained as Abel Gray stood opposite her looking deadly. 'Nothing . . . nothing.'

'I *said*, what were you doing?'

Terrified, Alice stepped back, but Abel continued to follow her, his eyes raging dark and black.

'What have you got in your hand?'

Abel stalked towards her as Alice, panicked, backed further away. Her body thudded into the wall and she pressed herself against it, trying to get as far away from Abel as she possibly could.

Rage danced in Abel's eyes, his voice gravelly, his cockney accent harsh. '*What's in your hand*? You'd better answer me, Alice, otherwise I won't be held responsible for my actions.'

Abel's breathing was hard as he stood in the wet grass of the night staring wildly, then Alice, glancing to one side of him, took her chance. She ran, but Abel, surprisingly quick, managed to grab her. He squeezed her arm tightly and Alice gasped from the pain, all the while holding onto Lola's phone tightly.

Far stronger than he looked, Abel threw Alice to the ground, standing over her as she tried to crawl away, but he grabbed her legs and pulled her back towards him as she screamed in terror. 'Give me what's in your hand!'

'No! No! No! Get away from me! Get away. You're hurting me!'

Abel wrestled her hand open and grabbed the phone away, scrolling through to the last number and pressed redial.

'Hello, Alice, what happened? You were cut off.'

Abel reeled, staggering backwards, images flashing through his mind as he clicked off the phone, recognising the voice. He leant against the tree trunk and vomited, retching violently, many expressions crossing his face before, in barely a whisper, wiping the sick from his chin, he murmured, 'Nico. You're speaking to Nico.'

Quaking, Alice was too scared to say anything as Abel leant over her, his screams rising into the air. 'Why are you speaking to him, *why*?'

'He's my friend, he . . . he understands me.'

The veins in Abel's face bulged as he hovered over Alice. 'How long? How long have you been speaking to him?'

'What's going on?' Alfie, having reached the opening of the rose garden, stared at Abel. 'What the fuck have you done to her?'

Lola, catching up to Alfie, pointed at Abel, her voice shaky. 'You'd better not have frightened her, do you hear me? She's just a kid, Abel. A kid!'

Abel stared, cold and hard, as he turned to Lola. Then, leaving Alice, he walked towards Lola and Alfie, his face twisting with rage. He tilted his head to the side, his eyes piercing.

'What is that?' He pointed his long sinewy arm towards Lola and nervously she looked behind her.

'What are you talking about?'

'*That*!' Abel screeched.

Lola looked down slowly, confusion etched on her face.

Walking even closer to Lola, Abel continued to shake. 'That! That! Get it off, get it off, now!'

Lola touched the white nightie she was wearing. 'I got it out of the drawer.'

'*Now*!' Abel suddenly lurched at Lola, ripping at the nightie, tearing at it, the force of his actions pushing her over into the grass.

Alfie dragged Abel off Lola, who covered her body with the torn nightie, and roared like a lion, 'What the fuck do you think you're doing, Abel?'

Although Abel had neglected himself over the years, he was still strong and still capable of handling a fight. He twisted out of Alfie's grip and before Alfie had time to react, smashed his fist into Alfie's face, the hard blow instantly splitting open his lip. Lola screamed as Abel expertly continued to slam his forearm into Alfie's throat, pinning him down on the grass, their faces nearly touching.

Spitting with anger, Abel growled his words. 'Tell her to take that off. Tell her, Alfie, before I rip it off her.'

'What . . . what are you talking about?'

Abel pushed down harder on Alfie's neck, stopping him talking further, his face turning scarlet. He hissed in a whisper, 'I'm talking about what she's wearing. *It's Natalia's.* She needs to get it off. You hear me? She needs to take it off, *now!*'

Alfie gave a tiny shake of his head as saliva spluttered out of his mouth. He pulled at Abel's arm, desperate to get away from the choking hold, then out of the corner of his eye Alfie spotted a small stone. He slid his hand to the side, stretching and straining towards it, but it was too far to reach. Suddenly, Alfie felt the weight of it placed into his hand gently. Quickly, he turned his eyes to see Alice crouching down, pressing the stone into his palm, her eyes filled with fear.

Exchanging the briefest of glances with Alice, Alfie brought the stone down hard on the back of Abel's head. Although it didn't knock him out, it gave Alfie the chance he needed. Grabbing Abel by the shoulders, Alfie turned him over and underneath him, slammed his elbow into Abel's face. He heard a crunch.

He leant forward and whispered into Abel's ear, 'Tell me why I shouldn't fucking kill you now, Abel?'

Just as venomously, Abel whispered back, 'Because it won't help you to kill me, it won't help Franny or Bree, it won't help anyone but Nico.'

Alfie pushed Abel as he got off him, sucking the blood from his lip. 'Make any more moves like you just did and I *will* kill you.'

'And like I told you, it won't help, but then, that's the least of your troubles when you have someone on the inside talking to him . . . Didn't I tell you to take that off?' Abel spoke calmly as he got up from the grass and looked at Lola coldly.

Lola glanced hesitantly at Alfie and he tilted his head towards the house. 'Go on, Lola, go and get changed.' She nodded and walked off as Alfie turned back to lock eyes with Abel. 'What are you talking about?'

'I'm talking about Alice. She's speaking to Nico.'

Alfie blinked, then blinked again, not quite registering what Abel was telling him. 'What?'

'She was on the phone to Nico, that's what this was all about.'

'What is he talking about?' Alfie shook his head as he turned slowly to Alice.

Seeing the mixture of confusion and horror on Alfie's face, Alice began to back away. 'I don't know.'

'Alice, I'll ask you again, what is Abel talking about?'

Alice glanced towards Abel, who stood in the moonlight holding Lola's phone. 'I . . . I . . .'

'What the *fuck* is he talking about?' Alfie's voice rose, making Alice jump.

Trembling, Alice's eyes danced from Abel to Alfie. 'He's my friend. That's all.'

Alfie didn't know whether to laugh or cry; instead, he chose rage. 'Friend? Nico is your friend?'

Alice nodded quickly. 'Yes, we talk, that's all, he understands me. How . . . how do you know him?'

Unable to speak another word to her, Alfie turned to Abel. 'Is she having a fucking laugh? *Is* she? Tell me this is some sick joke.'

Angrily, Alice spat out her words. 'He's a good man, but then you wouldn't know what that was, would you?'

Faster than she could have imagined, Alfie was suddenly just millimetres from her face as she cowered back against the stone wall. 'Are you being serious? Are you trying to do my head in?'

Her voice quivered. 'N-no.'

Alfie stared at Alice, his eyes blank and forbidding. 'Then tell me about Nico. Start talking.'

'I can't, he made me promise.'

Alfie grabbed hold of Alice and shook her hard. 'Promise! Promise! You've lost the plot.'

In floods of tears, Alice shouted at Alfie. 'He said you wouldn't understand!'

The rage in Alfie was out of control as he continued to shake her. 'You stupid, stupid little girl. Have you any idea what you've done? I could wring your neck.'

'Leave her, Alfie, don't do that to her.' Surprising himself, Abel stepped in, pulling him away from Alice.

'Have you any idea who Nico is? Where he is?' Alfie continued to rant, his face red, his eyes bulging.

Hurt and defiant, Alice stood up to Alfie. 'Of course I have, he's a friend of Dad's. Well, he was before Dad went off to work for some . . . some thug.'

Alfie snarled. 'And Nico told you that?'

'Yes.'

'But he missed out the part that *he's* the thug, he's the one banged up in prison.'

'No, you're wrong.' Alice shook her head.

Alfie laughed bitterly. 'No, *you're* wrong, Alice, because *he's* the murderer, the psycho, the one who ordered your dad to be killed, the one who ordered Franny and Bree to be taken.'

'What?' It was Lola who spoke, coming up behind Alfie in her old clothes.

He turned to her, his voice cracking at the edges, and nodded. 'Oh, yes, Lola, you don't know that part yet. The Russos have got them.' He stopped and shifted his attention back to Alice. 'But I haven't finished the story yet, I haven't told you the main point Nico left out. He's not really bothered about your dad or Franny or Bree, he couldn't care less. The person he *really* wants is you. It's you he wants to kill, Alice. You!'

'Liar! You're lying to me. I hate you! I hate you!'

Alice's cries cut through the air as she lurched forward, snatching the phone out of Abel's hands as she ran into the grounds of the house.

38

'Look, she can't have gone far. Lola, why don't you look over by the summerhouse and swimming pool, I'll go up to the woods towards the stables and Abel, you take the left side of the grounds and house.' Alfie's eyes darted as he scanned the land surrounding the large estate.

He hadn't got time to stand about feeling angry with himself for reacting like he did, or feeling sorry for himself, or feeling scared about Franny and Bree. All that *had* to wait, because the thing that mattered, the *only* thing that mattered right now, was finding Alice.

'Well, what the fuck are you waiting for? Come on, let's go!' Alfie shouted, worry taking over.

As Alfie and Lola headed off in separate directions, Abel watched them until they disappeared into the night. He turned slowly towards the house, strode across to the large stone-pillared front doors, kicked them open and stalked in.

By the side of the grand wooden staircase where walking sticks and umbrellas hung, Abel pushed a pile of faded coats aside. He pulled out a shotgun, then checked to see if it was loaded. Satisfied, Abel Gray went to go and look for Alice.

* * *

The private chapel in the grounds stood at the far corner of the wooded walkway. Seeing his way by moonlight, Abel entered. Urgently, he ran down the nave, past the coats of arms painted underneath the arch, to where a carved and painted reredos sat behind the altar.

By the rose stained-glass window was a large stone dais with a wooden crucifix and a portrait of the Virgin Mary staring down. And in the front wooden pew was Alice Rose, crying and shaking as she knelt, eyes shut, hands tightly clasped together.

'I thought I'd find you here. If you're looking for God, well, he moved out of here a long time ago.' Abel spoke gruffly.

Startled, Alice stood up, glanced at the gun, then back at Abel, his eyes haunted as he continued, 'I'm here to tell you about Nico.'

Alice made a move to go. She didn't want to hear it; she didn't want to hear any more lies.

'Where are you going, Alice? There's nowhere for you to run, you *have* to listen whether you like it or not.' Abel clicked off the safety, looking down at it then back up at Alice. 'Unless of course you want to take a chance, and don't think I won't use it, because I will.'

Afraid and bewildered, Alice answered Abel in a whisper. 'Why are you doing this? Why are you doing it in *here*?'

Abel laughed scornfully as he stepped closer to Alice. 'In *here*? This place is just old stones and bricks. There's nothing else, Alice. There is no God, only a burning, everlasting hell, and you would know that if you'd seen what I'd seen. I want *revenge*, Alice, and one day I will get that. *La mia vendetta*. I will bring down Nico for what he did.'

Scared, Alice shook her head. 'Stop! Stop! I don't want to know what you *say* he did, because it'll be a lie, like everything else, you're all lying.' Alice turned away, putting her hands over her ears as tears slid down her cheeks.

Abel wildly pulled one of her hands away, his whole body

shaking, the veins on his forehead bulging as his voice rose, echoing round the small stone chapel.

'Listen, you need to listen! I worked for Nico and by working for him I sold myself to the Devil. I watched evil hard at work. He destroys people, Alice, rips the soul out of their very life.'

Alice shook her head again, her tears pooling down onto the chapel stone floor. 'He's not what you say he is, he's kind, he's, he's . . . I love him.'

Shocked, Abel whispered hoarsely. 'What?'

'I love him.'

Abruptly, Abel grabbed Alice's hand, dragging her out of the chapel. She began to scream as he pulled her through the dark grounds and past the walled garden.

'What the hell are you doing? Abel! Abel!' Seeing Abel drag Alice, Alfie hollered at him as he and Lola came running from behind one of the summerhouses.

Still gripping Alice, whose eyes were wide in terror, Abel swivelled round and pointed the gun at Alfie. 'Stay back, Alfie, stay back if you know what's good for her.'

Alfie's face paled. 'Abel, for God's sake, just leave her alone, let her go. Whatever it is that's going on in your head, you've got to stop it. Abel, listen to me!'

Ignoring Alfie, Abel pulled Alice along as he marched into the house whilst Alice continued to scream, pleading desperately.

'Alfie! Alfie! Help me! Help me!'

As Alfie and Lola ran behind, they watched Abel, like a man possessed, drag Alice by her hand through the dusty wooden corridors, through the great oak wooden doors towards the west wing.

In the dark and dust of the once regal home, Abel kicked open a set of double doors and threw Alice into the room. His face strained and crazed, he raved, 'This is what Nico does. Destroying and ripping the soul out of people's lives. Look! Look!

Look, Alice.' He pointed, and Lola clung to Alfie's arm as they stood helplessly in the doorway.

Alfie stayed silent whilst Lola's eyes went wide as she took in the scene before her. 'Oh my Christ, Alfie! Oh my Christ!'

At the end of the long boarded-up room, lying in an open wooden coffin, was the mummified body of Natalia.

Abel opened his arms, spinning round to look at them as he walked backwards towards the coffin. 'I'm here, Natalia, I'm here . . .' He bent over the coffin, touching and kissing Natalia's face, her skin like old, worn, stretched chamois leather. He continued to speak, but this time it was directed at Alice.

'Look at her, look at her! This is my punishment, Alice. Natalia is my punishment, and I can't sleep, I can't rest until I have my revenge . . . I said, look at her!'

Petrified, Alice shook her head, covering her face with her hands. 'No! No!'

Before Alfie had time to stop him, Abel, in fury, ran up to Alice, picking her up off the floor and pushing her towards the coffin. Holding Alice's shoulders in his strong grip, he stood behind her, forcing Alice to look at Natalia.

Leaning forward, he whispered in her ear. 'They raped her, they cut her, they tortured her and they made me watch. Nico, Salvatore and Bobby. Then they left her to die like a wounded animal. I brought her here, back home. I tried to make her well again, but I'd already lost her. It was like she died that day in the lodge with Nico. She had no peace at the end. All she did was call my name and wander the house at night. I sat with her, tried to nurse her, but it made no difference. Then one day, I went into the chapel and she was hanging there, with a rope tied around her neck, her eyes bulging, her tongue hanging out.

'And when I buried her, I knew I couldn't leave her there, because she was afraid, you see, she was afraid of the dark, and I didn't want her to be afraid anymore. So I brought her into the house, to be with me. At least Natalia's safe here, where I can protect her and Nico can't touch her anymore.'

Abel's voice broke on the last words and his eyes rolled back until only the whites of them were showing as he dropped to the floor, his head in his hands, deep, racking sobs filling the room.

Alice stared back at Alfie and then at Lola in horror.

'Is it true, Alfie? Is it true about Nico?' she asked, her voice almost inaudible above Abel's cries.

Sadness preventing him from speaking, Alfie just nodded as he fought his own tears. Alice, shocked, walked to where Abel was slumped. She crouched down, took him in her arms and rocked him gently as she whispered into his ear. '*And the Lord says we will show no pity, no mercy for the guilty. Our rule will be eye for an eye, tooth for a tooth . . . Life for life. And then we, the righteous, shall bathe our feet in the blood of the wicked.*'

39

'Franny, do you want some water?' Bree kept her voice down, not wanting Bobby Russo, who was sitting dozing at the far end of the warehouse, to hear.

Just as quietly, Franny replied, 'No thanks, I'm fine. You have it. You need to keep yourself hydrated.'

'I'm not ill, Franny.'

'No, but you're pregnant,' Franny said matter-of-factly.

Bree blinked, staring at Franny in puzzlement. 'I don't understand you.'

Bristling, Franny hissed, 'What is there to understand, Bree?'

Bree shrugged. 'You do know it's okay to be upset?'

It was Franny's turn to stare in puzzlement, her tone hard. 'Upset about what?'

Raising her voice but seeing Bobby stir, Bree brought it back down into a whisper. 'Franny, we're locked in a cage, you've been beaten badly and you've just found out I'm pregnant by the man you love.'

The tiniest flicker of hurt, though it was too dark for Bree to see it, passed through Franny's eyes as she spoke coldly. 'I thought you said you didn't know who the father was.'

'I don't, but that's not the point. The point is there's a strong possibility that it could be Alfie's and you act like you're not upset about any of it.'

'I already told you before, I don't feel like other people feel.'

Bree shook her head. 'Don't give me that. That's just an excuse to bury your head in the sand.'

Scornfully, Franny leant in towards Bree. 'What do you know about me? You've known me for all of ten minutes and you think you can make a judgement on who I am? You have no idea about my life.'

'No, but what I do know is that you go around being aloof, pretending you don't care, when that couldn't be further from the truth.'

'Don't kid yourself, Bree, that's who I am, and rather that than be the martyr.'

'What do you mean?'

'All *you've* done since I've known you is tell anyone who'll listen that you're willing to give up Alfie for me. Well, let me tell you something, sweetheart, I've already given him up, so don't do me any favours.'

Tears pricked in Bree's eyes. 'That's not fair!'

'What is, Bree, what is?'

Bree shook her head again. 'This is what you do, isn't it? You try to be as mean as you can to push people away, but I'm not going to let you.'

Exasperated, Franny said, 'What do you want from me, Bree?'

'I want you to tell me that you care, that you care that Alfie cheated on you, that—'

'He didn't cheat on me. I'd told him I wasn't coming back, remember? We weren't together.'

'In your heart you were.'

'So, you know about my heart now as well as my life? Jesus, Bree, you're some kind of special.'

'Stop! Just stop being like this.'

'Why? Why do you care? Why do you care how I feel? You didn't before so why would you now?'

'What do you mean?'

Panicking at the rush of emotion beginning to churn inside her, Franny tried to turn her hurt into anger. 'What I mean is, no matter what he told you, it was obvious to anyone that there was still something between Alfie and me. I know him, and he wouldn't have been able to hide it, hide his hurt, and seeing as you think you're so fucking clever at knowing people, why didn't you see it when he talked about me? I'll tell you why, shall I? Because you didn't want to. Because it suited you for me to be out of the picture, so you could get in there, and Jesus Christ, didn't you get in there quick! What did you do, Bree, throw away the contraceptive pills the minute you stepped over the front doorstep?'

'It wasn't like that.'

'No, it never is with people like you. But you've got what you want now, so just leave me alone and maybe then I can figure a way to get you out of here, so you can play happy families with Alfie.'

Bree reached over to touch Franny. 'Please, don't be like this.'

'Get your hand off me. I don't need your pity.'

'That's not what I'm doing, I'm just trying to say—'

Swallowing her emotions, Franny cut in again. 'What, Bree? What are you trying to say? You're pregnant with Alfie's baby, so there isn't anything more to say, is there? But you know, it . . .' Franny stopped abruptly.

'What were you going to say? Franny, please, look at me . . . Franny,' Bree whispered, emotion catching in her throat.

'Nothing, I wasn't going to say anything.' Angry with herself, Franny felt tears brimming.

'Franny, don't push me away, talk to me.'

With tears now running down her face, Franny blurted out the words she hadn't known were there. 'It hurts, okay. It really,

238

really hurts, and the idea of you being with Alfie makes me feel like I can hardly breathe. I just wish that Cabhan hadn't got involved with the Russos, because then I wouldn't have had to choose between Alfie and helping Alice and Cab, and I wouldn't have lost Alfie. And I know it sounds crazy, but I wish . . . I wish if anybody had to be pregnant it was me, not you. So now you know, happy now? Now you know how I feel.'

Crying as much as Franny was, Bree pulled her into a tight hug, which Franny accepted gratefully as she wept quietly onto Bree's shoulder. 'I'm so sorry, Franny. I'm so sorry. If we get out of here, I promise it'll be okay, somehow I'll make it okay.'

'Nico, it's me, Alice. I'm sorry about before. They caught me calling you. They've been saying things, but I haven't listened to them. I pretended I did, of course, but I don't believe anything they say. Not anymore – *you're* the one I trust.'

With the sun streaming through his tiny cell window, Nico smiled and closed his eyes, feeling the warmth of the sun's rays as he imagined Alice.

'Good, good, because the only people who matter now are you and me. And Alice, did you mean what you said?'

Alice held the phone in her hand tightly and swivelled on her seat, lowering her voice as she spoke. 'When?'

'When you said that you loved me, Alice.'

'Yes, yes, I meant it.'

'Say it, Alice, say it. I want to hear you say it.'

In the quietest of voices, Alice murmured, 'I love you, Nico.'

Nico groaned down the phone, pleasure rushing through his body. 'You really are my special girl. Now not a word to anyone, not to Abel, not to Alfie, and although we've talked about how wrong it is to hold secrets, this is more about protecting what we've got, holding sacred our special bond . . .'

The phone clicked off and Alice sighed, closing her eyes.

'Well?'

Quickly opening them, she stared at Alfie. 'Well, he fell for it, he doesn't suspect a thing.'

Alfie nodded, glancing at Lola and Abel as they stood in one of the dining rooms in the south side of the house. 'I say we get out of here as soon as we can. Now that Nico knows that Alice is staying with Abel, it won't take long for Bobby and Salvatore to find their way here.'

Pacing, Lola shook her head. 'Why don't we just wait for them to come? Cos they think Alice won't say anything, so they won't be expecting any kind of ambush. We can take them by surprise.'

Abel stared coldly at Lola, his eyes void of emotion. He spoke in a deathly whisper.

'This ain't a game. We have no idea how many men they'll bring, what weapons they'll come with, and, unless you know something I don't know, I'm thinking you're not so handy with the old shotgun.'

'I'm not saying I am, but if we continue running, they'll continue searching, and if we do this right, it could be over with,' Lola bit back.

'Not an option.'

Feeling overwhelmed, Lola raised her voice. 'I don't understand, you and Alfie have done stuff like this before without even blinking. It's what you've done most of your life. I ain't asking anything out of the ordinary, but the truth is, I'm scared, and I want this done with. I realise that there are only the two of you, but if we're quick, we can round up some men. Surely we can? Alfie, why ain't you saying anything? Why aren't you agreeing with me?'

'Lola, listen to me. It will never be over whilst Nico is alive. He will keep on hunting, keep on searching until he's got what he wants. He won't stop until he has Alice.' Abel walked round the table to Lola as Alfie, deep in thought, continued to stare out of the streaked and dusty window. 'We have to think clearly, keep our heads, even if it feels like the long way around. We

240

can't go steaming in when there's the safety of Franny and Bree to think of. One call from Nico and they're both dead. Look, we have sixteen days to come up with—'

'What do you mean, sixteen days? Why sixteen?' Alice cut in, as scared as Lola looked.

From the corner of his eye, Abel saw Alfie shake his head, and, taking Alfie's cue, he answered Alice as casually as he could, his tone flat. 'It's just the timescale Alfie and me have put on things. Got to have some sort of deadline, that's the way we've always worked. Back in the day that was. Anyway, I think you and Lola should get ready to go, we don't want to be here when they come. But I have to go and do something. If I'm not back in half an hour, leave and I'll meet you in the village by the old mill.'

Alfie turned on Abel. 'What are you talking about?'

Uncomfortable with having to be in the company of people after spending so long on his own, Abel began to pace agitatedly. 'Like I said, I have to go and do something.'

'And I said, *what*?'

Coldly, Abel stepped towards Alfie, his face curled up into a snarl as he toyed with the knife hidden in his pocket. 'Just drop it, Alf, don't make me angry, understand?'

'Then tell me.'

'It's just something I need to go and do, that's all, it ain't got anything to do with you.'

'Since when? We need to stick together. What is it that can't wait?'

A dark shadow crossed Abel's face, his eyes narrowed. 'Natalia.'

'*What*?'

'I have to make sure Natalia's all right.'

Alfie's face screwed up, puzzled. 'What the hell are you talking about?'

Urgently, Abel hissed his reply, his eyes manic. 'I have to keep her safe. Bobby and Salvatore are on their way, I can't leave her for them to find. Don't you get it, Alf? They're her worst nightmare and I have to hide her somewhere safe, somewhere she won't be scared.'

Thinking Abel couldn't see her, Lola raised her eyebrows, but he caught a glimpse of her expression in the great dining-room mirror. He spun round, his face taut and tense. Snarling and wide-eyed, he pulled out his knife and pointed it at Lola.

'Maybe if you'd loved anyone the way I loved Natalia, then you might understand. Although she might not be with me as she was before, she's still in here . . .' He stopped to bang on his heart and his head. Then, suddenly gazing round the room, he heard Natalia calling him.

'Abel, are you all right, mate? Abel?' Alfie's voice cut through the air, bringing Abel back.

'I'm fine, but I pity her. I pity Lola, that she's never loved like I have, so save your ridicule, all of you. Even in death, my love for Natalia will be a greater love than you will ever experience.'

Abruptly, Abel left the room and, ashamed, Lola spoke, almost to herself. 'I never meant to upset him; I'd better go after him. Me and my big bleedin' mouth, when will I ever learn?'

As Lola hurried after Abel, Alice turned to follow but Alfie called her back. 'Alice, before you go, I want a quick word.'

Alice hesitated. She hadn't spoken to Alfie on his own since she'd run off at the quarry.

'Sit down, Alice, *please.*'

In silence, Alice did as she was told, pulling out one of the large wooden chairs, her mind on her dad as Alfie talked.

'I heard what you said – well, we all did – but I just want to make sure you're all right. I know I can come across as hard-headed, but as Franny and Cabhan ain't here, I feel . . . well, it's my responsibility to make sure you're all right.'

Alice brushed her corkscrew curls back from her face, feeling guilty and stupid and ashamed at herself for all the trouble she'd caused. 'What do you mean, Alfie?'

'That you loved Nico. You told me you loved him,' Alfie said, feeling just as uncomfortable as Alice appeared to be.

Embarrassed, Alice nodded. 'Yes.'

'And do you still love him?' Alfie cleared his throat. 'Because you see, Alice, even though they might've done bad things, I get it that it's not always easy to turn off our feelings for who we love, no matter how hard we try. Sometimes we end up loving people we shouldn't. Loving someone, as much as it can make us feel alive, can destroy us as well, it can be fatal. Look at Abel, darlin', look what love has done to him. I just don't want you to end up hurt.'

'I'm okay,' Alice answered, pushing away her sense of shame.

'Are you sure? Because—'

'I *said*, I'm okay. You don't have to worry, Alfie. I know you've got a lot on your mind and I don't want to add to that.'

Alfie paused, then awkwardly asked, 'Nico, well, did he ask you to send him any pictures . . . you know . . . pictures that you wouldn't want anyone to see apart from someone close, someone intimate?'

Alice stood up, her face crossed with anger. 'No, it wasn't like that! And I know Nico has done all these terrible things, so I'm not defending him, but . . . but at the time it felt special, pure. And I know now that wasn't real, but just for a moment, a tiny moment, I thought someone *actually* understood me – apart from my friend, Isaiah, and he's not in my life now – so Nico seemed like he was the *only* person around who understood me, because you clearly don't. And not having that understanding anymore, well, that's the part that really hurts. That's the part I really miss. But the worst thing is, the worst part of it all, is I know it was me.'

'Know what was you?'

'I know that it was *me* who killed Sister Margaret and all of my friends.'

Alfie looked shocked. 'No, Alice, of course it wasn't, what are you talking about? Why are you saying that, baby?'

Alice's voice soared to a scream, the pain she'd held rushing out of her. 'I was the one who told Nico where I was. Me! It wasn't anything to do with Dad, so no matter how much I try to blame him, and blame you, and everyone else, I can't. *I* killed them, and I don't know how to deal with that, I don't know what to do.'

'Alice—'

'Don't say "Alice" like that! Don't try to make it better, because you can't,' Alice shouted, her words tumbling out in a mixture of anger and hurt. 'You never will do. They're dead. They're all dead. It's like I can see the blood on my hands and I can't wash it off. It feels like it was me who pulled the trigger – I might as well have done! And I understand how Abel feels, I understand how the guilt could make you go mad. But I don't want to go mad, Alfie. I just want to make it better and I can't. If I could swap places with them I would, I'd do anything to make it all go away.'

Alfie reached out to hold her, but she pulled away. 'Please, Alice, I hate to see you like this.'

Pulling herself together, Alice wiped away her tears. 'Don't be nice to me, Alfie, I don't deserve it. Now, if you don't mind, I'm going to go and get ready to leave.'

Alfie watched Alice march out, leaving him in the silence of the cold, stark, vast room. He rubbed his temples, feeling the pressure building up and a sudden sense of loneliness.

Looking out of the window at nothing but the moon, Alfie let out a long, deep sigh before glancing at his phone. Impulsively he picked it up, checking quickly that no one was coming, before pressing redial. He waited for it to ring.

'Hello?'

Alfie didn't recognise the voice, but he replied with hostility. 'I want to speak to Salvatore. Put him on.'

'He's not here.'

'Then you call him, and you tell him it's Alfie. It's Alfie and I

244

want to speak to Franny. I need to speak to her. Tell him I know the deal and then you need to call me back on this number. Tell him I'm waiting.'

Ten minutes passed and Alfie still waited as Lola and Alice sat in the car. He paced the room and was just about to give up when the phone rang. He scrambled to pick it up. 'Hello?'

It was the same voice from before. 'Salvatore says okay. He also says, *Sei pazzo*. You're crazy . . . You've got five minutes . . .'

Then Alfie heard the voice he was desperate to hear. 'Hello? Alfie?'

'Franny, are you all right? Shit, that's a stupid question. What I mean is . . .'

Franny Doyle sat in the darkness of the warehouse, refusing to acknowledge the tears that threatened to fall as she listened to Alfie, her throat sore and her body aching from being huddled in the cage, as well as from the beating she had taken from Bobby. 'It's good to hear your voice.'

'Listen, Franny, I'll get you out of there, you understand me, I'll get you out of there. Somehow.'

Franny's voice was flat, 'Yeah, *somehow*.'

'Franny, please don't give up on me. I love you, I always have, but I haven't always been good at saying it.' He stopped, having to rub his face, feeling like he was trying to scrub away the tension. 'And Bree, how's she?'

'She's here, next to me.'

Alfie, acutely aware that Franny hadn't said Bree was fine, squeezed his eyes shut. 'It's always been you, you know that, Fran.'

'Alfie—'

With his voice breaking, Alfie interrupted. 'No, you got to listen, I want you to hear this; I fucked up. This mess, I let you down.'

'This wasn't to do with you, it was me, me and Cabhan, and

245

that's why . . . that's why I'm okay with the decision you *need* to make. Alfie, it *has* to be Bree.'

Alfie slumped down on one of the chairs, his body shaking with fear, the kind of fear he'd never experienced in his life. 'I can't live without you, Fran. I can't. Look, I'm going to find a way out.'

'Alfie, listen to me, there is *no* way, you know that as well as I do. You know it will soon be the end and there's nothing you can do. You have to try to accept that. If there's anything, *any* last thing you can do for me, that's what it is. Accept this.'

Angrily, Alfie shouted down the phone. 'What's wrong with you, why are you saying this? Why are you giving up like this? You've always been the fucking same – so calm and so controlled. Well, I don't want you to be, because I ain't coping, and the fact is I need you and I want you to show me that I ain't the only one who's falling apart.'

Sitting near a pool of her own urine, as Salvatore had refused to let them go to the bathroom, Franny pushed down her despair. She looked around, speaking in a whisper so as not to wake Bree, who was ill and sleeping fitfully next to her. 'Alfie, I'm being realistic. You know it's the truth and the truth is all I have left.'

Alfie cried out passionately, 'But it ain't all you've got left, cos you've got me, darlin'. You've got me. Always and forever and don't you forget that.'

'I love you, Alfie, I do, and I know you love me too, but even your love won't be strong enough to work this one out.'

'Franny—'

The line went dead.

'Franny! Franny!'

The door suddenly opened and Lola, looking tired and worried, stood in the doorway.

'Alfie, what's going on?'

Wiping away his tears, Alfie kept his back to Lola. 'Nothing.'

246

'Who were you talking to? Was that Franny? Alfie, was that Franny?'

Alfie swivelled round, glared at Lola and stomped past her. 'How the fuck could it be Franny if she's locked up God knows where? So do me a favour, Lola, and just keep your nose out of me friggin' business.'

At the old mill down by the tiny village, Abel climbed into the car, his clothes muddy. He nodded to Alfie, who asked, 'All done?'

'Yeah, Alf, all done. Where are we going?'

In the rear-view mirror, Alfie looked at Lola and then at Alice before quietly saying, 'To Soho. We're going to go to Soho.'

40

'Help me, she's being sick, help me!' Franny yelled as she rattled on the cage. She turned to Bree, who lay on the hard concrete floor, pale and dehydrated, vomiting up green bile as her body went into spasms. 'Somebody help! Come on!'

Stopping shouting for a moment to turn her attention back to Bree, Franny stroked her forehead, feeling how cold and sweaty it was. 'It's okay, Bree. I'm here, it'll be all right.'

Bree's eyes fluttered open to look at Franny, her expression pained as she held her stomach.

'Fran, it hurts, it hurts so badly.'

'I know, honey, just try to keep calm, it won't do you any good if you get stressed, just try to breathe deeply . . . Hello! Help! Hello, we need some help here!' Franny shouted again, shaking the cage harder as she tried to keep her own emotions in check.

The door of the warehouse slid open, allowing bright sunlight to rush in.

Gian Colombo, one of the three men who'd escorted the Russos to England, stood in the doorway, cigar in mouth and gun in hand.

Taking a deep lug of the large cigar, Gian casually sniffed before he spoke. 'What's all the noise for?'

'We need some help, there's something wrong . . . She's pregnant, please, you've got to do something.'

Gian, tall and muscular, strolled towards the cage and stared at Bree convulsing on the floor. 'That's where you're wrong, honey, I don't have to do jack shit,' he said in his thick New Jersey accent.

'She's ill! Can't you see?'

'Not my problem.'

Franny gripped hold of the bars whilst she spoke to Gian, trying to keep her temper under control. 'Don't you understand what I'm saying? She's *pregnant* and she needs help. *Now!*'

Sneering, Gian smashed the butt of his gun onto Franny's fingers. She screamed, reeling backwards in agony, falling on her side as she clutched her hands under her arms to try to stem the pain. Laughing to himself, Gian turned to leave.

'Wait, please, wait. I'm sorry, I'm sorry.' Franny crawled up onto her knees, the skin of her fingers ripped and ragged. 'At least bring her some water, she needs to keep hydrated.'

'Honey, look around you, look where you are. It won't make a damn bit of difference what happens to your friend because your time is running out already, sweetheart.'

As Gian turned his back on Franny, she panicked and shouted after him, 'And what will Salvatore say if you let her get ill? What if something happens to her, how will he play his games then? Are you sure you want to be responsible for letting something happen to her? Think about it, I know Salvatore and I've known him for a long time and he doesn't care if you're his enemy, part of his firm or his closest friend. If you mess up, he'll get rid of you like you're nothing. And you know what I'm saying is true.'

Gian stopped, mulling over Franny's words. He nodded thoughtfully then pulled out his phone and dialled Salvatore as Franny watched intently.

He shrugged. 'No answer.'

Frantically, Franny yelled, 'Then *you* have to do something.

You do something! Otherwise you'll be explaining to Salvatore why you let her become ill.'

Gian glanced at Bree, who moaned in pain quietly. He looked back at Franny then matter-of-factly said, 'Tell me what you need.'

Leaning her head on the bars in relief, her face covered with grime and twisted in pain, Franny whispered, 'Water and something to eat for her. Bring some towels, clothes, anything you have, and if you've got a blanket or something that can keep her warm, bring that as well.'

Without saying another word, Gian nodded, walking out, leaving a trail of cigar smoke in his wake.

With Gian out of sight, Franny, her fingers still throbbing, crawled over to Bree. 'Hey, Bree, help's coming, so hang in there, okay? We'll get you sorted.'

It seemed as if Gian was taking an eternity to come back as Franny watched Bree, her head in Franny's lap, breathing with difficulty and in considerable pain.

Eventually, the warehouse door slid open and Gian, arms full, walked towards the cage.

'Where've you been?'

Gian stared at Franny scornfully. 'Don't push it, baby, because Salvatore or not, I can walk the hell out of here and take these things with me, understand?'

Not wanting to ignite him and risk him carrying out his threat, Franny nodded whilst Gian began to unlock the top of the cage. He stopped suddenly, narrowing his eyes as he looked at Franny. 'Now don't do anything stupid, you hear me?'

'I hear you, but *please* hurry up.'

The cage top unlocked easily and Gian dropped a blanket and some biscuits, along with a couple of items of clothing, inside.

'What about the water? She needs water.'

Gian shrugged begrudgingly. 'Fine, I'll get it.'

He walked out, muttering under his breath as suddenly Franny froze in stark realisation. Gian had left the cage top unlocked. She glanced at the doorway and then back at Bree, and shook her awake.

'Bree, come on! Come on, we've got to go. Bree, please, come on.'

Bree opened her eyes and stared at Franny, her lips dry and dehydrated. 'What?'

'Come on, we haven't got long. It's our chance, but we have to go now!'

With tears in her eyes, Bree nodded whilst Franny tried to pull her up, but the pain in Bree's stomach was overwhelming. She cried out, gripping onto Franny's arm. 'I can't, Franny, it hurts too much. I can't move.'

'Yes, you can, you hear me? Now just take my arm so we can get out of here.'

Attempting a smile, Bree nodded once more but, yet again, as she tried to move, the pain ripped through her. Gasping, she began to cry. 'I can't, I can't do it. But you can. Franny, you need to go.'

Shocked, Franny shook her head. 'No, I can't leave you here, Bree. I just can't. Please just try again.'

'Franny, listen to me You're not going to get another chance. I want you to take it, *go*. There's no point in us both being here. Please do this for me. Think of Alfie. Like I said, he needs you . . . And there's my daughter, Molly, she needs you to look after her, too. Will you do that? Franny, will you do that for me?' Bree leant forward, gritting her teeth as her stomach cramped.

'Yes, but I just can't leave you here, I—'

'Just do it! Do it!'

Franny glanced at the warehouse door again, joining Bree in her tears. 'Bree, I—'

'Do it!'

'But—'

'I'm begging you. *Please*, just go.'

Fear for Bree rushed through her. 'Okay . . . okay, but I'll bring help, I'll go and get help. I promise. I promise.'

Then Franny bent forward and kissed Bree on her head before quickly jumping out of the cage and running from the warehouse into the bright sunlight. She ran along the path, panting and looking over her shoulder, and scrambled up the hill, seeing nothing but countryside.

Running ever faster along the road, Franny crossed over to a grass verge and up to a gravelled track. She glanced around, not knowing where she was and not knowing how far it would be until she could get help. Then quickly checking behind her, she sprinted over to a dense thicket and scrambled through bushes, making sure she was out of sight of anyone coming along the road.

Flinching at a thorn bush scratching mercilessly at her skin, Franny, dripping with sweat, rested against a large oak tree. Sighing, she glanced up at the blue sky, feeling the sunlight and the warm breeze on her face. The warehouse had been dark, cold and wet, the floor hard and grimy. She shivered at the thought of it, absentmindedly rubbing her leg where Bobby had brutally kicked her. But now, thank God, she was out of there; though Bree, of course, wasn't, and she had no doubt that Gian would be incensed, not only at her escape, but also at the impending wrath of Salvatore and Bobby, not to mention Nico.

Knowing the Russos like she did, she wouldn't be surprised if Nico gave orders for Bobby to dispose of Gian permanently, and she for one wouldn't be weeping at his demise. But what did worry her, the ever-nagging fear in the back of her mind, was what Bree would have to go through before Nico gave Bobby the order.

First, Gian would find out she'd gone – he probably had already – and undoubtedly he'd turn on Bree, demanding information, taking his anger out on her. And then what would he do next?

Call Salvatore, who'd insist that Gian hadn't tried hard enough to extract the information and because of that, Gian would probably step up the violence towards Bree, taking his own fear of the Russos out on her with every punch . . . or worse.

She gasped, overwhelmed by her thoughts . . . She had to stop, pull herself together. It was just her guilt, which anyone would feel if they'd left someone behind, and anyway, it was just her imagination, *wasn't it*? She couldn't be certain that Gian *would* hurt Bree, *could she*? Perhaps the Russos were too busy doing something to really bother with her, *maybe*. She shook her head, trying to dispel the doubt. What she needed to do was stop thinking and go and find help before it was too late.

But as Franny set off to run again, no matter how hard she tried to think of Alice, of Alfie, of Lola, of Molly, of her freedom, the only thought that filled her mind was of Bree.

41

Old Compton Street was packed and buzzing with tourists the next day as Alfie, Abel, Lola and Alice slipped unnoticed through a black door and up some stairs, bare and strewn with rubbish, to Alfie's old Soho flat on the top floor, having picked up the keys from an old, trusted acquaintance.

Putting the key in the lock, Alfie spoke to Abel. 'How does it feel to be back, mate?'

Agitated, Abel replied, 'To tell you the truth, Alf, I ain't so comfortable with it. I've been away for a long time, I've been holed up in my house for even longer, and I just hope I can keep it together.'

Alfie gave a quick sideways glance at Lola, wondering if she was thinking the same thing. Since they'd been in the car, Abel had been restless, nervous, and right now he seemed more a liability than anything else. In his time, Abel Gray had been unshakable, the most reliable face around. He'd been at the top of his game, smart and ruthless but loyal to his friends. Wealthy and powerful. Driven. Selling arms and money laundering, no one he knew even came close to his success. But then the mistake Abel had made was going into business with the Russos.

Alfie had never understood why he had. Abel was almost at the point where he could print his own money. Maybe it'd been ambition, wanting to control both sides of the Atlantic, or maybe he'd just been bored, wanting more challenges. But whatever the reason, it was the beginning of the end.

Then the second mistake, maybe the most *fatal* one Abel had made, was falling in love with Natalia. It'd given him a weakness, a chink in his impenetrable armour, and Nico had known it, seen it and used it.

And whatever the truth about the money was, he knew Abel had nothing to do with it and he had a feeling that Nico knew that, too. But Nico liked to play games, dangerous games, that destroyed people no matter what the cost. And it had cost. It had cost Abel his sanity and ultimately Natalia, who had been five months pregnant when they had raped her, only to lose the baby afterwards before she took her own life.

Sighing and not wanting to dwell on such tragedy, Alfie walked into the flat. He looked around: it was clean and bare, small but that's all they needed – a space where they could think. And somehow play the Russos at their own game.

Popping a couple of painkillers into his mouth, his leg aching and throbbing, Alfie sat down on the couch by the window with a clear view of Soho.

Lola, shuffling to put the kettle on in the kitchen, called to Alfie, 'So what's the plan?'

Alfie glanced at Alice. 'Ally, can you do me a favour? Can you make us some coffee? Barry says there's some instant stuff in the cupboards. It'll save Lola having to do it.'

'You mean you don't want me to hear what you've got to say.'

Alfie, in pain and not in the mood, narrowed his gaze. 'Just do as you're told.'

'Fine.' Alice turned and pushed past Lola as she came back into the room. She slammed the kitchen door behind her, and

Alfie, having lost all patience, yelled after her, 'Oi! Oi! Manners, darlin', remember them?'

Kindly, Lola looked at Alfie. 'Sweetheart, she's only a kid, she's done amazing. Think of what she's going through.' She paused to shoot an accusatory glance at Abel as she said, 'What she's been through with certain people. So just leave her alone, Alf, allow her a bit of moody.'

Plonking down next to Alfie, Lola slipped off her shoes, her feet swollen and her varicose veins giving her jip. 'Anyway, like I say, what's the plan?'

Alfie gave her a tight, sad, embittered smile. 'I have no idea. No fucking idea.'

Lola's voice was firm as she drew Alfie's head towards her, his face between her frail hands. 'Alf, listen to me. I can see you're exhausted, but I ain't going to let you get down. We are going to come up with something, we are going to work this out.'

Sounding defeated, Alfie said, 'Like what?'

It was Lola's turn to give Alfie a tight smile. 'I have no idea either, but we can't just give up.'

Abel stared at Alfie and Lola from the other side of the room, his eyes dark and his voice hoarse. 'Nico, that's what you've got to think about. You need to get into his head, think the way he does, that's the key to it. That's the way out. We've got fifteen days now—'

'No, we haven't.'

Both Abel and Lola looked at Alfie, puzzled, but it was Abel who spoke. 'What are you talking about?'

Swallowing hard, Alfie reached up to massage his throbbing temples and, avoiding any eye contact with Abel, said, 'Just that we haven't got that long now, that's all.'

Abel walked across to Alfie and towered above him, his mouth curled in a snarl. 'No, no, no. That ain't all. What are you talking about?'

Rubbing his stubble, Alfie, annoyed and guilty, raged, 'It's my business, all right. My fucking business.'

Abel grabbed Alfie and dragged him up off the couch so they were face-to-face, their noses touching, as he hissed, 'Nico ain't just your business, he's all of our business, you understand me?'

Furious, Alfie shoved Abel off him. 'You're wrong. This has nothing to do with you, because Franny is *my* business. Mine, not yours. You hear?'

'Just tell me what you've done.'

'I ain't done anything, all right. Now leave it.'

Abel's voice filled the flat as he charged at Alfie, pushing him hard into the wall. 'Tell me what you've *fucking* done!'

'I talked to them, okay. I talked to them.'

Abel sneered in confusion. 'Talked to who?'

'To Bree and to Franny.'

'I knew you were talking to her.'

Alfie turned to Lola, thundering out his words. 'Just shut it! Shut your mouth.'

Abel, not understanding, began to pace, the wildness coming back into his eyes, agitation taking over his whole body. 'How? What? I don't get it. You'd better start talking.'

'I made a deal. A deal with Salvatore.'

Abel spun round, his face white with anger. 'What?'

'I needed to talk to them, to see if they were all right, and the only way to do that was to forfeit a day for a conversation. Each conversation cost me a day. I spoke to them at the house and I spoke to them a few times when we stopped on the way here, though two of those times Salvatore wouldn't let me speak to them, but he still forfeited the days.'

The roar from Abel splintered the air. 'How dare you! This was my chance to bring Nico down! It ain't just about you. It's about *me*, it's about Natalia. It's about *my* revenge, my life, my love and you have tried to rob me of that . . . How long are we talking about? How long have we got?'

'Eight days.'

Abel's eyes were wild. 'What! Can't you see what you've done, Alf? Don't you get it? You've ruined everything; you've put them at risk. How are we supposed to do anything now? I hope you don't live to regret this.'

Alfie spat back in fury, matching Abel with his anger. 'No, *you* don't get it! You don't get it because those conversations could be the last ones I ever have with them. And no, I don't fucking regret it, and *no*, I'm not sorry I did it, so get out of my face!'

Abel hissed, 'You stupid, stupid bastard. You're crazy!'

'Says the man who keeps his dead wife in the bedroom!'

Abel flew at Alfie again grabbing him by his throat whilst Lola screamed, hitting Abel on his back as he growled, spitting through gritted teeth, 'Say that again, Alfie, say that again and I will snap your fucking neck right here, right now.'

Alfie's face turned red. He held up his hands in surrender, at which point Abel let him go. Holding his throat, Alfie spluttered, 'Abel, look, it won't do any good us fighting between ourselves. The damage is done now, so we just got to think, put a plan together to come up with the money at least. Get the one million for Nico – that way we keep him sweet or at the very minimum it gives us bargaining power. And I know you said you can't get any money because it's all caught up in a trust along with your house, but there must be something.'

Abel shook his head. 'Not in time for this. What about Vaughn? What about the business you just bought into?'

'Like I told Cabhan, there's no way Vaughn is going to help. He hates the fucking bones of Franny after she pissed off with our money, he's hardly going to come running to bail her out now, is he? And most of the money is wrapped up in the business, which would mean selling it, and, apart from not having the time to load it off, Vaughn would rather put a bullet in me than sign the business away for Franny. As far as he's concerned, when it comes to her, what goes around comes around.'

Lola, full of worry, said, 'So what now? You've just told us all things we *can't* do, but what are the things we *can* do, Alfie? I'm frightened. I'm frightened for Franny and Bree.'

Alfie pulled Lola in towards him and held her tightly. 'I have got an idea. I've got a hundred grand I can get me hands on, I've always kept it tucked away in a safety deposit box in case I ever need to make a quick exit, and I've got this friend. He owes me, runs a yard down in Newmarket. You know, a racing yard.'

Lola pulled away to stare at Alfie in disbelief as it began to dawn on her where he was going with this. Her expression said it all. 'Don't, don't tell me you're going to put your money on a bet to try to get Franny and Bree out. That's it, that's the bleeding plan? Have you lost all sense, Alfie?'

Limping across to the window to lean on the sill, Alfie stared back at Lola. 'It won't be just any bet, do you think I'm stupid?'

'By the sounds of it, yes. Yes, I do, Alf.'

'Well, I'm not, because the day after tomorrow, he's got two horses running. One's the clear favourite, Apache Flash, and the other one, Boo-boy, is a good runner. Not as good as Apache, but he can't beat him unless he gets pulled back in the race.'

Lola shook her head. 'No, Alf, I won't let you do it.'

'Fortunately, you ain't got no choice, darlin'. It's easy, we've done it before, lots of times, and although the racing board has tightened up, it's hard to prove unless you're obvious in pulling up a horse. All the jockey will have to do is look like he's trying, but he'll be able to use his body weight without being detected, maybe stand up a little bit higher in the stirrups to slow him down, use a different bit in the horse's mouth, one that doesn't suit him, so he's throwing his head a bit, which will make him lose pace. Feed him up beforehand, work the back legs off him the day before . . . With a good jockey it's easy, he'll be able to do one or a combination of those things, and Jack owes me a favour. It's going to be a sure-fire bet.'

'There is no such thing as a sure-fire bet, Alfie, otherwise the whole world would be bleedin' millionaires.'

'Look, I'm going to put me money on Boo-boy, get a fixed bet at ten to one, that's what they're offering at the moment. He's going to come in by a half a length, so no one will be any the wiser, that's just horse racing for you, and in the meantime my stake will bring in a million big ones. But I'll break it up, bet it online through a few different bookies, cos some of them have an upper stake limit. And I don't want to go into a bookmakers cos me face is too well known, I need to keep it discreet. I've already got a few accounts with the big bookies, so it'll not be a problem.'

There was silence before Abel began to clap, slowly and mockingly. 'Lola's right, this ain't a plan, this is a joke, Alfie. You gamble away the days and then you want to play a mug's game. There ain't no winners in racing apart from the bookies, and that's why you and Vaughn bought the business, cos it's a licence to print money. Yet here you still are, thinking it's going to save Franny.'

Under pressure, Alfie snapped. 'Then give me something better cos I'm all ears.'

'You fucked up, Alfie, you fucked up big time.'

Alfie roared as he hit his chest. 'I know! I know! You don't have to tell me that. I *fucking* know, but what am I supposed to do? It feels like it's hopeless, because let's face it, let's be honest here, even if I can pull this off, even if we do get the money, it's not going to work, because it's not really about the money, that's just part of his game. We both know unless I give Nico the money *and* Alice, it's all over anyway. Franny and Bree are both going to die. So there won't even be a choice to make. It's Alice he wants. It's not the money that will keep them alive, it's Alice. Without Alice they're dead.'

'Is that true?'

The room fell silent as the three of them turned to look at Alice, who stood in the kitchen doorway holding a tray with mugs full of steaming coffee.

Alfie, having forgotten Alice was even in the flat, spoke quietly. 'Alice, baby, listen to me—'

'I said, is it true?'

Lola stepped forward with tears in her eyes and nodded. 'Yes, Alice, I'm afraid it's true.'

42

'Where is she, where the fuck is she?' Gian Colombo slammed Bree like a rag doll against the wall, causing Bree's head to flip back and smash into the concrete, leaving a trail of blood on the wall as she slid down against it.

'I don't know! I swear I don't know.'

Gian bent over, pulling Bree up. He shook her. The pain in her body was excruciating. 'Stop playing games with me, you hear me? Just tell me where she's gone!'

'I can't tell you something I don't know. *Please.*'

Anger and panic rushed through Gian as he snarled, 'Then if you won't tell me the easy way, let's make it the hard way. Maybe then you'll start talking.'

From his back pocket, Gian Colombo pulled out a large jagged knife and laid it on Bree's cheek. 'Tell me where she went.'

Shaking with fear, Bree felt the cold, sharp steel on her skin. 'I'm not lying, I don't know.'

Bellowing, Gian's grip hardened. 'I'll give you one more chance and then I'm going to start cutting. Where is she? *Where's Franny?*'

'I'm here.'

Gian and Bree turned around to see Franny standing in the

door of the warehouse. She walked towards them, empty-handed, speaking firmly as Gian dropped Bree.

'Put the knife down, Gian.'

Gian stared in contempt and laughed coldly as he twirled the knife in his hand. 'You're giving me orders? You're in no position to give me anything.'

'That's where you're wrong, Gian. Let me ask you this, what did Salvatore say when you told him you'd let me escape?'

The look on Gian's face told Franny everything she needed to know. 'You haven't told him, have you? Why not, Gian? Afraid? Worried that something might happen to you if you did? Don't forget I know the Russos and I know what they do to people who betray them, break their trust. So, if I were you, I'd just be happy that I came back, because if you're not careful, I'll tell Salvatore and Bobby how I went on a little jaunt because *you* screwed up.'

Snorting in fury, Gian continued to stare. He glanced down at Bree, who was crumpled up on the floor holding her stomach, before he slowly lifted his gaze back to Franny. He waved the knife. 'Get over there and help her up. Both of you get back in the cage.'

Franny rushed over to Bree and held up her head in her arms. 'Hey, Bree, look who's back.'

Grateful beyond words, Bree, overwhelmed and still in pain, gave Franny a small smile, her voice weak as she whispered, 'You came back. You came back for me.'

'Yes, Bree, I did. Of course I did. There was no way I could leave you here on your own.' Franny paused, attempting a smile herself as she tried to make the unbearable moment slightly more bearable. 'And besides, to tell you the truth, the thought of Alfie's moaning and his pig-headed ways, well, it had me thinking – I'd rather be here with you. And if somehow there's a miracle and we do manage to get out of here, I want you to know, no matter what happens, I'll always be here. For you and the baby.'

And as the two women laughed through their desperate tears, holding each other tightly, Franny knew in her heart that although it really seemed like this would be the end for them both, she would never have any regrets about coming back to be with Bree.

Nico Russo paced his cell as he spoke on the phone to Salvatore, who was driving along a country lane back towards the warehouse, with Bobby asleep in the back seat.

'What do you expect me to say, Sal?'

'I'm sorry, Nico, when we got to Abel's she was gone, they all were, but you knew that might be the case. They're going to keep on running until they've got nowhere else to run. We hadn't wasted any time though – the moment you told us where she was we headed down there. Alfie obviously found out somehow. *Senza mancare di rispetto*, Nico, no disrespect, but are you sure you can trust this girl? After all, Alice Rose is not family, her loyalties aren't with you.'

Irritated, Nico chewed on the inside of his cheek. He stared at the photo of Alice on his wall. 'Do you think I don't know what I'm doing? Do you think that I've managed to run our family business for years and not know when I've got some sweet little bitch eating out of my hand?'

'No, but I just think—'

Nico roared, banging his fist into the wall, 'Understand this, Sal, whilst you're talking to me, I don't *want* you to think, I just want you to listen. You got that?'

'*Sì.*'

'Good. Now I want you to get Alice Rose for me, whatever it takes, but it's important we get the money from Alfie; we need to make the most of this. So maybe step up the pressure, so he knows we're not joking. Business could be better than it is at the moment, another reason why you need to get me out of here. Which reminds me, any word on the appeal?'

'I've spoken to our lawyer about it and—'

Nico interrupted as he lay back on his bed. 'I don't want conversations, that's all it ever is. Conversations. I want action. Those bloodsuckers are costing me a fortune, for what? I don't want to be in the slammer in another six months' time. *Mi capisci*?'

'Nico, I hear you, my heart goes out to you. Bobby and I appreciate everything you do and the sacrifice you've made for us.'

'So if that's how you feel, do something,' Nico snapped. 'This motherfucking place is beginning to creep up on me now. What's happening with my transfer?'

'Sal, it's not bad news. The attorney came up with some good points to appeal on overall and as for transferring you to a lower-category prison, it looks like that could be a real possibility. At the end of the day, Nico, the authorities should never have placed you in a maximum-security prison for tax evasion, and they know that. So, hopefully, the transfer could be any day now. I can send you the main legal and appeal points the attorney made if you like. It's quite extensive, so you'll need to read it. There are a lot of things to think about, but it's pretty positive. You want me to email them to Officer Johnstone, so you can have a look at them?'

'No, just send them to my phone.'

Salvatore paused a moment. 'You know your phone's not as secure as sending it to Officer Johnstone.'

'What's wrong with you, you think I'm fucking stupid? I know that, but I don't want anyone fucking this up for me. I don't trust Johnstone, he does what he's told here, but I wouldn't put it past him to tip off the parole board about what we're thinking.'

Parked up, Salvatore watched Gian Colombo eat a large salami sandwich at the entrance to the warehouse.

'You want me to arrange someone to go and pay Johnstone a visit? Remind him of his obligations?'

'No, leave it. Let's just concentrate on getting me out of here first, but in the meantime . . .' Nico stopped to smile. 'I'll give Alice a call, check in how she's doing, see if she's having fun. After all, she really needs to start making the most out of life, because it can be snatched away, just like that . . .'

43

It was early morning the next day and the last trace of mist was beginning to disappear as Alfie drove towards the town of Newmarket, sixty miles short of London. White wooden fences lined the roads and stud farm after stud farm with vast green grass paddocks came into sight. The roads were mainly clear of traffic, instead filled with racehorses, thoroughbreds, ambling along with their jockeys towards the training grounds and gallops.

Driving extra carefully, Alfie headed across a roundabout on which was a gigantic statue of a rearing horse and its groom by its side. He sighed, trying to put Lola's words out of his head, but he also knew desperate men did desperate things and, although he hadn't admitted it to Abel or even Alice, he knew this was certainly desperate. But what other choice did he have? It was a gamble both literally and metaphorically, because Nico was playing a game, a game of roulette with Franny and Bree's lives. So every decision he made had to be the right one, because the stakes were too high, and it felt like with one wrong roll of the dice he'd lose it all.

He gave a sharp intake of breath, not wanting to process his own thoughts, and instead tried to concentrate on where he was.

In the distance, he could see the grandstand of one of Newmarket's racetracks, Rowley Mile, rise up from the valley. He passed Tattersalls, the oldest bloodstock auctioneers in the world, then horse hospitals, veterinarians, farriers and saddle makers until he arrived at the long grass slopes of the training ground, Warren Hill, just off the Clock Tower and along the Moulton Road.

Alfie parked his car, wearily got out and made his way towards the straight uphill grades to the north of Newmarket.

Usually when he stood by the gallop rails watching a string of horses thundering past, ridden by the jockeys wearing the same jackets and matching helmet covers from one of the various yards, he'd get a thrill, feel the adrenalin rush and tingle through his body. But all he felt now was a desperation, a despondency, a sense of ever-impending doom.

Triggered to light a cigarette, he gazed at a sinewy, grizzled jockey sat smoking on his horse, no doubt trying to stamp down his appetite. As Alfie let his gaze roam, he caught sight of Jack Connell, an old friend, renowned horse trainer and owner, whom he'd known from the old days when Jack had wheeled and dealed with the best of them, earning his money from strip clubs and hookers.

Waiting for Jack to approach him, Alfie watched with interest as Jack's team of riders prepared themselves, shortening their leathers whilst trying to calm the excited sharpness of the athletic, charged-up young thoroughbreds.

By the time Jack had caught up with Alfie, the horses had set off, turning into turbo machines like Formula One cars. Side by side, they raced past Alfie, looking on top form as they rode in the crisp morning with the rising sun, racing up the mile and a quarter of the legendary Warren Hill gallops.

'Here, have a butcher's through this.'

As Alfie felt the ground rumble and shake, he took the binoculars from Jack, listening to him talk.

'The black one's Boo-boy, and the tall dapple, that's Apache Flash. Going to earn me a fucking fortune. Didn't pay more than ten grand for each of them, but they're turning out to be something of a touch. I had some Arab geezer from one of the yards down the road wanting me to sell him Apache, offered me hundred grand for him, well, you can imagine where I told him he could stick it. Anyway, Alf, I got your message, sounds ominous. By the way, you ain't looking so cushty.'

With the jockeys gathering at the ridge before walking back down again for another ride round, Alfie said, 'I'll get straight to the point, Jack. I need you to throw a race.'

Jack Connell laughed. His large red nose was scribbled with purple veins. 'I would say you're having a chuckle, but I know you, Alf, you're being serious, ain't you?'

'Is that a question or a statement?'

Jack – a man who was partial to too many whiskeys – dressed in riding boots, jeans and a pink Ralph Lauren shirt, shrugged at Alfie, his overweight body straining through his clothes. He looked around before poking Alfie hard in his chest.

'Whatever the fuck it is, the answer is *no*. Don't come here and start talking that shit, you understand, Alf? Those days are over. Now, if that's everything, why don't you just get in your car and fuck off back to London.'

Alfie wiped his shirt where Jack had prodded him. He sniffed with irritation, looking up to the gallops before trusting himself to turn back to Jack.

'I'll let you have that one, mate, but if you ever put your fat fucking fingers on me again, I'm going to knock you right out and you'll be over the finishing line before starter's orders. Now, here's what you're going to do for me. Tomorrow, you're going to get your best jockey to ride Apache, and then you're going to get your second-best jockey to ride Boo-boy, cos there ain't any room for fuck-ups. Boo-boy is going to win, not by much but just enough so the punters and the racing board don't suspect a thing. I've studied the form and there aren't any other horses that will come close to beating those two. So it won't be a problem, will it? It'll be like old times.'

Jack Connell, furious, leant forward as he puffed the smoke from his cigar right into Alfie's face and spoke in a low, dangerous tone. 'Let me tell you something. I'm offended, really *offended* that you think you can come here and give it large. Who the fuck do you think you are, Alf?'

'I'm someone you came to when you wanted a bit of the old nose powder to give your jockeys, so they could keep the weight down. And we're not talking just the once, are we? I don't think the board would take too kindly to one of their licensed trainers dealing coke to their jockeys, *especially* as it seems to be a pre-requisite for them.'

'Turn it in, Alf, you don't know what you're talking about.'

'Don't I? Come on, Jack, what's the alternative for them? You have influence, and everyone around here knows that all it takes are a few words from you and no one will employ them, then bang goes their dream of becoming a jockey. So, you tell me which young lad with ambition, who's also struggling with their weight and those hunger pangs that keep them awake at night, is going to turn down your offer? It's perfect for you though, ain't it? You get them lads wired and they're up for anything. They become fearless, taking risks on the training grounds, not stopping when they're tired, pushing the horses to the limit. But when those kids are burned out, hooked on the gear, what do you do then, hey, Jack? You just ship them back to Ireland and wait for the next bunch of poor fuckers to come across.'

'Fuck you, Alf! You need to be *really* careful who you go around accusing of dealing.'

Alf laughed scornfully, his eyes dark with anger. 'I hope that wasn't a threat, Jack. Let's face it, deal, give, provide, offer, coerce, they're all fucking words, semantics, mate. Cos you know as well as I do, when you're banged up, it will all boil down to the same.'

Stubbing his cigar out on the gallop rails, Jack glared at Alfie. 'I never put you down as a grass.'

'Needs must, mate, needs must. So, do we have an agreement?'

Waving over to his jockeys, Jack turned his back on Alfie and started to walk away. 'You've already had my answer, but if you want it again, like I told you in the beginning, just get in your car and fuck off back to London . . . I'll see you around.'

It was dark when Jack Connell, tired from the day, walked into his kitchen. Without needing to put the light on, he moved across to the cupboard, knowing exactly where to find the large, expensive bottle of whiskey.

Relishing the moment, he unscrewed the top and, not bothering to reach up to the shelf for a glass, took a large swig, feeling the burn of the drink hitting his mouth before it coated his throat with the citrus, peaty taste.

'You going to pour me one of those?'

Alfie Jennings switched on the light, smiling as Jack looked like he was going to have a heart attack. He clutched his chest, drained of colour as he leant against the dark oak cupboards.

'Fuck me, Alf, you looking to kill me?'

'Might be, that all depends.'

Regaining his composure, Jack snarled back, 'Get out of my house.'

Walking over to the middle of the kitchen, Alfie smirked nastily. 'But you said, *I'll see you around*, and here I am.'

Sweat prickled at Jack's forehead. 'Get out! I already told you that the answer's *no*.'

Taking a small handgun out of his pocket, Alfie placed it on the table and spun it round.

'You see, Jack, I thought that's what you might say, and consequently, I also thought I'd bring a bit of encouragement along.'

Finally, reaching for a tumbler, Jack, his hand shaking, poured himself a large glass of whiskey. 'Do you know what you're even asking of me? Do you know how much money I'll fucking lose? I've put me money on Apache and there's no way I'm losing it.'

Not interested, Alfie shook his head. 'Let me tell you something, Jack: you won't lose as much as me.'

Glancing down at the gun before fixing his gaze back on Alfie, Jack sat down, taking another noisy gulp, his voice strained.

'I don't know what's going on here, Alf, and to tell you the truth, I don't want to know, but what you're suggesting is *totally* out of the question. You've got this idea that apart from my two, the rest are donkeys. But that's not right – I could name at least four other runners who will give Boo-boy a run for his money. It's going to be a tight race.'

'Then you need to get your jockey to try harder, don't you? The fact is, Jack, on my side of the fence there isn't any room for messing up. I need Boo-boy to win, that's all there is to it. It's as simple as that.'

Jack Connell sat in silence for a moment using his finger to slosh around the whiskey.

'And if I still refuse, what then?'

Alfie leapt across the table, grabbing and pushing Jack's head down onto it. The glass smashed on the floor. He pressed the gun hard into Jack's temple, digging the nozzle into his skin.

'But you ain't going to refuse, are you? Because I'm going to do whatever it takes for you to see what's good for you. Because at the end of the day, Jack, if I can't sort this out, then I *really*, *really* ain't got nothing to lose, so I'll be more than happy to blow out your brains.'

44

The next day, Alfie Jennings sat by the window in the Soho flat smoking his fifth cigarette in half an hour. He tried to ignore the hostile, and what he saw as unhelpful, glares from Lola, who sat nervously opposite him on the large blue wing chair in the corner of the room.

Fed up with it, Alfie snapped, 'Do you have to keep staring at me, Lola? It makes me feel uncomfortable. I know how you feel about all this but it ain't helping. So do me a favour, darlin', and cut the eyeballing.'

Lola sniffed disapprovingly. 'Rather stare at you than speak to you. I ain't got any words to sum up what you've done.'

'Well, thank fuck for that, because that will save us all having to listen to you chewing off me ear.'

As Lola decided whether she was going to give any kind of comeback, Alice walked into the room carrying a glass of iced water. She smiled, but it was a distant smile; her mind had been on the ultimatum Nico had given Alfie.

Nico had called her twice, but she hadn't been able to answer, largely because she wasn't sure if she could actually hide her feelings from him.

Alfie had asked her again if she still loved Nico. Not only did she no longer love him, but she felt something new to her, something that she'd never experienced in her life. Hatred. Pure hatred.

She knew that hating someone was wrong. Her mother often told her and her friend, Isaiah, that hatred was not only a sin, but also one of the *gravest* sins, and she'd always tried to steer away from ever feeling such an emotion, even when someone had really upset her. But for once she didn't care. She didn't care at all.

Maybe it was because Nico had hurt her and like a silly little girl she had fallen for everything he had said. Maybe that was why the burning hatred smouldered and lived within her now, but whatever it was, if that meant she was a sinner, so be it, because like Abel she wanted to get her revenge, and she would, no matter what it took. Nico Russo would pay.

'Are you going to give me that or are you going to water the plants with it? I'm gasping, darlin'!' Lola broke through into Alice's thoughts, waving her hand for the glass Alice held.

'Sorry Lola, I . . . My mind was elsewhere.'

Lola nodded in understanding, her heart going out to the girl. 'You don't need to explain. I know, sweetheart, it's difficult for us all. Look, why don't you come and sit down with me? The race is about to start – maybe you'll be our lucky mascot because, believe me, we need all the luck we can get.' Lola tried to hold the smile, but at the thought of what Alfie had done with the little money they had made, it quickly faded, her expression turning pensive.

Trying not to upset Alice, Lola made another effort, trying her best to sound cheerful.

'Anyway, love, have you heard any more about your dad? Alfie said he was going to call the hospital.'

'He did, and Dad's still the same.'

'That's good though, isn't it? He's in the right place and he's stable.'

Alice felt the guilt and the worry rise up in her again as she fought back the tears. 'He's in intensive care, Lola!'

'I know, love, but it's just a precaution, they know what they're doing.'

'I just miss him.'

Lola nodded. 'I know you do, I know . . . Look, why don't we call the hospital later, maybe they'll have some more news?'

Alice tried to smile. 'I'd like that.'

Wanting to change the subject, Lola asked, 'Where's Abel, by the way?'

'He's asleep. He told me he never really sleeps at night so—'

'Here, look, it's about to begin.' Alfie cut into their conversation as he turned up the sound on the television, logging into his betting accounts on the iPad his friend had lent him whilst trying to ignore the sense of sickness and panic rushing over him.

'*A number of horses have halved in price as punters look to land a big-priced winner. Apache Flash is still favourite, Harlequin Rose who was 60–1 is now at 15–1, Boo-boy on good form is now . .*'

'Which ones are they, Alf?' As Lola asked the question she glanced at Alfie, seeing the fear and worry in his face, which only made her own anxiety worse.

'Jack Connell's colours are red and pink spots for Apache and blue diamond stripes for Boo-boy. There they are.'

With the sun shining through the window, Alfie pointed at the television. Ignoring it, Lola got up and shuffled across to where Alfie was, popping herself down next to him on the couch. She took his hand into her lap, shaking as she spoke.

'Alfie, are you sure about this? I just don't think it's a good idea.'

'Whether I am or whether I'm not, it's a bit late now, so ease off on the pressure, okay?'

'Alfie, lovie, listen to me.'

'I said, ease off!'

'Just two minutes until the starter's orders and then it's one mile and four furlongs to the finishing line. And they're in the starting gates for today's final race. Apache Flash not looking too keen to get in, they're having to call the stewards . . .'

'That ain't a great start, Alf.'

'Lola, just stop, it'll be fine . . . It has to be.'

'Here we go then – and they're off. Harlequin Rose is making the early pace before Big Man takes it on. Apache Flash is joined by Big Man and Harlequin Rose as Boo-boy, ridden by Tony McKay, is starting to make its bid now . . .'

'Alfie, listen to me, I'm worried about you. You've put everything, including your hope, on this race and if it doesn't—'

'Just stop talking, Lola. What is he doing? No, no, no, what the fuck are you doing? Come on! Come on!' Alfie stared at the screen as Boo-boy fell back. 'Come on, push him on, push him on, you cunt!'

'Apache is in the lead now with Big Man making up ground and Sunny Morning looking in good shape coming up from the inside. Rising Castle is now in the lead with Hello Soldier travelling well, but there's a huge amount of ground to make up, so too with BallyCry as Irish Rapper's jockey pulls him up . . .'

'He's not even making ground! Boo-boy ain't even making ground!' Alfie grabbed his phone and pressed speed dial to call Jack Connell. It went straight to voicemail, but as Alfie kept his eyes on the television, he snarled a message: 'I'm coming after you, Jack. Mark my words, I'm coming after you if you fuck this up for me.'

He threw the phone to the side and grabbed his iPad, trying to get into his betting accounts as Abel, disturbed by the noise, walked into the sitting room.

'What's all the racket for?'

Ignoring him, Alfie continued to log into his accounts. 'I've got to stop this! I've got to stop the money. I've got to get it back.

I'm going to lose all the fucking money! I can't lose it! I can't lose it!'

Crying, Lola shook Alfie's arm. 'You can't get it back, Alfie. It's too late, you know that. Oh my Christ!'

Alice, as worried as Lola, spoke quickly to Alfie. 'Not necessarily. If you know what you're doing, you can go through the back door.'

Unable to process what Alice was saying, Alfie shook his head, irritated, as he continued to stare at the screen. 'What? What are you talking about?'

Rushing her words and remembering what she'd learnt, Alice spoke passionately. 'I'm talking about the point of entry that circumvents normal security measures, which means you can get into their system, but if you—'

Alfie cut Alice short. 'Not now, Alice! Not now! For fuck's sake stop rabbiting nonsense, can't you see what's happening?'

With her brown skin turning red, Alice stood in front of Alfie. 'I'm only trying to help you, because I know if—'

'*I said not now!*' Alfie's voice roared, filling the room with anger and tension as he threw the iPad against the wall.

Lola tapped Alfie on his arm. 'Look, the race ain't over, there's still a chance.'

'*. . . Harlequin and BallyCry are in good shape, but Rising Castle is still the leader. But Apache is coming up from the outside. Apache's pushing forward and Sunny Morning is trying to catch him. Boo-boy's dropping further back but Apache's still going strong making the turn for the back stretch, moving just outside the leading three. But Boo-boy's coming back, giving them chase and off the bend . . .*'

'That's it! That's it! Come on, come on! Come on, my son! Come on, Boo-boy!'

'I told you, Alf, I told you it'd be fine. I told you . . .' Lola suddenly trailed off as she stared in dismay at the television.

'*. . . But Boo-Boy drops behind again as he makes the turn* *along the back straight and that leaves Sunny Morning giving chase and they're coming down to the final bend. Apache leads them towards it. He's looking strong a couple of lengths in front followed by Miners-strike now in second place. He's made ground from the back, but has he left it too late to catch Apache Flash who's . . .'*

'Look at that, look at the fucking horse, it's winning, it's fucking winning! What the fuck is he doing?' Alfie grabbed the phone again and this time he got through.

'Jack, what the fuck! What the fuck is your jockey doing?'

On the other end of the line, Jack Connell watched the monitor. 'He can't do anything else, Alf. Boo-boy's lost ground. If my jockey were to pull Apache up now everyone would know that's what he was doing. Apache's bloody strong, he's fresh, and there's no way he can pull him back now, not unless—'

'Shut up! Shut up! I told you! I warned you! I fucking told you that you were supposed to sort it!'

'And I told you what could happen. These are horses, Alf, not fucking machines!'

The line went dead as Alfie stared in shock, holding his head in his hands as, mesmerised, he watched Apache Flash thunder home towards the finishing ground.

'*. . . And Harlequin Rose is being chased by Boo-boy, but Apache wins comfortably and look at that smile from his rider, Rod James. Jack Connell should be pleased with that performance, though the look on his face doesn't say that . . .'*

Alfie turned to Lola, who stood looking at him pityingly. Traumatised, he spoke in a whisper. 'The money. The money.'

With tears in her eyes, Lola stretched out her hand. 'Alfie, the money's gone! You've lost it! It's over. Face it, it's over.'

Filled with guilt, Alfie suddenly surged with anger. 'And aren't you pleased? Now you can say, *I told you so*. Go on, let's hear it. Rub it in.'

'Alf, I'm not going to say that, am I?'

'Aren't you?' Alfie sneered, feeling the weight of pressure on his chest.

'No, I'm not, and okay, I thought there were better ways to go about it, but—'

Alfie, red-faced, pointed at Lola, visibly shaking as he raged. 'Shut up! Shut up! Don't say it. Don't say a word, you hear me? Just don't say a fucking word. I know, all right, I get it. I get what I've done. But I tried. I know you think I didn't, but I did. I just didn't know what else I could've done. What other way was there? And now look what I've done, I've single-handedly killed Franny and Bree, haven't I? I've basically handed them on a plate to Nico.'

'Alfie, no! Don't you think that, you hear me? Don't you dare! I know you tried, lovie, no one can fault you for that.' Lola grabbed hold of Alfie's arm, but he threw it off and stormed out of the lounge with Lola hobbling out after him.

Abel walked across to the window in silence. Eventually, he turned to Alice, his mind clouded in thought. He studied her face, looking deeply into her large almond eyes. 'What were you saying then to Alfie?'

Uncomfortable under Abel's intensity, Alice shifted from one foot to the other. 'What do you mean?'

'You were telling him that all wasn't lost, that if he went in through . . . through . . .'

'The back door?'

Abel nodded, his face the colour of snow, his cheeks hollow and gaunt. He spoke softly. 'That's it. What did you mean by that?'

'It's just that if you know what you're doing, he could've pulled back his bet, but it was probably too late, and he didn't have the right stuff anyway.'

'But if he did, what you're saying is he could've done that or something similar?'

Abel walked up to Alice, listening attentively to her reply as if she were speaking in a whisper.

'Well, yes, maybe. Not every site is easy to get into but . . .' She stopped, glancing from under her curly fringe, worried she'd said too much.

Abel stared at her again. The minutes ticked by until he eventually said, 'Alice, can I ask you a question?'

'Yes, of course.'

'How do you feel about Nico now? You can tell me. I know you think you can't but you can.'

Without a moment's hesitation, Alice said with venom, 'I hate him. I want to destroy him, Abel.'

At the corners of Abel's mouth, Alice thought she saw something resembling a small smile. He nodded his head in approval. 'Good, good, I'm glad. Maybe we have more in common than I thought . . . And, Alice, this stuff you're talking about, do *you* know how to do it?'

Alice shook her head. 'No, not really, not me. I just know that you can do it – well, some people can.'

It was like a light had dropped away from Abel's eyes and he turned away without saying anything else. He opened the door to leave, but he stopped as he heard Alice say, 'But my friend can. My friend, Isaiah Thomas, can.'

45

'Hello, darlin', fancy going for a drink? Oh, come on; don't be like that. Where are you going? Come back!' An old, scruffily dressed man, leaning on the door of one of the numerous strip clubs in the heart of Soho, cackled as he wolf-whistled and called after Alice.

Ignoring him, she hurried along the small alleyway of Walkers Court, full of sex shops and peep shows, a world away from the life she was used to.

'Oi! I'm talking to you. Think you're too good for me, do you? Stuck-up little cow!'

Hearing the man call after her again and starting to feel panicked, Alice began to run, the noise and the smells of the red-light district alien to her. Not looking where she was going, Alice banged into a group of tourists, sending her stumbling into a doorway, where she tripped and fell into the sticky, rubbish-strewn entrance hall underneath an arrow and a sign reading: *Big, busty model and massage this way.*

'Move out of the fuckin' way, love. Find a park bench some-where.' As Alice fought back her tears, a large, balding man shoved her out of the way with his foot and went up the stairs.

At the same time another man, doing up the zip of his stained trousers, came down, leering at Alice, making her feel uncomfortable.

Shivering, Alice quickly stood up and walked back out of the doorway and along another street, which was lit up by neon shop fronts complete with large blue signs advertising Viagra. Puzzled, and not knowing what it was – though she'd seen the posters everywhere – Alice wrapped her jacket round her tightly, trying to keep her head down as admiring glances turned to leering stares and the catcalls, so unfamiliar to her, created a deep unease.

A group of platinum blonde Thai girls dressed in tiny miniskirts smoked cigarettes as they stood outside a massage shop, their faces drained, mascara smudged, heavy make-up disguising their youth as they stared at Alice with hostility.

Alice's heart pounded and she began to wish she hadn't ventured out of the flat, but she was worried about Alfie, who hadn't come back after he'd stormed out.

Lola hadn't been feeling well, and Abel had refused to open his door, so that had left only her to come and find him. Not that she had any idea where he might be; she didn't even know where to begin. But she had to at least try; to make sure he was all right, to make up for all the mistakes she had made. And even if making amends began with searching every single bar and strip club in the area, then that's what she'd do. Somehow, she'd find Alfie.

Alfie Jennings sat like it was old times in Frankie Taylor's Soho club watching the strippers trying to entice the punters to part with their money. However, as drunk as he was, no amount of alcohol could make him forget that it was far from old times. Everything was so well and truly fucked up.

There was no turning back. No second chances. No choices, no decisions about which woman he was supposed to choose, because with one stupid, desperate measure he had basically signed Franny and Bree's death warrant. And what a death it would be. Slow and torturous, an agonising, brutalised end, everything that the Russos enjoyed.

Alfie squeezed his eyes shut at the images in his head before knocking back the whiskey and signalling for the bartender to fill him up again. 'Another drink, mate, but make it a double.'

The bartender, tall and slender, Turkish in origin, nodded his head as he stood behind the gold-and-red bar, pouring a drink for Alfie. 'That will be ten pounds, please, sir.'

Drunk and with his vision blurred, Alfie rummaged in his pocket for money as the bartender stared at him, cold and impatient, tapping his fingers on the bar as the strippers spun and gyrated around the pole in the background.

Having to hold onto the chair to stop himself falling over as he stood up, Alfie swayed on his feet. His words slurred as he patted himself down. 'I don't have enough; in fact, I don't have fuck all.'

Irritated, the bartender wiped up the sticky residue of a spilt drink on the gold-coloured till. 'Then next time don't order the drink if you haven't got the money. If you could leave the bar now, sir, I'd appreciate it.'

It was like a red rag to Alfie, the excuse he'd been looking for. He raised his voice, swaying precariously. 'Who the fuck do you think you're talking to, you cunt? Don't you know who I am? I'm Alfie Jennings. *The* Alfie Jennings. You understand? Ask anyone about me. They'll know who I am and they'll tell you that's the geezer who can sort *anything* out. *Anything.* That's me, that's who I am, the guy who's supposed to be able to sort out anything.'

'Sir, if you can kindly leave.'

Alfie banged his chest, seeing the barman in double vision. 'Didn't you hear what I just said? If anyone's leaving it's going to be you when I pick you up from your arse and throw you fucking out of here.'

'Sir, I'll have to get security.'

Smashing his fist down on the bar, Alfie shouted even louder. 'Come on then. Come on. Fuck security and fuck you. My friend owns this bar, so you'd better watch your mouth unless you want to be out of a job.'

'Well, he's not here now, is he?'

'So call him, tell him it's Alfie-fucking-Jennings.'

Then with petulant defiance, Alfie grabbed the whiskey glass, knocking it back in one.

Fuming and long weary of difficult punters, the barman leant towards Alfie. 'That'll be ten pounds, sir. Unless you want me to call the police.'

'The Old Bill? You're having a bubble, ain't you? I told you, I ain't got no money, fuck knows where it's gone. If you don't believe me, check in my pocket. I dare you. No? I thought not, you pussy.'

He turned to leave but immediately felt a strong hand grip his arm. An over-built bouncer stood towering over Alfie. 'You heard what the barman said, *ten pounds.*'

With his temper charged up to the max, Alfie snarled drunkenly, 'Get your hands off me.'

'*Ten pounds,*' the bouncer repeated.

'Oh, it's going to be like that, is it, mate? Fine by me!' Alfie lunged forward, grabbing and breaking one of the empty beer bottles sitting on the bar.

'Alfie, no! Don't! Please don't!'

He stopped dead in his tracks, hearing his name but unable to fully focus on where it was coming from.

'Alfie, *please*, let's just go.' Alice Rose, relieved at finding Alfie as much as she was relieved to not have to scour any more of the Soho bars, came to his side.

A wide, drunken smile spread across Alfie's face. 'Alice, what you doing in here, darlin'? You should be tucked up in bed, not in this poxy fucking place with this bunch of muppets.'

Ignoring the harsh glares that the bouncer was giving her, Alice put Alfie's arm over her shoulder, trying to support him. 'Come on, let's get you home.'

The bouncer stood in front of Alice and Alfie. 'Not until he pays, darlin', you ain't taking him anywhere.'

Not having any money herself, Alice went through Alfie's trouser pockets thoroughly before trying his jacket ones. Eventually she pulled out a ten-pound note, which Alfie snatched and waved around in the air triumphantly.

He pointed at the bouncer. 'See, you cunt, I told you that I had the money, didn't I? Now put it where the sun don't shine.'

Alice, giving an apologetic smile, began to lead Alfie out of the club, but as they headed for the exit, Alfie swaying, Alice stopped, hearing the barman calling after them.

'Sir, this must've dropped out of your pocket . . . Sir!'

Alfie, only just able to focus on the barman, spoke to Alice. 'Here, Ally, what is it? I'm fucked, I can't see straight, darlin'.'

Alice frowned as she took the photo.

'What is it? Alice, what is it?'

'It's Franny. It's just a photo of Franny.'

Alice pushed the photo into Alfie's hand, who stared at it, his drunken state causing even more confusion, his voice desperate. 'Where did it come from? *Tell me!*'

Taken aback by Alfie's reaction, Alice tried to keep Alfie calm. 'It's only a photograph; it must've just dropped out of your pocket. It's okay. Come on, let's go.'

Alfie's eyes filled with anger as he continued to stare at the picture of Franny. He raced across to the barman, grabbing hold of the barman's shirt, the photo in his other hand. 'Did you do this, did *you* do this?'

The barman looked terrified. 'What? No! It dropped out of your pocket.'

'It can't have done. It can't have done, you must have put it there. I know it was you.'

Stuttering, the barman shook his head, trying to get away from Alfie. 'I never . . . I've never seen it before. I just picked it up from where you'd dropped it.'

Alice tugged on Alfie's arm, but he threw her off as she pleaded with him. 'Alfie, I know you're upset, but nobody here has done anything. It's not them.'

Ignoring Alice, Alfie swirled round to the bouncer, crumpling the photo up tightly in his hand as he pointed accusingly. 'Then it was you? Is this your idea of a sick joke? Did you put this in my pocket? Trying to wind me up?'

The bouncer looked at Alfie oddly but before he was able to answer, Alfie turned to glare at the punters in the club, who looked on fearfully as he ran across to them and dragged a young man off his chair, shaking him hard. 'Was it you?'

'Alfie, don't! Let him go. It's not his fault.' Alice pulled on Alfie's arm.

'Don't you see, Ally, it's got to be one of them. One of you must've done it! One of you must've seen it! Someone here must've put it in my pocket.'

The punters stared blankly at Alfie as he continued to wave the photo above his head, his voice thunderous, filling the room. 'Answer me, you fuckers! Which one of you was it?'

'Alfie, come, let me get you back home. *Please*, just come with me.'

Alfie, still very drunk, tried to focus on Alice, his voice softer. 'But if it wasn't them, who was it? They must be watching us. They could be watching us now and it'll be you who's next. They're after you, Alice.'

With huge sadness in her heart, Alice stared at Alfie. 'Alfie, we're safe here, I promise. You're very drunk and everything's confused right now, but it's only a photo that you had in your pocket, that's all. I swear it is . . . Alfie, you're bleeding. Look, you've cut your hand.'

Alfie's head lolled back and forth as Alice took off her thin jacket and wrapped it round Alfie's hand gently. She bent down to pick up the photo but she trembled as she looked at it – Franny's face was now obscured by Alfie's blood and no matter what she told herself, she couldn't help but think it was a sign of things to come.

Back in the flat, Alfie staggered, supported by Alice, along the hallway. She led him into his room, where he sat down heavily on the chair.

She looked at him, her heart breaking for him, fully understanding now what he and her dad had gone through for her. At the thought of her dad she gave a sharp intake of breath. Since she'd found out the kind of life he'd led, she had shut him out of both her thoughts and her heart, but that was all going to change now. She was going to put it right. And with the help of her friend, Isaiah, she would get her revenge. Nico Russo would finally get the punishment he deserved.

'Alfie, are you all right? Will you be all right if I leave you now? I can stay if you want me to, though.'

'You shouldn't be looking after me; it's me who should be looking after you. I should've been looking after all of you, but look how that turned out.'

'Alfie, you're not to blame. Lola's right, we all know how hard you've tried. You've done everything you could possibly think of. You've been amazing.'

Too drunk to concentrate on what Alice was saying, Alfie rolled his head back and forth. His words still slurred as he spoke more to himself than Alice. 'How the fuck could I have chosen, though? And now I ain't even got that option. I fucked up and there ain't no way I can put it right.' He looked up suddenly at Alice. 'I'm not surprised you don't want anything to do with me.'

'Alfie, that's not true.'

'Ain't it?'

Recoiling slightly from the reek of alcohol but not from Alfie

287

himself, Alice smiled. 'I didn't understand. I was stupid. I see that now. *And you will know the truth, and the truth will set you free.* John 8, chapter 32. And it has, Alfie. The truth has freed me to see what needs to be done. I was blind before.'

Through his drunkenness, Alfie gave a wry smile. 'You know that I'm past redeeming, don't you?'

Alice gazed down at Alfie warmly and laughed as she gave him a big hug. 'It's going to be all right, I swear it is.'

Gently pulling away from his much-needed hug, Alfie shook his head, looking at Alice sadly. 'I wish I could believe you, darlin', and I appreciate your words, I really do, sweetheart, but they ain't going to help get Bree and Franny back, are they?'

Alice nodded as she pulled the duvet off the bed, covering Alfie with it. 'You're right, they're not.' But as Alfie slumped into a drunken sleep, Alice whispered into his ear, 'Words may not, Alfie, but action will, and I promise you, I swear on my Bible that I'll do whatever it takes to bring them back. *Whatever it takes.*'

46

Beads of sweat sat on Isaiah Thomas's forehead as he gripped the gun, his heart working overtime as he crept through the dark, wet tunnel, emerging onto a rooftop before waiting patiently, not making a move. Suddenly, seeing a movement over by the burnt-out car, he aimed his gun as a tall man, dressed in camouflage shirt and trousers, came into the cross hairs of his rifle's scope. Quickly, Isaiah pulled the trigger – a direct hit. The man's neck exploded and the blood splattered . . .

'Isaiah, come on, you'll be late for Bible class! Isaiah!'

'I'm coming, Mom!'

'Isaiah, I hope you're not on that computer still!'

'I was just finishing off a college assignment.' Isaiah Thomas sighed as he put down the game controller, switched off his Xbox and picked up his Bible ready for class. From downstairs in the kitchen, his mum shouted up again.

'Well, I'm sure that can wait, whereas God's army can't!'

Sighing, he rolled his eyes as he slipped on his red canvas trainers. 'Whatever, Mom!!'

Then, slamming out of his room and running down the stairs, Isaiah Thomas waved a quick goodbye to his mum, who stood in the hallway looking despairingly at her son.

It was just gone five o' clock in the afternoon and the Mississippi sun still sat high in the blue sky as Isaiah headed along the pebbled path with his Bible tucked firmly under his arm.

It was hot and he was tired, his pale white skin pink from the burning sun. In truth, he'd rather not go to another Bible study class led by Pastor Michaels, who constantly seemed to enjoy finding fault with him. This only reiterated to the other students that he was something of a laughing stock, an oddball, someone to be avoided at all costs, apart from when they wanted to stick his head down the john.

He'd thought that getting a mouthful of toilet water would've finished in middle school and his classmates would've got bored with it, then he thought the same when he was in senior school. Now he was a freshman in college, just turned nineteen, he'd long given up thinking it was ever going to stop and instead he just accepted it.

It didn't help him that he'd spent all his life wrapped up in a small religious community, not that the kids there had been any better or kinder to him, the only difference being that when they'd stuck his head down the john, they'd said a few extra Hail Marys at Mass.

He'd always been the tall, spotty geek with the bifocal lenses, the freak show to everyone – everyone apart from Alice Rose, the only friend he'd ever had. The best friend *anyone* could have.

Alice, who'd been special and kind, funny and vulnerable, hadn't minded that he was odd. They'd just hung out regardless and wow! how he missed her.

He sighed as he stood in the doorway of the small hall, watching as Pastor Michaels placed worksheets on every chair. At least when her dad had sent her to the convent she was able to sneak the phone out of the nuns' office and give him a call, but since the tragedy at the nunnery he hadn't heard from her at all – until a couple of hours ago. And he'd been delighted, so happy to hear from her, but what they'd spoken about and what she'd asked him had been even more exciting, because now life was just about to start getting interesting, very interesting, indeed.

Alice waited in the corridor listening to the hubbub outside in Old Compton Street. The bars, pubs and restaurants thronged with people – a constant stream of tourists, theatregoers and locals who shopped and ate, enjoying the warm, balmy night in Central London.

Hearing snores coming through Lola's bedroom wall, Alice smiled to herself as she crept past, not wanting to wake her. With the moonlight coming through the window, Alice slowly opened the door by the kitchen, carefully turning the gold handle, not wanting to make a sound.

Tiptoeing across the small white-painted room, Alice gently sat down on the end of the bed.

'Abel! Abel!' Alice whispered his name, surprised at how deeply asleep he was, then, shaking him gently, she tried again. 'Abel, it's me, Alice . . . Abel?'

Suddenly, Abel sat up in bed, grabbing Alice hard by her arm. Terrified, she screamed as he whipped out a jagged knife from under his pillow, his eyes dark and wild. He pressed the tip of the knife against her cheek, a spot of blood coming to the surface of her smooth velvet skin.

Alice sat perfectly still, taking sharp, shallow breaths, her eyes darting across Abel's face, but there was nothing there. No recognition. Terrified to move, Alice spoke in the quietest of voices. 'Abel, it's me. Put the knife down. It's just me, that's all.'

Then, tentatively, Alice moved her hand towards Abel's. She paused before touching it gently.

'Abel, Abel, it's okay. You're here, you're in the flat with me . . . It's all right . . . Abel?'

Abel blinked, tilting his head as he stared at Alice. His lips moved slowly. 'Natalia? Natalia, is that you?'

'No, Abel, it's me. It's Alice.'

Abel blinked again, then looked at the knife that he held against Alice's face, a sudden awareness coming into his eyes. 'Alice, oh my God, I'm sorry. I'm really sorry . . .' He let out a deep sigh, bowing his head as he dropped the knife on the bed.

'It's okay.'

'No, no, it ain't though, is it? None of this is okay. I could've hurt you.'

'But you didn't.'

'Alice, you got to promise me, you won't do that again, will you? You can't come in here when I'm asleep. You got to be careful, you understand?'

Alice nodded and it was like she was seeing Abel for the first time. Although his face was hollow, strained and gaunt, she suddenly saw the real Abel. The handsome, chiselled Abel. The man he would've looked like before the Russos entered his life.

'I ain't so good at this people thing, Alice. It's been a while since I've had company and . . .'

'It's all right, Abel, you don't have to explain. But I woke you up because I need your help. I need you to drive me to the hospital to see Cabhan.'

'What? Now?'

'We have to go quickly, we haven't got much time. I'll explain in the car, but Alfie's falling apart and we've only got a few days left, so we've got to move fast.'

'Alice, you're not making sense and it's late for you to be up. I'm sure this can wait until the morning. Why don't you get some sleep?'

Alice stood up to switch on the light. 'No. You've got to listen, you've got to help me. I've got a plan but I can't do it on my own.'

'What are you talking about? And why aren't you asking Alfie? Where is he?'

Getting Abel's shoes and bringing them to him whether he

wanted them or not, Alice sat back down on the bed. 'Alfie's drunk but even if he wasn't, I wouldn't ask him because I know what his answer would be . . . The thing is, I want to help get Franny and Bree back and I reckon I know how. It was something that you said that got me thinking.'

Abel pulled on the blue sweatshirt Alfie had picked up from the market for him, slipped on his shoes and tapped his head. 'I may not be all there some of the time, but I know what the Russos are like, and you, Alice Rose, are just a kid.'

'I'm not! I'm sixteen.'

'I don't mean your age – but that as well – I'm actually talking about *you*. You ain't lived, darlin'. Out there on the street there are some sixteen-year-olds who would give Alfie a run for his money, but not you.'

'You're wrong!'

'He's told me all about you and I can see for meself how fragile you are.'

'I'm not like that, not anymore. I'm strong, I know I am. Look at what I've been through. I've changed. You know that and you know that you can't go through the things I did and not see life differently.'

A faraway look came into Abel's eyes. He gazed towards the night sky. 'Yeah, I do, I know that.' He turned back to Alice, warmth for the first time coming into his eyes. 'You remind me of Natalia. You would've liked her and she would've liked you. She was pure, innocent, it was something I loved about her, but she was also strong; though turns out just not strong enough. Anyway, whatever it is you're thinking, I can't let you do it, Alice.'

Alice's eyes flashed with anger. 'I thought you wanted to bring down the Russos? Well, I want to go up against them as well. I want to bring them down, but I need your help, and you need me, so let's work together, along with my friend, Isaiah.'

'The one who can do all that technical stuff you were telling me about?'

Excitedly, Alice grabbed hold of Abel's hands. 'Yes, that's him, and it was you who got me thinking. We can do this, I know we can. What do you say?'

'I don't know, Alice. I don't even know what the plan is. I'm worried that . . . you might be hurt like . . .'

Alice shook her head. 'I won't, but if I am, that's the risk I'm willing to take. *Without the shedding of blood, there is no forgiveness of sins*. Hebrews 9 . . . Sometimes sacrifices have to be made, Abel.'

'Alice, stop! I know this is who you are, and it makes you special, I'm not knocking it, but you've got to understand that this ain't a Bible class where you sit in the comfort of some church hall reciting lines. This is real. The Russos make them Romans look like the Salvation Army. They will kill you, and kill you slowly and cruelly.'

'Don't you see, Abel, I can't live if something happens to Franny and Bree. And to my dad, look what they did to him. You of all people have to understand that. This is all my fault and I need to make it right. I don't care about me, I care about *them*.'

Abel shook his head. 'But you *will* care when they torture you, when you scream for mercy and all they do is laugh and hurt you some more, that's when you'll realise you care and that's when it'll become real to you.'

'Then if you won't help, I'll do it on my own. You won't stop me, no matter what you say.'

Abel stared at Alice, not seeing a broken bird in front of him but a strong, powerful eagle. He spoke to her, beginning to take her seriously. 'But if it'll just be you and me, we can't take them on.'

Full of passion, Alice shook her head. 'No, it'll be you, me and Isaiah, plus *we shall put on the whole armour of God that we may be able to stand against the wiles of the Devil*. Ephesians 6, chapter 11.'

Despairingly, Abel blew out his cheeks, not sure whether he should seriously begin to panic. 'You see, it's saying those kinds of things, Alice, which makes me think this ain't a good idea from the start.'

'Abel, please, trust me. Wait and just listen then . . .'

Alice pulled out Lola's phone from her jeans pocket and dialled a number. It rang before a familiar voice answered.

'Hello?'

'Hello, Nico, it's Alice, how are you? I've missed you.'

Abel went to grab for the phone, but Alice quickly turned away, putting her finger against her lips to shush Abel.

'Alice, I was just thinking about you. I was wondering if we'd ever speak again. I've tried calling you.'

'I know and I'm sorry, but I was afraid to answer it in case anyone heard me. I don't want them to know about you. They have their secrets; I don't know why I can't have mine. Everything's a lie. They don't tell me anything. Nothing at all. I wanted to know where Franny had gone and all they told me was she was away on business. But what business and where? But I'm through with it, it's going to be on my terms now.'

'You sound different, Alice.'

'I feel different. You've made me feel like that, Nico. I feel strong. If it wasn't for you I'd be doubting who I was, I would never have seen the person I was supposed to be. For that, Nico, I want to thank you.'

Nico groaned down the phone. 'Alice. Alice. It's a shame you can't be here, we could talk all the time.'

'That would be nice, Nico. We've spoken so much it's almost as if I know what you're thinking now. Even if you don't say everything to me, I know who you are now.'

Nico smiled, overwhelmed by wanting, *needing* Alice. 'I still have your photo next to my daughter's. I pray for you every day, Alice.'

Alice glanced at Abel, who watched her intently. 'I can't be too long, Nico. I have to go and see my dad in hospital. He's still at Addenbrooke's, but I got a call from one of the nurses to say he's not doing very well. It's touch and go.'

Without saying a word, Abel waved to Alice to get her attention. He shrugged, gesturing and looking concerned. She shook her head to let him know what she was saying wasn't real before waving him away as she continued to speak to Nico.

'I wasn't going to go and see him because of all the lies he's told me, but if he's not going to pull through, I think it's better I do visit. But I'm going to go on my own. I don't want the others coming with me. I'll have to sneak out though. What do you think? I value your opinion, Nico.'

Smiling again, feeling the rush of excitement in his stomach, Nico nodded as he spoke down the phone. 'I think that's a good idea, Alice. It's important you make your peace with your dad and if you go on your own, then you'll have space to be able to tell him everything that you want to say . . . Are you thinking of going now, Alice?'

It was Alice's turn to smile. 'Yes, but it'll take me an hour or so to get there. I'm going to jump in a cab and hopefully the nurses will let me stay as long as I like with him, so I'll be there for a while. Thank you, Nico, for helping me decide. I can always rely on you to give me the right answer.'

'So, where are you, Alice, where are you staying now? I thought you were at Abel's house?'

'I was but . . . Nico, I have to go, they've just walked into the kitchen.'

'Alice, no, wait!'

Alice clicked off the phone. She stared at Abel. 'There you go, the fly is about to come into our web. Game on, Mr Russo, game on.'

47

The drive down to Addenbrooke's Hospital was clear and quick, taking just over an hour as Abel sped along, listening to Alice telling him her plan.

Pulling up a few minutes' walk away from the hospital, Abel parked the car. He turned to look at Alice, who noticed there was a light in his eyes, something she hadn't seen before.

'Are you sure about this, Alice? When the others find out what we're doing, they'll go mental.'

'They won't find out though, will they? I don't want them knowing anything about this. Look, we can be back before they wake up. Alfie was so drunk he won't be awake for ages, and Lola won't come into my room and she *certainly* won't come into yours.'

Abel raised his eyebrows. 'That's true enough. But what happens if something goes wrong? Once you go in there, I won't be able to look after you. You're on your own.'

Alice gave a smile. 'No, I'm not.'

Abel shook his head, his shoulders slumping. 'Don't tell me, you've got some archangel by your side.'

Getting out of the car, Alice gave a small laugh, teasing Abel. 'Exactly! See, you're learning! We'll make a saint out of you yet, Abel Gray.'

Surprised and shocked at the sound of himself chuckling, Abel grinned. 'Saint Abel – you know what, that sounds proper pukka! . . . But seriously, Alice, I'm worried.'

'I know and so am I, but that shouldn't stop us doing what's right, should it? Come on, let's go. And you know what you have to do, don't you?'

Alice Rose walked along the corridor to the lift, which took her up to intensive care. Everything was quiet and except for a few of the night staff, the place was deserted, with an eerie calm in the air.

At the door of the unit, the nursing staff, who were expecting Alice, let her in and led her to where Cabhan lay in an induced coma, tubed up and ventilated, with the sounds of the machines quietly beeping in the background.

She gasped as she stared at her dad, looking at his bandaged stumps and battered face. Nervously she leant over, surprised at how warm he felt. She kissed him tenderly on his head, closing her eyes and feeling the rush of love and the now ever-present guilt surge through her.

She had missed him so much and when he did wake up, she wanted to make him proud. She wanted him not to have to worry about the Russos anymore, or about her. He had done so much to try to protect her, he had made so many sacrifices, and now it was time for her to make some, too.

'Dad, it's me, it's me, Alice. I came to tell you that I love you, do you hear me? I'm not sure what's going to happen to me, but they say *you're* going to be all right, which is great, really great. And I need you to know that having you in my life has been so wonderful. I'm so sorry that I haven't come to visit you before, I should've done, I was just being selfish, but never think I don't love you. I've always loved you . . . Will you forgive me, Dad? I know that you can hear me, I just know it.'

Alice's phone buzzed in her pocket. She answered it quickly.

'Hello?'

'Alice, it's me, Abel. They're here.'

'Okay, I'm coming down, and Abel, remember to keep out of sight.'

Alice hurriedly slipped her phone back in her pocket and held onto her dad, burying her face in his chest before kissing him again. She wiped the tears from her eyes. 'Dad, I've got to go, but everything's going to be all right, I promise. I'm going to make sure it is. I love you, Dad, *never* forget that.'

Running out of the unit, Alice then made her way down from the third floor, taking the lift to the service area. She called Abel, speaking fast.

'Where are they now?'

'They're just getting out of the car. Hold on, I can see Bobby but Salvatore's still in there. It looks like he's not getting out. Shit.'

Alice thought for a moment then said, 'Okay, stay where you are, you can't let them spot you, but what I'll do is when Bobby comes into the hospital, I'll go into the car park. That way Salvatore will be able to see me and I'll be able to lure him out of the car.'

'No, Alice, that's too dangerous, that wasn't the agreement! All you said was that you knew a way of bringing them to the hospital. Nothing else . . . Alice . . . Alice!' Abel looked at the phone, realising Alice had cut him off. Angrily, he spoke out loud to himself. 'For fuck's sake, Alice, what are you doing? What are you doing to me? Have you got some kind of death wish?'

In the A&E department, Alice stood in the shadows watching Bobby walk across the car park. He looked exactly like the photo Abel had showed her: heavy, muscular build and thick black hair, pockmarked face and a long scar below his eye.

He strode towards the main entrance with purpose and once Alice was certain that he was safely inside, she took a deep breath, steadying herself, before she walked out into the car park.

It was dark with only a couple of solar lights to brighten the area. Alice, not knowing which one was the Russos' car, walked slowly down the line of parked vehicles.

She could feel her heart racing and she jumped at every noise, aware that if this was going to work, she *couldn't* get caught.

Over at the far end of the car park, Alice heard what sounded like a car door open and close. Squinting, she thought she could just make out in the distance the silhouette of someone walking towards her, but she had to be certain it was Salvatore. All she needed was to get a quick glance at him, see his face, before she turned to run.

As Alice watched the person getting ever nearer, her phone buzzed in her hand. She glanced down and saw the first line of the text on her screen. It was from Abel and it simply read: *run!*

Alice sprinted back towards the entrance of the A&E, hearing footsteps running across the gravelled car park behind her, sounding like they were getting nearer and nearer.

Frantically, she flung herself round the door, banging into the pile of wheelchairs by the entrance. She skidded on the polished floor, her heart racing as she bolted down the corridor and turned the corner, fear pumping through her veins. She headed towards the lift, though she could see it was still on the top floor. Catching a glimpse of Salvatore pushing an elderly doctor out of the way, alarmed, Alice, not wanting to take the risk of being caught, began to run again, through some double doors and down the backstairs, descending into the darkness of the basement corridors . . .

Outside in the car park, Abel walked across to the Russos' car, all the time keeping an eye on the entrance of the hospital. He checked around, making sure that no one was about, before pulling out Alfie's wrench from the small canvas bag he was carrying.

Crouching down by the boot, he placed the wrench on the

300

ground and took from his pocket a piece of galvanised wire, which he expertly slotted into the lock. He wiggled it about until he heard a click, then, holding the wire steady with one hand, he scrabbled in his jeans pocket and yanked out a small flat-head screwdriver, sliding it into the lock along with the wire, which he still held in place.

Turning both the wire and the screwdriver anti-clockwise, Abel felt the latch connect and with one last turn the boot bounced open.

Checking again that no one was coming, his eyes darted around. Working quickly with the wrench to lift the boot's floor and liner, Abel managed to expose the empty space directly underneath the spare tyre.

After zipping open the side pocket of the bag, he pulled out Alfie's iPad, which they'd taken from his room, and made sure it was switched on, then placed it carefully against the side of the car in the empty well, jamming it in so it wouldn't move about.

Satisfied, he hurriedly replaced the floor and lining before shutting the boot, checking that the lock was still intact before jogging away into the darkness. Now all there was left to do was find Alice.

Ignoring her fear, Alice Rose crept along the vast corridor trying not to make a noise in the pitch-black when, suddenly, behind her, she heard the sound of running feet and the double doors at the other end swish open.

But the footsteps suddenly stopped. Alice, chewing nervously on her lip in the blackness, could hear the sound of heavy breathing. She couldn't see who it was but she just *knew* it was Salvatore Russo.

Crouching down carefully, conscious that she must not make a single sound, Alice, trembling slightly, hid under one of the steel trolleys left in the stone corridor and slowly, slowly, began

301

to crawl along, pausing every few seconds to listen for Salvatore's movements.

Backing into some doors that opened quietly, Alice felt a sudden temperature drop as she heard the footsteps again. They were definitely coming her way.

Quickly getting to her feet, alarmed, Alice – just able to see the outline of another door on the other side of the room – tiptoed across. Frantically she pulled the handle, but it was locked.

Panicking, Alice spun round and with her eyes adjusting to the dark, she realised where she was. She was in the hospital morgue . . .

There were four large steel tables with the bodies of the dead on them, all of them covered in green sheets, an empty post-mortem trolley and freezer drawers lining the room, but there was nothing else. Nowhere to hide.

Dashing towards the door she'd come through, Alice, frightened now, stood on tiptoe looking out of the small fire window, wondering if she could make a run for it, but the swish of another door just outside told her it would be impossible without being seen.

The footsteps were getting louder and she could hear Salvatore looking in the different rooms and offices along the corridor. Alice knew, any minute now, he'd find her.

With her fear rising, an idea suddenly came to her. She ran across to one of the tables in the darkest corner of the room and pulled back the heavy green cotton sheet, uncovering the body of an elderly man.

Making the sign of the cross and plucking up courage, Alice climbed onto the metal table, squeezing herself on, immediately feeling the cold clamminess of the man's body next to her. She shivered before quickly covering both herself and the man with the sheet. A moment later she heard the mortuary door open.

Alice held her breath, trying to keep as still as possible, as Salvatore Russo walked into the room. She could almost feel him next to her as she tried to push away the fact she was lying skin to skin with a dead man, the smell of death in her nostrils.

The footsteps paced about, and Alice prayed that the darkness would protect her and that he wouldn't notice the strange outline that no doubt she and the dead man created under the cotton sheet.

Suddenly, Alice sensed Salvatore coming closer, nearer, towering over where she lay. Fighting the urge to scream, she was certain that Salvatore would be able to feel her warm breath through the sheet or hear her heart pounding as he stood only inches away.

Then, after what seemed like forever, Alice eventually heard the squeak of Salvatore's shoe turning on the polished lino floor as he headed for the exit and walked away into the corridor.

Letting out a giant sigh of relief, Alice began to climb off the table when, unexpectedly, she felt her phone begin to jump in her hand, vibrating before it buzzed then beeped loudly. Echoing through the silence.

Outside in the corridor, hearing the noise of a phone, Salvatore Russo stopped in his tracks. He listened again before striding back to the room he'd just come out of, at the same time as Alice slid her mobile across to the far corner, diving under the table. She watched from where she hid as Salvatore walked back in.

For a moment he stood by the door, but seeing a phone gleaming on the floor in the corner, he walked across to get it. He bent down to pick it up, but as he started to open the message on the screen, a violent blow to the back of his head knocked him unconscious, sinking him to the floor.

Standing above him, holding a wrench, was Abel Gray.

48

'We did it! We did it! We'll be able to trace their location now from the tracker Isaiah sent to the iPad – we'll know where they are. It's brilliant!' Alice grinned at Abel, who stared at the road as they sped away from the hospital.

He didn't reply but sat gripping the steering wheel, clenching his jaw.

'Abel, aren't you happy? Don't you see? This is just the first part. The Russos won't know what's coming. We can do this, I just know it. See, I told you it'd be easy.'

Abel turned the car hard, skidding up the grassy bank and screeching to a halt. He turned to Alice, his eyes dark and thunderous. 'You think that was easy? Are you having a fucking laugh, Alice? What would have happened if I hadn't found you? You were so close to Salvatore catching you, don't you get that? You could've been killed.'

'*Know that God is—*'

'Stop right there! Just stop! I don't want to hear that shit. You understand me? We need to call this off. It's too risky. It's over.'

Frantically, Alice shook her head. 'No. No, it's not.'

Abel's face darkened. 'Alice, listen to me, Salvatore will know now that something's wrong.'

'He doesn't, he didn't see you.'

Frustrated, Abel banged his fist against the side of the car door. 'Oh, come off it, Alice, he got clumped round the head, what's he going to think? That it's some hospital porter taking the law into his own hands?'

'No, of course not, but I do know if I call Nico, I can straighten it out with him, I can play dumb.'

'And how long's that going to last, hey? He'll see right through it soon.'

Alice sounded defiant. 'No, he won't, you don't know him like I do.'

'Alice, listen to yourself, you don't know him at all. I do. What he's pretended to be isn't him at all.'

Alice's face was screwed up in anger. 'It's you who doesn't get it. *I'm* his weakness, it's *me* he wants and because of that, he'll make a mistake.'

'I've told you before, this isn't a game, Alice.'

Crossly, Alice stared back. 'You keep saying that like I don't know, as if I haven't been through everything I have, as if my dad isn't lying in hospital, Franny and Bree aren't taken and Sister Margaret . . . isn't dead.'

'Then if you know that, why are you behaving the way you are?'

Angry tears ran down Alice's face. 'Behaving? You sound like a teacher, Abel. I thought I was helping.'

Abel slammed down his hand on the wheel, his eyes wild. 'How is getting yourself killed helping? Look at me, Alice. I said, look at me!'

With Alice refusing to look at him, Abel leant over and grabbed her face, turning her head towards him. 'You know what they did to Natalia, why push it? Why risk it? You're acting like you're on some kind of mission. And don't say anything about God.'

Furious, Alice pushed Abel's hands away. 'How can you say that, *you* of all people? I thought you wanted to bring Nico down?'

'You know I do, Alice.'

'Then why are you acting like this? I don't understand.'

'Then don't.'

Alice's eyes darted across Abel's face, confusion wrinkling her forehead. 'Is it because you wanted to bring Nico down on your own, is that it? Because I don't want to take any of the glory, I just want to get Franny and Bree out of there.'

'Grow up, Alice,' Abel hissed through his teeth.

'Maybe that's what I should be saying to you!'

Abel shook his head, seeing the fire in Alice's eyes. 'Think what you like.'

'I will, and I know what I think. I think you're scared. I think that without Nico in your life you have nothing and that's why you hold onto him so hard. Admit it, Abel, you need Nico and you're afraid to let him go.'

The sound of the slap on Alice's face resonated around the car. Abel's voice was low and dangerous. 'How dare you. You don't know me, Alice Rose. You think you've got it all worked out, don't you? But you haven't. Be careful, you don't want to cross me, don't make me your enemy. I'm not Alfie, I'm not Franny, I don't forgive people so easily. I know I'm damaged but even before I was, I come from a place, a way of life that has silly girls like you for breakfast.

'Think about it, Alice, *I* worked for Nico. *Me*. I was his right-hand man, so what does that say about who I am? I learnt the error of my ways through a very painful lesson, one that haunts me to this day, but don't make the mistake of thinking, because I'm not like Nico now, that some part of me, when pushed, isn't still like him. So be careful what you say, Alice. Make sure that youthful exuberance of yours doesn't get you into trouble.'

Shocked, Alice rubbed her face, feeling the sting of humiliation more than she felt the sting of the slap. Then, annoyed that tears were rolling down her cheeks, she spoke in a whisper.

'I'm so sorry, Abel, I went too far. I shouldn't have said what

I did. I had no right and the stupid thing is I don't even mean it. I know how you love Natalia and what I said must be really hurtful to you. It was cruel. I got carried away because I just want to sort this out, but I'm really sorry about what I said. Will you forgive me?'

There was a long pause before Abel spoke. 'Thank you, Alice, for your apology. It means a lot. I shouldn't have slapped you, that was wrong of me. I'm just tired of it all. I want to sleep and never wake, but I can't, Alice, I can't. All I do is just continue to walk along the boundary between life and death. I'll have no peace until Nico is dead, so no, Alice, I want no glory, I just want it to end. But I also need *you* to be safe . . .

'I've never told anyone this before, but Natalia thought she could get Nico to listen to her, that she could convince him that I hadn't taken the money, and I hadn't, but she underestimated him. She didn't even tell me she was going to see him, but she did that for me. She loved me, Alice, and she walked into his trap. Nico knew I would come looking for her and I did.' Abel paused before adding, 'A man once said, *l'amore è fatale, condannato dalla vita stessa.* Do you know what that means, Alice?'

Alice, thinking hard, took Abel's hands and nodded. 'Yes . . . love is fatal, condemned by life itself.'

'That's right, so whatever you choose to do, be careful if you do it in the name of love.'

Alice smiled, the print of Abel's hand still on her cheek. 'I need you and you need me to do this, both for our different reasons, but only we can do it. Let me phone Isaiah, let's do this and whatever happens, happens . . . Agreed? Let's shake on it.'

Abel stared at Alice as she held out her hand. He glanced down then back up before hesitantly putting out his own. 'Agreed.'

'And no going back? Whatever it takes.'

'No going back, Alice, whatever it takes.'

* * *

Ten minutes later, Isaiah Thomas sat in his poster-covered bedroom. He had locked the door, but now his mum was furiously banging on it loudly.

'Isaiah, open this door, *now*! Have you any idea what time it is? It's very late. What are you doing in there anyway?'

Getting his earphones out of the drawer, Isaiah shouted back as he sat in front of his array of computers, radio transmitters, Raspberry Pi computers, network adapters and Ubertooths wired up to various keyboards and ports. 'Nothing, Mom! Now *please* go away.'

'Remember, Isaiah, you may be able to hide something from me, but don't forget, God can see it all!'

'Whatever, Mom!' He turned back to his computer screens, picking up the phone by his side. 'Sorry about that, Alice, Mom's on the warpath.'

Wistfully, Alice, remembering old times, said, 'It's fine. How is she anyway?'

Tapping some numerical data into one of his computers as well as biting into a giant Hershey bar, Isaiah laughed. 'Oh, she's still just being Mom!'

Alice smiled to herself, picturing Isaiah's mother, but quickly she turned her attention back to the conversation. 'Abel managed to put the iPad in the car. Can you get a signal? Can you pick up their location yet?'

Isaiah watched the screen of one of his computers, seeing a red flashing dot. 'Yeah, I can. All systems go.'

Alice turned to Abel, giving him a big grin. 'Hold on, Isaiah, I'm just going to put my cell on speaker . . . Where are they?'

'It looks like they're still at the hospital. The car hasn't moved, but don't worry, I'll track them all the way. I'm also streaming to one of my hard drives, so even if I have to go out to one of Pastor Michaels' Bible classes, I'll be able to play back their every move.'

Eagerly, Alice asked, 'And what about the emails? Have you

managed to do anything about them? Did you get into my dad's email account?'

Abel frowned, cutting into the conversation. 'Hold up. What email? I never heard anything about this. You need to tell me what's going on. I don't want you two keeping me out of the loop, understand? If we're going to do this, you run everything by me. And I mean everything.'

Isaiah Thomas, having been brought up with the best of manners, smiled as if Abel were in the room with him. 'Hello, Mr Gray, it's good to meet you. Alice has told me all about you.'

Abel glanced at the phone and then at Alice, raising his eyebrows. 'I doubt it and if she had done, I doubt you'd be so pleased . . . Anyway, son, just call me Abel. But tell me about this email.'

'I'll tell you.' Alice spoke quickly, talking both to Abel and the phone as she did so. 'Well, Isaiah is a genius when it comes to computers.'

Isaiah leant forward, speaking closely to the phone. He grinned and blushed all at the same time. 'Thank you, Alice.'

Ingenuously, Alice scrumpled up her nose happily. 'Well, you are, Isaiah . . . Anyway, what we came up with was this. Actually, Isaiah, maybe it's better for you to explain this part.'

Pushing his bifocals further up the bridge of his nose, Isaiah cleared his throat. 'Getting into people's email is easy, maybe not the President's, but even that's possible. So basically, what Alice thought was, if I get into Salvatore's emails via her dad's correspondence with him in the past, then I can send Nico an email looking like it's from Salvatore. Once he opens the email, not only will I be in Salvatore's files and accounts, but I'll also be in Nico's phone. So everything they do, every call they make, I'll be able to monitor it all on my screen and they won't know a thing. They won't know we're watching because within the email I'll plant some malware, so when he opens it, I'll get the payload.'

Abel frowned. 'Payload?'

Opening another Hershey bar, Isaiah spoke with his mouth full. 'Yeah, it's basically harvesting the information on his phone and Salvatore's computer. I'll have a mirror image of it – nothing they do will go unseen. I'll paint his whole set of files with spyware.'

'Isaiah, who are you talking to? Are you on that computer again?'

'No, Mom, I'm just talking to Elijah about the worksheets for Pastor Michaels.'

'I hope you're not lying to me, you know that the Bible says you shall bear no false witness.'

'Whatever, Mom! . . . Sorry, guys. The point is this is *real* easy for me.'

Alice turned to Abel, eagerness in her voice. 'What do you think?'

'I think I understand it. I basically get the main drift of it and it's clever, I'll give you that, but if we're going to do this, we need to do it properly. Let's use this email to our advantage. We need to keep thinking like Nico . . . What Nico likes to do is set a small stone rolling until it becomes a landslide. He has an impact on one person and in turn that impacts another, then he stands back and watches until whole families are destroyed. So let's play him at his own game. Let the Russos destroy each other.'

'How?'

'What is it that Nico hates, Alice? What is his Achilles heel, what will make him turn like a rabid dog on his own family? . . . *Tradimento.*'

'Betrayal?'

'Yes, Alice, betrayal. The harshest cut of all.'

49

Back in the flat in Soho, the next morning, with the dawn sun shining brightly through the window, Alfie Jennings lay fast asleep on the couch after having consumed the bottle of whiskey he'd found in the cupboard. Lola, having tried to sober Alfie up and getting nothing back for her troubles apart from a mouthful of abuse, feeling anxious and stressed about the whole situation, decided to retreat to her bedroom for a much-needed lie-down, leaving Alice alone listening to Isaiah's plan.

'I don't know, Isaiah, that sounds crazy. How do you know it will work?'

Isaiah Thomas spoke quietly so as not to wake his mother through the paper-thin walls.

'I guess it is crazy and I don't know if it will work, Alice, but technically, there's no reason it shouldn't. This could be amazing and everything with the Russos could all be over. And think about it: if you can believe what Nico says, at the most Franny and Bree have only got about five days left.'

At that thought, Alice felt sick. She frowned, nervously biting on her bottom lip as Alfie snored loudly. 'It's such a risk and such a rush. And what about you? If they catch you, you could be looking at twenty-five years in prison.'

'That would be worth it just to see my mom's face. Look, I've booked a flight already. It leaves Gatwick at 3pm UK time.' Isaiah stopped before adding sheepishly, 'I used my mom's credit card, but I'll pay her back . . . Alice, you need to get him on that flight. Trust me, I can do this. I can pull this off.'

'I don't know, it's a lot to ask and . . . Listen, Abel's coming, I have to go, call me back in a couple of minutes.'

'Will you think about it?'

Alice spoke hurriedly as she tried to finish off the call. 'Okay, okay. I'll think . . . Now I've got to go.'

'Who was that?' Abel walked into the lounge, glancing at Alfie through the bedroom door before turning back to Alice.

'It was Isaiah.'

Abel looked at Alice oddly. 'What's going on, are you all right? Was it about the email to Nico?'

Thinking of what Isaiah had just suggested, Alice answered tightly, 'No, it was about something else, but I'm fine, just tired.'

Not convinced Alice was telling him everything, Abel sat down next to her. 'This Isaiah, are you sure we can trust him? It's all a bit odd to me. The way he works is proper undercover.'

'He's not a black hat if that's what you mean, he's more of a grey one.'

Abel laughed, feeling more alive than he'd done since Natalia's death. 'No, darlin', I didn't mean that at all, not that I know what you're talking about.'

'Black hat hackers are people who do it for illegal purposes, like their own financial gain or even for the notoriety of it all, but the grey hat hackers, like Isaiah, they really only do it to be curious and to help out.'

Taking a sip of the drink Lola had made him before she'd headed back to bed, Abel shrugged. 'And his mum doesn't know anything?'

Alice shook her head. 'Mrs Thomas doesn't suspect a thing. She just brings his dinner and Hershey bars on a tray and as long as he attends Pastor Michael's Bible classes and he comes out of his room occasionally, she's happy.'

Before Abel could reply, the phone rang. It was Isaiah again. Alice put it on speakerphone.

'Hi, Alice, just me. Is Abel there?'

'Yeah, he's here with me now.'

'Cool. So I just wanted to let you know that the email to Nico is all done and awaiting your approval before I send it.'

Abel let out a long sigh. 'And you stuck exactly to what I said? It's got to be believable.'

Still in his pyjamas, Isaiah lay back on his bed. 'To the letter, Abel. The email is *exactly* how you wanted it. I can send you it if you like before I send it to Nico?'

Abel gave a wry smile as he squinted from the sun in his eyes. 'What? And have you crawling all over my phone? Inside me mobile? After what you told me you can do, no thank you.'

'Mr Gray, how do you know I'm not inside your phone already? For all you know I could be.'

'You'd better be having a laugh, son, let me tell you that. Atlantic between us or not, I'll come and sort you right out.'

Isaiah grinned as he held the phone closer to his ear. 'Just kidding, sir.'

Alice grinned as well, at which Abel scowled, not fully trusting that Isaiah actually *wasn't* kidding.

Isaiah continued: 'Once Nico opens the email, what he'll read will make it look like Salvatore's sent it to him by mistake. I'm guessing he'll then want to look at Salvatore's email account to see what else is there. If he does, obviously Nico won't have the passcode to get in, but that's okay, because he'll do what everybody else does – he'll try different passwords. But as I'm controlling his phone, I'll make it easy for him: I'll let him get into Salvatore's emails on the third or fourth attempt. But it won't actually be Salvatore's account I've let him into; although it will *look* like it is because I've created a mirror account.'

'What if he knows the actual password?'

'That won't make a difference because I've blocked the pathway from Nico's phone to Salvatore's actual email account to redirect to this fake one I've set up. But I've also copied some of Salvatore's *real* emails through and I've embedded fake ones as you suggested, Abel. So the point is, if Nico goes into Salvatore's emails, what he sees he'll think is real, it will look authentic, and what he reads won't make him happy at all.'

Abel stood up, looking out of the window. 'But what if he doesn't try to look at Salvatore's account, Isaiah?'

'Then it doesn't matter because he'll still have the email we sent him, but wouldn't you? Wouldn't you want to know what else a person close to you was doing behind your back?'

'I guess I would and knowing Nico, thinking like Nico, that's *exactly* what he'll try to do, which means—'

Alice cut in. 'Which means the landslide has started.'

'And I've saved the best till last, guys. I know where they are. I know where Franny and Bree are being kept.'

Alice jumped in the air, grabbing hold of Abel's hand. Her face lit up as she spoke. 'That's brilliant! That's amazing, you're my hero, Isaiah Thomas.'

Touched by Alice's words, Isaiah just smiled to himself. 'It was easy, the tracker in the iPad worked perfectly. My computer followed it to a place just outside Kintbury in West Berkshire. The location on these things is pretty darn accurate. I've pinpointed where they are. It's a disused farm, a good few miles from anywhere. But that's where they are or at least that's where the car is.'

Abel nodded. 'But we haven't got long. Time's running out, quicker now thanks to Alfie; though at least we've got the where-abouts of Franny and Bree. Maybe – and it's only a maybe – I can pull out some favours, get some men together. Hopefully I still can, but that will take a couple or so days. Then somehow we can try to get them out of there. But it's how to piece it all together, that's the main problem. Trying to do all this without risking Franny or Bree's life. I mean, what now?'

'Alice, why don't you tell him about my plan?' Isaiah said.

'What plan? Is this what you were talking about on the phone earlier? I told you you had to run everything by me.' Abel looked at Alice firmly.

'I just don't think it's safe, I don't think it's a good idea.'

'How about I be the judge of that, Alice. Come on, spit it out.'

Alice walked over to where Abel stood, looking out over Old Compton Street. 'Well, this is where Isaiah thinks you should come into it.'

Abel stared at Alice. 'What are you talking about?'

From his bedroom in Mississippi, Isaiah cut in. 'To stop an infestation of ants you have to get to the queen. Get inside her nest.'

Abel frowned at the phone. 'Isaiah, you've lost me.'

'Mr Gray, *you* are going on a trip.'

Standing in Old Compton Street by the door of the flat, Alice held Abel tightly in a big, warm embrace and hesitantly he moved his arms, self-consciously hugging her back. 'I don't want you to do this, Abel. Please stay here.'

Abel shook his head then pulled back so he could look at her. 'Alice, I have to go. Isaiah's right, this will stop it all. It'll be over. We need it to be over for both of us. I'm so tired, Alice, and you need to be able to stop running.'

'But Isaiah doesn't even know if it will work.'

Abel smiled at Alice, surprised that he could feel her warmth, her care, but even more surprised that he felt something back towards *her* after years of feeling numb. 'You have been so good for me, but you know this is the right thing. Do you trust Isaiah?'

Moving out of the way of a group of tourists, Alice stepped to one side. 'Yes, yes, of course. I'd trust him with my life.'

'There you go then. And that's what I'm doing, Alice.'

Desperate to stop him, Alice said, 'But what about the others, what will I tell them?'

'Tell them everything. They'll understand.'

Abel turned and walked away.

'But what about Natalia?'

Abel froze then slowly turned around to stare at Alice. 'What did you say?'

Alice swallowed hard. 'What about Natalia? What will happen to her if you don't come back?'

Abel tilted his head then walked back to Alice. He spoke in a low voice. 'She will understand, like you have to understand. Now goodbye, Alice, I have to go, otherwise I won't have time to get my things from my house.'

'Abel . . . Wait.' Alice grabbed Abel's hand, her corkscrew curls falling over her face. 'Thank you . . . thank you for everything you've done.'

'Alice, you're speaking like you won't see me again.'

She looked at him, her almond eyes full of kindness. 'But we don't know, do we? We may never meet again.'

'Alice, we will. I know we will. Like I shall meet Natalia again.'

Alice smiled at Abel sadly, her heart breaking as tears ran down her face. 'Isaiah will look after you.'

'I know he will, because he's a friend of yours, isn't he? It'll be fine. I'll be back before you know it.' Then, gently, Abel kissed her on her head. 'Now take care, Alice Rose. I'll let you know when I've got in contact with some of my old acquaintances, so they can come and help you. It won't be long until we get Franny and Bree back, I promise. Whatever it takes, remember?'

'Whatever it takes.'

Alice watched Abel walk along Old Compton Street and at the top, he turned around and waved before disappearing into Shaftesbury Avenue, leaving Alice with a sinking feeling in her heart.

50

In her house in Cranfield, Mississippi, Mrs Thomas stood on the landing outside Isaiah's bedroom. From out of her red-and-white apron pocket she pulled out a key and slotted it into the lock. Opening the door, she gasped at the scene in front of her, tutting and shaking her head. Coke cans, Hershey bar wrappers, coffee cups, dirty plates and dirty laundry were discarded and thrown around the room.

Sighing, Mrs Thomas, armed with a black bag and bucket, rolled up her sleeves, picked up the rubbish and threw Isaiah's dirty clothes outside on the landing. She dipped her checked cloth into the warm soapy water and started to clean, tackling the layer of dust that seemed to sit on every surface.

Ten minutes later, red-faced and perspiring, Mrs Thomas sang loudly an unrecognisable version of 'America the Beautiful' to keep her spirits up. She wrung out the cloth tightly before setting about cleaning Isaiah's computers and keyboards with great vigour.

'Mom! What are you doing? What have you done?' Isaiah stared in horror at the screens of his computers, which flashed and lit up brightly.

Mrs Thomas, small and petite with green eyes and a neat

blonde bob, stared at her son with annoyance. 'Isaiah Thomas, the state of your room, no wonder you didn't want me to come in. Cleanliness is next to godliness and you, Isaiah Thomas, are a long way from that.'

Isaiah, throwing down the Hershey bar he was eating, walked towards one of his computers.

'Mom, what did you do? What did you touch?'

'What I did was what you should've done a long time ago. Clean.'

Isaiah continued to stare at the screen, shaking his head. 'No, no, no, no, no, Mom!'

'Calm down, Isaiah!'

'Tell me you didn't press this button? Tell me anything but that, Mom.'

Frowning and not particularly interested in her son's computers, Mrs Thomas shrugged. 'I don't know, all I know is that I washed the keyboards for you and I tidied up all those wires over there. You really . . .'

Isaiah stopped listening to his mother as he watched one of the files on his computer show a 'read' notice.

'Oh my God!'

'Isaiah, do not take the Lord's name in vain.'

'Mom, believe me, it's not in vain, I need all the help I can get . . . Now, can you leave the room?'

'But—'

'*Mom*! *Go*!'

Hurt by her son's anger towards her, Mrs Thomas picked up her cloth and bucket, marching out of the room affronted.

Quickly picking up the phone, his eyes still glued to the screen, Isaiah pressed call.

'Hello?'

'Alice! Alice!'

'What's the matter, Isaiah, what's happened? Didn't you get the text that Abel got off okay?'

Isaiah whirled around, running across to the door to lock it. 'It's not that, it's about the email to Nico.'

'What about it?'

Isaiah closed his eyes before saying, 'It's gone.'

Sitting down on her bed, listening to Alfie stagger around the flat, Alice said, 'Isaiah, you're not explaining properly.'

'Okay, what I'm trying to say is the email has been sent to Nico.'

'What? But Abel told you *not* to send it, *not* until he got there.'

'I know, I know, but that's not the worst part. The worst part is, the wrong email was sent. Nico's got the wrong email.'

Alice leant forward breathing tentatively as she chewed on her fingernail, fear rushing through her. 'I don't understand.'

'My mom, she was cleaning and I hadn't locked my computer. I was only popping out for a Hershey bar, you know, the new milk—'

Raising her voice, Alice cut in, 'I don't care about what flavour chocolate it is, Isaiah, just tell me what you've done!'

Nervously, Isaiah pushed his glasses back up the bridge of his nose. 'Sorry, sorry, I know you don't. Look, I didn't lock my computer, so when Mom was cleaning, by mistake she hit the command key, which is linked to the file for the emails I created to send to Nico.'

'But you said the *wrong* one was sent.'

'It was. The file I'm talking about had the emails in it that Abel told me to delete.'

Bewildered, Alice snapped at Isaiah. 'But you didn't delete them!'

'I know, because I never delete, I just archive, it's something I've always done. But I hadn't finished archiving and I hadn't unlinked the pathway, so when Mom pressed the command key, it shortcut to send. I'm so sorry, Alice.'

With tears in her eyes, Alice shook her head. 'I don't want you to be sorry, I want you to undo it. Can't you delete it, so Nico won't see it?'

'No, well, I could, but I've got a "read" notice. Nico has already read it.'

'But don't you understand, that email, it makes out that Salvatore was betraying him with my *dad*. Isaiah, the reason Abel decided *not* to send that version was because he knows Nico well enough to realise that not only will Nico want revenge on Salvatore, but also my dad. But he *can't* get to Dad at the moment, so the closest person to him is Franny. You knew that, Isaiah, but look what you've done. That email could put Franny in *more* danger than she already is. These are real people, Isaiah – their lives depend on us.'

'Alice, please don't cry. I'll sort this out. I promise.'

'How, Isaiah?'

Not feeling like eating his chocolate anymore, Isaiah stared at one of his computer screens. Excited, he suddenly sat forward, watching as the virus he'd embedded in the fake email started to download, copying the details from Nico's phone, sending files and contacts and numbers to Isaiah's computer.

'Alice, we're in. I'm in Nico's phone, our malware bug has worked . . . Wait, wait, I can see he's making a call . . . He's calling Bobby.'

Alice, just as excited, said, 'Will you be able to hear what he says?'

'No, I only get a mirror image of his phone screen on my computer that shows who he's calling. It'll also show me any texts he sends or receives. Basically, anything he does on the phone I'll see it, but I can't hear. Alice, the only way to find out anymore is for you to call him. You need to call Nico and see what he says. It's the only way.'

'Nico? Hey . . . Nico? Are you there?'

Alice held the phone close to her ear, listening to Nico's staggered breathing as she sat on her bed. She waited for another couple of minutes or so before she tried again.

'Nico, are you all right? You're not saying anything. Are you ill? Is there a problem? It's making me nervous.'

In his prison cell, Nico Russo, edgy and dripping with sweat from the hot Colorado evening, leant his head against the off-white walls, his eyes closed as he whispered venomously, 'And why would you be nervous, my *sweet* Alice Rose? What have you got to be nervous about? Have you done something that you shouldn't? Have you, Alice?'

Trying her best not to feel uneasy or paranoid, Alice kept her voice as light as she could.

'No, well, I hope not, Nico.'

Grinding his teeth, Nico hissed, 'And how do I know you're not lying? How do I know precious little Alice isn't just like her precious father?'

Standing up and checking in the hallway that Lola wasn't near enough to overhear, Alice shut the door of her bedroom. Her heart thumping, she walked across to the small window that looked out over Soho's rooftops.

'Nico, have I upset you in some way?'

'You tell me, Alice.'

Trying to play it carefully, Alice said cautiously, 'I'm just confused, because I don't know what my dad has got to do with this. You seem so angry. Different to how you normally are.'

'I'm not angry, Alice, why should I be *fucking* angry when all my life I've just given to others, looked after them, taken care of my family and looked after my friends as if they were my own blood.'

'I'm not sure, I don't know.'

Nico banged his head against the side of his brick cell, bursting open the skin on his forehead to leave a trail of blood to run down the off-white wall. 'You don't know? I thought you were cleverer than that, Alice. But maybe I'm wrong about you like I've been wrong about other people. Maybe you're just like your stupid, stupid father.'

'Nico, you're not making sense.'

Raging, Nico began to pace. 'Aren't I? What a shame, Alice. What a fucking shame for you.'

Doing her best to keep calm, Alice continued to speak gently. 'I don't know why you keep talking about Dad. Has something happened?'

'Not yet, Alice, but it will, trust me, it will.'

'Nico, you're beginning to frighten me.'

'My mother used to tell me, beware of the half-truths, Nico, they're more dangerous than lies because you never know which half you've been given . . .' Nico stopped and chuckled scornfully to himself before adding, 'But then look what happened to her. We all get the punishment we deserve in the end, Alice.'

Not knowing how to steer the conversation, Alice, desperate but feeling sick at her words, said, 'I love you, Nico, and you can tell me anything.'

Agitated, Nico shook his head as he stared up at the sky through the bars of his cell. 'No, Alice, I can't.'

'But you *can*, Nico, we're—'

Nico interrupted her, screaming down the phone, the veins on the side of his head pulsating. 'I said, I can't! Don't tell me what I can do, Alice. I need time to *think* . . . Do you know what it's like to give everything? Every part of you?'

'No.'

'No, I didn't think so, but I do and what do I get in return for all my efforts? I'll tell you, shall I? *Tradimento. Tradimento. Tradimento.*'

With a shiver, Alice thought of what Abel had said as she quietly whispered the word down the phone. 'Betrayal.'

'Yes, and what has to come after betrayal, Alice?'

'I don't know.'

Nico laughed scornfully again as he stared at Alice's photo on the wall. 'After the rain comes the sun, Alice, and after betrayal comes *vendetta* . . . revenge!'

And with that Nico Russo clicked off the phone, leaving Alice Rose frozen with fear of what was about to begin.

Biting down on his fingers hard enough to leave teeth marks, Nico stared at the screen of his phone, rereading the email from Salvatore to Cabhan, which must've been sent by mistake when Salvatore had forwarded all the various emails from his attorney regarding his prison transfer and his appeal.

The email spelt out what had crossed his mind a few times whilst he'd been in prison: that Salvatore was trying to take over the family business with the help of Cabhan. Though when he'd questioned Salvatore about it, of course his brother had just made excuses and denied any such accusation. But now he knew the truth. The *full* truth.

The email was dated a few months ago and for some reason, between then and now, Salvatore had turned his back on Cabhan. Perhaps it was because Salvatore had thought Cabhan knew too much, wanting to dispose of him before it was too late, or perhaps Cabhan had just become surplus to requirements, but whatever the reason, he didn't care, it made no difference. The damage had been done. The writing was now on the wall. He knew the truth.

With a surge of hatred running through him, Nico spat on the floor, mixing his spit with the blood from his head. He made an oath to himself. From this moment on, Salvatore Valentino Russo was no longer his brother. He was dead to him and he would pay heavily. Vengeance, Nico told himself, vengeance would be his.

51

The buzzing of her phone woke Alice. She was exhausted, having only slept fitfully in the night, but reaching over to the bedside cabinet she answered quickly. 'Isaiah? Has something happened?'

'Alice, there's been a text from Nico to Bobby. It came through on my computer just a few minutes ago. I'll read it for you.'

Alice sat up in bed, listening as Isaiah cleared his throat.

I want you to go through with what we discussed last night. Don't fuck it up. Call me when it's done. There's no more time left, everyone has had their chance.

Having finished reading the text message, Isaiah leant back on his chair. 'That's all there is, Alice, there's been no reply from Bobby.'

Feeling sick, Alice closed her eyes to steady herself. 'It can only be about one thing. It can only be the fact that he wants revenge because of what he thinks my dad has done. He's going to do something to Franny, I know it. I just know it.'

Not feeling as convinced as he sounded, Isaiah said, 'No, we don't, Alice, it could be about anything.'

Fighting back tears, Alice shook her head, her hands trembling. 'No, Isaiah, you didn't hear him last night. You didn't hear how Nico sounded. Nothing I said made a difference. He didn't say anything about the emails, but he was so angry, and he talked about betrayal. I just know it was about the email. He's planning to do something, Isaiah . . . What have we done? We've made everything worse, haven't we?'

'Alice, we're doing all we can already. Abel is coming; he'll have landed by now.'

Desperation ran through Alice's words. 'And what difference will that make to Franny and Bree? Isaiah, don't you see, we've got to do something before it's too late.'

'Alice, there *is* nothing. You don't even know if he was talking about them.'

'Yes, I do, and I can't just leave them. It's already my fault and all I've done is gone and made it worse.'

Isaiah, feeling Alice's panic as well as responsible for what his mum had caused, said, 'Why don't you just wait to speak to Abel? He'll know what to do.'

Becoming angry, Alice began to get dressed, putting Isaiah on loudspeaker as she did so. 'I haven't got time to wait for him! Think what the text said: *there's no more time left.* How can you want me to risk it? How can I sit back and do nothing when there's a chance that Bobby is going to hurt Franny?'

'But—'

Beside herself now, Alice shouted down the phone, racked with sobs. 'Don't give me a *but*! Look, we know where they are, don't we? So that means we can do something.'

'Alice, Abel said that he wouldn't manage to get any of his old acquaintances together until Wednesday, just wait a couple of days.'

'I don't care what he says, and I don't care what you say. I've already told you, it'll be too late by then. And I don't want you saying anything to Abel. You understand? I don't want you telling Abel. You owe me that, Isaiah Thomas.'

Isaiah rubbed his face, more stress than he'd ever had in his life hurtling through his body.

325

'Please, Alice, just wait, okay. Don't do anything silly. I'm scared for you. I'm over here and so is Abel, and you can't just do this on your own.'

'I'm not on my own though, am I?'

Isaiah spoke quickly. 'Alice, I love God as much as you do, but I don't think he's going to help you right now.'

Alice, furious, snarled down the phone as she laced up her trainers. 'I'm not talking about God, Isaiah, I'm talking about Alfie.'

Sceptically, Alice stared at Alfie, who was drunk and half asleep. Frowning, she shook him hard, looking up at the clock as she did so.

'Alfie, get up! You need to get up. I need your help. Alfie!'

'Leave me alone, Alice.' Alfie's voice was slurred.

Shouting at him, Alice shook him harder. 'Alfie, you've got to wake up, now!'

Lola hobbled through to the lounge and looked at Alice as she continued to shake Alfie awake.

'What's going on, love?'

'I just need to wake him up.'

Leaving Lola looking baffled, Alice quickly ran into the kitchen, filled one of the pans with water and ran back into the lounge. Without hesitation, she threw the water over Alfie.

Spluttering in shock, Alfie sat up raging. 'What the fuck! What the fuck do you think you're doing? Fucking hell!'

Alice stared at Alfie and spoke with a new kind of firmness. 'Alfie, you need to sober up. You hear me? Alfie!'

Staggering to his feet, Alfie sniffed loudly. 'Leave me alone, Alice.'

She shook her head. 'No, I'm not going to leave you alone. You need to get yourself sorted and have a clear head.'

Alfie went to reach for the almost empty bottle of whiskey, but Alice snatched it away. 'No more drinking, Alfie. Understand?'

Dripping wet, Alfie contorted his face in fury. 'What is this, some fucked-up intervention? I bet this is something to do with you, Lola, ain't it? Is this your idea of the twelve-step programme? What are you going to do, hey, Lola, grant me the serenity to accept the things I cannot change? Well, I've got news for you. I'll never accept it, I'll never accept what's happened to Franny and Bree, so why don't you do me a favour and fuck right off!'

Alice slapped Alfie hard on the face. Her own face was red and angry. 'Don't you dare speak to her like that, do you understand me, Alfie Jennings? The only thing that Lola has done is try to help. Everyone here is hurting, everyone is scared, but it's only you who's drunk. So stop feeling sorry for yourself and get yourself sober.'

Alfie rubbed his face, not quite knowing whether to laugh or bawl Alice out. He smirked. 'What is this, one of your crusades? Cos I've already told you, I ain't no angel.'

Stepping right up close to Alfie, Alice held his glare, her almond eyes hard and steely. 'What this is, Alfie, is me doing what I can to save Franny, like Abel is, like we all are, and if you want to do the same, I'd get in a cold shower and get dressed. But in the meantime, Alfie, why don't you just shut the *hell* up.'

It was past two o'clock as Alice, Alfie and Lola sat in the car on the way to West Berkshire with Alice telling them an edited version of what had happened in the last twenty-four hours.

Lola, driving as smoothly as Lola could, shook her head. The car immediately swerved and Alfie had to put a helping hand on the steering wheel. She sounded bewildered as she spoke to Alice.

'I can't believe it. I feel like I've let you down. All I've done is hide in me bleedin' room and feel sorry for meself.'

Alfie, feeling ashamed, looked at Alice, who was squeezed into the barely-there back seat. His head still swam, and the swirl of alcohol still sat in his blood, but he knew that although it was

327

far from ideal, Alice was right, *this* was the only way and they couldn't risk leaving it until Wednesday – no matter what the danger, no matter what happened, they at least had to try.

'Have you spoken to Isaiah yet?' The tension in Alfie's voice was obvious as he checked the chamber of one of the guns Abel had brought from his house.

Alice glanced at her watch before she replied. She had to trust that Isaiah would contact her if there were any more texts or calls between Bobby and Nico. But maybe, rather than *no news is good news*, maybe it was a bad thing that there hadn't been any more communication between the pair, because it could only mean one thing: that the final decision had already been made. There was no going back. Nico had made up his mind that Franny was going to pay for what he thought was Salvatore and her dad's betrayal.

Answering just as tensely, Alice said, 'No, I haven't, and I haven't spoken to Abel either. I just don't think it's a good idea, not for now anyway. He can't help from where he is, so the only thing Abel will do is worry and . . . Lola, turn here. The farm is just along that road.'

Alfie glanced out of the window, looking concerned. 'We need to ditch the car, it's hardly discreet, is it?'

Lola nodded as she pulled over, driving the Ferrari carefully off the road to park up behind a large thicket. She swivelled round to face Alfie, her forehead creased with fear. 'What now, Alfie?'

'You got to stay here, darlin', just keep hidden.'

'No, no way! There's only two of you, you'll need all the help you can get.'

Alice leaned over the seat and kissed Lola gently on her cheek. 'Lola, please do as Alfie tells you. It really will be better if you stay here.'

'You mean, I'm no good for anything?'

'That's not what we're saying at all,' Alice said warmly.

'I can still do my bit, you know. Look at Alfie, his leg's bust up, he's hardly up to it himself. Look, I can't just do nothing. What would Franny and Bree think if I was just kicking back and doing nowt helping out? I just wish I could be of use.'

Nervously, Alice's eyes darted about before she beamed a smile at Lola. 'Listen, we couldn't have done any of this without you. You've played your part, you really have. It was only because of you that I didn't run off. You came searching for me and you made me see sense, showed me that I was being selfish. You've been amazing and I love you, but we need you here, so *please*, Lola, let Alfie and I do what we have to do.'

Lola's eyes filled with tears, panic embedded into her voice. 'But what if you don't come back? How long should I stay here? Should I come looking for you after an hour, should I call someone, what should I do?'

As Alice looked at the road ahead, catching a glimpse of the farmhouse far in the distance, she simply muttered, 'Just pray for us, Lola, just pray, because right now that's all you can do.'

52

'Sal, hey, Sal, can I have a word?' Bobby Russo smiled at his brother as he sat on one of the broken chairs in the warehouse, next to the cage where Franny and Bree were being kept.

Nonchalantly, Salvatore shrugged, got up and walked across to Bobby. 'Yeah, sure, what's up?'

Bobby tipped his head to one side, his eyes darkening. 'See, the thing is, I've got a little problem.'

Suddenly concerned, Salvatore frowned. 'Yeah?'

Bobby looked around, bringing his voice down to a whisper. He smiled again, holding Salvatore's stare as he placed his hand gently on the back of Salvatore's neck. 'You little fucking creep, you think you can betray us?'

'What!'

Then, without warning and with vicious fury, Bobby kneed his brother hard in his stomach. Shocked and taken by surprise, Salvatore fell forward, sprawling on top of the cage, causing Bree to scream in fright.

'Come on, Sal, get up! Get up, you motherfucker.'

Bewildered, Salvatore staggered up and edged back towards the warehouse entrance with Bobby bearing down on him.

'Where are you going, hey, Sal? Huh?'

'What's wrong with you, Bobby? What the fuck is wrong with you?'

Bobby laughed as he brought his fist slamming down again, his New Jersey twang loud and aggressive. 'What's wrong with *me*? What's wrong with me? You motherfucker. You creeping motherfucker.'

Bobby launched into another attack, kicking Salvatore hard over and over again, knocking him out of the warehouse and back out towards the ditch as he continued to yell at him, wild-eyed. '*Ci hai tradito.*'

Salvatore, panting and wiping the blood out of his eyes, struggled to get up but slipped back down into the ditch by the stream. Breathless, he gasped, 'What are you talking about, Bobby? I've never betrayed you, I wouldn't. I love you. *Ti amo.*'

Incensed, Bobby dragged Salvatore's head up by his hair, spitting in rage as he slammed his fist into his face so hard that he split open Salvatore's lip.

'We know about the emails, Sal. We know about you and Cabhan. Thought you'd get away with it, huh? Thought you were smart, did you? But you're not so smart now, are you?'

Punching Salvatore again, causing him to splutter and cough as his mouth filled with blood, Bobby stared at his brother with disgust. 'You make me sick! Does family mean nothing to you?'

'I don't know what you're talking about, I swear.'

In agony, Salvatore tried to crawl away, but another well-aimed brutal kick from Bobby left him groaning on the floor. Spitting the blood out of his mouth, Salvatore watched in horror as Bobby took a gun from his back pocket and aimed it at him.

'Bobby, no!'

To which Bobby Russo smiled and pulled the trigger.

'*Brucia all'inferno*, Salvatore. Burn in hell.'

Alfie and Alice hid behind a copse of trees, the farmhouse still some way in the distance.

'What was that, Ally? It sounded like a gunshot.'

Alice, feeling the tension, shook her head. 'I don't know, but it came from over there, near the buildings.'

Alfie listened again but, hearing nothing more, turned his attention back to Alice, feeling nervous himself.

'So have you got it now? Do you understand? There's really not much to it. But it's got a massive kickback, and it's heavy, and of course these shells don't travel far, so you need to be up close and personal.'

Alfie handed one of the shotguns to Alice, grimacing at the pain in his leg, which was throbbing now the alcohol had begun to wear off.

Alice nodded as she stared at the gun, hearing the anxiety in her own voice. 'Yep, I understand. How hard can it be, right?'

Alfie saw the fear in Alice's eyes, and a surge of guilt and concern hit him. 'Listen, darlin', why don't you just go back to the car, sit with Lola? I think that's the best thing, don't you? It's not right, you shouldn't be doing this. You're sixteen, for Christ's sake, no young girl should be holding a shotgun in their hand. Please, Alice, just go back. I can do this. I got it, I promise.'

Wishing she could do just that, Alice gave Alfie a small smile. 'No, Alfie, we're in this together. I'm not leaving you.'

'But, Alice, this is dangerous. This isn't a game, someone could get hurt. And like Lola says, we might not be heading back tonight, if you know what I mean. I can't let you do this.'

'You've got no choice. This is my decision. I'm under no illusion, Alfie, I know what's waiting for us, but I have faith. I have faith that somehow Bree and Franny will be okay, but not if I back out. This is something I have to do.'

Alice stopped talking and tried desperately to get her shaking under control. She wiped away the tears that were rolling down her face. These past few days she'd cried more than she had in her entire life.

'I'm sorry, I don't know why I'm even crying, it's stupid, that's all I seem to be doing.'

'Alice, it's okay. I've been around for a long time and even I'm bricking it. We're going into the unknown and you, well, Jesus, Alice, I've never met anyone so brave. But this is going to be tough, we're up against it.'

'I know, I know, but we *have* to finish this. Whatever it takes, Nico won't stop it so we have to, Alfie.'

Alfie stared at Alice for a moment before he took her in a tight embrace, holding her closely and kissing her on her head. 'Alice Rose, have I ever told you how much we all love you? . . . Now, if we are going to do this, come on, let's go and kick some ass.'

Alice and Alfie ran through the trees and bushes as fast as they could. Alfie, pouring with sweat, stopped occasionally to lean on a tree, pain from his leg shooting through his body. But, determined, he darted through the woods a few feet behind Alice, the farmhouse coming into sight.

On the mound of the hill that overlooked the farm, Alice, fear and adrenalin pumping through her, lay on her stomach next to Alfie, a gun by her side.

As Alice kept her eyes on the farmhouse, Alfie surveyed the area, staring at the large derelict warehouse situated by the other farm buildings. Then he suddenly ducked, pulling Alice down with him.

'Alice, someone's coming! Stay still!'

Breathing hard, Alice and Alfie stayed frozen on the ground for a few moments before, fear pricking him, Alfie warily raised his head again.

He watched as two men, both armed with semi-automatic weapons, walked around the building in deep conversation, then stopped to smoke their cigars by an old burnt-out tractor.

Worried, he whispered quickly to Alice again. 'We should really wait until it's dark. If we run down now, try to get to the warehouse or have a look inside any of the other buildings, we'll be so exposed they'll see us straightaway.'

'But we can't wait, you know that.' Alice looked at Alfie in panic.

Deep in thought, Alfie fell silent until eventually he said, 'Maybe what we need is to cause a distraction, do something that will make them all come running out. That way we'll have a good chance to see how many of them there are.'

'Lola. Why don't we call her? She can drive the car, they're sure to come out.'

'I don't know, it could be risky.'

Alice's voice was urgent. 'Look, we have to do something, what else is there? Just get Lola to drive to the top of the hill and then she can turn back. Like you say, all we need is a distraction that will give us a chance to go and see what's down there. See if Franny and Bree are even there, because we don't know that for certain. Alfie, just call her. *Please.*'

With his eyes still trained on the men, Alfie, knowing there were no other options, pulled his phone out of his pocket. He hesitated just for a moment to glance at Alice before pressing call.

'Lola, you've got your wish, darlin', we need your help.'

From over the horizon, Alfie and Alice saw the red Ferrari swerving and weaving, snaking and spinning, spitting up dirt and smoke along the gravel path. Alfie could only guess at how fast Lola was going, but it was clearly too fast. Even from where they were waiting, they could see the smoke billowing up and out of the car and the sound of the engine revving, turning over at high speed, was booming out like a beatbox.

Terrified for Lola, Alfie muttered, 'Fucking hell, what's she doing? She was supposed to just stop there. Christ almighty, why ain't she turning?'

He stared in horror. It was clear Lola was completely out of control as the Ferrari hurtled down the track, careering on, heading for the farm.

Scrambling up with some difficulty, Alfie yelled to Alice, 'Come on, Alice! Run! Let's at least make the most of it.'

The pair set off, sprinting down the grassy verge in the direction of the car. Alice, her heart racing, caught a glimpse of one of the Russos' men rushing up the hill towards the speeding vehicle, but there was nothing she could do to help – only hope that somehow Lola would be able to regain control . . .

Inside the car, Lola, terrified, pushed down on the accelerator, trying to turn the Ferrari back around. But feeling like the vehicle was in control rather than her, she gripped the leather steering wheel as if she were in some kind of fight.

The smell of burnt rubber and engine fumes filled the air. Her head flicked back as one of the wheels hit a stone, making the car veer and spin, speeding it along the dirt track with the dial hitting 120 and dust blowing from underneath the wheels as if the Ferrari were on fire.

With the wind streaming around the car and the noise of the gravel hitting the underside like hailstones, Lola, petrified, screamed over the blare of the roaring engine as she tried to keep the car straight, smoke and dirt clouding her vision. Suddenly, in front of her, she saw a man running from behind the warehouse, gun in hand.

Frantically trying to manoeuvre the car in a different direction, Lola spun the steering wheel hard. But all she managed to do was send the Ferrari careering into a skid, spinning it round and round into a powerful tight circle before it came to an abrupt, grinding, stalling halt by the side of the warehouse wall.

Without having a minute to catch her breath, Lola watched in terror as the man came nearer towards her. Almost hysterical, Lola, crying hard, pressed the start button. 'Come on, come on, come on, start! Oh my Christ!'

Horrified, she began to shake as she watched the man raise

his gun and aim it straight at her whilst she tried desperately to get the car going again. She let out a blood-curdling scream as she ducked down, throwing herself to the side as the bullet shattered the windscreen. Lying on her side, she glanced up, and there at the passenger window was Gian, holding his gun.

She stared into his eyes and held her breath in terror as he smiled.

'Please, no, *please*.'

'*Addio signora.* Goodbye.' As he went to pull the trigger, Gian's eyes suddenly rolled back, the whites showing, a bullet hole through his head as he fell forward, his body smashing against the car before dropping onto the dirt track.

Traumatised, Lola looked up, blinking away the spots of blood that had splattered onto her face. A few feet away she saw Alfie holding a smoking gun. He opened his mouth to say something but, as he did, Lola screamed again.

'Alfie! Look out!'

The pain in Alfie's shoulder told him he'd been hit as he whirled round too late to see another of the Russo men behind him. Desperately, he tried to shoot back, but his arm, his shoulder didn't have the strength to raise his shotgun.

He staggered forward as Lola continued to scream whilst the man aimed his weapon directly at Alfie.

'Put it down. I said put it down,' Alice Rose shouted as she crept up unnoticed and shoved the muzzle of her gun hard into the man's back. 'I said put it down. *Now*!'

Immediately the man dropped his gun, throwing it on the muddy ground as Alice continued to give instructions.

'Put your hands up and turn around. Go on. Turn!'

Slowly, the man, small and well-built, turned around. He stared at Alice Rose, who stood by the warehouse holding a sawn-off shotgun. Her hands trembled as she glanced at Alfie, who was bleeding heavily and lying on the ground in agony.

'Stay where you are. I said, stay where you are!'

For a moment the man hesitated as he watched Alice intently before a large grin spread across his face. He spoke with a heavy New Jersey accent. 'You can't do it, can you?'

Alice shook, her hands still trembling. 'I can, and I will.'

'Come on then, little girl, I'm waiting.'

The man walked confidently towards her, holding her stare as Alice's fingers wavered over the trigger. Terrified, her voice broke into a whisper. 'Stay back! Stay where you are. I've warned you.'

The man's grin contorted into a sneer. 'What are you going to do, *shoot me*?'

'No, but I am.'

Taken by complete surprise, the man quickly spun round to face Lola, who held Alfie's gun in her hands. She looked at him with contempt. 'And I have no problem with doing it, mate, none whatsoever.'

And with that, Lola Harding pulled the trigger.

Chucking the gun to the ground, Lola hobbled across to where Alice stood. 'Are you all right, lovie?'

Distressed, Alice looked at Lola wide-eyed. 'I'm sorry, I'm sorry, I couldn't do it. I tried, but I just couldn't. I've let you down, I'm so sorry.'

'Hey, hey, stop that. No need to be sorry, don't even say that.'

Before Alice could reply, Alfie shouted to them. 'Can you hear that? It sounds like someone's calling.'

He spoke through gritted teeth, the pain showing in his face as he pushed himself up against the warehouse wall, cold sweat running down his forehead. Lola and Alice hurriedly went over to him, with Lola wrapping her neck scarf tightly round his shoulder to try to curb the bleeding. Alfie frowned, speaking quietly as the pain soared round his body.

'Sshhh, there it is again. You must've heard that?'

Lola nodded. 'Yes, I can hear a voice. I think it's coming from in there. Alfie, it is.'

Without waiting for the others, Alice, her hopes rising, ran to the end of the building and popped her head around the corner, making sure no one was there.

'Alice! Be careful!' Lola shouted after her as Alice crept along the wall until she came to a large wooden door. She waited there as Alfie, helped by Lola, came up behind her. 'Are you sure you don't want to stay here? I'll go in if you like.'

'It's fine, Lola.'

Alice smiled as she slid open the door, recoiling at the smell that hit her. She covered her nose and, side by side with Alfie and Lola, walked into the gloom of the warehouse.

'Hello?' A voice came out of the darkness.

'Bree? Bree, is that you?'

'Alfie?'

'Yes, I'm here, baby, I'm here!' Alfie's voice was filled with relief and despite his pain, he ran towards her. He stopped in his tracks as he saw Bree, covered in blood and bodily fluids, trapped and locked like a dog in a cage.

He fell to his knees, sick at what he was seeing, anger welling in him. 'Bree, oh my God, Bree. What did they do to you?'

Bree's fingers touched Alfie's through the bars. She spoke, her lips parched and cracked, her voice hoarse and frail. 'You found me. You came for me, Alfie.'

'Yes, darlin', of course we did, of course, but it was Alice and her friend who found you . . . Where's Franny? Bree, where's Franny?'

Weak and dehydrated, Bree tried to answer but her head nodded forward.

'Okay, don't talk, it's okay, baby.'

Alfie turned to Lola, trying not to worry about the amount of blood he was losing, focused instead on what he needed to do. 'We've got to get her out of there. The others will be around here somewhere. Let's get back in the car as soon as we can. But we can't shoot the lock off, it's too small a space, she'll get hurt.

Lola, why don't you go and check the men's pockets for the keys? It's best you do it rather than Alice, they'll be in a bit of a mess.'

Distraught at the sight of Bree, Lola nodded and shuffled off without saying a word.

Before Alfie had time to say anything else, his phone rang, buzzing in his top pocket. 'Get that for me, Alice. I can't move me arm.'

Quickly, Alice pulled the phone out. The call came up as private.

'It might be Isaiah or Abel, I'll take it outside.'

She ran to the warehouse door and stepped back into the sunlight as she answered.

'Hello? Isaiah?'

'No.'

Alice paused, then carefully said, 'Who is this?'

'I should ask you the same question, but it's Bobby, I was calling to speak to Alfie about Franny, I thought he might want to say goodbye.'

Alice's head spun, her voice breathless. 'Bobby?'

Bobby laughed, sounding very much like his brother Nico. 'Yes.'

'Bobby, Bobby Russo?'

'That's right. Who are you?'

'I'm Alice, Alice Rose, and I understand you've been looking for me.'

53

'Where's Alice?' Alfie asked Lola as she walked back into the warehouse carrying a bunch of keys.

'I thought she was with you?'

Panicking, Alfie shook his head. 'She was, well, she was a few minutes ago, but she went outside to take a call.'

'I didn't see her when I came in, she wasn't there.'

'She must've been there, she just went outside.'

Lola hurried to the warehouse entrance and looked around. Her face drained of colour as she turned back to Alfie. 'She's gone, Alfie. She's gone.'

Alice Rose ran as quickly as she could along the gravel path, up the hillside to the trees at the top, listening to Isaiah on the phone as she ran.

'Alice, I've got some bad news, I'm sorry but—'

She cut in, speaking quickly, her words rolling on top of each other. 'I know about Franny already, I've just spoken to Bobby. He's given me an hour but that's all. We've got to come up with something by then, otherwise it's all over. He obviously doesn't know what's happened back at the farm and that's good. I haven't told Alfie, though, because he's hurt, and anyway, he'd try to go in all guns blazing and Bobby will kill Franny then for sure. She won't stand a chance, that's why I need to speak to Nico. I *have* to talk to him, I'm the only one who can try to sort this out.'

'What? What are you talking about? Alice, you're not making sense. What's happened? What's Franny got to do with this? And what do you mean, *the farm*?'

With the sun beating down on her face, Alice slowed down to a walk. Puzzled, she frowned. 'I . . . I thought that was why you were calling, to tell me about Bobby having Franny.'

In his bedroom, Isaiah sat down on his chair, his voice full of anguish. 'Oh my gosh, Alice, I didn't know.'

'So, if that's not why you were calling, what are *you* talking about?'

'It's about Nico; he's being transferred on Wednesday. I just saw an email from his attorney, so the plan with Abel can't go ahead.'

Thinking for a moment, Alice quickly said, 'Then bring it forward.'

'What?'

'Just listen to me. Get Abel on standby, but he needs to be ready in the next fifteen minutes.'

Isaiah shook his head. 'Alice, you're asking the impossible. You're crazy!'

'Just make it happen, Isaiah, and don't do anything until I call you back, but make sure he's ready.'

Alice clicked off the phone and immediately dialled another number.

'Hello?'

'Nico, it's me. It's Alice.'

Nico purred down the phone. 'You took your time, Alice Rose. When Bobby told me he'd spoken to you, I expected your call straightaway. After all, I thought we were friends.'

'Well, I'm here now, and just for your information, Nico, I thought we were friends too, but *even Satan disguises himself as an angel of light.* However, I do want to talk about a deal I've got for you.'

In his room, Isaiah Thomas felt butterflies in his stomach as he read Alice's text:

> Do it. But you've only got half an hour. Call me when it's done.

Reaching across to his phone, Isaiah, feeling like one of Pastor Michaels' prayers would come in useful right now, called Abel. 'Okay, it's on, are you ready?'

Abel, dressed in a janitor's uniform, sat in the hire car he'd picked up from the airport, the windows open and the dead heat of the Colorado day coming in through the window. He could feel the sweat dripping down his back and the sense of anticipation running through his veins.

He spoke quietly. 'Believe me, Isaiah, I've been ready for this moment for a long time.'

Abel closed his eyes, letting the emotions run over him as he listened to Isaiah talk, as he expertly – from his small bedroom in Mississippi – began tapping various data and numbers into his computers.

The monitors lit up and a series of binary programming codes flashed green, whirling down the screens as Isaiah took a deep breath, readying himself as he glanced at his notes.

'Abel, you need to drive down to the visitors' car park, which is on your right. Then wait for the prison alarms. I'm going to set them off in –' Isaiah paused, feeling a mix of nervousness and excitement as he glanced up at the clock and at one of the processor screens in front of him '– in four minutes thirty-six seconds . . . And remember, there are three main sections within the prison: two of them are for general prisoners, the other for high-security ones.

'There are four electronic security rings around the prison and one at the main gate. The perimeter one and the gate, I'll deactivate first, then close it behind you. The last thing anyone needs is a bunch of prisoners running out, so you've got to be quick getting in. But you do understand, Mr Gray, once you're in, you won't be able to get out for another sixteen minutes and then you've only got a one-minute window.'

'What about all the guards when I go in?'

Knowledgeably, Isaiah said, 'There are two towers. Tower one is where the systems are and in tower two, that's where the armed guards are based, but they'll be too worried about people trying to get out than in. As we discussed, I'll hack into the communication system, so the guards won't be able to speak to one another around the prison, which will make it harder for them to seize back control. And anyway, Mr Gray, you're dressed in a janitor's uniform *and* going *in* towards the centre of the prison rather than out, so you won't be their main target; in fact, I'm certain they'll ignore you altogether.'

Abel rubbed his head, swatting away a fly. 'How do you know this is even going to work?'

'I don't.'

'What?'

Isaiah shrugged as he sat back in his chair. 'The only thing I do know is since I came up with the plan, I've timed myself getting into the prison computer system. I've got it down to a good time. It's not guaranteed, but if it's any consolation, I shouldn't be detected as I'm going in on a zero-day attack.'

Driving up to the visitors' car park, Abel frowned. 'You've lost me.'

'What I'll be doing is using a previously unknown vulnerability to get into their system. I'll be the first one to exploit it, well, at this prison anyway. Look, that's just technical stuff, you don't have to worry about that. The point is, Mr Gray, it will be very difficult for them to try to identify the problem, so I'll gain

343

administrator control to their system while simultaneously camouflaging the takeover. They'll think there's just a blip in the system rather than someone hacking into it.'

'And getting out?'

Isaiah blew a large bubble from the gum he was chewing. 'Well, that's easy, all you need to do is run.'

Glancing again at the clock, aware there wasn't much time, Isaiah began to talk quickly. 'You've got the physical fence, the detection ring, the inner ring and around a thousand cameras as well as thermal sensors installed throughout the penitentiary. I have to shut them down section by section, otherwise I might be bounced out of the system. It'll be like the lights going out at Christmas.'

'And once you've done that?'

'Basically, the inmates will be able to come out of their cells and it'll be dangerous in there. They'll be running riot, apart from the prisoners in wing 10, that's where you need to be. I'll keep that wing shut, but after eight minutes I'll open the door to the wing. I won't be able to keep it closed for any longer, so keep an eye on your watch.'

'Okay, I got it.'

'Don't forget, Mr Gray, that an emergency military unit will be deployed to come to the prison as backup, and once they've been contacted, it'll take just twenty-two minutes for them to get there. So, you'll have to be in and out before that time. It's tight but doable.'

Isaiah Thomas took a large sip of lemonade as he sat with the air con on, tapping into his computer again. He spoke again, cracking his knuckles, slipping on his *Mission Impossible* baseball cap.

'Mr Gray, in one minute's time you'll hear the prison alarms; that will be your cue to run towards the main doors, which will then open. After that you're on your own. But don't worry, I was born to do this, you'll be fine . . . You've got the screenshot I sent you?'

344

Having parked up, Abel checked his phone. 'Yeah, I've got it.'

'Good, but make sure everything else is shut down on your phone. Just follow the route as if it's a map. It'll be like *Call of Duty*, Mr Gray, and you're my player.'

With the sound of the prison alarm screaming out, Abel Gray quickly darted through the main gates, feeling the sweat running down his back as he charged along the side wall, watching the prison officers and staff running around bewildered.

Rushing to the left of them, Abel, full of adrenalin, ran towards the main block of the prison. Spotting all the doors beginning to open, he instantly sprinted down the corridors as the sounds of the prisoners began to get louder, with the shouts and cries of the officers echoing around the long stone corridors.

Chaos descended and surrounded Abel, and he could feel his heart pounding in his chest as he sped along, aware he had to keep on schedule.

Cell door after cell door came open and the inmates charged out like a herd of stampeding buffalos. All around him there were shouts and screams and bangs, clanging metal upon metal, but Abel, undeterred and without fear, continued to run as the prisoners pushed and shoved, barging him out of the way as they rushed for freedom.

With his top wet with sweat, Abel ran against the tide of men, charging along with steely determination down the dark corridors. Out of the corner of his eye, he saw three prisoners attack a warden as they threw their things out of their cells. More fights and screams and fires broke out around him, the acrid smell of burning mattress lying heavy in the air.

Hurriedly checking his phone, Abel followed the map Isaiah had sent him, which took him past the gymnasium and up a flight of metal stairs, where a group of Mexican inmates threw a screaming fellow prisoner over the balcony.

The sounds of the prison were deafening: clanking, clattering noises filled the air. At the top end of the corridor, Abel glanced at his watch and began to slow down as he headed for a door that read 'Wing 10'.

He pulled on the large metal handle of the security entrance but it was locked. Suddenly remembering what Isaiah had said, he looked at his watch: *After eight minutes precisely, I'll open the door to the wing.*

Keeping his eye on his watch, Abel began to count down. 'Five, four, three, two, one.' He smiled to himself as the door sprang open and, talking to himself, he walked into the small corridor of wing 10.

'Nice one, Isaiah, nice one, mate.'

It was surprisingly quiet, a stark contrast to the rest of the prison as Abel ran along, peeping in through each of the cells' tiny windows, pressure beginning to mount as the minutes ticked down.

Suddenly he stopped, standing motionless before he stepped back a few paces to the cell he'd just looked in. A wave of nausea rushed through him as he closed his eyes to ready himself. A moment later, Abel Gray opened the door of cell number five.

'Hello, Nico. It's been a while. Remember me?'

Nico Russo spun round, his face a mass of confusion and incomprehension. He blinked several times, almost as if what was in front of him wasn't quite real. Then he narrowed his eyes as he stared at Abel, a pulsating vein twitching at his temple as his voice gave away only a trace of alarm.

'Abel. It's good to see you.'

Ignoring Nico, Abel stalked into the small cell, hearing the shouts and cries outside in the corridor becoming louder. He stopped to stare at the wall, looking at the photo of Alice before ripping it off.

Holding Alice's picture in his hand, Abel studied it for a moment before glancing back up at Nico who stood in the corner of the cell.

'You couldn't break her, could you? You underestimated this one, didn't you, Nico?'

Nico smirked to himself. 'Nothing's over until it's over . . . How is Natalia, by the way?'

Abel Gray, with the strength and fervour of a lion, lunged at Nico, slammed and smashed him against the wall, gripped his hair and banged his head against the window bars.

Panting, Abel stared at Nico then closed his eyes as he continued to push and grind him hard against the wall. Images of *that* day rushed through his head. Screams of Natalia begging him to make the Russos stop echoed in his mind.

Breathing heavily, Abel tried to regain his composure, his reality, his sanity. Refusing to give Nico the satisfaction of learning what had really happened to Natalia, he whispered the words he so wished were true. 'She's fine . . . Natalia's just fine.'

Nico grinned. 'That's good. Natalia, from what I remember, was certainly *special*.'

With a vice-like grip, Abel squeezed Nico's face in his hand. He hissed through his teeth, the sound of his short, shallow breaths filling the cell.

'I had so much to say to you, Nico. For years I'd planned it, every day I thought about you, you were all I could think about. You haunted my dreams, my waking hours. I couldn't feel myself, Nico, but I could feel you, smell you. You lived within me like my heartbeat, but now I see there really isn't anything to say. I once told you, I once promised you, *avrò la mia vendetta*. I will have my revenge. However long it took, whatever it took, I knew that somehow, some time, I'd have my day of reckoning – and that time has finally come. And now, Nico, you shall burn in the fires of hell . . . This is for Natalia and for Alice.'

From under his jumper Abel pulled out a large jagged knife and swiftly dragged it across Nico's throat, pushing down hard, cutting through his windpipe.

Wide-eyed, Nico held his neck, the blood pouring and

spurting as he gurgled and gulped, gasping desperately to catch his breath. And as Abel stepped back and watched, Nico dropped lifeless to the ground, a pool of blood spreading quickly over the cold concrete floor. Then Abel Gray checked the time and turned to run.

In Mississippi, Isaiah paced around his room, checking and occasionally inputting numbers into his computer as he watched the screens blink and update, refreshing constantly. He glanced up at the clock.

'Come on, Abel, come on. You can do this, I know you can do this.'

He closed his eyes as his phone buzzed, too nervous to look at it. Then, taking a deep breath, with beads of sweat trickling down his back, Isaiah ran to read the text and almost immediately he punched the air in delight and spun his baseball cap across the room.

'Mission completed!'

'Isaiah, what's all that shouting for? Don't forget, Bible class starts soon.'

Biting into a Hershey bar, glowing with pride and relief, Isaiah rolled his eyes. 'Whatever, Mom, whatever.'

54

From behind the tree on the hilltop, Alice was able to see Bobby.
Next to him, only a few feet away, was Franny, standing by the
Russos' car, her hands tied together behind her back. Alice saw
Bobby look at his watch. Feeling sick, she took a deep breath as
she paced, the stress and pressure building up inside her.

Muttering to herself, trying to find comfort, sick with nerves,
she waited to hear from Isaiah.

'Please give me strength, somehow give me strength. Please
somehow make this okay.'

She closed her eyes, putting her hands together, feeling her
body shaking, trembling as the minutes ticked by. Then, suddenly,
after what seemed like years, Alice felt her phone buzz through
a text in her pocket. Pulling it out quickly, she read:

It's done. Abel did it! Mission accomplished.

Alice smiled and, overwhelmed, her eyes filling with tears,
she bent forward, catching her breath, feeling the relief flow. But
almost immediately she began to tense again, a cold fear creeping
all over her body.

She stood up straight and walked across to the brow of the

hill again, where she stared down to the bottom of the steep grassy slope. With her hand shaking and only a slight hesitation, Alice Rose pressed call.

'Bobby, Bobby, it's me.'

'Hello, Alice, just on time. Another minute and it would've all been over.'

Knowing that Bobby had yet to find out about Nico, Alice, her voice edgy and overwrought, asked, 'You know what the deal is?'

Bobby grinned as he looked up at Alice standing by the tree at the top of the hill. Chuckling, he spoke into the phone. 'I do, and I think you've all got a bargain. I think Nico was very generous.'

'So let her go . . . *now*!'

Without saying a word to Franny, Bobby placed his phone on the bonnet of the car and untied Franny's hands. She looked at him, puzzled, as he nodded his head and said, 'Go on, you're free to go.'

Rubbing her wrists, her face swollen from bruises, Franny stared with hatred at Bobby.

'What? Why?'

Bobby Russo stepped forward, pushing the gun hard into Franny's stomach. 'I said go. Otherwise we might change our minds.'

'What about Bree? What about . . .'

'*Go*!'

Franny began to run as Bobby picked up the phone again to Alice, who was still on the other end of the line. 'Don't do anything stupid, don't try any games, Alice, I still can kill her from here.'

'I won't.'

'Well then?'

Alice took a deep breath and then, her voice shaking, said, 'I'm ready.'

Trance-like, she dropped her phone and began walking down the hill as Franny ran up. Halfway to the top, Franny slowed down and stopped. Perplexed, she stared at Alice, not understanding why she was walking towards her.

She turned to glance at Bobby then back at Alice before running over to her and grabbing her by the arm. 'What are you doing, Alice? What the hell are you doing?'

Not looking at Franny as she tried to carry on walking, Alice's voice was a monotone. 'I've made a deal. Now just let me go, Franny.'

Franny shook her head furiously, running in front of Alice. 'No, no, no. You are not doing what I think you're doing.'

Alice's eyes were full of fear as she looked intensely into Franny's face. 'He would never let you go otherwise and now it's over. Nico's dead, but once Bobby finds out he would kill you too. Trust me, Franny, this is the only way.'

'Alice, it's not. It's not! It's not down to you to save me. I'm going back to Bobby, I'll tell him not to take you, to keep me instead.' Franny's voice was desperate.

Weeping, Alice shook her head. 'It's not you they want. It's me, and this way it'll be over. This way you'll be safe. You've all made sacrifices for me and now it's my turn.'

Franny began to cry, something she had rarely done until this week, as her words tumbled out. 'Alice, no, it'll never be over if you do this. What do you think we're going to do without you? Alice, see sense, this is crazy. This is not going to happen. You don't have to do this. Where's Alfie? You need to speak to Alfie.'

Trembling, her legs knocking together as she spoke, Alice shook Franny off. 'Franny, please, this is the way it's got to be. It'll be all right. I have to go, Bobby's waiting. I love you, Franny.'

Losing her usual cool, Franny gave in to the tears. 'Jesus Christ, Alice, no! Don't you understand what they're going to do to you? They're animals, Alice!'

Frantically, Franny turned to Bobby, ran back down the hill

and, with tears still streaming down her face, screamed at the top of her voice, 'I won't let you do this to her, you hear me. You leave her alone, you fucking well leave her alone. Take me, come on, Bobby, take me!'

Then, running to Bobby's car, she opened the door, threw herself in and quickly pulled the door closed, but Bobby, with one hard tug, yanked it open and dragged Franny out by her hair as Alice came running down the hill.

Kicking Franny aside as he pointed his gun at Alice, Bobby yelled, 'Get out of the way, Franny. You hear me?'

Alice grabbed Franny's hand, her beautiful almond eyes full of pain. 'I love you, Franny. Here . . .' Alice pulled off the cross she wore around her neck, placing it in Franny's hands.

Franny was hysterical with panic.

'Alice, please, please, don't do this! You really don't understand what they're going to do to you.'

Holding Franny's stare, Alice trembled as she got in the car, Bobby holding the door open for her whilst she talked calmingly to Franny.

'*Even though I walk through the valley of the shadow of death, I will fear no evil, for you are with me. Your—*'

The door slammed shut, cutting off Alice's words.

'Stop, Alice, stop!'

The car sped down the gravel track with Franny chasing after it, tears streaking her face.

'Alice, no! Alice, no!'

From inside the car, Alice, terror-stricken, listened to Franny's screams, the reality of what was happening and what she'd agreed to suddenly hitting as Bobby continued to drive at speed. Panicking, she banged on the window. 'Franny! Franny!'

'Alice!'

Franny's voice faded away and Alice herself began to scream, scrambling over the car seat to the back as Bobby looked at her in the rear-view mirror, a large smirk on his face as he switched on his music, Italian opera blaring out to drown out Alice's cries.

Turning his attention back to the road, Bobby, alarmed, abruptly took his foot off the accelerator. There, standing in the middle of the track, bleeding profusely but still alive, was his brother Salvatore Russo.

From the track, Salvatore screamed inaudible words as he raised the semi-automatic gun he held in his hands. He fired at Bobby and blinding flashes of light flared out as a hail of bullets ripped through the car and windscreen, exploding Bobby's head into thousands of bloodied pieces. Alice screamed in horror as the car swerved, hitting Salvatore and throwing his body up into the air.

The car plummeted towards the ditch, pitching and bouncing over the rough ground before nosediving to an abrupt halt as it hit a tree and the engine burst into flames.

'Alice! Alice!'

Alice heard her name as Franny began tugging frantically at the buckled rear door, forcing it open as Lola, who'd run out from the nearby warehouse, helped Franny drag Alice out of the burning wreckage, pulling her to safety. The dead body of Salvatore Russo lay only metres away.

Alice, with a large gash on her forehead, traumatised by her ordeal, burst into desperate tears. Sobbing uncontrollably, she buried her head in Franny's chest.

'Alice, oh, Alice Rose, you silly, special, wonderful, brave girl, why did you do that? Why would you do that, for me?'

'Because I love you, Franny, I couldn't have let anything happen to you.'

'The things we do for love, hey?' Lola smiled, stroking Alice's hair as she winked at Franny.

A moment later, Alfie and Bree stumbled up together with Bree looking ill, her face drawn and pale as she tried to push down the pain.

Sitting down next to Alice, Alfie kissed her on her head and didn't care that his voice was breaking and that tears were falling down his cheeks. He smiled. 'It's over, Ally, they've destroyed themselves . . .' He stopped and grinned. 'But of course, they could only have done that with a little bit of help from you – and I say, Amen to that.'

Alice, Lola and Alfie laughed as they clung to each other, until Alfie, glancing up, saw Bree walking away.

'Hold up! Where are you going?'

Struggling to his feet and thankful that the bleeding from his shoulder seemed to be under control, though he was still in an incredible amount of pain, Alfie frowned as he walked towards her.

'Bree, what's going on? Where are you going?'

'I just thought it was best if I left you to it.'

Alfie frowned, though his eyes were warm. 'Why? You're part of the gang now.'

Bree shook her head. 'No, Alfie, I'm not.'

'Look, I know it's all a mess, but after what happened it puts everything in perspective.'

'I know and that's my point.'

Alfie grimaced at the sudden pain that shot through his shoulder. 'What are you talking about?'

Bree took a deep breath, watching as Franny walked over to them. 'I'm leaving, Alf. I need time to be alone. I need to get my head straight. I should . . .' She stopped to take a quick breath, finding the words difficult to say, knowing that she didn't really mean them.

'I should never have got together with you in the first place, I made a mistake.'

Panic hit Alfie's eyes. 'I don't believe you. I know you better than that, Bree, I know you love me, so what's going on?'

'Alfie, I just need time for myself.'

'This has been difficult for all of us. What you went through, well, Jesus Christ, I'm not surprised your head's a mess, but you don't have to make a rash decision.'

Smiling sadly, Bree shook her head. 'Being in that cage gave me time to think, it made me realise what I want.'

'Is everything okay?' Franny asked, looking concerned, as she walked up to Alfie and Bree.

Hurt and in pain, Alfie snapped, 'No, everything ain't all right. She's trying to tell me that she wants nothing to do with me anymore. I know this is all a mess and I'm so sorry for that, but somehow we can sort this out, I know we can. And what about the baby, there's the baby to think of?'

'Alfie, there is no baby.'

Both Franny and Alfie stared at Bree, but it was Alfie who spoke first.

'What are you talking about?'

Looking uncomfortable, Bree gave Alfie a tight smile. 'I lost the baby a couple of days ago. I was bleeding heavily and there was nothing I could do, that's right, isn't it, Franny?'

Franny stared at Bree in bewilderment, but she quickly said, 'Yeah, that's right, Alf.'

Alfie's expression turned from shock into anger. 'This is because you were locked up in there, isn't it? It's my fault, ain't it? If I'd found you quicker, if I'd been able—'

Bree cut in, placing her hands on his. 'Alfie, stop, *please*, these things happen and who knows, maybe it's for the best.'

Alfie's eyes darkened. 'Best for who, Bree? That could've been *my* kid, doesn't that mean anything to you? I was actually looking forward to being a dad. Even if it wasn't mine, it wouldn't have mattered, I would've loved it all the same. You're talking like it ain't a big deal but, you know what, it's a big deal to me.'

'Look, Alfie, I'm sorry, but if you don't mind, I don't want to talk about it anymore. As soon as I get back to the house, I'm going to get my stuff and move out. The sooner I do it the better, it'll make it easier for everyone.'

Angrily, Alfie spat his words. 'Just like that? That's it?'

'Alfie, please—'

It was Alfie's turn to cut in, his hurt, as it always did, making him say things he would later regret. 'You've got it all worked out, ain't you? Well, let me tell you something, darlin', I was going to get shot of you anyway, so you've saved me the trouble. I'm only sorry I bothered getting together with you in the first place. I should've just left you in that trailer park. And you know something else? Franny is more woman than you'll ever be.'

And with that Alfie stormed off, leaving the women standing by the car.

Immediately, Franny turned to Bree. 'What's going on? What was that about?'

Bree wiped away her tears. 'Leave it, Franny.'

'No, I won't leave it! I want to know why you said all that to Alfie. Why did you tell him you lost the baby?' Franny's tone was hard.

Unable to look at Franny, Bree's voice cracked with emotion. 'Because I can't do this. I can't do what comes hand in hand with Alfie. Look what's just happened, we were lucky to get out alive.'

'The Russos were nothing to do with him though.'

'But if it isn't the Russos, it'll be someone else. Don't you get it? I can't be like you and I don't want to be scared anymore. I've had so much chaos in my life and Molly's life already, the last thing I want is to bring another child into this. It wouldn't be fair. I just want peace, Franny. And Alfie, he's never going to change, and I wouldn't ask him to. Even though I love him so much, I just can't do it.'

'So, what about the baby?'

Bree swallowed hard, but she didn't say anything, she just stared at Franny, pools of sadness in her eyes.

'You're going to get rid of it, aren't you? Bree, is that what you're going to do?'

Bursting into tears, Bree nodded miserably. 'I've got no choice.

If I did stay, I couldn't look Alfie in the eye knowing that I've got rid of the baby behind his back. And you heard him, if I did have the baby he'd want to be involved, so then I couldn't get away, but I have to. I have to get myself sorted, everything just feels too much . . . and besides, I can't really afford to have another child, not on my own . . . Franny, *please*, don't look at me like that, I need you to understand, I don't want you to hate me.'

Taking Bree's hand in hers, Franny stared intently at Bree. 'I don't hate you and I do understand, and I get that you should have a chance to live your life how you want to, but I also know getting rid of the baby isn't what you want.'

Unhappily, Bree said, 'That's just the way it is.'

'It doesn't have to be though, not if you let me help you. I told you already, no matter what, I'd be there for you and the baby.'

'What are you talking about?'

Franny glanced over her shoulder, making sure that Alfie was completely out of earshot. 'I'll help you. I'll give you some money, so you can find a flat and look after yourself until you get back on your feet, no matter how long it takes. Getting that kind of money isn't a problem. And then you and Molly and the baby can get on with your lives. That way you'll never have any regrets, and I'll be there for you, whenever you need me.'

Bree looked shocked. 'This is crazy, Alfie would never agree to it.'

Franny lowered her voice. 'But we don't have to tell Alfie. We *never* have to tell him.'

'Franny, I might not know Alfie as well as you do, but I do know if he ever found out what you were doing, that you were helping me behind his back, that you were keeping his baby away from him, he'd kill you, no question, because family is everything to him.'

'I know he would, but as long as he doesn't find out, I don't need to worry, do I? It'll be fine. And in the future if you want to tell him about the baby you can, but all you need to do is keep my name out of it, then it should be fine.'

Glancing at Franny and then across to Alfie, Bree said, 'I don't know, it's a lot to ask of you.'

'You're not asking though, I'm offering. I want to do this. Please, let me do this for you.'

Fear came into Bree's eyes. 'But if I agreed to it, I'd be frightened for you, worried that Alfie *would* somehow find out and then how could I live with myself if something happened to you, if he—'

Franny cut in. 'Let me worry about Alfie, and anyway, like I said, that's not going to happen, because he's not going to find out . . . So what do you say, Bree? Have we a deal? Will you let me help you?'

Unable to fight back her tears, Bree, overcome by her emotions, nodded and simply said, 'Yes, Franny, and thank you, we have a deal.'

Franny smiled, but, catching a glimpse of Alfie, an uneasy feeling suddenly began to creep over her.

One Week Later

55

Franny walked into the hallway with Alfie and Alice as the sunlight streamed through the window. Seeing the morning post on the doormat, Franny bent down to pick up a padded envelope, which was addressed to Alice, along with a couple of bills for Janine and a letter each for her and Alfie.

'Here you go, these are yours.' She smiled as she handed the padded envelope to Alice, who looked at it curiously, then, handing Alfie's letter to him, she quickly opened hers. It was from Bree.

Franny,
I thought I'd write to you rather than text, I wouldn't want Alfie seeing it. I found a flat, it's perfect. I don't know how I'll ever thank you. I'll give you all the details when I see you next week at the place we arranged, and I promise, I'll never breathe a word to anyone that you helped me.
x

'Who's it from, Fran?' Alfie broke into her thoughts as she crumpled up the letter and shoved it into her jeans pocket.

'Just a bit of junk mail from a health clinic.' She smiled innocently at Alfie, hoping not to give anything away as he ripped open his own letter. 'Alf, are you okay?'

Alfie's face paled, his voice wavering. 'Yeah, I'm fine.'

'Bad news?'

Blinking back a rush of nausea, fear crept over Alfie as he stared down at the letter, unable to stop his hand shaking as he struggled to answer Franny.

'No, don't be silly; it's not bad news. It's just junk mail, like yours.'

Distracted, Franny nodded as she turned and headed for the kitchen, her thoughts on Bree.

'Good, I'm glad, I'm just going to make myself a drink.'

As she walked away, Alfie, feeling his chest tighten, reread his letter. There was no name on it, but Alfie Jennings knew *exactly* who it was from:

Hello Alfie,

Remember me? I hope so. Twenty-two years inside – thanks to you – is a long time, but I'm out now, what do you think about that? I thought a lot about you over the years, every day in fact. That's the thing about prison, there's a lot of time to think. The other thing is there's a lot of time to do is write, so I thought I'd write you a poem – hope you like it.

Roses are red,
Violets are blue,
I'm your worst nightmare
And I'll be coming for you . . .

As Alfie stood frozen, fear etched onto his face, Alice, not noticing, tore open the seal of her padded envelope:

My dearest Alice,

I hope this finds you well.

Sometimes in life we meet people who touch us to our very soul. I have been fortunate to meet two people who have done that to me: Natalia was one and you, Alice, were the other. And whilst I certainly may not be religious in the traditional sense, you have converted me. You gave me my faith back and you took my hand and led me out of the darkness into the light. You gave me life and you gave me your kindness, and yet you asked nothing in return. As I told you before, when Natalia died she was pregnant. What I didn't tell you was she was expecting a girl. Many tormented nights I have spent imagining what my daughter would've been like and whilst I will never get to see that joy, in my dreams now I imagine that she would be just like you. You live in my heart and if it is God who I have to thank for you, then I thank him for sending you to me. I have not lived a good life, Alice, not a worthy one, and I have several regrets, but one of my biggest regrets is that Natalia never got to meet you.

These keys are for you, Alice. I no longer want to live in my house, it is time to move on, but I want you to have it. There were so many special memories, both good and bad, and I know it'll be in good hands. I just ask you two things. The first, never change from who you are, and secondly, come and visit me, you'll know where to find me.

Your servant,
Abel Gray

Frowning, Alice tipped up the envelope. At the bottom was a set of keys, as well as two single gold wedding bands, inscribed with the names Natalia and Abel.

There was a light summer storm as Abel Gray, dressed in his wedding suit, adjusted his tie in the mirror. Satisfied, he carefully positioned his grey top hat perfectly on his head before walking out of the house and through the vast grounds of his estate.

He passed the chapel and walked through the wet, lush green grass until he reached the tiny gravelled path, which took him up to the rose garden. There, he stopped to pick a single yellow stem, popping it in his buttonhole, smelling it as he looked up at the light blue sky, keeping his eyes open as the rain fell, watching the cotton-white clouds float by as he thought of Alice Rose. An angel who had given him life and freed him from his tortured existence.

He made his way to the bubbling stream, wading across to where the willow trees swayed and bent in the warm breeze. By a small earth mound with a pebble stone upon it, Abel lay down, draping his arm over it.

'Natalia, I'm here. I'm back.'

Then from one of his pockets Abel took a bottle of sleeping pills, tipping them all into his mouth. He swallowed them and smiled.

'Natalia, I'm coming. I'm coming to be with you. It's finally over.'

And with peace in his heart, Abel Gray closed his eyes, ready to join his Natalia.

And the devil who had deceived them was thrown into the lake of fire and sulphur where the beast and the false prophet were to be tormented day and night for ever and ever.

Revelation 20:10

ACKNOWLEDGMENTS

A huge thank you to the fabulous team at Avon books who have supported me and cheered me on from the sidelines – what a difference that makes. It's such a team effort it's great. Thanks to Victoria Oundjian for helping me with this book and thanks to my new editor, Katie Loughnane, for taking over so seamlessly and filling me with excitement for what the future holds. A big shout out to Sabah Khan who continues to work her magic and of course Dominic Rigby, who assures me he'll never rest until we have world domination……!!!!!! And as always huge thanks go to my agent, Darley, his wonderful assistant Pippa, the readers who have been so supportive and my amazing family. And lastly but by no means least, my horses, who make me smile each day. Happy days.

Bree Dwyer is desperate to escape her husband,
take the children and run. But he's always watching.
And she always gets caught. Until now . . .

Some relationships
are good for you.
Others are . . .

Toxic

Jacqui Rose

'Gritty and gripping – a star in the making' Kimberley Chambers

Available in paperback and ebook.

A gritty Romeo and Juliet story of bitter feuds and unbreakable bonds from bestselling author Jacqui Rose . . .

Available in paperback and ebook.

**'I was hoping you'd be able to help me.
I'm looking for my baby.'**

Another compulsive thriller from bestselling author
Jacqui Rose . . .

Available in paperback and ebook.